MW00465791

MADELEINE'S INQUISITION

The Irrational and Inhumane Treatment
of Women by the Church of Rome

PAUL R. DIONNE

Madeleine's Inquisition

The Irrational and Inhumane Treatment of Women by the Church of Rome

Copyright © 2020 by P.R.D. Publishing

ISBN: 978-1-6606085-4-6

All rights reserved. No part of this publication may be reproduced or transmitted in any form or by any means without permission of the author.

I dedicate this book to all the people who have helped me reach this goal — my loving wife, my incredible family and my loyal friends. Thank you!

Chapter 1

Dark clouds hung heavily over Paris, once the most celebrated city in Europe. The gray, stone buildings smelled dank, as faint sunlight brought a thin layer of warmth to the early morning. News of Napoleon's setbacks in Russia trickled into the city from the wounded and bedraggled soldiers who had deserted their unit weeks before, when defeat was obvious.

It was the end of a common dream for Napoleon, his soldiers, and the people of France. The *Grande Armee* of 600,000 soldiers had marched and fought its way into the heart of Russia. It arrived at Borodino low on ammunition, supplies, and morale.

Jean Marc Moreau had been a foot soldier in the *Grande Armee* since the Italian Campaign, fourteen years before. He was tall, powerfully built, and ruggedly handsome. Due to his courage and skill, he rose steadily through the ranks and was now a sergeant leading a platoon on this pivotal march to Moscow.

He was on the side of resting the troops but when the order came down from above, he prepared as best he could. As he walked about his soldiers, he observed that many were sick, exhausted and half starved by the endless marches that had outstripped the supply convoy. When he gave the order to march onward, they rose to their feet listlessly. He urged them to ration what little water remained, and when they exhausted their supply, he encouraged them to drink horse urine to quench their thirst. But soon that supply was exhausted as most of the horses died of starvation. He bolstered their morale not by his words but by sharing their hardships. He was assigned to the lead unit, and as they approached Borodino, he observed the Russian army heavily entrenched on the edge of the village. He halted the column and sent word back to the commander. As he awaited his orders, he observed the open farmland that led to the village, broken up by streams and ravines, and beyond thousands of soldiers in fortified bunkers, and redoubts, and hundreds of cannons all aimed at the open field. He surmised that they would attempt a flanking movement and avoid a direct assault, which would be suicidal.

When the order to assault was not given that day, he told his men to rest and sent a few soldiers into the night to fetch water from the streams. It was two days before the order to assault was received.

"What fool would order a direct assault?" Jean Marc asked when he received the order from his commander.

"Napoleon himself," the commander responded. "Your unit is being held in reserve until the tide turns in our favor."

Jean Marc watched the slow progress of the assault over the open ground. "The Russians outnumber us but we have superior leadership," he mumbled to himself. He looked for Napoleon, usually in front of his army exhorting and inspiring his men. He was nowhere to be found.

The field of battle looked chaotic, but the assault was gaining ground on the right flank; yard by yard they kept moving forward. But the rest of the assault was stalled. "Look to the middle of the field," he ordered his men. "The large redoubt is stalling our movement. The army is bogged down. That is where the reserves will be sent. Observe the terrain... take advantage of the ravines and the slopes for cover... move from cover the cover... don't get pinned down," he said as he looked around and saw fear on the faces of the soldiers. "Prepare yourselves; the time is near!"

At around noon, a massive shelling of the redoubt by the French cannons started and lasted for over an hour.

"Be ready," Jean Marc hollered to his men, over the loud booms of the guns. As soon as the cannon fire ceased, the reserve units, except for the cavalry, joined in the charge. Jean Marc directed his men from one ravine to the next, alternating his units to provide cover for the unit on the move. It was a fearful three hundred yards, and as they approached the redoubt, the cannon fire from the Russian side fell like hail and ripped into the oncoming army. The smoke was so thick they could hardly make out the redoubt. The murderous battle went on for hours, until the French troops were forced to retreat, over the fallen bodies of their comrades.

Jean Marc pointed to the right flank and saw that the French troops had penetrated the village and were making a turning movement to assault the redoubt from the side. At the same time, the French cavalry charge began. "Check your weapons," Jean Marc ordered. "We will follow the cavalry into the fight."

The horses started at a slow pace, then to a brisk trot, and when the redoubt was close, they charged toward the enemy line. "Follow me," Jean Marc ordered, "and follow the cavalry into the fight." At the head of his platoon, he led the charge into the heart of the enemy force. After a second great battle, the Russian line broke and retreated to the village.

The French line was halted, to the dismay of Jean Marc. "We can finish this battle now… we must pursue the bastards, they are on the run," Jean Marc hollered, waiting for the order which never came.

During the lull, Jean Marc trained his field glasses on the ground around him, and what he saw sickened him. On the once tranquil pasture, the dead and wounded bodies formed a braided rug covering the ground completely. "Thousands are dead, and thousands more are wounded," he grieved. "Luc, care for the wounded," he ordered his medic. He watched as the young medic moved from body to body, applying bandages and tourniquets. "They will all be dead by morning," he murmured to himself.

The field of battle had become a field of the dead and the dying, and it beckoned him. Seeing the open eyes on a young soldier's face, he felt for a pulse, then closed his eyes with his fingers. A few of the wounded gasped for air. "Luc, come here quickly," he called.

"I can't sergeant; there are too many calling for help here."

"Go help the medic," a voice from behind him said. "I will console the dying."

He recognized the voice of the chaplain and without looking back, he rose and walked toward Luc and beyond. "My God, how many brave soldiers have died here today?" he asked himself as his eyes scanned the field toward the village of Borodino. There was scarcely an area not covered by a corpse. He was hardened to the casualties of war, but today he was horrified by the slaughter. Wounded men screamed out in pain begging for help — or for an end to their suffering. As he walked over the bodies toward the village, his eyes swelled with tears. He ignored Luc's pleas to return and seemed oblivious to the dangers ahead. He entered the village and saw bodies, twisted and dismembered, littering the muddy roads — the carnage running throughout the village — the wounded pleading for help. The extreme horror suddenly unbearable, he sat in the blood-soaked mud beside the mangled bodies of Russian soldiers, their faces contorted and twisted in the throes of death, and he did not stir until Luc arrived, urging him to return to his unit.

He stared into the distance and said weakly, "The Russians have abandoned the village and are retreating to Moscow... that is were we will face our final bloodbath."

The next day, without burying the dead and leaving thousands of wounded soldiers to die, Napoleon pursued and drove his army toward its objective, which he believed would be the final battle of the war. When at dusk on the seventh day, the army arrived within sight of the cupolas and the onion domes of Moscow, Jean Marc turned to his men and said, "Napoleon has brought us to Moscow, and it is our destiny to capture the city and bring glory to France." Exhausted, most of them fell asleep not grasping the significance of his words.

Before dawn the next morning, as his soldiers awakened, Jean Marc rallied his men, "Moscow will be ours soon, and our reward is close at hand." The stakes were high, and he knew they had to be inspired to dig deep within their soul to summons the strength to fight what he surmised would be a bloody battle. He knew they would follow him in the assault, but he felt that a hint of booty would provide added incentive.

The battle at Borodino, a few days earlier, had been the bloodiest of the war with the slaughter of eighty thousand men; but due to Sergeant Moreau's skillful leadership, few in his unit suffered casualties. "The Russians lost thousands of soldiers in the last battle. But do not be foolish enough to think that they are beaten. They will fight fanatically tomorrow for they are fighting for their homeland. Follow my orders, and I will get you through the day!" Jean Marc said as they marched toward Moscow.

Sergeant Moreau was good at bolstering the morale of his men, but the gods seemed to conspire against him. The morning's foul weather and pelting rain only aggravated what the soldiers had seen a few days ago when they walked into the charred, ruined village of Borodino with its gruesome piles of dead and dying, causing even the most hardened soldiers to turn aside and vomit.

But the horror of Borodino was not to be repeated in Moscow, during the night the Russians retreated but not to a second line of defense. The army retreated beyond

Moscow leaving behind arsonists and saboteurs who set fires and planted explosives throughout the city. Independent fires were started simultaneously, and soon a great fire engulfed the city and raged unchecked for three days. The French soldiers watched from a distance as the heavy smoke rose toward the heavens, their booty, safety and glory evaporating like an early morning mist. Jean Marc was disappointed, not for the loss of booty but for the victory that had been snatched from their grasp.

The *Grande Armee* no longer had the resources to pursue the Russians. Its soldiers were sick, exhausted and starved. The supply lines were broken. The city that was to be their salvation was now their deathtrap.

As the French army entered the city, the soldiers took their revenge on the few inhabitants who remained and the few buildings not destroyed. But Jean Marc ordered his men to maintain discipline and not partake in ravaging the city for they would need whatever strength remained for the long and arduous retreat out of Russia.

"We fought bravely ... let us not dishonor France," he cautioned his men. Most heeded his command.

Napoleon remained confident that Alexander would still seek peace, but as the emperor waited in Moscow, the czar reinforced his troops and created two new armies. As the Russian numbers increased, the French numbers dwindled. The czar waited patiently for the emperor to start his retreat. Napoleon's generals, realizing that the army lacked the resources to stay in Russia, urged the emperor to begin the withdrawal. Napoleon vacillated for over a month, wasting precious time, then, when hope was lost, ordered the hazardous trek back to France.

Jean Marc ordered his men to travel lightly. "The Cossack cavalry will harass us constantly, and we must move swiftly if we are to survive."

They soon outdistanced the overburdened units but were ordered by their commander to slow their pace. As the retreat stalled, the harsh winter swept in early and brought bitter cold. Many of the exhausted soldiers simply gave up, fell asleep, and died in the snow. The mobile Cossacks harried the survivors, and the infantry pursued them relentlessly. The constant assaults further debilitated the French soldiers, as many were killed, wounded, captured or deserted.

It was this news that trickled into Paris in the winter of 1812.

Chapter 2

When she opened her eyes, she saw only darkness. It was too early to awaken the children and too late to return to slumber. She remained still, lying on the floor in a bed of straw. Her children lay next to her, breathing softly. The room was crowded, but it was all she could afford. She was thirty years old now with three children and a missing husband. She stared into the dark, trying not to think of what frightened her most — how to provide for her children. The dreams of the farm, the vineyard, and the lovemaking were gone, not likely to be replaced. Many of the young men in Paris had been killed, crippled, or emotionally scarred by the wars of the past decade — Napoleon had seen to that. She was penniless, with little food in the cupboard and nowhere to turn. Her prayers brought some solace, but little else.

As the day's light crept into the room, she was reminded of the squalor of the neighborhood, the rank air, and the danger to her children. Her hand moved gently to her side, groping for the feel of her husband, finding only emptiness. She sat up and gazed at her children huddled for warmth. All three were sleeping, and their calm breathing consoled her. At eight, Jean was the oldest. He would grow up tall and strong like his father. Next to him was Marc, who was seven. He was precocious and his intelligence would keep him out of harm's way. And there was Angeline, a year younger than Marc and blessed with fine features. She would become a beautiful young woman. Or maybe these were the thoughts of all young mothers, that their children would grow up to be strong, intelligent, and attractive.

People in the neighborhood were starting to move outside to stretch and relieve themselves. She could hear them talking, lighting smoking pipes, and shuffling about.

Hundreds of shacks had sprung up almost overnight as the families of soldiers were left without funds. The shanties were so close they seemed to support each other. The streets were rutted and muddy. No sanitation measures had been taken and disease was rampant. It was Sunday morning, and Madeleine had saved a few *sous*. She would take the children to mass at Notre Dame followed by a *petit dejeuner*. It brought hope to her soul and would take them away from the drudgery of this hovel, at least, for a few hours.

"Come on children, it is time for church, and we must not be late!" she urged. When they arrived, she stopped and admired the glorious façade of the cathedral, decorated with statuary, its towers rising towards the heavens, its imposing doors open to its parishioners, with the chant of the choir drifting to her ears. The Gothic cathedral had been completed in the fourteenth century and was the pride of Paris.

As the young family crossed the threshold from the brightness of the sunlight to the darkness of the candlelit cathedral, the children hesitated. Madeleine, sensing their fear, held the hand of Angeline and Marc, while Jean led them down the aisle. As Madeleine's eyes adjusted to the darkness, she realized that Jean had gone beyond the section of the commoners and had entered the area reserved for the elite of Paris. Embarrassment fell upon her as she contrasted the haute couture of the bourgeoisie with the rags of her children.

"*Ici, ici* ..." the kindly voice of an elderly lady enjoined as she gestured for them to come into her pew.

"*Merci*, Madame," Jean responded as if the pew had been reserved for them. From this vantage point, Madeleine was able to observe the splendor of the high mass and the opulence of the altar. The children, too small to see above the adults, seemed content with the warmth of their surroundings until the booming voice of the preacher broke their seclusion. Marc and Angeline slid toward their mother while Jean slid toward his newfound friend. As the preacher droned on, in a fire and brimstone manner, not about faith, hope, or charity but about the sinful ways of the congregation while intimating how redemption could be found through generous tithing. How Madeleine wanted to be back with the commoners, who rarely tithed for they had no money. But now, in the company of the bourgeoisie that surrounded her, it would be embarrassing if she did not. When the tithing basket arrived, the kind lady took money from her purse and motioned to the collector that it was for those in her pew.

Love of God and love of neighbor, that is the message of Jesus...not tithing, Madeleine thought. The kind stranger had done more in that instant to reflect the message of love than the preacher had in his drawn out and tiresome sermon.

As mass ended, the lady handed Madeleine a note, which she put in her pocket, and with her head held high she left the church. Madeleine and her family followed closely, her eyes catching the beauty of the spectacular stained-glass rose window to the rear of the church, the sunlight bringing it to the pinnacle of its beauty.

Outside many formed a queue to compliment the Monsignor on his wonderful sermon. Madeleine caught his eye, and it was cold and lustful. Shivering, she moved the children along rapidly until they reached le Petit Pont crossing the River Seine. And as they reached la Rue St Jacques, her thoughts turned to food as they passed the *fromageries*, the *creperies*, and the open markets. She bought a baguette, a slice of ham, and a bit of cheese. The family settled in at Place St Michel, overlooking the river, for a picnic and play.

As she watched the children having fun, her mind wandered to better times, growing up in southern France. Her father, with the help of a rich relative in Paris, had purchased land in the area and was cultivating a vineyard. She and her brothers learned the trade by working in the fields in spring and summer and the winery and cellars in the fall and winter. When time permitted, they attended parochial school, where they learned to read and write. The family enjoyed good fortune, and their wines soon became a local favorite. She enjoyed every aspect of winemaking, and her father never limited her curiosity.

"Mama, mama, we have made friends!" Jean shouted as he ran by, interrupting her daydream. She looked at the dozen or so children, all in rags, briefly oblivious to the hardships of the times. Her mind wandered back to her younger days. The French Revolution had had little impact on their wine producing, but Napoleon's rise to power did. One by one, the men of the area were conscripted into Napoleon's army, until very few remained to harvest the vineyards, produce the wine, and tend to the cellars. The larger vineyards had the capacity to pay higher wages to the available laborers, but the smaller vineyards did not. Their vines withered, production lapsed, and the wine soured.

"Mama, mama come play with us," Angeline's sweet voice called. She rose from the comfort of the shade to join in the excitement of her children and their newfound friends.

The day came to end too quickly, and as the family trekked back to their shabby quarters, the fears of tomorrow came rushing back to Madeleine. She hoped to get home before nightfall, for the streets were most dangerous at night. She needed to find work, but even if she did, who would care for the children? The preacher had earlier spoken of damnation, but that did not scare her, starvation did.

There was nothing left for them to eat but broth and a few stale biscuits. They would hunger for days unless she caught a pigeon, squirrel, or rat for the pot. She had seen women steal in the open market, but when caught, they were imprisoned, leaving their children to fend for themselves. And, others resorted to prostitution, also with bad consequences.

As they arrived at the slum where they lived, fires had been lit, which cast an eerie red glow. Many were huddled around the fire for warmth and none paid attention to them as they walked by. *They are consumed by their own feelings of suffering and hopelessness*, she thought, just as the church bells of Notre Dame tolled in the distance, bringing no solace to the wretched crowd. "Madeleine," a voice called from behind. As she turned, she noticed it was Henri, her neighbor, and he seemed agitated.

"What is it?"

"I have a message for you, Madeleine!"

"Is it about my husband?"

"No. It is from Notre Dame."

"Notre Dame?" she asked.

"Yes. It is from the Monsignor. He said for you to meet with him after mass on Sunday.

"Why me?"

"I don't know, Madeleine," he said as he turned to walk away, then stopped suddenly. "Oh, and he said to be sure to bring the children."

Chapter 3

The French Revolution had dealt a severe blow to the Catholic Church, but when Napoleon ascended to power, he restored much of the Church's authority and prestige, not for religious reasons but to maintain the widespread support of the peasantry. Once securely ensconced as the Emperor of France, he dealt more resolutely with the Church and the papacy. When Pope Pius VII refused to implement one of his directives, Napoleon ordered his troops to capture the papal palace and arrest the pope. Thus, the clergy silently rejoiced at Napoleon's defeat in Russia and covertly supported the alliance that had been formed by England, Russia, and Prussia in its holy war to rid Europe of Napoleon.

The clergy in Paris became particularly assertive, feeling its newfound strength. The Monsignor, following suit, became fixated with both his status and Madeleine Moreau.

Father Martin, a recently ordained priest, had been assigned to the parish of Notre Dame as an assistant to the Monsignor. As Martin engaged in his morning prayers, the Monsignor burst into his room. "The woman I mentioned to you the other day, Madeleine … Madeleine Moreau, she is a witch!"

"But, Monsignor, she is but a poor woman struggling to provide for her children. It is our responsibility to help the poor, not to condemn them," he said tepidly.

"She haunts me, and if she influences me in that manner, imagine the spell she casts on weaker men."

"What would you have me do Monsignor?"

"I will let you know Sunday. I have requested that she join me following the Sunday services. I shall order that she place her children in the orphanage, where they will be properly cared for by the nuns."

"And if she refuses?"

"Then, I will inform her that I have witnesses who will testify to her odd behavior."

"The witnesses will testify before whom, Monsignor?"

"Before a Dominican Inquisitor, of course," he said in an annoyed tone of voice. "And, in the next few days, research for me, from all of these books you have been reading, the proper procedure to present an accusation to the Grand Inquisition," he said, as he abruptly left the room.

The young priest, shocked by this behavior, wondered anxiously what would happen to Madeleine Moreau. *Her husband is away and cannot help. She is determined, but there is no work...and the children are precocious, but too young to be of assistance*, Father Martin thought.

He stood up from behind his desk, went to the bookshelf, and took down a text on the Inquisition. What he discovered was helpful. The popes had appointed inquisitors since the thirteenth century. The Inquisition was established to preserve orthodox religious beliefs from the attacks of heretics. Unfortunately, many inquisitors, through intimidation and torture, used their position to limit religious beliefs, intellectual freedom, and political liberty. All the Inquisitorial Courts in Europe were abolished by the start of the nineteenth century, but Rome still had the capacity to convene a tribunal within the Papal States.

He had never seen the Monsignor in this frenzied state of mind before — obsessed and vindictive. He hoped that by delaying the appointment of an inquisitor, he could dissuade him from his course of action. However, he knew better than to take issue with his superior while he was in a foul mood. He returned to his research, intent on making the process as long and tedious as possible, time would be his ally.

He soon learned that the history of the Inquisition was replete with examples of religious intolerance and the excessive use of force in matters of heresy. The entire process lay in the hands of a single inquisitor — from investigation and accusation to conviction. The actions were directed not only at heretics but also at the practitioners of magic and witchcraft. Punishment ranged from public humiliation, mutilation, imprisonment, and death.

The procedure was initiated by a person of good reputation reporting the heresy to Rome without having to support the accusation with evidence. The pope would then appoint an inquisitor to ascertain whether heresy had occurred. Eyewitness testimony was taken and, if none, the inquisitor would receive partial evidence, which could lead to a confession. The inquisitor was allowed to use torture to extract a confession. A confession made during or after torture had to be freely repeated the next day without torture or would be considered invalid.

Father Martin rose early the next day curious about why witchcraft was considered heretical. He entered the library and went to the area reserved for the clergy. Many books, banned by the Church, were available only to the clergy. Martin found them enlightening, but he often wondered why the Church was so restrictive. Within a few minutes, he had gathered a number of books on the subject and had settled in to do his research.

The Third Lateran Council of 1179, which was viewed by many as the start of the Inquisition, produced several canons condemning heretics. In 1199 Pope Innocent III issued a decretal, which constituted a major step in the formalization of the prosecution of heretics. The goods of heretics were confiscated, and their children castigated for the sins of their parents.

With the spread of heresy in Europe, the severity of the laws against heretics increased. During the thirteenth century, the inquisitorial procedure became the standard form of prosecution throughout Europe. The popes believed they were responsible to protect Christians from heretics and, in the year 1220, they founded the Dominican Order to teach doctrine and combat heresy. They were well trained and reported directly to the Papacy. A few years later, Pope Gregory IX directed the Dominicans to broaden the scope of the Inquisition to suppress the spread of heresy, which he linked to Satan.

The Council of Tarragon of 1242 instituted directives that shaped the authority and procedure of the Inquisition. The mission of the inquisitors was to save the souls of heretics while protecting the orthodoxy of the Church. The inquisitors determined whether the heresy occurred and whether it was punishable. They soon broadened their purview to include the practitioners of magic and witchcraft.

Throughout the following centuries, thousands of women were accused of sexual relations with the devil, subsequently inflaming an uncontrollable sexual desire in men. Women's sexuality and eroticism seduced both men and women away from God. The basis for this rationale was founded in Augustine's philosophy.

Saint Augustine was lauded as a Father of the Church, a distinction of the highest order, Father Martin mused. He reasoned that men and women were created in the image of God, and they possessed a rational soul. But this soul had two elements, a masculine element capable of contemplating God, which he referred to as *rationality,* and a feminine element oriented toward bodily life, which he referred to as *sexuality.* And, as sexuality became viewed as demonic, a new concept of woman evolved — the medieval witch.

Father Martin pushed the books to the far side of the

reading table. *My God,* he thought, *Madeleine Moreau is in real danger.*

Chapter 4

The children had not eaten in two days, and Madeleine did not know where the next meal would come from. The church would provide food, but she feared the Monsignor. The families in the area could not help, for they faced the same plight. She looked for work daily but to no avail. "Mama my stomach hurts!" Angeline cried.

"Mine too, mama," Marc said weakly.

Jean sat stoically but looked pale. She felt a painful mix of frustration and helplessness.

"When will Papa come home?" Marc asked.

"He will soon be back... there will be food on the table... a home to live in... a yard to bring friends... and a family to grow up with," she responded, with little enthusiasm. Jean-Marc had been gone for over a year and Madeleine was losing hope that he would return, but she did not want to worry the children.

Crime was rampant in the shantytown, and she feared for their safety. Whether help would come from God or from within, she was not sure. So she prayed as she gathered her belongings and led the children from the shanty for the last time.

They walked through the muddy streets toward the marketplace, already bustling with vendors setting up for the day's trade. The rutted streets eventually turned to cobblestones bordered by neat wooden houses, with gas streetlights to rob the night of darkness and gendarmes to secure the streets. These were the homes of craftsmen, traders, and bankers, with neighborhood squares, where people gathered for leisurely times and celebrations. "God, I will find a way to bring my children to a place like this," she murmured, loud enough for Jean to hear.

"I will help, Mama," he responded.

They crossed the bridge to *l'Ile de la Cit*e and

walked by *l'Hotel de Ville* and went directly to the convent housing the nuns, next to Notre Dame cathedral. She rapped on the door. A nun opened the door and greeted them warmly.

"My name is Madeleine, and these are my three children. I ask that you care for them while I look for work. I will return for them at day's end."

"And if you do not find work what will you do then?"

"I don't know; I just don't know, sister."

"The children could be placed in our orphanage. They would be well cared for."

"I could never let that happen, sister."

The nun motioned for the children to come in and reached out for Angeline's hand, but the children rushed by her as the sweet smell of food wafted from the kitchen.

"Au revoir, mama," Jean hollered without looking back.

Madeleine walked to the front of Notre Dame and entered the cathedral. As she prayed, she thought of the lady who had been so kind to them in church. Recalling the events of that day, she rummaged through her pockets and found a scrap of paper with an address written upon it. "God, could this be the answer to my prayers?" she asked, as she rushed from the church.

The Monsignor, walking from the shadows of the altar, observed her leave. He was obsessed by this woman and wondered why she had such a demonic hold over him. Nonetheless, he resolved not to let this devil-of-a-women tempt other men into sinfulness.

Arriving at her destination, she saw the soft glow of candles behind the wooden shutters of the luxurious stone mansion, bordering a large public square with benches, gardens, statuary, and a stately fountain in its center. She walked briskly to the rear of the building to the servant entrance and using the large doorknocker rapped the door.

A uniformed doorkeeper opened the door. *What must he think of this ragged woman,* she thought, as she handed him the scrap of paper.

"Oh, this looks like Madame LeBlanc's handwriting. Wait outside, I shall get you her personal attendant," he said brusquely.

"Bonjour Madeleine," an elegantly dressed woman said, as she opened the door and motioned for her to follow. As Madeleine walked behind the attendant, she noted the marble floor, the wainscoting, the domed ceiling and the artwork on every wall.

"My name is Sylvie, and I am in charge of Madame LeBlanc's staff," she said as they arrived at her bureau.

"How did you know my name?" Madeleine asked.

"Your son whispered it to Madame LeBlanc during mass. She hoped you would come."

Madeleine beamed.

"Madame LeBlanc is at her country estate because of the political unrest in Paris. She would like for you to serve as a handmaiden. Is that satisfactory?"

"Yes, yes, more than satisfactory!"

"Then follow me to the servants' quarters where you will be fitted for a uniform. All of the attendants wear similar attire. Your day will begin early and end late, and often your services will be required beyond that time. Is all satisfactory thus far?"

"Yes, Madame," she responded.

Once fitted for her clothing, she shadowed a long-time employee, learning her daily tasks and responsibilities. At the end of the workday, she made her way back to Sylvie's bureau, and as she waited in the anteroom, she looked at the *Gazette de France* lying on the table in front of her. The headline read: **Napoleon Deserts Army**. She picked up the newspaper and read the article:

Napoleon led his army out of Moscow on

October 19, realizing that it could not survive the winter. When he first entered Russia, he had 600,000 soldiers. He is now down to 100,000 — the rest having died, deserted, been wounded, captured, or just left behind. All forage along the route of retreat had been either consumed or scorched. When the army arrived at Smolensk it found that stragglers had confiscated the food left there. Horses were dying in droves, and the army's flanks and rear guard faced constant attack. Winter set in early, with high winds, sub-zero temperatures and lots of snow. On many bad nights, thousands of men and horses succumbed to exposure. Stories abound of soldiers splitting open dead animals and crawling inside for warmth, or stacking dead bodies in windows for insulation.

In late November, the Grande Armee narrowly escaped complete annihilation when it crossed the frigid Berezina River, but it had to leave behind thousands of wounded. It was under these conditions that Napoleon deserted his army and sped towards Paris amid rumors of a coup d'etat.

Madeleine put down the newspaper and sobbed. As Sylvie returned, she rushed to her side, trying to console her. She glanced at the *Gazette*, which she had read earlier, and understood.

On her way back to the convent that evening, Madeleine felt ambivalence. She had a job and Sylvie had found her an apartment in a nearby neighborhood. She could now provide for her children and live in a safe place — but her husband was either dead, wounded, captured or on the run.

She soon settled into a daily routine. She rose early, prepared breakfast for the children, brought them to the convent, left them with the kind nuns, prayed at Notre Dame, put in a full day's work, and returned with her children to their new tenement. Sundays were reserved for mass and family.

She was not the only one in a routine, for every morning, the Monsignor, hidden in the shadows of the altar, observed Madeleine as she rushed into the church, knelt at the same pew, mumbled a few words and rushed off. She had also disregarded his request to meet with him, which enraged him all the more.

One day as she walked through the bustling square on her way to work, something caught her eye. A sculptor at the edge of the square, with a hammer and chisel in hand, sculpting a marble block; his thick curly hair, either gray or whitened by the marble dust; his physique exposed from the waist up, muscular and taut; and his movement nimble in carving the hard white stone. She slowed her pace to admire his artistry. *He is older than me, but his body belies his age*, she thought.

She hesitated at the base of the wooden platform. The sculptor turned his eyes from the cold marble to Madeleine. Her heart filled with a sensual feeling, one she thought had left her forever. His eyes locked on hers and he smiled cheerfully.

Embarrassed, she looked down and walked away. She could not catch her breath, her heart beat rapidly, and a pang of desire filled her soul. But as she entered her workplace, the ecstasy of the moment quickly dissipated, replaced by a deep sense of guilt.

Chapter 5

The Monsignor stood smugly under the Arc de Triomphe with Father Martin at his side. "Napoleon commissioned the Arc in 1806 after his victory at Austerlitz. How ironic that his enemies will march through its vault once the emperor is defeated," the Monsignor said sanctimoniously.

Father Martin nodded as he admired the sculptural group, on the inner side of the Arc, called *Le Triomphe of 1810*, which featured Napoleon being crowned by the goddess of Victory.

"All reports indicate that since Napoleon slithered back from Russia, he appears out of touch with reality and seemingly unaware of the scale of his losses. He continues to ignore the truth even as the facts pour in, much to the dismay of the people grown accustomed to the emperor's invincibility. His enemies organize against him, including the European powers, the French nobility, and the Catholic Church," the Monsignor said.

"He finds little support outside the Army. The French people are upset that their support of the emperor has been in vain. They financed his armies, their businesses are in ruin, their sons fought the wars — with nearly four million of them killed in his military campaigns," Father Martin added.

"Even though many oppose the restoration of the Bourbon Kings, they fear the revolutionary extremists even more. The Legislature convened to censure Napoleon for continuing the war and adopted a charter criticizing him. He refused to initiate peace talks, declined to circulate the charter and even dissolved the Legislature."

Father Martin seemed to acquiesce.

"Emboldened by France's defeat in Russia, the countries of Austria, Prussia, and Sweden joined Russia and Great Britain in the fight against Napoleon. But in spite of these setbacks, Napoleon formed another army to confront the Allied forces as they advance from the east with 800,000 battle-tested soldiers, eager to engage Napoleon's smaller and less experienced military."

Leaving the area, Father Martin picked up a newspaper and read the lead story aloud. *"Napoleon led his newly formed army to Germany to engage the enemy. The armies clashed at Leipzig for four days. The combat ebbed and flowed with both sides letting the opportunity to achieve total victory slip from their grasp. Ultimately, the sheer number of the invading forces won the day. It was a catastrophe for France, which suffered 38,000 casualties with another 30,000 taken prisoner. As the French army retreats, Lord Wellington, leading the British Army, has entered France from Spain. Events are turning against Napoleon on every front, and his very survival is at stake."*

The Champs Elyses was bustling with traffic as the two strolled down the avenue.

"There is also good news from Rome. Both the Index of Forbidden Books and the Holy Office have been expanded. We again have the tools to pursue heretics," the Monsignor said enthusiastically.

"But as we become less tolerant are we not perverting the message of Jesus?" Father Martin asked.

"The perversion comes from the heretics. We must rid ourselves of those who are attacking the orthodoxy of the Church, which reflects the true way of Jesus."

Father Martin did not respond. The reasoning of his superior often confused him.

"File an accusation of witchcraft against Madeleine Moreau with the Holy Office," the Monsignor said abruptly.

"Paris is in a state of turmoil. The Allies are assaulting from all sides. The government is crumbling. There are more important matters to deal with than an

28

accusation of witchcraft against a blameless person," Martin said tepidly, for he knew his superior could be unyielding.

The Monsignor glowered, resenting his insubordination, then said derisively, "Prepare the accusation, and let those more qualified than you worry about Paris, our enemies, and the government."

Many Church leaders abused their authority, much like his superior. But, he had taken the vow of obedience and knew he must comply, he thought.

"As you wish Monsignor," he replied.

"Without delay, Father Martin," he ordered with a sinister look on his face.

Later that day, Father Martin went to the library to review the directives from the Holy Office. To his surprise, the librarian, at the request of the Monsignor, had set aside certain books for him to review. He quickly perused the titles.

"It is ironic that the Church has changed the name of the *Inquisition*, an institution that brought such terror to Europe, to the *Holy Office*, a name implying sanctity," Father Martin said, obviously annoyed. He felt comfortable with the librarian, Father Thomas, often times expressing his frustration to this young, liberal-minded priest.

"Father Martin, the Church makes these subtle changes to enhance its credibility. For example, if the Church were to say, *Augustine of Thagaste declares women to be inferior to men*, it would not have the same impact as, *Saint Augustine declares women to be inferior to men*. Sainthood endows the speaker with a greater degree of credibility. So the theory of the inferiority of women becomes more powerful coming from the mouth of a *Saint* than it does from the mouth of a mere *mortal*."

"And what are your thoughts about the Vatican reestablishing the Inquisition?" Martin asked.

"The history of the Inquisition is shameful in regard to the treatment of both men and women. When studying for the priesthood at the novitiate in Rome, I was selected to become a librarian because of my love of literature. I was privy to secret archives at the Vatican. I came upon documents recording four centuries of atrocities committed by the Church. In its attempt to control heretical behavior, it persecuted, punished and, with the cooperation of civil authority, executed hundreds of thousands of heretical Catholics as well as adherents of other faiths."

Father Martin knew that many young priests were challenging the teachings of the Church, but he always accepted the word of Rome. He now wondered about the young librarian. "You sound cynical about your calling Thomas. Why then have you chosen the priesthood as your vocation?"

"Because of my family," he responded. "I am from a very wealthy and influential Roman family. My father chose my eldest brother to run our family businesses; the next eldest is pursuing a political career; the next is serving as an officer in the army; the rebellious brother is an artist; and, being the youngest, I was chosen to be ordained as a priest and eventually to rise to the position of cardinal or even pope. I also have a sister, who is the brightest of the lot, but our society does not look kindly on the leadership of women, so she will marry well."

"Does your family have the influence to make this happen?" he asked.

"Yes, but I would rather make my own way."

Even though we are of different backgrounds and our families of different circumstances, we share a mutual respect, Martin thought.

"And what would you say about the accusation of witchcraft against one of our parishioners?" Martin asked.

"Witchcraft is a myth that the Church perpetuates. A woman accused of witchcraft will always be convicted.

The inquisitor has many tools to extract a confession from the accused, including torture. Most countries, as well as France, no longer permit the prosecution of witchcraft within their boundaries."

"Then there is no need to worry?" Martin questioned.

"The popes perpetuate the Inquisition in territories governed by the Church, which does not include France. At least, so long as Napoleon is its emperor."

Chapter 6

Madeleine's life had turned around, and each day she prayed at Notre Dame thanking God for her new life, still oblivious to the Monsignor observing her every move. On a particular morning, she forgot in the pew a book she had borrowed from Madame LeBlanc's library.

The Monsignor pounced on it as soon as she left. It was *Candide,* by Voltaire. Throughout his writings, Voltaire attacked the tyranny of the Church, and as a result, his books were on the Index of Forbidden Books. *Only a heretic would bring a forbidden book into a church. I will include this transgression in my accusation as further proof of her witchcraft,* he thought.

As Madeleine entered the square in front of the LeBlanc mansion, she smiled at the sculptor and he smiled back. This had become a daily ritual, and although they never spoke, they seemed to have developed a bond.

"What is your name?" he asked, much to her surprise.

"Madeleine," she responded as she continued her walk towards the mansion.

"Madeleine, that is what I will call my statue. You have been my inspiration!" he shouted.

She halted momentarily and said, "And how many women have you told that to today?"

"Only one, Madeleine," he responded flirtatiously.

She was still blushing as she entered the servants' quarters. "Madeleine, your complexion is flush," Sylvie said.

"The sculptor spoke to me this morning."

"It is time, Madeleine. You have waited long enough for your husband to return. You must think of yourself and the children."

"No, no, it is too soon!" she said as she put on her

apron and left the servant's quarters for her day's work.

As she departed the mansion after the workday, her heart sank when she approached the platform, and the sculptor was not at work.

"Madeleine, sit with me under the tree for a while," came his soft voice.

"No, I will be late to pick-up my children," she said with a smile

"Then I will walk with you!" he persisted.

"As you wish, but first tell me your name."

"Michel Bois... and how many children do you have?"

"I have three, and you?"

"I have no children, which is one of my biggest regrets. I spent too much time in Napoleon's army."

"My husband was... is a soldier also."

"Is he missing?" he inquired.

"Yes, and I have not heard from him in months. My hope is that he is a prisoner and will soon be released."

"Then he will be freed when the Allies defeat Napoleon," Michel said with little conviction.

"What else have you heard?' she asked sensing his reticence.

"Like all prisoners, they will be treated brutally, but the brave ones will survive," he said, "and now I must leave you to your thoughts."

"*Au revoir*, Michel," she said as she approached her destination.

"*Au revoir*, Madeleine."

For a moment, she had been carried away from her grief. Maybe love, joy, and happiness would re-enter her life. The thought was short lived, however, realizing that *Candide* was not with her. The last time she remembered seeing the book was in church that morning. She quickened her pace and when she arrived at the pew, the book was gone. She scanned the church and saw a robed figure dash toward the sacristy, to the rear of the church.

"Oh, no, the Monsignor found my book!" she gasped.

An enraged Monsignor burst into Father Martin's office. "I have damning information to include in the accusation against Madeleine Moreau," he said, flinging the book onto the desk.

"Ah, Voltaire's *Candide*. I have been meaning to read this comedy. I know it's on the Index, but how can we condemn a book without reading it?"

"Rome tells us what to read!" the Monsignor responded. "To do otherwise is blasphemy."

"Voltaire was a leader of a recent movement, including great writers like Diderot and Jean Jacques Rousseau. He is a gifted poet, novelist, satirist, historian, and philosopher. He has a broad and provocative view of humanity and its predicament. He rejects intolerance and condemns fanatical churchmen," Father Martin responded.

"Do not deceive yourself. When Voltaire wrote, *Ecrasez l'inflame*, he meant that Christianity must be wiped out, root and branch, Christ and clergy. That is why my accusation against Madeleine Moreau is even stronger now than before. When will you be ready to deliver it to Rome?"

"In a few days. But I have a request."

"Yes… yes, what is it?"

"I would like our librarian to accompany me on this dangerous journey."

"Why?"

"He knows the way the Rome."

The Monsignor nodded his acquiescence. "But, do it quickly."

"Yes, but keep in mind Monsignor, the jurisdiction of the Vatican does not extend into France. Even if your accusation is officially accepted, the tribunal will not have the authority to try Madeleine Moreau in France."

"Just deliver the accusation, and let me worry about getting Madeleine Moreau before the tribunal."

Eager to tell his companion the good news, Martin rushed off as soon as the Monsignor left. They had conspired to go to Rome together even though they realized the trip was fraught with danger: The British army had invaded southern France, the sea voyage on the Mediterranean was hazardous and many highwaymen stalked the roadways.

They wasted little time. "Thomas, you will map out our route while I gather the supplies."

"We need two riding horses, a mule, and provisions for two weeks. There are monasteries where we can stay overnight for companionship, direction, and food … and possibly local wine," Thomas added.

Martin laughed at his friend's levity.

"Let us also bring a few books about the Inquisition. They will provide background information for our mission in Rome. Once there, I will take you to the archives to study the history of the Inquisition. You will then understand that the purpose of the Inquisition went far beyond its avowed mission of saving the souls of heretics and protecting the unity of the Church. You will be shocked to learn of the thousands upon thousands of women who were persecuted and executed for the heresy of witchcraft," Thomas explained.

"And who directed the Inquisition? Martin asked.

"I will explain along the way how the papacy authorized and the Dominicans implemented the Inquisition, which led to the persecution of heretics, Protestants, Jews, Freemasons, and witches."

"I have known heretics, Protestants, Jews, and Freemasons, but I have never met a witch."

Madeleine's Inquisition

"Nor have I, but astoundingly, over the centuries, the inquisitors executed hundreds of thousands of women for the heresy of witchcraft."

Chapter 7

The retreating *Grande Armee* moved out of Smolensk concerned that the bridges over the Beresina River were already in enemy hands. Sergeant Moreau's platoon was assigned to the advance guard to find a way across the river. As they left, it was snowing heavily, and the temperature plummeted to minus 30 degrees. The commander forced the pace ordering fourteen hours of marching a day. There was no shelter and little rest, and their clothes, wet from the snow, froze on their bodies. When they stopped for the first night, Sergeant Moreau ordered his men to find fire wood, and once the fires were lit, he admonished them: "If you are too far from the fire you will freeze to death, but if you are too near you will suffer gangrene to your arms and legs."

They awakened before dawn and were soon dragging themselves through the snow. Some soldiers refused to leave the warmth of the fires and were left to fend for themselves. "They will soon be killed by the Cossacks," Sergeant Moreau said as his platoon marched by the deserters.

Following days of travelling in blizzard conditions, an unusual thaw gripped the region. The soldiers' morale improved, but Jean Marc worried that the frozen river might also thaw and impair their crossing. His premonition was right, when a few days earlier the army could have crossed the river anywhere with complete safety, it had now become a furious torrent.

As they stumbled upon the Beresina River, two units were sent in opposite directions to check if the bridges were intact. Sergeant Moreau's platoon reconnoitered the southern area. They returned two days later to report that all the bridges had been destroyed, and enemy soldiers were entrenched on the opposite side. The other unit returned an hour later with a similar report.

"I do have some good news," Sergeant Moreau told the commander. "A few miles down river, we located an unmarked ford near a village."

"Are you certain that the army could ford the river at that location?"

"From a distance, we observed the villagers shoring up the river bed. And we observed no Russian soldiers on the other side."

"Show me the village on the map," the commander directed.

"Here, right here," he responded, pointing to the village on the map.

"Ah, the village of Studienka."

Sergeant Moreau nodded and awaited the order from the commander.

"Send word to the main force that we will cross the river at Studienka. Tell them to bring the engineers and the bridging equipment immediately," he said to his aide.

"We should send a diversionary force down river to confuse the Russians."

"Yes, trick them into believing that we will cross elsewhere as we build the bridges for the heavy equipment and soldiers to cross. That is an excellent idea, Sergeant."

As soon as word reached the main force, the engineers and the bridge equipment were diverted to the village. A number of feints were ordered to distract the Russians, who took the bait moving their troops south of Studienka. When the engineers arrived, Sergeant Moreau's platoon was assigned to the rear guard. From the top of a hill, he observed the work being performed by the engineering units in the freezing waters. He watched as the engineers destroyed the buildings in the village for wood to build the bridges. They worked day and night to secure the framework and set the planks. By morning's light, the first bridge was completed. Soldiers rushed over the bridge to set up a defensive position on the opposite side.

The engineers started work on a second and larger bridge and within twenty-four hours it was ready for crossing, with still no sign of the Russians. Jean Marc heard a rumbling from the north, as he looked up the road, he saw thousands of French soldiers marching toward the bridge. The soldiers were directed to the smaller bridge, the artillery and horses toward the larger one. All seemed to be proceeding in an orderly fashion as soldiers and artillery reached the far bank. He took out his field glasses to get a closer look at the operation.

"Jesus," he exclaimed. "The supports on the artillery bridge are collapsing."

He watched helplessly as soldiers, horses and artillery were dumped into the icy waters and either sank to the bottom or were carried downstream by the raging river.

Soldiers on the nearer bank panicked and made a mad dash to the remaining bridge. Hundreds of soldiers were knocked into the water and drowned, with only a few making it to the far side. When order was finally restored, the engineers worked feverishly through the night to shore up the shattered bridge. Few of the workers survived that night, dying of exposure or being swept away by the powerful currents.

The Russians arrived early the next morning and attacked at once. The rear guard fought valiantly, keeping the Russians at bay, so that the crossing could go on unabated. As the battle ebbed at dusk, the crossing continued under the cover of darkness. At dawn, the rear guard was ordered to cross the river. But the Russians renewed the attack before they could cross. Heavy artillery fire destroyed the larger bridge as the Russians pushed forward.

Sergeant Moreau led his platoon to the bridge. Coming off the hill, he noticed thousands of wounded soldiers stranded and with no way to cross the river unaided. "The engineers will blow up the bridge as soon as we cross," Sergeant Moreau told Luc.

"What will happen to the wounded?" Luc asked.

"They will be slaughtered by the Cossacks."

"But there are thousands of wounded soldiers... lying there powerless... we must help."

"We can't stop, the engineers are ready to detonate the bridge to prevent the Russians from crossing," he said, even as every instinct in his body told him to stay.

As he stepped off on the other side, Jean Marc looked back through the smoke seeing the Cossack hordes charging from the hills to slaughter the helpless soldiers.

"Ten thousand wounded were left on the other side," Sargeant Moreau heard the commander say to someone nearby. But, his thoughts could not linger on the slaughter, as enemy artillery rained on their position. "Move, move, move... find cover," he ordered, as the battle continued until the Russians broke off the fighting. The engineers failed to blow up one bridge, allowing the Cossacks to cross the river in hot pursuit of the retreating army.

The army reorganized and formed a column for its forced-march to Vilna, 160 miles away. "We are ordered to the rearguard to protect the column," Sergeant Moreau told his men. He watched them fall in after the last unit of the column.

The cold weather came back with a vengeance. Sergeant Moreau checked his men regularly for signs of frostbite. Whenever he spotted white skin, he ordered his medic to treat the soldier immediately. All the while, being harassed by the ever-present Cossack cavalry.

"The men are fighting tenaciously, both against the weather and the Cossacks, but we are losing more men to gangrene than to enemy bullets," Luc reported.

"It grieves me to see them falling to their deaths in the deep snow. Look at the men Luc: dressed in rags, breath freezing on their beards, the heavy snow making every step an ordeal, no boots, no food, no water, no sleep... and the fucking Cossacks attacking like a swarm of bees. Do what you can Luc," he said with resignation.

Chapter 8

Paris was a city of hope and expectation, of courage and valor, but on this day, all of Paris was fearful — France was being invaded. The Prussians were attacking from the north, the Austrians from the east and the British from the south. Initially, Napoleon was brilliant in his defense of France but his smaller army was soon exhausted, and there were few new recruits.

Eligible young men inflicted serious injuries upon themselves to avoid the draft. Some married much older women to gain an exemption and many dodged the draft by joining deserters in the countryside. To compound the problem, a severe shortage of horses deprived the army of an effective cavalry.

Still, Napoleon led his army to Leipzig to confront the forces coming from the east, where a sad fate befell him. Over four days he took 38,000 casualties and 30,000 were taken prisoners. The battered army broke contact and retreated back to France.

Now badly outnumbered, events turned against the French on all fronts. The British were victorious in Spain and trod onto French soil. The Allies depleted the French army on the eastern front. And, before Napoleon could react, 180,000 enemy soldiers advanced from the Marne to Paris. In the final battle, fought at the base of Montmartre, the French fought courageously but were overwhelmed by the superior numbers of the invading force. When defeat was inevitable, Paris capitulated.

As Madeleine left work, she was shocked at the sight of a military encampment in the nearby square. Armed soldiers guarded the perimeter, unfamiliar flags fluttered overhead and tension filled the air.

As she approached Michel's worksite, she noticed a few foreign soldiers milling around. Their attention was diverted as she approached. "She is my model," Michel said protectively.

"Will she pose nude for us?" a soldier quipped, to the laughter of the others.

Michel glowered at the soldier, jumped off the pedestal, took her hand and walked away.

"This is no place for you. The soldiers are on the verge of looting and pillaging Paris."

"What is keeping them from doing that?'

"Napoleon's army is but a few miles away awaiting the terms of the peace talks. But he is still in a position to attack the occupying forces."

"What will happen next?" she asked anxiously.

"The legislature has formed a provisional government and will move for Napoleon's deposition."

"What will he do?" Madeleine asked.

"It depends on the concessions of the Allies. "

"What will become of France?"

"Charles Maurice de Talleyrand, the French Foreign Minister, is negotiating with the Allies. He is no friend to Napoleon and is amenable to his deposition."

"Will Napoleon abdicate?"

"For the time being?'

"What do you mean?"

"I am not sure, but I recently met with Napoleon's staff," Michel responded.

'Why, Michel?"

"I was asked to serve as a secret agent so that Napoleon can keep in touch with developments in France."

"Why would he need secret agents?"

"Many of his followers believe he will be exiled but will return as soon as possible. We have been told to prepare for his homecoming."

"But, why you?"

"I was an officer in Napoleon's army and… "

"No, I cannot lose another to war!" she said, as she ran off crying.

A few days later, the Treaty of Fontainebleau was signed, forcing Napoleon to abdicate and exiling him to the island of Elba.

In the depths of Russia, the French stragglers experienced further hardships. The march to Vilna had been wearying, and the rear units were bogged down. "We are falling behind the main unit," Sergeant Moreau told his platoon. "We will soon be cut off by the Cossacks."

"Sergeant, let's leave the rear guard and catch up to the main unit. Otherwise, we will be slaughtered... or, worse, captured by the Cossacks."

"Corporal, our orders are to stay with the rear unit, but somehow we must catch up to the main force. Take two men and move up the column until you find the commander who is fucking up this march. Tell him of the danger that we are facing and push him to pick up the pace."

"Jacques and Louis come with me," the corporal ordered, anxious to leave as soon as possible.

As the rear guard approached Molodetchno, a squadron of Cossacks descended upon them with such speed and fury that it was cut off from the rest of the unit and captured without much of a fight.

Sergeant Moreau huddled with his captured soldiers and whispered, "The Cossacks have something in mind for us; otherwise, we would all be dead."

The Cossacks remained on their horses, which responded to their every move. Horse and warrior were like one. The prisoners were told to drop their weapons and ordered to march forward. Surrounded by the horsemen, they walked north for about an hour. When they arrived at their destination, they were quickly turned over to Russian guards, and the Cossacks disappeared into the night. Each prisoner was given a blanket and a wooden board and herded into a crowded barrack.

"Stay together," Sergeant Moreau ordered.

They found an open space, placed their boards on the frozen ground, and wrapped the blankets around their cold bodies. They were awakened before dawn by the shouting of a Russian soldier.

"You will work from dawn to dusk, seven days a week. Now that we have defeated the French, we will conquer Poland and pursue the French scum all the way to Paris. You will broaden the roads and reinforce the bridges for us. Anyone who does not do his share of the work will be shot on the spot." And to prove his point, three prisoners were brought to the front of the group, told to kneel, and shot in the back of the head.

That is the reason we were spared — to be worked to death or shot, Jean Marc thought.

They were given rice and bread and then ordered out into the bitter cold to work on the roadway. The prisoners walked bent against the bitter winds that blew in off the fields.

Jean Mark thought back on the past year: *He was part of the preparation for the Russian campaign; he left Paris with fifty men in his platoon; he now counted ten; he was 1400 miles from home and a prisoner of war.* But still, he was determined to bring his men back to Paris. *I will observe the guards, memorize their routine, and discover their weaknesses until I can develop a plan for our escape. But in the meantime, I must keep the spirit of my men up, as well as mine.*

"Do what is asked of you, but save your energy," he would say as he passed through his men. "Don't fight back... don't get angry... save your energy," he kept repeating.

Each night he planned for the escape. He memorized the earlier route they had taken through

Belgium, Germany, Poland and Russia and reversed the order in his mind: Vitebsk, Kamen, Klubokoje, Vilna, Kovno, Konigsberg, Danzig, Hamburg, Brussels, and Paris. He visualized the dangers to be faced along the way in crossing rivers and skirting cities. He thought of the Russian army clamping down all likely routes of exit. Exhausted, he would fall asleep reserving his last waking moments for thoughts of his family.

Chapter 9

The Treaty of Fontainebleau brought a dismal end to a dynasty that once cast a long shadow over Europe. "The treaty has settled the fate of Napoleon. He has been given sovereignty over the island of Elba. This was a compromise, for some of the Allies wanted Napoleon under house arrest on the British fort of St. George, while others wanted him exiled to the United States," the Monsignor told Father Martin, while seated at his large wooden desk.

"Will he have to abdicate as Emperor of France?"

"But, of course, the treaty mandates his abdication," the Monsignor responded smugly.

"What if he refuses to sign the treaty?" asked Father Martin.

"He is resigned to his fate. The Gazette carried parts of his speech to the Army: *Soldiers of my Old Guard, I bid you goodbye. For twenty years I have found you continuously on the path of honour and glory... I have sacrificed all of my rights and am ready to sacrifice my life, for my one aim has always been the happiness and glory of France... If I have chosen to go on living it is so I can write about the great things we have done together and tell posterity of your great deeds. Goodbye my children!"*

A few days later, Madeleine, Sylvie, and the children walked to the Champs-Elysee to see Napoleon's departure from Paris. A convoy of carriages, Polish lances, and a battalion of guardsmen escorted Napoleon out of Paris and to the Mediterranean island of Elba.

Madeleine scanned the grande boulevard and observed the crowd on both sides standing five to six rows deep. "There are so many people along the route to bid farewell to their former emperor," Madeleine remarked.

"There is still much support in Paris for Napoleon, but much of France supports his abdication and a return to the Bourbon kings," Sylvie responded.

"I have been told that the *Grande Armee* would rally behind him if he decided to return to Paris."

"The *Grande Armee* would follow Napoleon to Hades, if Napoleon so ordered."

"Mama, mama, there is Napoleon's carriage!" Jean exclaimed.

Madeleine turned toward a passing carriage and saw a somber Napoleon waving to the crowd. "He has devastated France, and still they hail him as their savior. He abdicates in glory not infamy," Madeleine remarked.

"The crowd remembers his victories and the pride he brought to France, Madeleine," Sylvie responded. "And they will rally to his cause when he returns."

Madeleine looked down at her children waving wildly as the emperor passed. And as they walked away, Jean tugged at his mother's sleeve and said, "Mama, mama, I will be a soldier when I grow up… just like papa, Michel and Napoleon!" Hearing these words, her heart sank.

Chapter 10

On the day of their departure, Thomas chatted idly about the matters they were about to explore. "Truth should direct the course of the Church. If Augustine was wrong in regard to the inferiority of women and if the Inquisition was amiss about the demonic nature of women, then these falsehoods should give way to the truth. This would return the Church to its roots in Christ. But the papacy and the bishops are adamant about the inferiority of women."

"Napoleon has been deported to Elba. Paris is in a state of fear. Foreign soldiers are looting the city. Let's pack our bags and talk about these matters at a later time!" Martin urged.

But Thomas persisted. "Just a generation ago, the *Philosophes* brought reason to our world. They were the intellectuals of the eighteenth century. They championed progress and tolerance and denounced superstition. They attacked organized religion and the medieval institutions."

Martin nodded and continued packing, not paying much attention to what was being said.

"These enlightened philosophers had the courage to think for themselves. And, that is why the Church denounces them."

"Enough chatter, let us leave now before the roads out of the city are blocked."

"You are right. Let us go."

"We must meet with the Monsignor before we leave" Martin said impatiently.

Thomas grabbed both bags and led the way. Martin followed while observing his friend. He had a rugged physique, olive colored skin, black, curly hair, and a youthful glow about himself. Even though they were quite different, he was delighted to have him as a travelling companion.

As they entered the rear of the cathedral, Martin spotted his superior in a darkened area of the church, "Monsignor, we were told we could find you in the cathedral. It is an odd time of day to be here," he remarked.

"Madeleine Moreau has not been in church since she left the banned book in that pew. Doesn't that make you suspicious, Father Martin?"

"Not at all, Monsignor."

"I have a better nose for heretics than you do. Here is the official accusation. It is under seal and signed by me. Be sure to file it with the tribunal as soon as you reach Rome and return with the judgment without delay."

Martin nodded his acquiescence

"The accusation was reviewed and approved by the Bishop of Paris yesterday. He agrees that we should now be more aggressive in prosecuting heretics."

"Now that we have the accusation, may we take our leave, Monsignor?" Father Martin asked.

"Yes, be on your way," he replied, turning his attention to the rear of the church.

As the two stepped outside, Martin was pleased to leave the scrutiny of the Monsignor.

"Good morning Madeleine," Martin said to a passerby.

"Good morning Father Martin," she responded.

"Martin, is that Madeleine Moreau?" Thomas whispered.

"Yes it is."

"She certainly does not look like a witch to me... just a very attractive, young woman," he said, as he turned to watch Madeleine walk away.

Madeleine continued on her way to work. She had not seen Michel in several days and the sight of foreign soldiers patrolling the streets hardened her opposition to Michel's involvement with Napoleon.

As she approached the park, she observed Michel chipping away at his sculpture.

"Bonjour Michel!"

"Bonjour Madeleine," he said, while turning toward the sculpture, "Madeleine, you are emerging from the marble."

As her gaze focused on the sculpture, she was amazed at the resemblance in the face and the hair. "That is quite remarkable, Michel!" Disarmed momentarily, she quickly regained her composure. "Much better that you sculpt than spy Michel."

She noted the anguish on his face as he responded hesitantly. "I love the people of France, and I cannot bear to see them under foreign rule, or the tyranny of kings, or the oppression of popes. I must follow my heart Madeleine."

"Too many have perished due to Napoleon's foolish wars… and many more will die if he returns to power."

"He has the support of the people, and they will support him if he returns."

"You have served France in war, now serve her with your artistry."

He looked back at the marble statue but said nothing.

"I must leave for work; let us talk tonight."

His eyes followed Madeleine as she walked away hoping that somehow he could both serve France and win her love.

"Tend to your work sculptor," a Prussian soldier said gruffly, as he walked by with rifle in hand.

Madeleine could see the anguish in his face as she approached him after her day's work. "The day has not been good to you," she said.

"Both passions pulled at my heart today, those of the woman I care for and those of the enemy I hate. After you left this morning, I wandered the streets of Paris, with soldiers at every corner, some looting stores, others accosting Parisians, all creating intolerable tension."

"And what will you do?"

"I cannot run away from people who need me, even if it means losing something very special to me."

"One day a man walks into your life, and you fall in love, and the next day he is struck down in battle, and is gone forever."

"Men and women have different dreams," he said sadly.

"And, maybe we can reconcile the two... "

"There is a curfew," came a harsh voice from behind them. Startled, they turned around to see two Prussian soldiers striding in their direction.

"I was just inquiring about the sculpture," Madeleine said furtively.

"Get your answer and be on your way," the soldier ordered.

She held her breath, then asked, "What will the rest of the sculpture look like, Michel?"

"A nude goddess," he whispered.

"Then best to leave it unfinished."

"If you posed for me, you would remain young forever."

She thought about it for a moment and said, "I have a better idea, and if it is acceptable, I will model for you but not in the nude."

"Tell me."

"Your sculpture will be that of Mary Magdalene, fully clothed."

"But, why Mary Magdalene?"

"Because she was the most beloved of Jesus' apostles."

"Surely, Mary Magdalene was not an apostle?" he said.

"Many believe that she was, but the others were so jealous they concealed the fact. In any event, she was His most beloved disciple."

"If it will give me time with you Madeleine, then this block of marble will become Mary Magdalene."

"When do we begin?"

"Come to my studio Sunday. The children can play as Mary Magdalene emerges from the marble."

"Why not in the park?" she asked.

"There is too much chaos in the streets, so I will take my work into the studio," he replied.

"Then we will come to your studio. I will bring a *petit dejeuner* for you and the children."

"You must leave now before the curfew," he said, loud enough for the soldiers to hear.

The next day when she arrived at the servants' quarters, she ran into a buzz of activity. "Madeleine, a messenger notified us that Madame LeBlanc is on her way back to Paris."

"Why would she return now when Paris is occupied by our enemies?" Madeleine asked.

"If you knew her like we do, that would be obvious. A few decades ago, she was caught up in the French Revolution. She rebelled against the monarchy and embraced the cause of freedom, liberty, and democracy. She was ostracized by the notables, which did not phase her, for she was more concerned about human dignity than her status with the aristocrats."

"Did you know her then, Sylvie?"

"No, but I have heard the stories. The Bastille, a prison, had become a symbol of Louis XVI's tyranny. One morning in July 1789, a small number of people gathered in protest before its outer gate. As word spread through the districts, the crowd grew in numbers and excitement. At one point the throng stormed and captured the Bastille.

Jeannette LeBlanc was one of the rebels. It was the start of the revolution of the common people against the king, the aristocrats, and the Catholic Church."

"Why the Church?"

"The Church was an integral part of the old order. It supported the king and opposed democracy"

"And why was it so opposed to democracy?' Madeleine asked.

"The clergy and the nobility were the privileged classes at the time. They owned much of the land. The Church was concerned about preserving its own material wealth even at the expense of its followers."

"So different than Jesus, whose simple message was to bring faith, hope, and love to the downtrodden."

"While people were clamoring for greater freedom, the Church clung to the past, like a predator clinging to its prey," Sylvie responded.

These thoughts of freedom tumbled through Madeleine's mind for the remainder of the workday as she tried to reconcile the Church's action with the words of Jesus. She also wondered, if the Revolution had brought about so much change, how did the Church maintained its influence.

As she left for the day, she sought out Sylvie, "How did the Church retain its status if it was on the losing side of the Revolution?"

"Napoleon knew that the Church wielded considerable influence over the peasantry, from whom he derived much of his support. So he entered into an agreement with the pope." Sylvie answered. "The agreement, called the Concordat, was popular with the peasantry and a good compromise for the Church. However, through the agreement the Church was forced to cede land and influence — which it is now trying to recover."

Chapter 11

On Christmas Eve, a few months after Napoleon was exiled to Elba, rumors were rampant of his return to the mainland. "He has been told of the discontent in France," Michel Bois told a group of veteran soldiers gathered in a small café in the heart of Paris.

"We have also informed him that there is dissension among the Allies. It seems that Austria and England want a Bourbon king while Russia and Prussia loath them, " added a group member, referred to as Colonel.

"There are thousands of veterans who have returned from the fields of battle convinced that they were sold down the river and finding that there is nothing left for them in France. They are bitter and eager for revenge."

"The sergeant is right, and there will soon be thousands of returning prisoners of war in the same mood. And, I am prepared to lead them again in battle," said an officer from the group."

"Napoleon is encouraged by the information he has received from his spies," Michel said.

"Does he have a plan?" the sergeant asked.

"He has seven hundred soldiers from the old guard and a squadron of cavalry with him on the island. That is sufficient for a landing on the mainland. The Allies anticipate Napoleon will take a direct route to Paris, and they plan to ambush him along the way," Michel answered as he observed his comrades.

"If that is the case, they will easily defeat him and his small band of soldiers," the sergeant remarked.

"But instead, he will go through the Alps to Grenoble. It is much more treacherous but will provide good cover," the colonel explained.

"Will he advance in the winter?" the sergeant asked.

"The plan is to leave Elba within the next few

months," Michel responded.

"We estimate that once he reaches Grenoble, the city gates will open, and the soldiers will pledge their allegiance to him. When he leaves Grenoble, he should have close to ten thousand soldiers under his command," the colonel added.

"Still not enough of an army to confront the Allies," the sergeant argued.

"He will then march to Lyons, where the sentiment for the emperor is strong. Marshall Ney, who hates the Bourbons, will defect to Napoleon, along with his army." Michel responded.

"Our mission in Paris is to unite the veteran soldiers and the returning prisoners of war, so that we can join him between Lyons and Paris," the colonel explained.

"Each of us will be assigned a different section of Paris to recruit veteran soldiers. We will meet once a week to report on our progress. Always in a different café, for some of us are being followed," the colonel said as he pulled out a map of Paris and designated the various assignments.

"Hail the Emperor," one from the group shouted.

"Hail the Emperor!" the rest responded.

"And, Joyeux Noel!" the colonel said to all, as they prepared to leave.

Michel ordered another beer and sat alone at the long, wooden bar.

"Are you not going home to celebrate Christmas with your family, Michel?" the colonel asked.

"I chose Napoleon instead of love, and it is days like these I regret that decision."

The colonel ordered a beer and sat beside him. "My family — a wife, two sons and three daughters — were killed by the Prussians as they invaded France, for no other reason but that I was a colonel in Napoleon's army."

Nothing more was said for a while, as the two

warriors sipped their beer in a darkened bar, lost in thought.

"The curfew is but a few minutes away, let us finish our beer and leave," Michel said, breaking the silence.

"I must travel a long distance to return to an empty house."

"Then stay with me. My studio is only a few blocks from here."

As they walked out of the bar, Michel noticed a checkpoint at the first intersection they encountered. They were searched and sent on their way.

"That is why we do not carry weapons, colonel."

"And that is why you should not call me colonel, Michel."

"Then tell me your name."

"Roger Gravel."

As they entered the studio Roger admired the sculptures as Michel poured a glass of brandy for his guest.

"You will soon be a renown sculptor, Michel."

Michel joined him, sipping brandy as they ambled from one sculpture to the next. "Your themes range from love to war; these must reflect the experiences of your life."

"At first, I experimented with religious themes like a pieta and biblical figures. Then came these sculptures, which reflect the themes you mention. And most recently, I returned to the bible for Mary Magdalene. Here she is. What do you think?"

"Such a controversial figure. Hailed by some as a saint and by others as a sinner, which one will you portray?"

"Both... the redeemed sinner who exemplifies Christ's mercy."

Michel brought the bottle of brandy to a small table near the Magdalene. They sat down, poured more brandy and admired the beauty of the Magdalene.

"Madeleine, the one I spoke to you about, was my model."

"Is she married?"

"Yes, to a soldier who has not returned from the Russian campaign."

"Do you love her?"

"Why do you ask?"

"Because you cannot conceal the love I see in your eyes."

"She is the most wonderful person to ever enter my life... but all I have now is a lifeless, cold block of marble."

"Why can't you be with her?"

"She does not want me to go war."

"Then don't..."

"I have this need to be true to myself. I can never run away from people who need me."

"The circumstances of war brought you together and now they separate you."

"What should I do, Roger?"

"I recently buried my family and now I have only the memories and a life of melancholy ahead of me," he said, as tears came to his eyes.

He remained silent for sometime, and then said, "You, however, still have hope."

The Allies had clamped down on people coming in and out of Paris. It took the two travelers longer than expected to pass through the armed checkpoints on the perimeter of the city.

"We will find an inn on the outskirts and leave early tomorrow morning," said Father Thomas. "The traffic will be heavy because of the holiday and the soldiers returning to link up with Napoleon."

"Why at an inn when a monastery is so close by?" Father Martin asked.

"Let us make this journey a true pilgrimage. The

pope, cardinals and bishops are all older men. They cling to the old order. We are the future of the Church. We must learn from the common people how we can better bring the message of Jesus to them."

"Martin Luther brought about a Reformation because the Church corrupted the message of Jesus. Now Christians are divided between Catholics and Protestants, warring against each other, but all with the same basic beliefs. How many more schisms must the Church undergo before it returns to the ways Jesus?"

"If you're willing, we will dress as lay travelers and mingle with the commoners; and, in that way, they will be more honest with us."

"We may shed our priestly clothes but not our priestly vow," insisted Father Martin.

"I will call you Martin, and you will call me Thomas."

"So be it, Thomas!"

"And about our vows, those that can be attributed to Jesus, we shall honor. Those that are man-made, we shall debate. And those that are nonsensical, we shall challenge."

"Our pilgrimage begins, today, Thomas."

Once at the inn, they checked into their room and changed to street clothes.

"Where shall we eat?" Martin asked.

"At the tavern."

"The tavern?" he asked incredulously.

"Where else are we going to meet the common man... and the common woman?" Thomas responded with a broad smile.

They sat at a small table in the crowded tavern. "It's a lively place," Martin remarked.

"Do you mind if I join you boys?" a man with a tattered uniform asked.

"Yes, yes, please join us," Thomas responded.

"Henri, shall I get you an ale?" the waitress asked.

"For now, of course, and later what will you get me?"

"For you nothing but for your young friends the possibilities are endless," she responded, bringing laughter to all but Martin.

"Are you on your way to join Napoleon's army?" the soldier asked as he ordered a round of ale for the table.

"No, we are on our way to Rome," Martin responded.

"What the hell's the matter with you boys? The enemy occupies Paris, Napoleon is our only salvation, and you're running away to Rome!" exclaimed the soldier as the bawdy waitress delivered the ales to the table.

"Here are your ales, Henri," she said as she kissed him on the cheek, which seemed to mellow him.

"Why Rome, boys?"

"To pray for the salvation of France, Henri," Martin responded.

"What are you, priests?"

Martin gulped his ale fearing their ploy had been exposed.

"God can't keep the enemy at bay. Only brave soldiers can under Napoleon's leadership," Henri responded for all in the tavern to hear. "I am on my way to Paris to join the resistance. *Sauvé la France!*" he exhorted, as he stood with his pint held high, toasting the crowd.

"*Sauvé la France!*" came the loud response.

"You see, all we need is a leader and young soldiers like you. Come with me," he urged.

"Blessed are the peacemakers," Martin responded.

"The peacemakers are not worth crap when the enemy occupies your homeland. When you cowards return to France in a year, you tell that to the widows and children of the dead soldiers... tell that to the crippled soldiers begging for alms... and tell that to our countrymen who are living under foreign rule!"

The crowd fell silent.

"Now run your scared ass to Rome before I plunge a fucking bayonet through your peacemaking heart!" he said as he slammed his pint on the table.

"Henri, Henri, please sit down. We did not mean to insult you. Explain to us the life of the soldier, so we might understand," Thomas pleaded.

Slowly Henri sat down, his face still flush with anger. "What is it you want to know?"

"Does God help soldiers in warfare?"

"At first, a soldier prays to God to protect him in battle. But once he experiences the terror of combat, he wonders what kind of god would allow this to happen. Gradually, he becomes hardened as his friends die and the enemy is killed. The soldier witnesses more horror in one day of war than most people experience in a lifetime. God goes swiftly from a soldier's heart... and the Church does little to soothe a soldier's soul."

Thomas sat stoically as he watched the old soldier drift off to where he knew he had never been... and would likely never go.

Chapter 12

Each day, Jean Marc saw the prisoners marching greater distances, working longer days and getting less food and water. Stronger prisoners were not permitted to help the weaker ones. Frail men were thrown in the snow to die a slow death. The recalcitrant ones were beaten and kicked to death. Most were suffering from malnutrition. And all were becoming weaker and more depressed.

"We must break out before it is too late. I have surveyed the area, and during the next storm, we will jump off the road at a ridge a little way from where we are working," Jean Marc told his men.

"If we're captured we'll be killed on the spot," said Dennis, one of the group.

"Better than dying in this fuckin' rat hole," another responded.

"Eat and drink whatever you can," Jean Marc urged. "Sleep well, and if it's stormy tomorrow, we will start our escape."

Jean Marc had also noticed a guardhouse near the work area, which lodged about a half a dozen soldiers. *This could be our salvation,* he thought.

It was snowing hard at the end of the next workday. "Take any tool you can as a weapon. Go closely behind me on the way back. When I leap off the ridge into the snow, do the same. Do not hesitate... twelve of us must jump at about the same time. I have talked to other soldiers, who will close the gap behind us," Jean Marc said, just as they received the order from a Russian guard to fall-in for the march back.

A prisoner in front of them stumbled to his knees and was bayoneted by a guard. A shot rang out to the rear as another prisoner was killed. "The guards are in a foul mood. Many more will be killed tonight... do nothing to attract their attention," Jean Marc cautioned his men.

As they rounded the bend, Jean Marc jumped and landed in the soft snow at the bottom of the ridge. He counted ten thuds. "One more, just one more," he sighed. He could hear the prisoners shuffling and the guards berating them. They waited silently for the column to pass.

"Give me a roll call," Jean Marc ordered. "Dennis... Bertrand... Jean... Philip... Albert... Joseph... Norman... Claude... Eric... Jacques..."

"Luc is missing, Sergeant," Albert said.

All froze as they heard a sound to the rear. A few moments passed before an outline appeared.

"Over here, Luc," Jean Marc whispered..

"I jumped late... I'm afraid of heights," he responded.

"There's a grove of trees a few hundred meters from here. Let's move out," Jean Marc ordered.

From the grove they could see the guardhouse. Smoke was rising from the chimney, the warm glow of fire was in the window and one guard patrolled the perimeter.

"I can get to the guard without being seen," Eric said.

"How?" Jean Marc asked.

"I am from the Alps. I traveled in the dark every night."

"Why?" a soldier asked.

"To go to the outhouse," which brought a muffled laughter from the group.

"Once you silence the guard, take his gun. We will run to your side and rush the cabin. You will enter first. Shoot anything that moves."

Eric nodded.

"We will give them time to fall asleep. Huddle together and keep warm."

At about midnight, Jean Marc gave the order. Eric left not making a sound and was soon veiled by the falling snow and dark night.

"Where is he?" Luc asked.

Minutes dragged on with no sight of Eric. Suddenly, the guard moved from his post looking in the direction of the grove.

"Eric is in trouble, let's rush the guard... ''

"No, hold your position," Jean Marc ordered.

The guard advanced tentatively, his rifle moving from side to side. He stopped, cocked his weapon, and took aim.

The soldiers tensed up, ready to charge, awaiting an order from Jean Marc.

Jean Marc broke a branch. The guard turned in the direction of the noise. Eric sprang forward and lunged at the guard, forcing his head deep into the snow and snapping his neck. When his friends arrived, Eric had the rifle in hand and led the assault on the guardhouse. He smashed the door open and shot at the first motion he saw. The others rushed in and quickly overwhelmed the Russian soldiers.

Jean Marc saw Eric drop to his knees and went to the side of the young soldier. "God forgive me," he prayed. "He has, Eric...", then he turned and ordered: "Our best marksmen will take the rifles and put on the Russian uniforms."

"Sergeant, here is the storage area... food, water, boots, jackets and ammunition," Claude yelled.

"Fill the back packs and stuff your pockets with the rest."

"Leave room, Sergeant. Here's a case of vodka," Philip bellowed.

"Good for cold nights," Jacques added.

"Philip, open a bottle and pass it around. We'll eat, catch a few hours sleep and get the hell out of here."

After the soldiers ate, all bunked down on the beds and the floor, except for Eric, who walked out the front door.

"I will keep watch, Sergeant."

Over the snoring of the men, Jean Marc could hear Eric sobbing by the front door. *God, don't ever let my sons go to war,* he pleaded.

In Paris, the city was abuzz with news of Napoleon's landing on the mainland. An army of sixty thousand was mobilized by the King and sent to intercept Bonaparte. The Allies declared Napoleon an outlaw and pledged to provide 150,000 soldiers to destroy him. Their strategy was to form a cordon from the Alps to the English Channel and set the trap for Napoleon. The forces in Paris were ordered to withdraw to the outskirts of France. These were the thoughts that tumbled through Michel's mind as he entered the tavern.

Michel and the others watched as the foreign soldiers made preparations to leave Paris. "We have informed Napoleon that Marshall Ney's support for the King is wavering. His defection would bring his army to our side and sway others. A meeting is scheduled between the two at Auxerre in a few days," Michel told the group.

"Michel, is he aware that the Allies are leaving Paris?" a voice from the bar asked.

"A messenger is on his way to deliver the news."

"Our recruiting effort in Paris is strong, and soldiers are flocking to the city from all of France," the colonel added.

"Is war inevitable?" the sergeant asked.

"Napoleon sent an envoy to meet with the Allies to broker terms and avoid war," the colonel explained.

"In that case, there is still a chance," the sergeant persisted.

"But Napoleon was rebuffed. The Allies called him an enemy of humanity. They said he would be banished from Europe if captured," the colonel responded.

"Then it will be a fight to the finish," the sergeant said, now resigned to the battle lay ahead of them.

Silence filled the room as the members weighed the finality of these words.

"What will happen to King Louis XVIII?" the sergeant asked, breaking the silence.

"The Allies placed him on the throne to support their effort in France, but he is weak and will flee before Napoleon enters Paris," Michel responded.

"Now that we have raised an army, let us arrange our volunteers into platoons, companies and battalions with officers and sergeants in charge of each. In that way, the army will be at the ready when the Emperor arrives," the colonel directed.

"Michel... Michel!" came a cry from the front door.

All turned to see who was interrupting their meeting.

"How did you know I was here, Marie?"

"I heard the soldiers talk of an ambush before they broke into Madeleine's apartment."

"How many, Marie?"

"Three, Michel."

"Michel, take me and the sergeant to the apartment. The rest of you set a trap for the Prussians," the colonel ordered. "Our war has begun!"

The three hurried toward the apartment, poorly armed but emotionally charged.

"There it is," Michel said pointing to the second floor of a building.

"Through the front door and up the stairs as fast as we can."

"Yes sir," the sergeant replied, leading the group.

Screams were heard coming from the apartment. "You fucking pig," the sergeant yelled as he busted through the door and thrust his saber through a soldier's chest.

Michel saw the colonel tackle the second soldier as

66

he rushed to the bedroom. He smashed through the door seeing a soldier rolling off Madeleine's naked body, reaching for a gun. At once, he was upon him driving his knife deep into his body until it reached his heart. The soldier gasped and his warm blood poured onto Michel's hand. He turned to see Madeleine covering her naked body and crying out, "The children... where are the children, Michel?"

"In the kitchen, Madeleine," he said, as the sergeant led them into the room. They rushed to her side and she held them tight, shielding them from any more harm "Merci, merci Michel."

"Michel, bring Madeleine and the children to your place, where they will be safe."

Where will you go?"

"We will drag the bodies to the cellar and then join the ambush at the tavern."

"I will join you after I bring Madeleine and the children to the studio."

"No, Michel. Stay with your family."

"But..."

"That's an order, Michel."

Later that evening, as the children and Madeleine slept, Michel answered a rap on the door to find the colonel.

He entered and said somberly, 'They're dead... they're all dead."

"Who is dead?"

"As we arrived, I saw squad of Prussian soldier rushing into the tavern firing their rifles."

"Oh, no!"

"Then suddenly from the alley across the street, a group of our soldiers pushed a carriage up against the tavern, barricading the door they had just entered. Two others lit torches and tossed them inside through a small window. Within seconds the tavern was ablaze. All that could be heard, over the sounds of the inferno, were the screams of those inside."

"Who, colonel... who was inside the tavern?"

"As the Prussians tried to escape through the back door, they found it barricaded. They were trapped as the torches fell upon the floor covered with kerosene."

The two embraced as the colonel said, "They're safe... our men are all safe, Michel... but our war has begun!"

Chapter 13

"Louis XVIII is vacillating as to whether he will remain in Paris or flee to a friendly country. But he does not waver about his support of the clergy. He longs for the old regime: The absolute rule of monarchs, the Catholic Church, wealthy aristocrats, and powerless commoners. He abhors the new creed of liberty, equality and fraternity. He assured me that he will return the Church of Rome to a singular place in France," the Bishop of Paris told a gathering of clerics.

"If he leaves France, how will he be able to help us?" the Monsignor asked.

"He is convinced that the Allies will defeat Napoleon and return him to the throne. And, in turn, he will restore the alliance of throne and altar. It was Henri IV, the first Bourbon King, who affirmed Catholicism as the official religion of France. Louis would like to emulate his ancestor."

"Your excellency, the Revolution has brought about significant change, freedom is in the air, which includes the freedom to worship according to one's personal choice. Many Catholics have left the Church and become Protestants, while others are searching for a religion of reason. We have lost touch with our followers by trying to defend the past. Instead, of a throne and altar policy, we should adopt a people and altar policy," a priest from a nearby parish said.

"Those words are blasphemous," the bishop retorted. "Saint Augustine said 'that liberty comes by grace and not grace by liberty.' And, in Corinthians it is said: 'The grace of God, not earthly wisdom, guides our conduct.' We are the successors to the Apostles, and only through us can people find salvation."

"Man can find salvation only through grace and the

help of the clergy, and the Revolution has not replaced the grace of God," the bishop continued.

"Your Excellency, I understand that both grace and the clergy are needed for salvation, but Jesus was dedicated to the people and not Caesar, as we should be dedicated to the followers and not the king!" the priest replied.

"Before we can convert the Protestants, heretics and witches, we must condemn religious toleration. The liberal uprisings must be suppressed by force, if necessary." the Monsignor interjected.

"The King is aware that the pope despises the thought of religious freedom. I will reinforce this thought when I meet with the king tomorrow. God be with you," the bishop said as he adjourned the meeting.

On the way back to Notre Dame, the carriage turned onto a side street. "Stop, stop right here," the Monsignor ordered. The carriage stopped. He exited and looked up to the second floor. It looked vacant. He walked toward the front door, but hesitated when he heard a company of Prussian soldiers marching towards his carriage.

"Halt!"

The Monsignor froze.

"Oh… good morning, Monsignor. I could not tell it was you."

"Good morning. How did the mission go, Captain?"

"We found three bodies in that cellar and lost a squad of soldiers at the tavern… the mission was a disaster."

"Is that why you are on the march now?"

"No, Monsignor. We are departing Paris to join up with the Allied army on the eastern front."

The Monsignor shook his head dejectedly.

"After we defeat Bonaparte, we will come back."

"Do not delay; France needs you!"

"We've a long way to go!"

"Before you leave, where is Madeleine Moreau?"

"We have not seen her," he said, as he returned to his unit.

Upon his command, the company marched toward the boulevard.

As the Monsignor arrived at Notre Dame, he thought: *Overnight, my world has changed. I am a confidante of the bishop, a friend to the Allies, and now have the influence to promote my agenda. Since the time I was ordained, I believed the destiny of the Church was somehow intertwined with my life... I will not allow this opportunity to pass.*

"Tomorrow, find out the whereabouts of Madeleine Moreau," he called to the coachman, over the noise of the carriage on the cobblestone street.

As Napoleon approached Paris, Louis XVIII assembled an entourage and fled to Ghent. The Emperor entered Paris a few days later and was greeted by exuberant crowds lining the route to the palace. He had made good on his boast to reach his destination without shedding a drop of blood. But realizing war was looming, he met immediately with his military staff, which urged him to lead a war of liberation against the enemy. He assured them that his goals were not unlike theirs and that he would soon raise a fully trained army.

"The Emperor's strategy calls for a preemptive strike in Belgium. He plans to drive a wedge between the Prussian and British armies and then destroy each in turn. Then, he will turn his attention to the Russian and Austrian armies in the east."

"And what are your plans, Michel?" Madeleine asked.

"I have been given a commission of major in the

Grande Armee. It is the elite corps..."

"I know the Grande Armee, Michel," she interrupted. "Jean Marc is... or was... a career soldier in Napoleon's army. I am asking whether you are going to Belgium?"

Michel walked to the window and looked outside, seemingly oblivious to her question.

"Well, Michel..."

"Yes, I depart in a few days."

"You are leaving three children, who adore you... and a woman, who loves you, to fight a war you can't win."

Michel's internal struggle was evident on his face.

"Maybe I should just accept the fate of women, to be subservient to men, society and the church — but I cannot," she continued. "Go to war Michel, but I will not be here when you return."

Chapter 14

The two young travelers stopped at an inn in the Orleans region. It was located in the center of a small village. Once the travelers had secured a room, they went to a nearby pub, sat in a quiet corner and ordered the local wine.

"There is a much-loved personality in this region who died for the glory of God and of France. As we mingle with the villagers this evening, we will learn more of this heroine. Tomorrow we will return to our priestly garb when we visit the library at the Cathedral of Sainte Croix," Thomas said to his friend.

"And who is this heroine?" Martin asked.

"Why, of course, Joan of Arc!"

"Tell me about her," Martin urged.

"You will learn first hand from the villagers. The children of the village learn about Joan of Arc at the same time they learn about Jesus."

It was a warm summer evening and many of the villagers were wandering into the small pub. A middle-aged woman brought their wine, and asked, "What brings you to our village?"

"We would like to learn of your local heroine." Thomas responded.

"Ah, yes, I will send my daughter to your table. She will tell you the story of our brave Joan as you enjoy the local delicacies," she said warmly.

Moments later an attractive young girl appeared at their table. "Bonsoir! My name is Marie. Welcome to our little village. I hope your stay is pleasant."

Martin was struck by her natural beauty, but was uncomfortable in her presence. Thomas, however, joined the conversation immediately. "Marie, you and your mother are very gracious. May I ask your age?"

"I am sixteen, and my mother believes I should already be married. She introduces me to all the young men who travel through our village. My father, however, is not of the same mind and keeps a very close eye on me. But I am the same age as Joan of Arc when she saved France, so I believe I am old enough to make my own decisions."

Martin smiled wryly, thinking that young girls saw everything too simply. "And how old are you monsieur?" she asked Martin.

"I … I am twenty four years old," he responded awkwardly.

"Your friend is shy, but so handsome," she said to Thomas.

Martin was offended by her brazenness. He had never been told he was handsome; especially by an attractive young woman. He thought instantly of the Monsignor's warnings about the sensual spell women cast on men leading them to sinfulness.

"It is time for us to leave … come on, Thomas," he whispered as he stood up to leave.

Taken aback, she clasped his hand and gently pulled him back toward the table. "Sit down Martin. I will no longer tease you. Let me tell you about our local heroine as you sip your wine and enjoy my father's fine food."

"Martin … Martin, she is only being hospitable. Her father stares at us as we speak. Let us enjoy the evening and learn about this brave woman, Joan of Arc," Thomas urged.

"Forgive me." Martin said earnestly. "That was rude."

"Please continue, Marie," Thomas said as they settled in for their lesson in local history.

"Joan of Arc was born in 1492 in the little village of Domremy in eastern France. During her childhood she heard voices from heaven telling her to free her country from the armies of England and Burgundy."

"Why would God choose a women for this grand task?" Martin asked skeptically.

"You will see. Be patient," Marie responded. "France was divided into two factions. The Orleanists led by the Duke Charles of Orleans and the Burgundians led by Duke John the Fearless of Burgundy. As the French fought their civil war, King Henry V of England invaded France and defeated the French army at Agincourt. The English soon gained the support of the Burgundians, who recognized Henry as the heir to the French throne."

"How did Joan become involved in this conflict involving dukes and kings?" Martin asked.

"Her visions of saints and angels increased in intensity. They included visions of St. Catherine, St. Margaret, the archangels Michael and Gabrielle. Others witnessed the apparitions but could not hear the voices." She paused and stared at Martin as if looking for a response.

"I cannot comprehend why saints and angels would appear to a young girl," he said, still incredulous that saints and angels would appear to a woman, let alone a young girl.

"You are too cynical, Martin, but let me continue. The situation became more crucial as the English troops advanced to the Loire River Valley. The city of Orleans now became the objective of the advancing armies. The situation for Charles, the heir to the throne of France, looked bleak. And at this time Joan's apparitions called for her to go to the local commander to escort her to Charles."

"No commander would escort a young girl to the king. He would be laughed out of the royal court," Martin said facetiously.

"You are right, Martin. The local commander refused to listen to her even as the enemy was closing in on Charles."

Martin nodded proudly.

"It was not until Joan had accurately predicted a defeat of French troops several miles north of Orleans that the commander agreed to bring her to the king."

"Was she clairvoyant?" Martin asked, still cynical about the tale he was hearing.

"Would you feel differently if Joan had been a boy?" Thomas asked.

Martin did not respond, and after a short pause, Marie continued. "Joan's voices told her that God supported Charles' claim to the throne and had taken pity on the French population for the suffering they had endured during the war. Her escort disguised her in male clothing to protect her from being raped by the soldiers. After eleven days on the road, she presented herself to Charles. She informed him that God had sent her. He was doubtful at first, but he took her seriously when she recounted a dream he had had months earlier. She also reassured him that he was the legitimate claimant to the throne."

As Marie's mother served the main meal, she asked, "Very inspiring isn't she?"

"Joan of Arc is very inspiring," Thomas responded.

"I was talking of my Marie."

"Mother!" Marie exclaimed.

"Please Marie, please continue," Thomas urged.

"Very well Thomas," she responded with a smile. "Charles was not yet convinced that he should let someone lead his troops in battle, let alone a young woman. So he had her examined by a group of theologians for three weeks. They concluded that she held her own against the learned theologians. And her reputation began to spread as many referred to her as another St. Catherine come down to earth. With Charles' consent, she wrote an ultimatum to the English commander at Orleans, expressing that God supported Charles claim to the throne and instructing him to return to England, or she would drive the British Army out of France."

"What happened?" Thomas asked.

"The British commander ignored her entreaty."

"I believe any commander in his position would have done the same thing," Martin said.

"Yes, but it did not dissuade Charles. He had her suited with armor and brought her to the army south of Orleans. She expelled the prostitutes, required the soldiers to confess their sins, and had them attend mass. Their confidence grew as word spread that a *saint* was now at the head of the army."

"I am enjoying your story Marie," Thomas responded as he finished his meal. But Martin remained aloof.

"The French Army moved out from Bois with the *Maiden* at its head holding a banner with the picture of the Savior and two angels," Marie continued. "A few days after her arrival, Joan's army assaulted the enemy army, which was heavily entrenched at the church of St. Loup. The battle was carried when Joan rode up to the front line, with the banner in hand, encouraging the infantry to scale the ramparts while exposed to enemy arrows."

The villagers in the restaurant had heard the story many times, but still they gathered around Marie, listening intently to the story of their heroine.

Following a slight pause to get the sense of her audience, she continued. "She carried a banner in battle instead of a weapon because she did not want to harm anyone. And in future battles, she always led her troops with banner in hand and at the front of the attack."

"Brave indeed for a woman," Martin interjected.

"Brave indeed for anyone," a person in the crowd corrected.

"On the following day, she met with her generals outlining a plan for a series of assaults against the English fortifications. However, she did not order the charge until she had given the enemy one final chance to leave France, which it immediately rejected. Joan then led the French troops against the fortified church of St. Jean LeBlanc, which was taken with little resistance. She pursued the English and at the head of the charge, stormed and overran the heavily fortified fortress of *Les Augustins*, taking very few casualties. On the following day, wounded by an arrow while scaling a wall on the fortress of *Les Tourelles*, she was taken from the field of battle to have her wound treated, but returned to rally her demoralized soldiers to victory with the enemy in full retreat from Orleans."

"Did the invading Army retreat to England?" Martin asked.

"Unfortunately, no. After the King and the *Maiden* met the next day, she convinced him to take an army north to pursue the English. They caught up to the retreating army at *Jargeau* with Joan ordering the soldiers to storm the ramparts while leading the charge and shouting, 'Friends, friends, up! Our Lord has condemned the English!' The fortifications were taken, and the English were driven back again. The French pursued, spurred on by Joan with a cry to chase the enemy from France."

The two armies met again south of *Patay*. The *Maiden* was at the head of the cavalry, which overran the English infantry and routed the rest of the enemy army."

"Were there many casualties?" Thomas asked.

"The *Maiden* was certainly blessed. The English lost 2,200 men while the French suffered only three casualties. The French marched to Troyes, which was garrisoned by Burgundian troops. Joan ordered the generals to besiege the city, predicting the army would gain victory in three days *either by love or by force*. Troyes surrendered the next day without a fight."

Marie's mother brought out strawberries and fresh cream for dessert while trying not to interrupt the storyteller.

"Joan convinced Charles to travel to Reims to be crowned as custom required. She again led the charge at Reims, and the English retreated with little resistance, now convinced the French Army was led by a saint."

"Was she truly a saint?" Martin asked.

"She has never been canonized," Marie responded.

"If ever there was a saint it was the *Maiden of Orleans!*" a villager exclaimed.

Marie nodded and said, "These are the words she spoke tearfully at Charles coronation: '*Noble king, now is accomplished the pleasure of God, who wished me to lift the siege at Orleans, and to bring you to this city of Reims to receive your holy anointing, to show that you are the true king, and the one to whom the kingdom of France should belong.*'"

"There is more to the story, but that will be studied in the archives in a few days." Thomas said. "Shall I order more wine?"

"Not for me," Martin responded. "I am going back to the inn. Thank you Marie for a very interesting evening."

"And you Thomas, will you stay for another glass of wine?" Marie asked.

"Yes, Marie," he responded flashing an enticing smile.

Chapter 15

"Our families are related," Madame Leblanc said to Madeleine. "I have been to Bordeaux and discovered that your grandmother and my father were siblings. When I first saw you, that Sunday at Notre Dame, I noticed a striking resemblance to my family. I did a little poking around and learned that you were from the same village as my parents. I informed my staff that I was going to the country estate, but instead I went to Bordeaux. Although not many of our relatives remain, I was able to piece together our family tree."

Madeleine was shocked and could not speak.

"I think I developed the blood of my father, the soldier, and you developed the blood of your grandmother, the peacemaker," Madame LeBlanc said.

"I was brought up in a very loving household, but the wars ravaged our family. The men went off to war — most did not come back, and those who did were not the same."

"There is one who wanders around the village aimlessly. I spoke to him briefly, but he was too inebriated to make much sense."

"He is like the vines in our yards withering away because of lack of care… "

"And lack of love," Madame LeBlanc added.

'So there are very few of us left."

"Which makes our reunion so much more important. Tell me about yourself, Madeleine."

"Well, I am still shocked by this revelation, but as you know I have three lovely children. Their father is Jean Marc Moreau, and he is a sergeant in Napoleon's army."

"Is he here in Paris?"

"He was part of the Russian offensive. I have not heard from him in over a year. He could be a prisoner… or he could be…"

'It must be a terrible burden not knowing."

"I was lonely, and I longed for love and someone came into my life."

"And who is that person?"

"Michel Bois."

"The sculptor?"

""You know him?"

"I know of him. As an artist, he is the talk of Paris," Madame LeBlanc said admiringly. "And, where is he now?"

"He has volunteered in Napoleon's army and will be leaving for Belgium in a few days."

"Do you care for him, Madeleine?"

"I fell in love with Jean Marc because of his strength and courage. I always felt secure with him. But, Michel gives me confidence. He compliments the things I do, respects my point of view, supports my endeavors, and helps me grow as a person."

"Sadly, you might not be in charge of your destiny."

"Yes, as for so many in France… our destiny is in the hands of Napoleon's war."

Madame LeBlanc poured tea for the two and then asked, "Where are you living?"

"I am looking for an apartment that is safer and closer to work."

"I suggest you and the children moved in with me. Not only is it safe, but it close to work," she said with a chuckle. "I will send someone to get your clothes and property."

"No, let me do that. I must tell Michel something before he leaves." She stood, hugged Madame LeBlanc and left.

When she arrived, she noticed the colonel leaving the studio. "Madeleine, it is nice to see you. What are you doing here?"

"I need to talk to Michel, Colonel."

He looked confused.

"Where is he?"

"He is gone to the front to gather intelligence for Napoleon."

"Oh, my God," she said. " You can't mean that he left Paris. Colonel, tell me he is not gone!"

"He volunteered for the mission yesterday and left this morning. He said there was nothing left for him in Paris."

Tears streamed down her cheeks. He held her in his arms to console her.

"Will you see him soon?" she said at last.

"Yes, Madeleine. I have been assigned as a battalion commander and Michel is my adjutant. I will see him in a few weeks."

"You must tell him something for me."

"But, of course."

"Tell him I have had a change of heart. It is Napoleon's war I oppose not France's warriors."

He smiled and said, "I will tell him you are concerned."

"Yes, please do."

As he walked away, he turned and said, "By the way Madeleine, a priest came by yesterday asking for your whereabouts."

"What did he want?"

"He did not say."

Madeleine was sad when she returned to the LeBlanc resident.

"Come to the gardens Madeleine and tell me what is wrong," Madame LeBlanc said.

"Michel is gone and I did not have the chance to talk to him."

"Where is he?"

"On his way to Belgium with the advanced group."

"Then we will pray and come up with a plan for you. The worst thing you can do is to sit around and feel sorry for yourself."

"What kind of plan?"

"Sylvie will continue to manage the staff, but I have a special plan for the outdoors. Come walk with me around the gardens, and I will tell you of my thoughts. I am quite impressed by the artwork of Michel Bois, especially his sculptures, and I would like to commission him to do artwork for me."

"That is such a pleasant surprise. What is your idea for the changes?"

"As you may know, Madeleine, I was involved in the Revolution. I have read the works of Voltaire, Rousseau, Diderot, Montesquieu, and Locke. They brought about an age of reason and opposed superstition, intolerance, and abuses of power by the monarchy and Church. These are the public figures I want memorialized in marble!"

They meandered through the gardens together observing every sculpture but saying little.

"The sculptures are very pleasing to the senses, but they are all in the baroque style and limit the viewers experience," Madame LeBlanc said.

"And, what is the baroque style?" Madeleine asked.

"It is very religious and many great works have a religious theme, but the baroque pits Catholics against Protestants. I find that troublesome."

"What would you do?"

"We will include more classical and neo-classical sculptures. They will better reflect our society."

"Then, you would include statues of Voltaire, Diderot, Rousseau... '"

"Yes, it would add balance to the gardens."

"Which one will you start with?"

"My favorite, of course, Voltaire."

"And, what role would I play?"

"You will rearrange the gardens to unify both themes."

"I will begin rearranging the gardens immediately. They will be ready when Michel returns."

"Be guided by the words of Voltaire: *It is evident that it is our souls which are under the clergy's care, solely in spiritual matters. The clergy should not have any temporal power. And, no coercive force is proper in the ministry.*"

Madeleine's mind wandered, not responding.

"What is the matter, Madeleine?"

"The last words. *No coercive force is proper in the ministry*. The Monsignor is searching for my whereabouts."

"Do you fear the Monsignor?"

"Yes."

"I will let the bishop know that I am concerned. I am his largest benefactor. No harm will come to you, Madeleine."

Chapter 16

The journey through Russia was arduous and slow. The small band of soldiers traveled only at night, using the stars to navigate a course due west. Without a map, they encountered many obstacles, such as, marshes, lakes and rivers that forced them to backtrack. Sergeant Moreau sensing the frustration mounting in his soldiers ordered the unit to travel on the roadway. The strategy was not as safe, but it increased the pace significantly. He sent the uniformed soldiers ahead with the others a few hundred yards behind.

The road led them to a hill overlooking the city of Minsk. Once the rear group caught up, Jean Marc scanned the area. "Large parts of the city were destroyed during the fight with the Russians. The forest borders the edge of the city, especially in the eastern and northern parts. Most of the fortifications are on the hills to the west. Our safest route is through the forest to the east." Jean Marc said.

"It is also the longest route," Philip added.

"Night is about to fall. We will camp in the forest tonight. At daybreak, we will head to the eastern part of the city under the cover of trees." Jean Marc ordered.

"I am heading to the northwest. We are wasting too much time circling villages and cities. Who's coming with me?" Philip asked.

A few men moved in his direction. "Stand down!" Jean Marc ordered.

"You are no longer giving the orders, Moreau," Philip asserted, as he raised his rifle in the direction of Jean Marc.

"You'll give away our position if you shoot me."

"Then we will just walk away."

"How long will it take by the eastern route?" Luc interrupted.

"Look in the direction Philip wants to take. There are three or four rivers that will have to be crossed. Look to the east. There is only one river."

The men nodded and moved toward Jean Marc. "He has gotten us this far. Let's stick together. It's our only chance," Luc said.

Philip lowered the rifle and fell in behind the others.

Within a few days they had circled Minsk and crossed the border into Poland.

"We must be more vigilant now."

"But, why, Moreau? We are out of Russia," Philip said.

"Russia and Prussia have been stealing lands from Poland for decades. What remains of Poland is but a strip of land. The Poles are outraged, but they do not have the capacity to repel the invaders. As we traverse what was once Poland, we could be assaulted by Cossack cavalry, Prussian infantry or Polish guerrillas."

"Do we revert to travelling at night?" Eric asked.

"Yes, and you will be at the point. We will also cover our flanks and rear. It will be slow but secure."

"What about you, Philip?" Luc asked.

"Count me in… at least, for the time being."

"Let's bunk down until nightfall. Then, we will begin our journey through Poland."

"How long a journey, sergeant?" Luc asked.

"Over four hundred kilometers, as the crow flies. We will travel southwest to the Vistula River, follow the Vistula as it winds it way to Warsaw and then west to Germany."

"We have no maps, cannot ask for directions and have no compass. How will we ever find our fuckin' way back?"

"Claude, by the sun, stars and landmarks," Jean Marc responded.

They traveled cautiously at night and kept to the

roadside for their bearing. The feel of warmer weather and the smell of spring were encouraging, but the longer days and down time gave them ample time to bicker.

"I worry about the men, sergeant. When you are not around, they quarrel about your leadership. Philip seems to be gaining support," Luc warned.

"These are trying times for all of us…"

"Sergeant, Sergeant … look who I captured," Jacques said excitedly, while holding a rifle to a goliath's back.

"Do not fool yourself Frenchy, you would be dead if I did not want to meet your leader. Dat is you sergeant?" the burly man asked pointing to Jean Marc. He had a thick Polish accent and walked menacingly towards Jean Marc. He stopped abruptly, opened his arms and embraced him.

Jean Marc thought he would suffocate from the bear hug.

"I need you, and you need me sergeant," the man said in a gruff voice as he loosened his embrace.

"I need you to put me down, so I can breathe!" exclaimed Jean Marc.

"He's an animal… he loves you sergeant!" Claude roared as the men broke into laughter.

"I ave been with better looking livestock," the stranger responded, further encouraging the laughter. "My name is Jacek Pabst. I ave been following you for days and you are lost."

"Why have you been following us?"

"Sergeant, I am Polish, and I ate da fukin Russians and Prussians, da bastards are raping our country."

"Then we both hate the Prussians… and the fuckin' Russians even more!" Claude barked.

"Why do you need us, Jacek?" Sergeant Moreau asked.

"Our enemies… dey ravage our land… dey rape our women… dey want our country. We have many men to fight dem but no army... no leaders like you, sergeant! Der are a hundred Cossacks west of ere... dey sack our villages at will... I want to kill dem all... but I need you to lead us."

"And why do we need you, Jacek?" Jean Marc asked.

"You travel tree kilometers a day... by da time you reach France you will be old men... da French women will not wait for you... you'll get der just in time to die!"

"He's right," Philip added.

"How will you get us there faster?"

"Da Russians dey need us as dey move to France... we bring dem food and labor as dey move west. Hundreds, no tousands of Poles do dis every day. We can make you into us... we can make you Poles. Dey tink we are dumb, so you Frenchies will fit right in!" he said as he roared with laughter. "When we do dat job, we travel tirty or tirty-five kilometers a day ... ten times more den you do in one day ... and der is no danger. You will get back in time to protect Paris and screw your women!" he exclaimed, and again broke into a loud laugh.

The soldiers looked at each other like they had been given hope by a big, ugly angel from heaven. "He might be our salvation," Claude said.

"Where are the Cossacks now?" Sergeant Moreau asked.

"Ten kilometers west from ere."

"Jacques, take a man with you and scout out the Cossack. Check out their every move. Then report back to me, as soon as possible"

"Yes sergeant. Claude, come with me!"

Two days later, Jacques and Claude returned and found Jean Marc instructing Jacek. "First I will teach you tactics, then I will teach you strategy," Jean Marc said as he spotted his two scouts approaching.

"What do you have to report?"

"About fifty Cossacks all well disciplined. They

station sentinels every night about five hundred meters from camp. They sleep near their horses. At the slightest sign of danger they are on their horses in a heartbeat. It will be very difficult to surprise them."

"How many men on horses can you have ready, Jacek?" Jean Marc asked.

"Maybe, fifty or sixty."

"And how many foot soldiers?"

"Maybe, da same number."

Jean Marc thought for a few seconds and said, "We can only beat them if we keep them off their horses!"

"How we stop dat?" Jacek asked.

"I will take my men south of the encampment. You will bring your foot soldiers north of the encampment. And the cavalry will come in from the west."

"How will that keep the Cossacks from getting on their horses?" Claude asked.

"Our timing must be perfect. We will attack first from the south. That will cause a distraction, but they will hesitate for only a few moments, Jacek. That is when you must attack from the north, which will cause more confusion."

"I understand!" Jacek responded.

"If you attack too soon, you are dead. If you attack too late, we are dead. If the Cossacks get to their horses, we are all dead."

Jacek nodded.

"The horsemen waiting one kilometer to the west will attack as soon as they hear the first shot. They will go directly to the Cossack horses and scatter them... then they will attack from the rear to assist the both of us."

"Dat is a good plan sergeant... the Cossacks don't move good on da ground, slow as sheet on der feet!"

"Your soldiers must not hesitate, Jacek."

"Der more scared of me den dey scared of the Cossacks... dey will not delay... if dey do, dey get my foot up der arses!"

"We attack at sunrise in two days. Be sure your men are in place, Jacek."

"Yes, sergeant. I go now to get my men. Tank you."

At the designated time, Jean Marc's unit moved into position. "I said my prayers last night, sergeant," Jacques whispered. "I prayed so the Poles will follow your plan … you know the stories about the Poles always being late."

"We are fucked if they are not in place," Jean Marc responded just as the sun was peeking over the horizon to the east. "Move out men! Shoot the sentinels as soon as you see them, then double time to the encampment."

"Moments later a shot rang out, and the soldiers hurried toward the encampment. As Jean Marc rushed forward with his men, he listened for a shot from the north. "Come on Jacek… attack now… or we're all dead!" Jean Marc said to himself. No shot was heard.

"It's too late to turn back," he yelled to his men. "Keep moving ahead!" As the last word left his lips, he heard the gunfire to the North. "Yes, Jacek … yes Jacek … kick some Cossack ass!"

His men also heard the gunfire, the adrenaline rushed through their bodies, and their pace quickened. They were soon upon the enemy as their gunfire erupted. None of the Cossacks had reached the horses. Men fell on both sides, but the surprise attack created chaos with the Cossacks. Jean Marc looked beyond the battle to the west just as the horses were scattering. The Cossacks ran towards their horses but were swarmed by the Polish cavalry, who slaughtered them mercilessly.

Jean Marc ordered his soldiers to the north to help his newfound ally. As they turned, he sensed the Cossacks were winning that fight. He hurried his men to the objective ordering them to maintain their assault formation. They came upon the enemy just as they were about to overtake the Poles. The Cossacks turned to face them. As Jacek noticed the change, he rallied his men and they attacked the Cossacks with vengeance. Overwhelming the enemy from both sides, the friends met on the victorious field of battle. Jacek gave his friend a big hug.

"I would rather face the Cossacks then be hugged by you, Jacek." But as he put him down, Jean Marc noticed that his friend had been wounded.

"Luc, Luc take care of Jacek while I survey the field!"

When Jean Marc returned, he could see Jacek. He lay face up on the ground, his chest heaving. Jean Marc knelt beside him. Jacek pulled him forward with his huge arm. "What we ave done today will ripple tru Poland tomorrow. We ave beat da Russians... it will bring hope to my people!"

"Your men were very brave. They fought with courage because of you! Rest now my friend," Jean Marc whispered back.

"Everybody dies... but not everybody make a difference... we make a difference for Poland today, sergeant," he said, with his last gasp.

Chapter 17

Notre Dame Cathedral was beloved by the Parisians and Sunday masses were always well attended, especially when the Bishop of Paris delivered the homily. And on this particular day, he stood tall in the pulpit, attired in his most opulent clothing, and eager to deliver the word of God to his flock.

"God has freed the Church from the heresies of the Revolution. The heretics, the so-called *Men of Reason*, profess that God does not involve Himself in our everyday lives — how sad, how forlorn and how wrong. They call themselves deists and compare God to a watchmaker, who makes a watch, winds it up, and lets it run. They disregard the hand of God in miracles, in our every day lives, or in special revelations of the Bible.

The *French Encyclopedia* by Diderot and the works of Voltaire substitute science for God and condemn Christianity. Their objective is to destroy the Church. Therefore, their books are on the Index of Forbidden Books.

The deists assume they know all about God's wisdom and purpose. They substitute reason for faith. Their reasoning is filled with obscurities, ambiguities, and lies. The Church, on the on other hand, is guided by God and prefers religious truths and faith to scientific formulas and the reasoning of mortals." The bishop paused to allow his flock to absorb the gravity of his words.

Madeleine scanned the crowd. It appeared content with the bishop's explanation. However, she had read that the deists did not condemn God, but rather, the priests who had concocted the myths and doctrines of religion to enhance their own power. Her eyes caught those of the Monsignor, and she understood what the deists meant.

"Reason has no explanation for the evils and

disasters of life," the bishop continued, "but faith helps us to accept these unexplained mysteries of life. The deists believe there are certain patterns in nature that direct our lives. But, look around you, life is not a pattern, it is filled with confusion, mystery and problems. God, and not reason, is the answer to these mysteries."

The bishop descended the stairs of the pulpit and was handed his staff by an aide. He walked to the altar and sat by the Monsignor looking out at the flock, which he believed had been enlightened by his words

The Monsignor, attending the bishop, watched closely as Madeleine approached the communion rail. *She is taking communion without confession;* he thought. *I will have her followed after mass to see where she now lives.*

As the people filed out of church, Madeleine spotted the bishop and the Monsignor greeting the parishioners. Madame LeBlanc took her hand and approached the bishop. "Bonjour, Madame LeBlanc!"

"Bonjour, your excellency. I would like to introduce to you my niece, Madeleine Moreau."

Madeleine bowed and kissed the bishop's ring. When she rose, she looked directly at the Monsignor, whose face had blanched.

"When the Monsignor does his parish visit this year, he will meet with Madame Moreau about my contribution to Notre Dame. She is being trained to handle my financial affairs."

"I do hope you will be present, Madame LeBlanc," the Monsignor interjected.

"Madame Moreau will not need my assistance in such matters."

"And, Madame Moreau, how are you related to Madame LeBlanc?" the Monsignor asked.

"Our families are from Bordeaux. My grandfather and her mother were siblings."

"How fortunate," the Monsignor said sardonically.

"Yes, how fortunate," Madeleine repeated.

It gave Madeleine profound satisfaction that she had confronted the Monsignor. She was beaming in the back of the carriage on the ride home.

"Do not think you have heard the last of him, Madeleine," Madame LeBlanc said, interrupting her daydream.

"Why do you say that?"

"He had a sinister look on his face."

"Yes, but the bishop had a concerned look on his face."

"The bishop will keep him in tow for awhile. At least until he gets my annual contribution."

"Why do you make these large contributions to the Church, Madame LeBlanc?"

"I guess I am like the deists, who the bishop mentioned in his homily. I am searching for the original religion of Jesus, whose message, I believe, has been distorted by the clergy. They concocted the theologies, myths, and doctrines of Catholicism to both enhance their power and subjugate others. *Love God and love thy neighbor* is the central message of Jesus. But the men of the Church have placed so many trappings on this simple message that it is no longer recognizable."

"Then your contributions empower those who have corrupted the message of Jesus."

Madame LeBlanc thought about this for a few moments. "Well, if my future contributions go directly to my neighbor, God will be pleased."

"But the bishop will not!"

Madame LeBlanc nodded her agreement.

"I must confess that I prayed for Jean Marc today," Madeleine said impulsively.

'As you should… and as you should daily."

"But I feel I am betraying Michel."

94

"Jean Marc is a brave man, and he might just survive this ordeal. If he does, then your love and fidelity should be to him. Your children talk to me about him all the time. If Jean Marc is alive, you should be with him."

The two were quiet for a while, but as they arrived at the carriage house, Madeleine said, "I also prayed for Michel."

Chapter 18

"Where were you last night Thomas? You did not come back to the room," Martin said with disdain.

"A brief worldly flirtation, Martin… that is all."

"Do you feel the need for confession?"

"But, of course not. I am learning how people outside of the clergy live, so that I can be a better priest. However, I do feel the effects of the wine this morning."

"How will carousing make you a better priest?"

"Martin, how old were you when you left home to become a priest?"

"I was fourteen."

"You have never worked for a living, never been married, never had children, never fought in a war and never encountered the hardships of life. How do you expect to give guidance to those who are penniless, to couples with marital problems, to abused children, to a depressed veteran and to the masses who face hardship daily?"

"God will provide the answers."

Thomas shook his head and headed toward the stable to get the horses. A few minutes later as they trotted by the pub, Marie waved to Thomas from a second floor window. Thomas waved back and smiled. Martin looked down wanting no part of this escapade.

During the short journey to Orleans very few words were exchanged until they turned onto the main street.

"Oh, my God!" Martin exclaimed, as his eyes focused on the beauty of the cathedral at the end of the avenue.

"It is the Cathedral Ste. Croix, a beautiful gothic church. The interior is just as spectacular, and the stained glass windows depict the story of Joan of Arc. Go, go ahead and visit while I meet with the librarian, Bertrand, who is a close friend. Join us in the library at noon."

"Merci," Martin said as he hurried towards the magnificent cathedral in front of him.

Thomas felt uncomfortable in his priestly garb. He felt so much more at ease in lay clothing. He looked toward his friend tethering his horse and racing up the stairs of the cathedral, his robe flowing gracefully with his every step. The priestly robe looked so natural on him.

Thomas admired the fascade of the cathedral for a few moments and left for the library to find his friend. Once in the library, he tugged at his robe that seemed to weigh him down.

"Bertrand, it is so nice to see you again," he said as he entered his friend's office.

"Thomas, what a wonderful surprise," Bertrand said, as he rose from his chair to greet his friend. "And what brings you to Orleans?"

"A witch-hunt my friend … a witch-hunt."

"What in the world are you talking about, Thomas?"

"The Monsignor in Paris believes one of his parishioners is a witch. He has commissioned Father Martin to file an accusation against her in Rome."

"And who is Father Martin?"

"Father Martin is visiting the cathedral and will join us at noon. He is a good person and has the potential to be an exceptional priest, but he is very naïve, especially about the Church's prejudice toward women."

"I do not believe in witches, and I have little patience with young, naïve priests… so what would you have me do Thomas?"

"Tell him of the persecution of Joan of Arc, and later I will teach him about the treatment of women by the Church."

"I should have known… and one of these days we will be caught, found guilty of heresy, defrocked and burned at the stake!" Bertrand said in jest.

"But if this scandal is not exposed by young priests then the Church will continue to fail in Jesus' mission."

"Tell me Thomas, what would you do if you were defrocked?"

"I would marry and have a dozen children. And you?"

"I don't know. It has always been the goal of my family for me to be a priest, a bishop and a cardinal, however, more for worldly reasons than spiritual ones."

"Then I will take the blame if we get caught and return to where I really belong."

"The things we do for our families, Thomas!"

"Yes, yes indeed... but getting back to Father Martin, he knows of the chauvinism of his superior but does not yet believe that the same prejudice permeates the Church."

"And how will we teach him that lesson?"

" You will reveal to him the injustice of the inquisitors towards Joan of Arc. And, I will teach him about the bigotry of the Church against women."

At noon the three young priests met in the library. Following an exchange of amenities, Bertrand started to recount the story of Joan of Arc. "After her glorious victories, Joan experienced a reversal of fortune when her army assaulted Paris. When attacking the city's inner moat, an arrow wounded her. Over her protests, she was taken from the field of battle. Just as her army prepared for a second assault, Charles unexpectedly ordered the army to stop its advance and return to the Loire valley. The event was devastating to both Joan and her army.

Around Easter, her apparitions returned and told her that she would soon be captured. The *Maiden* never feared battle with the enemy but was terrified of betrayal by her friends."

"Why would they betray their heroine?" Martin

asked.

"Jealousy... fear... or maybe just because she was a woman," Thomas answered.

"In any event, with the consent of the king, she led his army to free Compiegne which was under siege. Joan and a small group slipped into the city. Later in the day, she led a raid against the enemy but was forced to retreat. She stayed with the rearguard until a drawbridge was raised behind her unit. Their backs to the river and separated from their army, they were overrun and captured by the enemy."

"Many claim that the drawbridge was raised intentionally so she would be captured," Thomas interjected. "All attempts to rescue her failed, and the enemy refused all ransoms."

"She was transferred to the English, charged with heresy, and scheduled for an inquisitorial trial. The tribunal consisted of priests obligated to follow ecclesiastical law and serve as impartial jurors."

"Why was she not tried by a military tribunal... and what heresy did she commit?" Martin asked.

"Because they knew they would get a conviction from a tribunal of bias priests," Thomas responded.

"The charges ranged from sorcery to horse theft," Bertrand continued. "Even though she was nineteen and illiterate, she was not allowed an advocate; and, though accused by an ecclesiastical court, she was confined in a secular prison. Tribunals were supposed to hear witness testimony against the accused and base their verdict on their testimony. In this case, the only witness called was Joan herself. The inquisitors questioned her incessantly. The trial lasted for many months. The tribunal declared Joan's visions and voices to be false and diabolical. The priestly inquisitors threatened that if she refused to retract her version, she would be handed over to the secular authorities — to be burned at the stake."

"Was the tribunal unanimous?" Martin asked.

"A court of thirty-seven judges decided unanimously that Joan must be treated as a relapsed heretic and condemned her to death," Bertrand responded.

"The execution was carried out the very next day," Thomas added.

"She was allowed confession and communion and marched outside before a subdued crowd. She forgave her accusers," Bertrand continued. "She was tied to a tall stake well above the crowd. As the fire was lit, she asked for a crucifix, which was held up in front of her on a long pole until the flames were too intense. She screamed in a loud voice the name of Jesus and implored her saints to save her, right up until the flames consumed her."

Martin gasped, "What an injustice!"

"The Church recognized the injustice fifteen or so years later, ruling she was convicted illegally by a corrupt tribunal," Bertrand added.

"Then it was just an aberration." Martin suggested.

Thomas responded morosely, "It is not an aberration, Farther Martin, if repeated thousands... no, hundreds of thousands of times against women under the guise of heresy, witchcraft and sorcery!

Chapter 19

The Monsignor sat alone in his room dejected by the news he had received about Madeleine Moreau. He took pen and paper in hand and wrote a letter to his friend in Bordeaux. He sealed the letter and urged the carrier to deliver it as soon as possible.

"Are there any instructions to go along with the letter, Monsignor?"

"No, the pastor will know exactly what to do with the records once he reads the letter."

She seduced the sculptor with the lure of female sexuality and now she defrauds the wealthiest woman in Paris with the guile of female deceit. She is surely the tool of the devil! the Monsignor thought.

He believed that women were weaker than men and, therefore, they were more susceptible to the temptations of the devil. And once possessed, their sexual appetite was insatiable.

The Monsignor went for a walk beyond Ile de la Cite. He crossed the bridge over the Seine to the narrow streets of the Latin Quarter. His thoughts wandered between Madeleine Moreau and his future in the Church, *somehow they seemed intertwined.* The Bishop of Paris was old and upon his death the pope would appoint a new bishop. He was a logical choice, but the pope was not yet familiar with his accomplishments. If he were to convict Madeleine Moreau of witchcraft he would gain notoriety and come to the attention of the pope. He was lost in thought when he arrived at the magnificent gardens of the Luxembourg Palace. He sat on a bench in one of the gardens but was oblivious to its beauty. Like a predator, his focus was on his prey.

"I would like the sculptures to capture not only the

101

essence of the Age of Reason but also your personal role in that important period. For that to happen, you must tell me of your experiences during the Revolution," Madeleine said as she sat in the garden with Madame LeBlanc.

"I am a private person, but I understand the reason for your request."

"Tell me of your early life," Madeleine asked.

"So distant, yet so near. I experienced the excitement of youth during a very tumultuous time in Paris, which, of course, served to heighten the experience. My parents, whom I loved, were part of the nobility, which I despised. As part of my rebellion against the excesses of the aristocrats, I read the writings of Voltaire, Diderot, and Rousseau. I was intrigued by Rousseau's ideas of democracy, the right to participate in politics, to vote and to a greater freedom of expression. These were revolutionary thoughts of those whose lives had been controlled by kings and popes. In his book *The Social Contract,* Rousseau opens the first chapter with: 'Man is born free, and he is everywhere in chains', which became the clarion call for those of us who wanted change."

"And how were the chains broken?" Madeleine asked.

"The will of the majority was to replace the will of the king. Rousseau says there is a social contract of individuals to subordinate their judgment, rights, and powers to the needs of the community as a whole. The sovereign power in any state should be the general will of the people."

"The will of *all* the people prevails?" Madeleine asked.

"No, the will of the majority becomes the rule of the community, but in turn, the majority must afford all its citizens the protection of the communal laws. So even though a citizen might be in the minority, that person still has the right to participate, vote and express himself."

"Obviously, the king did not support that change." Madeleine inquired.

"The king and the nobility were vehemently opposed to democracy. But the fervor of liberty, freedom and democracy had infected the rest of the population."

"Was Rousseau calling for a revolution against the kings?" Madeleine asked.

"While the other philosophers were calling for piecemeal reforms, Rousseau was a revolutionary. In his words, 'It is impossible that the great kingdoms of Europe should last much longer. Each of them has had its period of splendor, after which it must inevitably decline. This crisis is approaching: we are on the edge of a revolution.'"

"And what were your dreams, Madame LeBlanc?"

"I was consumed by Rousseau and the revolutionary spirit. I would miss classes at the University to attend meetings with groups fomenting revolution. I was absorbed by the protests against the monarchy. Many tasting of liberty for the first time rallied to the cause. But it wasn't without danger. Oftentimes, our protests were allowed to exhaust themselves, but at others, the king's cavalry rained down upon us, inflicting deaths and casualties, which only served to motivate us all the more."

"The king had soldiers, cavalry, guns, and cannons. How did you combat that?" Madeleine asked.

"French soldiers who had fought side-by-side with the Americans during their Revolutionary War came back to France to oppose the king. They had participated in a war for freedom and independence, and they came home with a changed attitude toward the monarchy. They joined our cause and taught us how to fight back."

"Were you part of the fray, Madame LeBlanc?" Madeleine asked.

"Many women were part of the fight… but I also had another reason to be involved."

"And what was that?" Madeleine asked.

"I fell in love with a young officer. He was a few years older than me and very handsome, very worldly. I was smitten the first time I saw him walk into the room, so confident, so composed. He taught us how to fight in the streets of Paris, how to avoid direct conflict, how to care for the few weapons we had. All things he had done while fighting in America. But, more important, having seen it first hand, he reinforced our thoughts of freedom, liberty, and democracy."

"Oh, Madame LeBlanc, this sounds like the making of a beautiful love story."

"I was not always old, Madeleine. In my youth, I was quite attractive… and, the lieutenant thought so. He stayed after that gathering and spent time flirting with me! I was swept off my feet and could not wait to see him again. I left the university and spent my days both advancing the cause of liberty and falling more deeply in love with the handsome lieutenant."

"What did your parents think of all of this?" Madeleine asked.

"They were very concerned about the changes evolving in France because their way of life was threatened. They supported King Louis XVI and Marie Antoinette. They continued to attend the lavish social functions, and they resisted the rabble-rousers with all the means at their disposal. They were as involved in resisting the cause as I was in supporting it. All along they thought I was attending the university and supporting their cause. They referred to it as an insurrection of the peasantry and believed it would soon be quashed. But where they went wrong is that it was not only the peasantry that was rebelling, it was a combination of the peasantry and the bourgeoisie. It was the common people of Paris who were revolting — peasants, artisans, students, shopkeepers, soldiers, writers, philosophers — the men and women who wanted some say in their lives. It was these common people who marched upon the Bastille and then upon the king and queen in their palace at Versailles."

"You created a democracy," Madeleine interjected.

"Not only did the movement revolutionize our government, it dramatically transformed our society. There was so much fervor and hope among the people. It was a new world filled with men and women, all equal, with a future brighter than the past. Not only did we emulate the Americans, we surpassed them by adopting a Declaration of Rights that went beyond the American Bill of Rights."

"Why then did the Revolution fail?" Madeleine asked.

"For a number of reasons. The monarchs of Europe took it upon themselves to defeat our cause, and even though we knew how to rebel, we did not yet know how to govern. When the king and Marie Antoinette were executed, Robespierre became our leader and decreed death for all he considered enemies of the revolution — thousands died beneath the guillotine during the months of terror. Great purges were undertaken to weed out the members of the old society who were unwilling to accept the new regime, including my parents."

"How sad."

"The revolution which I supported led to the execution of both my mother and father," she said sadly. "Because I was part of the revolution, I was allowed to keep their property."

"And what happened next?" Madeleine asked.

"France was repulsed by the horror of Robespierre and the new regime. It found its savior in Napoleon, but he became intoxicated by his newfound power and within months crowned himself Emperor. France again had an absolute monarch. Our experiment with democracy crumbled faster than it had evolved."

"And, what about your romance with the young lieutenant?" Madeleine asked.

"We became very disillusioned with Robespierre's leadership. It was not what we had fought and died for. Many were afraid to speak out against the horrors of Robespierre, but my brave lieutenant was not." Madame LeBlanc paused to regain her composure.

Mesmerized by the story, not a word was spoken by Madeleine.

"One night as we slept, supporters of Robespierre broke into our bedroom and ripped him away from me... it was the last time I held him in my arms."

"Oh, my God!" Madeleine gasped.

"He was guillotined the very next morning in the Place de la Revolution, before my very eyes," she said tearfully as Madeleine held her tightly in an attempt to console her.

The sculptures will reflect the themes of *reason, revolution and love*," Madeleine whispered to her. "...especially, *love.*"

Chapter 20

Michel made his way to Brussels, the capital of Belgium, to gather intelligence for Napoleon. The country had been captured and annexed by France in 1795, and its residents were hostile toward the French. Everyone was desperate to know what the Allies would do and rumors were rampant. Michel went to the Grand Place, surrounded by shops, restaurants and taverns. He spent his nights in the pubs and days in the artists' quarters, astounded by how loose the talk was about the enemy units.

"Wellington has 120,000 British and Dutch soldiers on the outskirts of Brussels. Blucher is at Liege with a similar number of Prussian soldiers. The Austrians are west of the Rhine with an army over 200,000. And the Russians are marching through Germany with an army of over 150,000," Michel overheard a group of British soldiers boasting in a popular tavern.

"And more are being held in reserve," another chimed in. "We have close to a million soldiers to destroy the little monster."

"Do you think he might surrender?" another asked.

"This is a fight to the finish. We'll hang him as soon as we destroy the *Grande Armee*," the first soldier said.

Michel winced but retained his composure.

That night, he sent a courier to Paris with information for analysis by the general staff.

A few days later, the *Grande Armee* crossed into Belgium with 122,000 soldiers. Michel joined his unit that same day.

"Michel, it is so good to see you. I saw Madeleine, and she wanted me to tell you that she understands."

"All the more reason to win this war… how did she look?"

"Beautiful… very beautiful."

"Then we must get back to Paris soon. Tell me, what is the plan of attack?" Michel asked his friend.

"The Emperor was briefed yesterday and while he kept nodding off during the presentation, he has come up with a solid strategy."

"He is better asleep than the Allied generals are awake."

"Yes, but he is not the same general who led us in the past. When his army passed in review, he did not seem too healthy. He is obese and appears lethargic."

"What is his strategy?" Michel asked.

"The plan is to divide the British and Prussian armies and attack the Prussian army first. Once it is destroyed, we will turn to meet Wellington."

"He knows that Wellington is cautious and will assume that the movement to the east is a feint to trap him."

"Speed is of the essence in defeating the Prussians because, at some point, Wellington will react."

"How is our battalion being utilized?" Michel asked

"We will be kept in reserve to lead the charge against Wellington once the Prussians are defeated."

At first, the battle went as planned. The French cannons devastated the exposed Prussian infantry. "We are doing well," a courier informed the colonel.

A few hours later, the same courier delivered the news that the tide has turned and the colonel's battalion would join in a counterattack.

"Major, our battalion has been ordered to attack the center of the Prussian line," the colonel informed Michel. "Prepare the assault formation."

The artillery company fired its cannons to soften up the point of attack. The other four companies advanced under the cover of high rye grass until they reached an open field. The cannon balls continued to pound the enemy position. The French soldiers were ordered to double time across the open field. As they approached the enemy line, the cannon fusillade ceased. The enemy soldiers stood up from their bunkers and greeted the French soldiers with a barrage of rifle fire. Michel saw soldiers around him drop to the ground, wounded and dead. The charge halted momentarily, they took aim, fired into the Prussian position and with fixed bayonets rushed forward to meet the enemy. Michel was suddenly in the thick of it, avoiding deadly bayonet thrusts, swinging his sword as much to wound as to kill. The fighting was fierce. Men fell all around Michel, hacked down by swords, bayonets and gunfire. The Prussian center gave way but the flanks held their ground.

"Major, take two companies to attack the left flank. I will take the other two to attack the right," the colonel ordered.

As both flanks were attacked, the two battalions that had been ordered to support the assaults of the flanks, and deliver the coup de grace, halted before reaching their objective. The Prussians delayed for the last hour of daylight then conducted an orderly retreat under cover of darkness.

"We lost the opportunity to defeat the Prussians and turn our forces against Wellington," the colonel told Michel, once they reassembled.

The next day, the colonel received orders from headquarters. "Napoleon has divided the army. He is sending a third of the soldiers to pursue the Prussians. He will lead the rest of us against Wellington. Take out the map and find the fastest way to the town of Waterloo," the colonel ordered Michel.

"How are the men, Michel?" the colonel asked.

"Morale is low. They believe that they were the sacrificial lamb yesterday. They are upset at the timidity of the two generals who could have won the day for us."

"One of the generals is in pursuit of the Prussians

— as we speak he has been ordered to insert his unit between the two Allied armies to prevent them from joining forces."

"Who is that general?" Michel asked.

"Field Marshall Grouchy."

When they arrived at the outskirts of Waterloo, Michel noticed that the enemy army was well ensconced on the high ground.

"There it is, colonel," Michel said, pointing to the low ridge of Mont-Saint- Jean.

"We have been ordered to the rear of the formation next to the Imperial Guard. Napoleon must be pleased at the way we fought yesterday," the colonel said to Michel. "Will the men fight as bravely tomorrow?"

"For you they will, colonel."

The next morning, Mont- Saint-Jean was bombarded by a tremendous fusillade of cannon fire. Michel observed the infantry move into position for a frontal assault. As the French units advanced, they were raked by devastating volleys from the enemy cannons but were soon engaged in close combat with the British infantry. When they broke through the enemy lines, the British cavalry charged down from the hill, broke through the French line and continued their charge towards the French cannons. Napoleon timed the countercharge to perfection and decimated the cavalry.

As the tide turned for the French, Michel noticed that two French brigades were being detached to the east.

"Grouchy fucked up, and we are being attacked by the Prussian army," the colonel shouted.

Michel saw thousands of soldiers being redeployed to engage the Prussians. When his gaze returned to Mont-Saint-Jean, he saw the French cavalry charging the ridge and being cut to pieces by the British guns. "The battle ebbs and flows," he mumbled.

The order came for the colonel's battalion to assault a British redoubt at the base of the hill. They rushed to the fortification, battered down the huge door and slaughtered the enemy within.

The colonel spurred his men up the slopping hill. Michel joined the front ranks of the unit. They made good progress and overran the advanced unit. Michel noticed that the Imperial Guard had joined them. Together, they assaulted two artillery batteries. They opened fire and swept away the gunners. The cannons silenced, they clawed their way to the crest of the hill sensing victory within their grasp.

But just as quickly, Wellington ordered his reserve units to assault the surging French troops. The reserves stopped the French cold and drove them down the slope. The hand-to-hand combat was fierce. Napoleon threw in more units of the Guard, and the French again moved up to the crest of the hill. Michel spotted a fresh British force on his left flank. His unit was met with a scorching volley followed by a bayonet charge. He saw the colonel fall to the ground fatally wounded. His heart sank. He moved towards his friend but was beaten back by the surge of British soldiers. Tears came to his eyes as he saw his friend's body trampled by the onslaught of soldiers. Instinctively, he moved to the center of his unit to take control, but they were giving up ground. The French line broke. Then he heard the order he had never heard before, the order for the elite Guard to retreat.

At the same time, the Prussian army broke through the French line to the east and marched towards Mont-Saint-Jean. Thirty thousand fresh troops came rushing onto the field of battle. Michel saw Wellington on the crest of the hill waving his hat for all units to advance. A torrent of soldiers came rushing down on the French troops. Michel backtracked as fast as he could but knew he must take a stand to avoid a complete rout. Once he reached the flat ground, he halted his unit as it stood side by side with the Old Guard.

They rallied for a last stand and slowed the onslaught enough to cover the escape of their comrades and Napoleon. The British brought up the cannons, concentrating their fire on the resisting units, mowing them down. Most were killed and wounded while the others were surrounded and isolated. Michel turned to see the enemy cavalry pursuing the fleeting soldiers, retreating in panic. He surveyed the field of battle and saw a mass of corpses strewn about. There were heaps of wounded men with mangled limbs unable to move and dying from their wounds. The sight was too horrible to behold, and he felt sick to his stomach. "All is lost," he said in desperation.

Chapter 21

Word of Napoleon's defeat at Waterloo spread with lightning speed throughout Paris, France and Europe. In Paris, the Monsignor thought: *Sometimes the enemies of the state do our work for us. Soon, instead of having to work around the emperor, I will work directly with the king.*

"The emperor was defeated at Waterloo. The Allies are closing in on Paris from all sides. The king will soon return to France. Napoleon has no choice, he must abdicate," the Monsignor told his entourage.

"The change and decay of the last decades will be swept away by the resurgence of the Church. We will revive the orthodoxy of the past, appoint conservative priests to head the parishes, restore the Inquisition and censure heretical books." Father Leon, a supporter of the Monsignor, said to a group of like-minded priest assembled by the Monsignor.

"And, let us eradicate witchcraft in the process. We will bury ourselves in the writings of the past and lead the charge against the enemies of the Church," the Monsignor added.

"The Monsignor is in a powerful position both as an advisor to the bishop and as the head of Paris' largest parish. The bishop is old and will soon be replaced. Monsignor is the likely successor if we do our work well," Father Leon added.

"It is important that you be educated in the ways of the Inquisition, which now exists only in the Papal States. At one time, it existed in every country in Europe, and we will return it to its former status. It is a process developed over the centuries and intended to save the soul of heretics. Father Leon is well versed in its history and tradition. Today will be our first step in the journey to restore this sacred institution," said the Monsignor.

"The *Decretum* of Master Gratian is one of the most influential text in Ecclesiastical Law. It was compiled in the twelfth century, and it circulated quickly just as the authority of the popes became established throughout Europe. And to reinforce their authority, the popes appointed judges to carry the papal presence to every corner of Europe." Father Leon instructed the priests assembled in the Monsignor's lavish office.

"All to combat heresies?" a priest asked.

"Not necessarily, many cases dealt with the implementation of Ecclesiastical Law, but the prosecution of heretics became more widespread as the papacy's influence grew. Extensive powers were delegated to the bishops, which made the process more pervasive and efficient. The Dominican and Franciscan Orders were founded, in part, to judge these cases and report to the pope. As the number of prosecutions increased so did the severity of the penalties — to include death." Father Leon responded.

"However, the purpose of the Inquisition, to save the soul of the heretics and protect the orthodoxy of the Church, never faltered."

"That is correct, Monsignor, and to ensure that truth prevailed, the doctrine of torture was introduced to the process. But, its use was rigorously defined by Master Gratian."

"In my opinion, the use of torture should now be expanded because the heretics are more clever, more secretive, and more dangerous than ever!" the Monsignor responded. He then asked, "When is torture to be used?"

"The process commences when a person of good reputation makes an accusation to an inquisitor. The inquisitor then takes evidence and calls witnesses to determine whether the incident occurred. This is called the *general inquiry*. Torture is not permissible in this phase. Once the person is identified, the *special inqu*iry begins.

The accused is served with a written account of the charges. The prosecutor introduces either a *full proof* or a *partial proof.*"

"And what is the difference?" a priest asked.

"The *full proof* requires the testimony of two eye witnesses, or catching the accused in the act, or a confession. Torture is not required in these cases." Father Leon asserted.

"That's understandable," the priest commented.

"All other evidence is *partial proof.* A person can never be convicted with a *partial proof.* But if there are enough *partial proof*s then the inquisitor can seek a confession."

"And how is that done, Father Leon?" the priest asked.

"The inquisitor can ask the accused to confess."

"And if he or she does not confess?"

"Then the inquisitor can use the doctrine of torture to extract a confession," Father Leon responded.

"And if the confession is given, is the accused then found guilty of the heresy?" the priest persisted.

"Not yet, a confession made under torture must be freely repeated the next day for it to be valid... and without torture."

"And if the confession is repeated, what is the punishment?" a priest asked.

"If the convicted heretic does not recant, he or she is turned over to the civil authorities for punishment — usually burning at the stake."

"Does the punishment apply..."

"Yes Monsignor, it applies to witchcraft!"

People were in a frenzy running toward the village as if something important was about to happen.

"Let's follow them," Thomas said, as they wheeled

their horses toward the village and followed the crowd. In the small square Martin saw a soldier reading from a scroll.

"Napoleon has been defeated by the Allied army. The king will soon return to Versailles," he said, as people filled the square.

"Will Paris be defended?" one from the crowd asked.

"Napoleon still has enough soldiers to defend Paris, but the Allied forces are advancing on the city."

"Can Napoleon withstand an assault on the city?' another asked.

"The British and Prussians are twice as numerous as the French, and the Austrians and Russians are not far behind. He might resist for a few weeks, but eventually the siege will wear him down."

"Our beautiful Paris will be destroyed by the bombardment of the Allied cannons," another said, as the two travelers looked at each other. Thomas was the first to speak, "We must return to Paris. Our parishioners need our help," Thomas urged.

"Our superior has given us strict orders to deliver the accusation to Rome," Martin responded.

"But circumstances have changed dramatically."

"We have taken a vow of obedience. Let us resume our journey," Martin said as he spurred his horse toward Avignon.

Madame LeBlanc was incredulous. The hope of a week ago had turned to despair.

"The children play in the gardens as the world crumbles around us," she said to Madeleine.

"It is the innocence of youth… why must we lose it as we grow older?"

"I can only hope that the city will not be defended. Otherwise, its buildings will be wrecked, it boulevards cratered, its shops and cafes turned to rubble and its people butchered."

"The city should surrender... we have seen too many wars... we have lost too many brave young men," Madeleine said emotionally.

What we ave done today will ripple through Poland tomorrow. We ave beat the Russians... it will bring hope to my people. These words reverberated in Jean Marc's mind as his band of soldiers traveled toward Warsaw with its new Polish comrades.

"Our dream of a free Poland will never die, Sergeant Moreau," the Polish captain said. "In 1797, after a heroic effort by our people, we were defeated, and our country was partitioned by Russia, Prussia and Austria. But the spirit of Jacek Pabst and the Polish people demand that we shed this yoke of suppression.

"Napoleon always supported Poland," Jean Marc responded.

"There are thousands of peasants who have left the cities and the farms armed with pikes and scythes to join the fight to free Poland."

"Poland is occupied by foreigners. It has fewer soldiers and weapons, it has limited resources, but it is fighting for its homeland and that could make the difference," Jean Marc rejoined.

"Napoleon has been defeated at Waterloo," a horseman travelling at a fast pace cried as he approached the group.

"What do you mean?" the captain hollered back.

"Napoleon is retreating to Paris after a massive defeat in Belgium. The Allies are in hot pursuit."

'We must get back to defend France," Jean Marc said frantically.

"We will help. The Poles are being forced to help the Russians in their march to France."

"The next caravan leaves tomorrow, captain," the messenger interrupted.

"Then, let us move quickly to Warsaw to get our friends on the caravan. But do not forget us when you get to France, sergeant."

That night Jean Marc dreamed not of Poland but of being united with his beautiful Madeleine and his three lovely children. It was the same dream that kept him going during the Russian campaign. The same dream that brought him hope in the prison camp. The same dream that inspired him during his escape. But the dream was different tonight and he awakened with a blast of fear — like a cold wind touching his soul.

Chapter 22

It was around noon when the two travelers emerged from a wooded hillside within sight of Avignon. The lavishly decorated Palais des Papes, Petit Palais, and Cathedral de Notre Dame-des-Dons dominated the city landscape. These structures were testimony to the influence of the papacy in Christian Europe. Thomas' horse picked his way along the rutted road toward the city. Martin followed and reflected upon his new friend — poised, confident and capable. *Thomas has carefully planned the whole trip. He is gracious when we encounter people. There is something to learn at every stop, and somehow, it all seems directed toward me.*

"Tell me about Avignon," Martin said anticipating Thomas' next lecture.

As if on cue, Thomas responded, "The splendid buildings ahead of us were all built by the popes during the previous centuries."

"And why in Avignon and not in Rome?"

"Because the popes abandoned Rome for a time, and Avignon became the City of Popes. In 1309 a French pope refused to go to Rome. Instead, he installed himself in Avignon. Seven popes were to reign there before the papacy was returned to Rome in 1423."

"And what lesson are we to learn from Avignon?" Martin asked.

Thomas looked back at Martin quizzically, "Why do you believe there is a lesson?" Thomas asked as Martin spurred his horse to come alongside. He smiled but said nothing.

"A political lesson, Martin," he responded as they crested a hill that brought them in sight of the Rhone River, south of the city.

"Were the popes political?" Martin asked.

"More political and more Machiavellian than all the

119

princes in Europe. The popes bought Avignon from a local prince in 1348 for a pittance and ruled the area for four hundred years, until they were expelled by the French Revolution and Avignon became part of France."

"From what I see of its beautiful buildings, their reign must have been very successful." Martin remarked.

"Quite the contrary, the Church in Avignon was driven to corruption by its greed for money. It did build these spectacular buildings but at the expense of its spiritual mission. And, over time, it came under attack from various groups urging the Church to give up its wealth and follow the example of Jesus and the Apostles."

"To be less materialistic?" Martin asked.

"Yes, and to be more concerned about its flock than amassing great wealth."

"Did it change?" Martin asked.

"The Church failed to recover its spiritual traditions and recapture its moral authority," Thomas responded.

"So, it could not abandon its worldly ways," Martin commented.

"While in Avignon we will learn about the Great Schism and take away a valuable lesson — as in today's world, the Church should have shed its worldly garb and donned its spiritual clothing."

The following morning, they met at the library at the University of Avignon. "I will research the Italian texts as you research the French ones dealing with the Great Schism. In that way, we will both gain perspective as to the political events that tore the Church apart," Thomas explained to Martin.

"I am on my way to delve into the relevant books," Martin responded.

From his research, Martin learned that the Catholic Church of the Middle Ages was a very powerful institution: implementing laws, accruing material wealth and imposing taxes. Gifts were exchanged for special favors including entry into heaven. And, kings and princes bowed to the bishops of Europe.

The Inquisition and excommunication were powerful tools in silencing its critics. Excommunication deprived a person from attending mass and receiving the sacraments. The Inquisition prosecuted heretics. In both instances, the offender was sentenced to eternal damnation.

Even the cardinals turned against one another. When Gregory XI, a French pope died, the cardinals elected an Italian pope under pressure from an Italian mob. The French cardinals fled Rome, invalidated the election, and elected one of their own to rule from Avignon. The competition created a schism between the two areas.

Martin learned, to his disappointment, that the two popes were notorious in matters of splendor, gifts, bribery, patronage, and corruption, which drained the resources of both sides. But what he found most egregious was that half the population was following a false pope and would thus be condemned to hell.

That evening, when Martin returned to the *Petit Palais* for dinner, he felt distraught about the revelations of the day. History had revealed to him that the Church he so loved had a very unsavory past.

Thomas, anticipating his friend's disappointment, greeted him with a bottle of red wine. "Sit down, Martin. Sip your wine as I try to reinvigorate your spirit. I knew this morning that what you were about to read would sadden you, as it did me when I first studied the dark history of our Church. But before I can reassure you that there is hope, let's explore the negative impact the break-up had on the Church and its followers."

"The wine, if not the explanation, should help," Martin said with a little levity. "It appears to me that the popes were undermining not sustaining the teaching of

Jesus."

"The Church had two leaders, one in Rome and one in Avignon, a situation that was untenable. A number of alternatives were proposed: Several kings were asked to exert their influence but feared the wrath of the popes. Theologians were invited to decide the issue but worried about excommunication. Saintly men were polled but could not reach consensus. The words of influential writers fell on deaf ears. And, calls for both popes to abdicate were ignored."

"Was no one interested in the spiritual needs of the faithful?"

"The faithful became very resentful of the actions of the papal rivals, and they attached themselves to a movement placing priestly powers in the hands of the individual."

"I read today that these initiatives gained favor with many disaffected Catholics," Martin interjected.

"A few reformers called for a general council to determine the true Vicar of Christ. The cardinals convened the Council of Pisa. When the rival popes refused to attend, the Council deposed them. The cardinals then elected another pope, which only exacerbated the problem, instead of two there were now three claimants to the papacy."

"When did the comedy of errors end?" Martin asked.

"The Pisan Pope called for another general council which met at Constance, Italy. The Council declared that it represented the universal church and that all Christians, including the pope, were subject to its jurisdiction. The Council moved swiftly: deposing both the Pisan and the Avignon popes, forcing the Roman pope to abdicate and electing a cardinal who took the name Martin V. This sequence of events brought an end to what came to be known as the Great Schism. However, the schism had done untold harm and intensified the hostility toward the pope throughout the Christian world."

"Did it bring about reform in the Church?" Martin asked.

"It was an opportune time for the Church to change, but it failed to seize the moment and continued to reflect God as wrath not love. The Church shunned reform and dealt harshly with its critics, creating a climate for a gathering storm which was about to transform Christianity — if not the Catholic Church!"

"And, what was that gathering storm?"

"Martin Luther and the Protestant Reformation."

Chapter 23

"There is something I have to explain to you," Thomas said to Martin as they left Avignon. "You will soon discover that at certain times the Church lost its way, striking out against Jews, Protestants, and women. As we explore the historical roots of Christianity keep in mind that Jesus loved Jews, women, and would have loved Protestants."

"Are we going back to its beginnings?" Martin asked.

"What was founded by Jesus Christ is not the Church that we know today. He did not establish a religion with a specific organization of churches, doctrines, and canon law. However, the Church does have its origin in Christ in his proclamation of the *Kingdom of God* and his call to *Discipleship*."

"Are you saying that Jesus was not the founder of the Church?"

"It is better to say that the Church has its origin in Jesus and was founded by the disciples. During the first two centuries of its history, it was essentially a private religion practiced in households not basilicas; consisting of house churches, loosely organized and with the congregation always involved in important decisions. And, wherever Christianity spread, women were leaders of house churches."

"Why did it fail?"

"It was not until the third century when Christianity had a widespread appeal, that male leaders demanded the same subjugation of women in the churches as prevailed in the society at large. That argument was reinforced in 323 when the Emperor, Constantine, made Christianity the religion of Rome, and its leadership positions became prestigious and lucrative."

"Are you implying that the male leaders forced women from these leadership positions because of status and money?" Martin asked.

"Women were marginalized, in part, for these very reasons. And the society of the time was not ready to accept Jesus' revolutionary idea of absolute equality, which made it easier for the Church to discard the leadership of women. During this period, the established roles of women as house church leaders, prophets, priests and bishops were challenged. The male leaders demanded the same limited stature for women as prevailed in Roman society."

"So women had to battle not only the male leaders of the Church but also the prejudices of society?"

"The societies of the time had strong ideas about the superiority of men to women." Thomas responded.

Martin pondered this for a long time and finally spoke, "When I was ordained, I promised to obey my superiors. Through this obedience, we give God the possibility of making complete use of priests in carrying out the mission of the Church. God embraces the priest who is obedient."

Thomas persisted, "By all means, remain obedient to your superiors, but keep an open mind, Martin."

"I will keep an open mind so long as I can remain true to my vow of obedience!"

"As for me, Martin, even if the pope tells me otherwise, I cannot accept that Jesus intended to exclude women. I cannot ignore that women were leaders in the early church. And, I yearn for their return — to everyone's benefit."

As the two travelers neared Marseille, Thomas explained, "A few years after the death of Jesus, Mary Magdalene, who had been expelled from the Holy Land, crossed the Mediterranean and landed in Marseille, then known as Massilla. Within a few years, Magdalene, her brother, Lazarus, and a handful of disciples converted the entire region to Christianity. She then retired to a cave on a hill near Marseille where for thirty years she gave herself up to a life of penance."

"She was certainly an important figure in the spread of Christianity," Martin added.

"When Jesus gathered disciples to spread his message, women were prominent in that group... Mary Magdalene, Mary of Bethany, and Mary the mother of Jesus. Paul's letters reflect a Christian world in which women were well-known evangelists, apostles, leaders, and prophets."

What argument was made to subordinate their status?" Martin asked.

"Although women's leadership was a widespread phenomenon in the early Christian churches, such independence on the part of women conflicted directly with the social conventions of a Roman society. It was during this period that we heard for the first time the argument that Jesus chose only male apostles, and therefore, women cannot serve as priests."

"Was any official action taken by the papacy to exclude women from the priesthood?" Martin asked.

"Not until nearly two-hundred years later, in the year 493, when Pope Gelasius issued an Epistle demanding that outlying churches cease the practice of ordaining women as priests."

"What did the Epistle say?"

"The Epistle reads, in part, 'Nevertheless we have heard to our annoyance that divine affairs have come to such a low state that women are encouraged to officiate at the sacred altars, and to take part in matters imputed to the male sex, to which they do not belong.'"

"The tone as much as the content reveals Gelasius' feelings toward women," Martin added.

"The Epistle goes on to condemn not only the

actions of the bishops who ordain women but also those bishops who seem to be favoring them by not denouncing them publicly," Thomas continued.

"Did Gelasius' Epistle find support in Scripture?"

"Not in Scripture but in the ecclesiastical canons promulgated by male bishops." Thomas responded.

"But Scripture is the basis for Christianity and reflects the inclusive attitude of Jesus." Martin remarked.

"All of the attacks against women were initiated by men who disregarded the example of Jesus. It was Augustine who created a philosophy intimating that women are inferior to men. It was Gelasius who prohibited the further ordination of women. It was the men of the Church who suppressed and concealed the leadership of women. And, it was the male clergy who prosecuted and persecuted women for heresy and witchcraft."

"Do you believe they betrayed the legacy of Jesus?" Martin asked.

Thomas smiled at him and spurred his horse to a full gallop toward Marseille, leaving Martin to answer his own question.

Chapter 24

Michel stumbled off the field of battle along with the few remaining French soldiers who had fought so valiantly to protect the retreating army. Making his way over the dead and dying bodies, he was utterly sickened. The ground before him was glistening with the blood of thousands of men and horses. *What drives men to such madness?* He saw shattered skulls, dismembered bodies, smashed rib cages, organs oozing from slashed abdomens. He heard calls for help coming from wounded soldiers. He saw the less severely wounded hobbling off the field, hoping to escape the bloody mopping-up operation of the enemy.

He fell to his knees. A bloodied hand reached out from a mass of bodies and grabbed his arm. "Help me, for God sake!" came the cry from a trembling voice.

"God has abandoned you," he said, as he pushed away. "He has abandoned all of us!" He stood and walked on limp corpses that moments earlier were alive. He felt a sharp pain in his right arm and saw blood covering his sleeve. Every movement caused him pain. He took off his jacket and saw a jagged gash across his bicep. "Shrapnel from the exploding cannon ball," he mumbled. He bandaged it up as best he could. "A one arm sculptor... is this what it has come to?" He walked over the bodies until they thinned out and then walked around them. It was getting dark. He had to rest. He needed water.

He saw clouds of dust coming in his direction. "The fuckin' cavalry is coming back!" He scampered to the edge of the woods and dove under the low hanging branches of a pine tree. He felt a sharp pain in his arm as he hit the ground but lay motionless as the horsemen passed.

Exhausted, he fell asleep. But sleep did not comfort him. The nightmares of the day's events rolled through his head. His body shook. His eyes opened. He saw only darkness. The stench from field filled his nostrils. "I must get away," he mumbled. He pushed with his right hand but fell to the cold ground as pain tore through his arm. "I need water to clean the wound."

He saw the red glow of campfires in the distance. He struggled to his feet. Slung his rifle over his left arm. And, walked away from the massacre — but not from its images.

"The battle is not lost for Napoleon. Field Marshall Grouchy still has his army intact. There are thousands of artillery pieces for the defense of Paris. The National Guard is available. And, thousands will volunteer, if called."

"The Russian and Austrian armies are still weeks away. The British have lost over 50,000 men and will have to re-assemble. Napoleon must rally France."

"He is depressed and exhausted. He may not have the energy to bring us together, one more time."

"Where are you getting this information?" Madame LeBlanc asked the two barristers.

"Madame LeBlanc, my son is on Napoleon's staff. He has just returned from Belgium. Our defeated army is not far behind."

"Will Napoleon return to Paris?"

"His generals are encouraging him to remain with his army to avoid the treachery of the officials in Paris. But it appears that he is determined to negotiate with the politicians."

Madame LeBlanc nodded.

"The ministers, the legislature and the Church are aligned against him. Without his army he is doomed."

"However, if he takes a stand, the people will support him, and his army will rally behind him."

"Why does he hesitate?" Madame LeBlanc asked.

"He has been heard to say that to rally the people to

his cause would plunge France into a civil war just as the Allies begin their invasion."

"What will happen, now?" she persisted.

"The Legislature will demand his abdication and form a provisional government. His army remains in northern France awaiting his orders."

"Oh, my God, I need to give Madeleine this news immediately. Please inform Monsieur l'Heureux that I will return later to sign my Last Will and Testament."

When she arrived, she found Madeleine in the parlor sobbing. "You have heard the bad news?" Madame LeBlanc asked.

"I was in the park with the children when I heard of Napoleon's defeat."

"We must continue to hope that those we love are still alive, but we must also plan for you and the children. I was at the bureau of my advocat when I heard the news of Napoleon's defeat. I rushed home to be with you."

"Is there something wrong?" Madeleine asked.

"No, Madeleine. Before you and the children came into my life, my thought was to give my fortune to the arts and struggling artists."

"Not the Church?"

"If ever I had an inclination to bequeath anything to the Church, it left me last Sunday when I listened to that despicable Monsignor deliver his homily."

"What was the homily about?"

"Witchcraft, Madeleine… witchcraft."

A cold shiver went down Madeleine's back.

"He asked the parishioners to be aggressive in the hunt for witches. He called upon us to report the strange behavior of families, friends, neighbors and, even, complete strangers."

"We all act strangely, at times," Madeleine added."

"Now people will attribute a sinister motive to these

actions. It could very well cause a frenzy in Paris."

"He is an evil man," Madeleine responded in a tremulous voice.

"I did not mean to upset you, Madeleine. This is not the time to discuss the Monsignor. This is the time to be concerned about you and the children. I am at an age where I sense my mortality. A few months ago, this feeling troubled me. But today, I have the opportunity to carry on my family's legacy, for I am now blessed with you and three children. Tomorrow, I will execute my will which reads that upon my death, I bequeath to you my entire estate."

Madeleine was lost for words but finally said, "All I really need is your love."

Returning from mass at Notre Dame, the Bishop of Paris and his entourage were in good humor. The Monsignor finding himself next to the bishop took the opportunity to voice his opinion. "If Napoleon abdicates, it will be a grand day for the Church."

"And the provisional government will ask the king to return to France."

"It was Henry IV, the first Bourbon King, who made Catholicism the official religion of France," the Monsignor said.

"It was indeed, and I understand that Louis desires not only to compensate the Church for its loss during the Revolution but also to restore Catholicism as the official religion of France."

"The money will serve us well, the recognition will enhance our stature and the Protestants will flee to Germany."

"They need not flee from France, but they must accept the authority of the Pope."

The Monsignor smiled, and said: "The Pope is the

successor to Peter, and the bishops are the successors to the apostles, and only through us can the Protestants find salvation. Since the time of the Reformation we have been on the defensive, and now is the time to crush the Protestant heresy. Pope Pius must condemn religious toleration and re-institute the Inquisition beyond the Papal States. This will give us the weapons to combat the heretics."

"But, Monsignor, let us not get ahead of ourselves, Napoleon is on his way to Paris as his army grows in numbers under Field Marshall Grouchy's command at Laon."

"We will tread lightly," the Monsignor responded, "until the Allies force Napoleon to abdicate."

Chapter 25

The bishop believes that I am clairvoyant now that the Spanish Inquisition has been reestablished. He has also been told that the vestiges of the Portuguese Inquisition are undergoing a resurgence. He will be supportive, as I work toward returning the French Inquisition to its former standing and power, the Monsignor thought as images ran through his mind of women incarcerated, before the fire, and on the rack, in various stages of nakedness.

"It is only through the Church and its priests that the faithful can find God," the bishop advised a number of priests convened at his command. "But there are obstacles placed in our way by Satan. The Monsignor alluded to one such obstacle in the Sunday homily — witchcraft. Even though they cannot be prosecuted in France at this time, sorcerers, witches, and magicians must be identified and shunned. And as more and more heretics are identified, the civil authority will recognize the danger and return the Inquisition to France."

"In the meantime, perpetrators can be prosecuted by the Church if they are brought to Rome," the Monsignor added.

"Publish not only the names of the heretics who are identified but also the names of concealers, those who know heretics but do not denounce them; of hiders, those who prevent heretics from being discovered; of suspects, those who are present at the preaching of heretics and participate in their ceremonies; and, of defenders, those who defend heretics so as to prevent the Church from eliminating heretical depravity!" the bishop directed. "And, do not forget the relapsed, those who return to their former heretical ways after having formally renounced them," the bishop added with loathing in his voice.

"And, how will we identify the heretics?" a young

priest asked.

"There are six ways to identify a heretic," the Monsignor responded. "A heretic is one who creates a false opinion in matters of faith, interprets literature differently from the sense of the Holy Spirit, is separated from the sacraments of the Church, perverts the sacraments, is dubious in faith, and attempts to remove the Roman Church from the summit of all churches."

"These are rather general; shouldn't we be more specific to better identify the heretics?" the young priest persisted.

"They are the standards that have been in place for centuries. The standards that identified millions of heretics, that foiled hundreds of thousands of sorcerers and witches, that saved souls and preserved the unity of the Church. These standards are specific enough, father," the Monsignor responded, glowering at the young priest.

"There are priests who are opposed to this effort," the young priest responded, obviously not intimidated by the Monsignor's reaction.

"You will be obedient to the orders that come from my office," the bishop interceded.

"I have recently met with the Order of Preachers and the Order of Friars Minor and both are prepared to resume their roles as inquisitors as soon as France reinstates the Inquisition," the Monsignor added, still glowering at the recalcitrant priest.

"The pope recognizes that heresy, of whatever kind, cannot be tolerated. Return to your parishes and expose the wrongdoers. There is no salvation beyond the Church and no need to compromise," the bishop ordered, leaving little doubt as to how the priests should proceed.

The Church will again bask in the glory of the old order. The priests will be obedient to the call of the Bishop of Paris and his order will spread through the region, like a wildfire raging through dry fields, the Monsignor thought as he returned to Notre Dame, fondly recalling days gone by.

"The soldiers are gathering at Laon to await Napoleon's orders," a soldier on horseback hollered to Michel.

"What direction?"

"Follow this road for a few kilometers, where you will find food and water," he responded. "Here, this will help quench your thirst 'til you get there," he said, as he tossed a canteen in Michel's direction.

Michel sat on the side of the road removing the bandage from his arm. He poured water over the wound, removed the pus and covered the infected area with the used bandage. He looked back and saw soldiers coming up the road with a little more spring in their step — inspired to put defeat behind them and rally to the cause, one more time. *What drives these warriors... where do they find the courage... how can they recover from such horrors?*

"Major, lead us to victory," came the cry from a limping soldier.

His mind wandered. *My sculptures and, maybe, even Madeleine await me in Paris. But, I cannot betray France to her enemies... I cannot desert my men in time of crisis.* He pushed himself up with his left arm, stepped in line with the soldiers and called to all who could hear, "Our retreat has ended... destiny awaits us in Laon!"

As they arrived at the fork in the road, medics waited to tend to the wounded.

"That's a bad injury major. It's infected, and I am worried about gangrene," the medic said after examining the wound.

"What do you recommend?"

"I have salve to put on the wound, but if that does not work, you will need to be bled."

"What is that?"

"A barber-surgeon will bleed the bad blood from you."

"How is that done?"

"The barber cuts into a vein, which drains the body of bad blood."

"And, also good blood," Michel responded.

"Or, he might cut into the skin slightly to better control the bleeding."

"Is there another procedure for blood letting?"

"A very simple one, major. Place leeches directly on the lesion and let the blood-suckers draw the bad blood directly from the wound."

"Leeches are abundant in the countryside. It is the one thing that French cuisine has not made delectable."

The medic chuckled.

"Give me the salve, and I will find the leeches. I am going to join my brothers at Laon."

As he arrived at Laon, he was impressed by the organization of the army. Even though Field Marshall Grouchy failed Napoleon in the field, he was now poised to save the emperor. Michel was directed to the officers' quarters, where he was given his orders.

"We will cross the Somme River and destroy the bridges behind us. We will construct our fortifications on its southern bank. It will be a treacherous crossing for the Allies, coming from the north. Once we defeat Wellington's army, we will march the army to the eastern front, to meet head on with the oncoming Russian and Austrian armies."

"When do we deploy?" an officer asked.

"On the order of Napoleon," was the response.

Chapter 26

The partition of Poland by Russia, Prussia, and Austria led to instability within the country. Jean Marc Moreau found the Poles to be extraordinarily brave but undisciplined. They were disorderly in military conduct, lax in obeying orders, and unmanageable in military assaults. As he mingled with the officers, he emphasized discipline, restraint, and the chain of command to help bring order to a disorderly army.

During the march to Warsaw, Jean Marc was consumed with instructing his counterparts. But when he returned to his cot late at night, fear gripped his heart. He desired to be with Madeleine but worried how he would be received. Had she changed? Did she still long for him? Did she still love him? Was she with another? He longed to hold Madeleine, make love to her, and wake up in the morning to the laughter of his children.

They were so young when he left. Would Angeline remember him? Would Marc be angry with him? Would Jean mind him? Why had he not listened to Madeleine when she asked that he not leave for the Russian front? The time away from his children was gone forever, never to be recaptured. He rarely cried, war had deadened his emotions, but he sobbed that night as these thoughts ran through his mind.

The next morning, Jean Marc was asked to meet with the Polish officers. "We have gathered intelligence about the Russians in Warsaw. Initially, their security was sound, but recently, it has become lax. Based on this information, we have planned an assault on our enemy in Warsaw. Will you and your soldiers join us?"

Jean Marc thought about the request before he responded. "You may gain a quick victory against the Russians in a surprise attack, but you are not prepared for the Russian reaction. They will hunt you down, kill innocent Poles, and will be merciless in their retaliation."

The officers, obviously disappointed, said nothing.

"You are not yet ready to confront the Russians, and you might not be for many years. You must first train your officers, non-commissioned officers, and recruits; and they, in turn, must train others, until you have formed a formidable army."

"But that will take time, sergeant," an officer responded with cynicism.

"And it must all be done surreptitiously, which will take even more time. It will take years, but you have no chance against the Russians until the Polish Army is adequately prepared. And, only at that point, will the Poles be ready to defeat the enemy and reunite Poland."

"Can we be that patient?" another officer asked.

"Train your army, build your arsenal, and keep the thought of Poland alive. Time will pass quickly as your strategy evolves."

"Will you then come to help us sergeant, as Lafayette helped the United States?" an officer asked.

"It is your homeland and that is your greatest strength. Only you and your countrymen can take it back from the enemy. Dream of a reunited Poland and pass the dream on to your countrymen."

The next morning, Jean Marc was awakened early. "We have received more negative information from France," the captain announced.

"Is all lost?" he asked anxiously.

"The casualties are staggering on both sides."

"How many dead and wounded?"

"We were told, over a hundred thousand loses."

"How many from the French army?"

"More than half."

"Has Napoleon surrendered?"

"Napoleon has gone to Paris to state his case. His army is reassembling at Laon. No, he has not surrendered"

"Captain, it is urgent that we find a way to join our army in France."

"The Russians are also anxious to reach France, but they need our help. We will do our best to get you on the next convoy to leave Warsaw."

"How will that be done?"

"Our Jewish friends, sergeant."

"Can they be trusted?"

"Let me teach you a little about Polish history. Four or five centuries ago, many Jews came to Poland to escape persecution elsewhere. Here they were given the right to own land, conduct business, and preserve their unique culture. Through succeeding centuries, Poland opened its borders to Jews fleeing other lands. Within this tolerant climate, they thrived as nowhere else in Europe. But now that the foreign powers are in control of Poland, they are initiating anti-Semitic policies."

"But, how does that help us?"

"The Russians are making use of the Jews in critical positions, such as, organizing the convoys going to France. They will assist us in getting you assigned to the next convoy."

"And, if they fail?"

"It will be weeks before the next convoy departs."

"Which means that we will miss the battle for France's liberty."

That night, they slipped into Warsaw. Once the French soldiers were left with Polish families, Jean Marc was escorted to the home of Ludwik Goren. Following the introductions, Jean Marc said: "I have been informed of Poland's tolerance toward the Jews."

"Poland is known to us as the 'Jewish paradise'. Thousands of Jews have come here fleeing the persecution in other European countries. But our paradise is in jeopardy, much like yours in France. The Allies are closing in on both of us."

"I know of the dangers facing my country, tell me of those facing your culture." Jean Marc inquired.

"There were three partitions of what was known as the Polish-Lithuanian Commonwealth. The partitions were conducted by Russia, Prussia and Austria. They took place between 1772 and 1795. With the third partition, the Commonwealth ceased to exist; Poland had been erased from the map of Europe."

"A very short period for the death of a country."

"Russia controls over fifty percent of our land and population with the rest pretty evenly divided between the other two countries."

"But later, France interceded," Jean Marc remarked.

"After the third partition, there were many revolutionaries who fought for the freedom of Poland. Our hopes were resurrected in 1807 when Napoleon gained a decisive victory in eastern Prussia."

"I was involved in the battle of Friedland," Jean Marc said. "The Russians had their backs to the Alle River. We made a massive assault and broke their defensive line. Many drowned trying to escape. They sustained over thirty thousand losses."

"The Russians came to the peace table and signed the Treaties of Tilsit," the captain added. "And, Napoleon formed a Polish state, the Duchy of Warsaw, with lands ceded by the Russians."

"When Napoleon attacked Russia in 1812, we expected a French victory and the restoration of the country of Poland." Ludwik said. "Now, the Russians are back and will soon dissolve the Duchy."

"Unless, we defeat the Allies in France," Jean Marc responded. "It is our only hope for France... Poland... and the Jews."

Chapter 27

With tension running high, it was largely a question as to who would blink first. Napoleon had plenty of support. His followers pleaded for him to impose martial law and dissolve the Legislature. They pointed out that the people were on his side, evidenced by the rallies held on his behalf. The Legislature, instigated by the Emperor's enemies, declared itself in permanent session, indissoluble except by its own action, and called in the National Guard for its protection. Napoleon refused to use force against the Legislature. He refused to shed blood and was unwilling to lead a revolution. The Legislature was not as reticent, and charged Napoleon with the death of three million Frenchmen and demanded his abdication.

The situation was confusing, and it did little to settle the anxiety of Parisians. For Madeleine, it served to obscure the fate of Jean Marc and Michel. A problem she struggled with daily. However, she now had a confidante. "Madame LeBlanc, what should I do?"

"You are married to a man you love and who is the father of your three children. Before you move on, you must find out whether he is still alive."

"But others have told me that I have waited long enough."

"There is still too much uncertainty, too much undiscovered."

"How would I go about doing that?" Madeleine asked.

"You can wait, and time will eventually provide the answer, Madeleine."

"I am not very good at waiting, Madame LeBlanc."

"We can inquire at the Ministry of Foreign Affairs to determine what information they have about missing soldiers. I know the Minister, and I am certain he will cooperate."

"That is a good start but what else can we do?"

"My gardener, Pierre, is a veteran of Napoleon's early campaigns. I will have him work the streets for any news from the Russian campaign. And, if we find other avenues, we will explore them, also."

That evening, they met with Pierre and explained their plan. "It would be very helpful if you could assist us in this venture, Pierre." Madame LeBlanc explained.

"Madame LeBlanc, I know the streets of Paris, I am a veteran of Napoleon's wars.

"Will the veterans talk to you?" Madeleine asked.

"Yes, they will talk to one of their own. Yes, they will talk to me."

"How will you do this?" Madame LeBlanc asked.

I will do my job in the gardens during the day and work the streets at night," he responded.

The next morning, they met with staff members at the Ministry, who explained how difficult it is to get information from enemy countries. They were solicitous, due to Madame LeBlanc's influence, but not helpful.

"I will contact Charles Maurice de Talleyrand-Perigord tomorrow," Madame LeBlanc said. He is a former foreign minister and is trusted by the Allies. But he is also an adversary of Napoleon, who considers him to be a traitor, not only to himself, but to France. He served as Napoleon's Foreign Minister until he fell in disfavor with the Emperor."

"Is he in a position to help us?"

"He is presently the leader of a movement in the Senate to oust Napoleon and form a provisional government, with him as President."

"Can we influence him?"

"Yes, he is very susceptible to bribes."

As they left their last appointment, they came upon the bishop's entourage, which included the Monsignor. Their eyes met, and even though the encounter triggered an inner fear, she did not break her eye contact until he did.

"Be careful Madeleine, he is a vengeful man." Madame LeBlanc said while smiling at the bishop.

As soon as the bishop's meeting was over, the Monsignor went directly to the bureau where he had seen Madeleine exit.

"Why were Madeleine Moreau and Madame LeBlanc visiting your bureau?' he asked the official.

Surprised by the question, the official responded, "With all due respect Monsignor, it is none of your business."

"You will soon know whose business it is," the Monsignor responded dismissively.

As he caught up with the bishop, he said, "What do you know about Madame LeBlanc, your excellency?"

"She is very charitable, especially, to the Church!"

"It is truly amazing how deceptive the devil can be!" the Monsignor responded.

The bishop nodded his acquiescence.

Pierre was appalled by what he found in the streets of Paris. The once proud soldiers of the *Grande Armee* begged for money, slept in the alleyways, went without care, and wandered aimlessly. However, they were not reluctant to talk to one of their own. "Pierre, so many were killed or seriously wounded, many starved, some froze to death, others drowned, and a few were taken prisoners. I did not know Sergeant Moreau, but if he is not in Paris by now, he is dead!" said a homeless soldier, drunk on cheap wine.

"My guess is that the fucking Cossacks killed him

as he retreated on foot. They were everywhere like mosquitoes in a swamp," another said.

"They took no prisoner… they exacted revenged… they tortured their enemies and left them to die in the snow," still another remarked.

The stories went on endlessly, all with the same ending — death.

Pierre stopped at a tavern for a brief respite. The bartender, wearing a black patch over one eye, asked, "You are not from the neighborhood, what are you doing here?"

"Give me an ale and then I will tell you," Pierre responded.

When the ale arrived, Pierre said, "I am looking for Sergeant Jean Marc Moreau, who has not returned from the Russian campaign."

"I was there. It was a fuckin' nightmare. In three days during our retreat over twenty thousand soldiers died."

"How did they die?"

"From extreme cold, lack of food and supplies and the Cossacks. We would cluster around a fire at night and by dawn those on the outside were dead. Our extremities froze and in a few days were gangrenous. Thousands died of gangrene. There were no winter clothes, no blankets, no medication, no shelter, so they died. Your friend was probably one of them."

"How did you make it back?" Pierre asked.

"I ran faster than my friends, but one night a Cossack caught up to me and slashed my face with his saber. I feigned death until the Cossacks left, patched my wound, and walked through the cold night to a village, where the Poles nursed me back to health."

"Pierre, is that your name?" a patron asked who had been listening from a few stools away.

"Yes, it is."

"I served with Jean Marc Moreau in two campaigns. He might have died from a Cossack's saber, an infantryman's round, the shrapnel of a cannonball, or from the cold winter; but, believe me, if he is dead, he died bringing his soldiers home!"

Chapter 28

Marseille was a beautiful sight, nestled between the sea and hills, its warm, light blue waters alluring to both travelers. "Marseille was founded 2600 years ago and has served as the cradle of commerce and Christianity for much of Europe," Thomas explained to Martin. "We will visit the old port section, where many early Christians entered France, to view the artwork of the Inquisition, which has been amassed from the area between Rome and Paris."

"When do we depart for Rome?" Martin asked anxiously.

"I will book passage for us today."

"The trip has taken longer than anticipated. I am sure the Monsignor is eager for us to file the accusation against Madeleine Moreau."

"We will take advantage of any time we have. There are many museums in Marseille which will enlighten us as to the conduct of the Church toward women."

"You are not a believer of witchcraft are you Thomas?"

"I was a believer when I was younger," Thomas responded. "But as I explored the subject, I learned that people were very reluctant to talk about it, and it concerned me that educated people shied away from that conversation. Like the sly spider, the Church had woven a web so broad that people avoided the subject for fear of being snared in its mesh, either as a witch or as an abettor to witchcraft."

"Why should anyone fear being charged with witchcraft when they have the opportunity to defend themselves before one of God's servants?" Martin asked.

"For two reasons: First, many of the inquisitors were prejudiced against women; and second, torture. Prejudice and torture, Martin."

"Are you accusing the Dominicans and the

Franciscans of prejudice and torture?" Martin asked incredulously.

"I will let you be the judge of that tomorrow, Martin. But for now, I will book passage to Italy while you make arrangements for us to stay at the rectory of Notre Dame de la Garde."

"How will I find it?" Martin asked.

"It was built on the highest point in Marseille. Just look up to God, Martin, and you will find it."

The following day the two priests left the rectory early to spend time visiting Marseille's museums. "If we are leaving Marseille in two days, we should have ample time to visit most of its museums," Martin said.

"Marseille has more museums than most European cities and we do not have the time for all of them. However, we will visit the ones most relevant to our trip. We will avoid the more popular museums and visit a few of the smaller ones."

"Why avoid the more popular ones?" Martin asked.

"Because they are influenced by the Church. The Church limits the books we read through the Index and restricts the artwork we view through its influence. The Church does not trust us to use our God-given intellect to make these decisions."

"I will follow your lead today but will reserve judgment until I visit the others tomorrow," Martin asserted.

"Ah, here we are, Martin."

"This looks more like a house than a museum."

"Let us go inside, the artwork is more impressive than the building."

Within seconds, Martin observed a painting that was prominently displayed at the entrance. "*The Murder of the Inquisitor Pedro Arbues* is its title, and it depicts the vengeance of a wronged woman who has waited for this opportunity for many years." Thomas explained.

Martin nodded.

"The next painting depicts the execution of Arbues' murderess," he added as Martin shifted his focus to the painting. "*The Vengeance of the Inquisition* is its title."

"Of the two, I prefer the *Vengeance* but, in my opinion, it should be entitled the *Justice of the Inquisition*," Martin remarked.

The two drifted into the next room observing a number of drawings of nude and half nude women being interrogated, tortured, and tormented — the men in the background feigning disinterest.

Martin's discomfort with the nudity was obvious.

The next room was filled with large, graphic paintings of women being burned at the stake, seared with hot pokers, and tortured with strange instruments. "Such cruelty," Martin whispered under his breath.

"The cruel and erotic nature of the Inquisition is displayed in the large room to the rear of the building," Thomas explained, as he led his friend to the location. "This artwork displays the intolerance of the Inquisition, the abuse of ecclesiastical power, the lust for young women, and the sadism of the inquisitors."

"Why does the Church deny its role in the Inquisition?" Martin asked.

"Hypocrisy, arrogance, and denial are all possibilities."

"What should be done?"

"The Church could ask women for forgiveness! A mea culpa perhaps!" Thomas suggested.

Following a *petit dejeuner* in an outdoor café overlooking the bay, the two walked a few minutes to another museum. "In the Middle Ages torture was used for punishment, interrogation, and deterrence. The museum we are about to enter is very depressing to most people.

Torturing devices are exhibited, and you may be appalled by what you see today."

"I believe the cruelty of the Inquisition was well depicted in the museum we visited this morning."

Thomas did not respond and ushered Martin into the museum. The first display was called a *head crusher*. Martin read the description and walked away. Thomas read the description to himself: "The device was attached to the head and chin and the top screw of this gruesome device was slowly turned compressing the skull tightly. First, the teeth were destroyed, shattering into the jaw. Then the eyes were squeezed from the sockets. Lastly, the skull fractured and the contents from the head spilled out."

The next device was named a *cat's paw* and the inscription noted, "It was an extension of the torturer's hand. In this way it was used to rip and tear flesh away from the bone to any part of the body."

Thomas observed the color draining from his friend's face as he read the inscription for the third device, "The *knee splitter* does what it's called; it splits the heretics knees and renders them useless. Two large screws connecting the spiked blocks are turned causing the blocks to close towards each other and crush the knee."

Martin was speechless and went to an open window to catch his breath. When he returned, Thomas was reading the description below a device called the *Judas chair*. "The witch is lifted up by ropes hanging from the ceiling and lowered onto the point of the pyramid in such a way that her weight will rest on the point positioned in the vagina. The executioner, according to the pleasure of the inquisitor, can vary the pressure from zero to the total body weight. The victim can be rocked or made to fall repeatedly onto the point."

"Repulsive!" Martin exclaimed.

"Even more repulsive is the *Spanish Don*key. It consists of a main board cut with a wedge at the top and fastened to two cross beams. The naked victim is placed astride the main board as if riding a donkey. Weights are attached to the witch's feet. In many cases, the wedge slices entirely through the victim as a result of the immense weight attached to her feet."

"What is this?" Martin asked as he went to the next instrument of torture.

"That is called the *pear of anguish* and was reserved for women guilty of sexual union with Satan. It was forced into the vagina of the witch and expanded by the force of the screw, mutilating the vagina and, oftentimes, killing the victim."

"And this gruesome device is called a *breast ripper*. 'It was used on women convicted of heresy, blasphemy, adultery, erotic white magic, and any other crime that the inquisitors selected. The claws were used, either cold or heated, on a females exposed breast, rendering them into bloody pulps.'" Thomas read.

Martin turned away quickly from the gruesome looking instrument and ran out of the museum. Thomas followed and found his friend vomiting in the street. Martin straightened up, wiped his mouth with the sleeve of his cassock, looked harshly at Thomas, and said angrily, "You should never have taken me to this hideous place."

"Don't be angry with me, be angry with the priests who falsely accused the victims, at the inquisitors who employed these dreadful devices, and with a Church that condoned torture!" he exclaimed, as his friend rushed away.

"Running away will not diminish the cruelty, Martin," he hollered.

Chapter 29

Madeleine and Madame LeBlanc visited the Ministry of Foreign Affairs regularly to inquire whether there was any news concerning Jean Marc Moreau. The news was always the same and never positive. However, it was important that she find out whether Jean Marc was alive — no matter how difficult.

She thought it ironic that fate had cast her in this role. She had always followed convention, never been rebellious, and never questioned authority. But somehow things had changed, and she was now single-minded about discovering the truth. Madame LeBlanc had observed this quality and had nurtured it on a daily basis by giving her more and more responsibility for her vast holdings. She had also exposed her to proper etiquette, developed her social skills, and taught her the art of conversation, although she did not need much help in this area.

"Have you sent anybody to the Allied countries to determine whether French soldiers are still alive?" she asked a deputy minister after he had informed her that there was no trace of Jean Marc or other French soldiers.

"No, we have not Madame Moreau."

"And why not?" she persisted.

"We are still at war with these countries, and it is too dangerous," he responded.

"Then it should be done clandestinely. French soldiers should never be abandoned, especially after they have given so much for their country."

"The Allies patrol the borders of France. It is difficult to send Frenchmen on this mission without the proper credentials."

"And, what does it take to obtain the proper credentials?" Madame LeBlanc asked.

"Bribes!" The deputy minister responded curtly.

"How large a bribe?" Madame LeBlanc asked.

"Ten thousand francs, maybe."

"And how many men would be allowed into these countries?" Madame LeBlanc persisted.

"Maybe a dozen or more."

"And what would their status be?" Madeleine interrupted.

"They would be classified as envoys which would provide them security and, of course, the liberty to move through the countries freely," the deputy director responded.

"I suggest we send veteran soldiers, who are both familiar with the territory and motivated to find one of their own," Madeleine suggested.

The deputy minister pondered the proposal for a few moments. "There are many well qualified veterans who would be willing to undertake this risky mission. If the Minister authorizes the plan, I will assemble the soldiers."

"When can they be ready?" Madeleine asked.

"Within a few weeks," he responded.

"Can we cut the time back?" Madame LeBlanc asked.

"It will cost more money, maybe closer to twenty thousand francs," the deputy director insisted.

"We will meet a week from today. You assemble the soldier, and I will bring the twenty thousand francs!" Madame LeBlanc said.

"Very well. We will meet in the Bureau of the Minister. Bonjour."

"Au revoir."

"Now, let us meet with Talleyrand. He is a crafty diplomat who has ties with all the foreign powers. It is rumored that he had secret talks with them — and accepted large bribes."

"When did he have his falling out with Napoleon?"

"Seven or eight years ago, when he openly objected to Napoleon's foreign wars. He resigned as foreign minister. Napoleon's response was to dress him down publicly and to call Talleyrand 'shit in a silk stocking.'"

"What is their relationship now?" Madeleine asked.

Talleyrand has joined with Fouche and Lafayette to force Napoleon to abdicate and to restore the Bourbons to the throne. Lucien, a brother of Napoleon, and Lafayette are scheduled to debate the issue in the Senate within the next few days."

Talleyrand was waiting at the door when they arrived. "Jeannette, it is so nice to see you. And who is this beautiful woman accompanying you?"

"She is my niece, Madeleine Moreau."

"Well, come into my office and tell me why you are here. Unless you have come for just a social call."

"Charles Maurice, you are always the gentleman. And I do wish we were here on a social visit. But it is much more serious. Madeleine's husband is a sergeant in the army. He was in the Russian campaign and has not returned."

"I have had numerous discussions with the Russians about prisoners of war. I am informed that they have very few prisoners left. What is your husband's name, Madame Moreau?"

"Jean Marc Moreau... Sergeant Jean Marc Moreau, Monsieur Talleyrand."

"Let me see if he is on our list," he said as he picked up a packet of papers.

Madeleine looked at Madame LeBlanc, amazed not only that a list existed but wondering why it had not been made public.

"Why has the list not been published?" Madeleine asked.

"It was just received, Madame Moreau."

"Is my husband's name on the list?" Madeleine asked anxiously.

"I do not see his name but do not despair. The Russian official did say that a few French soldiers had recently escaped. It is believed that they were on the run to Poland."

"What can we do Charles?" Madame LeBlanc asked.

"Be patient. Once Napoleon abdicates, I will represent France in negotiating a peace treaty with the Allies. I will inquire as to the whereabouts of French soldiers."

"We have already met with officials from the Ministry of Foreign Affairs. They will help once they receive my money."

"And, what will they do for you once they receive the money?"

"They will allow a group of veteran soldiers to cross the border into Prussia as envoys in search of Sergeant Moreau."

Talleyrand shook his head and said, "As soon as they cross the border, they will be captured and killed. The officials from the ministry cannot give them any protection. Here is my advice: If you are determined to send a group of veterans across the border into enemy land do it clandestinely without the assistance of the Ministry. But I urge you to be patient and wait for me to negotiate with the Allies."

"Charles, your advice is always sound. We will consider both options."

"Jeannette, before you decide, wait until after the debate in the Senate, the situation will be much clearer at that time."

"Thank you, Charles. It was so nice to see you again."

"As it was for me, Jeannette. And keep in mind that

my office is here to assist you in any way it can."

Madeleine observed their interaction and wondered what their relationship had been in the past.

On the ride home, Madeleine asked Madame LeBlanc, "What should we do, work with the Ministry or with Talleyrand?"

"I trust Talleyrand, but I do not trust the Ministry. I would do nothing until Napoleon's status is determined. However, I suggest we work with Pierre to gather a group of veterans to cross into Germany in search of Jean Marc. We could use the bribe money to train and pay the veteran soldiers."

"Many soldiers are looking for work," Madeleine added.

"However, I am upset that we did not come up with a plan sooner, we have lost valuable time." Madame LeBlanc said.

As the carriage arrived, Madeleine spotted the children waiting outside. "Mama, mama," they cried out as the carriage approached. Marc and Angeline rushed toward their mother as she stepped from the carriage. Jean, however, waited for Madame LeBlanc to disembark and rushed to her side. "Any news about Papa?" he asked.

"Not yet, Jean... but we have a plan."

The maidservant observed as both women hugged the children, all beaming with delight! "Come Madame LeBlanc, I have prepared a special dinner."

Following the dinner meal and after the children had been put to bed, the women discussed their plan with Pierre.

Pierre was beaming. "I can assemble veterans, who are hungering for work and would eagerly undertake such a mission."

"Then, assemble a dozen or so men and start

training them." Madame LeBlanc directed.

"I am on my way, Madame LeBlanc."

"Merci, Pierre," Madeleine said.

"Let us take a little leisure time for ourselves and view the sketches Michel delivered before he left," Madame LeBlanc suggested.

"That is a wonderful idea; they are still in the library."

"Candide is impressive, but Mary Magdalene has waited nearly two thousand years to emerge, she is glorious." Madame LeBlanc commented.

"She has been ignored and defamed for too long, it is time to bring to Magdalene her just recognition." Madeleine added.

"She has been called a sinner, a prostitute, and a whore... but, Jesus said to her, 'Neither do I condemn you. Go and sin no more."

"And I do not believe there is direct reference to her as a prostitute anywhere in the Gospels!"

"And what is that in her hand?" Madame LeBlanc asked.

"It is unfinished marble. Rumors have been rampant in southern France for centuries that Mary Magdalene inspired a Gospel that, for whatever reason, has not seen the light of day. I believe that one day it will surface, and when that occurs, Michel, or another sculptor, will chisel the lost Gospel in the hand of Mary Magdalene."

Madame LeBlanc thought about this for a few seconds and said, "If Mary Magdalene was an *Apostle*, as many say she was, she was part of the Apostolic Succession and could ordain priests, both male and female. And if she was the *Apostle to the Apostles*, as many also say she was, she was the first head of the Church, the first *Pope*, equal to or above the others. And that, I believe, is the message Jesus wanted to impart and that Michel will captured through Mary Magdalene."

Chapter 30

In Rome, the pope was concerned with the restoration of the prestige and status of the Church in European countries, in particular, France. The papacy recognized that the French Revolution had brought about a wave of democracy, liberalism and humanism, which were in direct opposition to the views of the Church. The pontificate became extremely conservative condemning religious toleration, reinforcing the Index of Forbidden Books, restoring the Inquisition, reestablishing the feudal system, confining Jews to the ghettos, outlawing Freemasonry and resorting to mysticism."

"I receive regular directives from Rome," the bishop informed the Monsignor. "The directives clearly express the pope's aversion to the liberalism of the modern world. He is appointing moderate cardinals, imposing press censorship, creating secret societies, and supporting conservative governments."

"Protestants, Jews, Freemasons, heretics, and witches will feel the wrath of Rome. The conservative papal theology will emanate from Rome to France, Europe, and the Western world. The Church will once again lead people to salvation while eradicating the world of heretics," the Monsignor said coldly.

"We will keep current with the directives from Rome and make the necessary changes for their implementation. Initially, we will preach the conservative theology from every pulpit in France. We will display the Index of Forbidden Books in all our churches. And we will publicly support the restoration of Louis XVIII," the bishop asserted. "And, of course, remind the parishioners that the Pope, and the Pope alone, is the guardian of orthodoxy."

"I will restore the Inquisitorial courtrooms and refurbish the torture chambers. It will be the first steps in bringing justice back to France."

"As soon as the king reinstates the Inquisition, we will invite the Dominicans to return," the bishop responded.

"Do you expect resistance from the King?"

"Louis is not confrontational. He will leave the difficult decisions to his ministers and the bishops."

"Then where will the opposition come from, your excellency?" the Monsignor asked.

"From the liberal writers, the philosophers, and the middle class — all infatuated by democracy."

"They include those who wish to replace the Christian faith with science and human reason."

"A philosopher, I met with the other day, had the gall to say to me that the Church's history was one of bigotry and bloodshed in the name of Christ."

"That is despicable, and how did you respond?'' the Monsignor asked.

"I quoted God's words in Jeremiah: 'I have this day set thee over the nations, and over the kingdoms, to root out, and to pull down, to destroy and to throw down, to build and to plant.'"

"Did he cower at that point?"

"He was dismissive — typical of those who undermine the faith and promote heresies."

On the carriage ride back to Notre Dame, the words of Jeremiah kept rolling through the Monsignor's mind: *I have this day set thee over the nations and over the kingdoms, to root out, and to pull down, to destroy and to throw down....*"

Upon his arrival, he went directly to the room of an older priest, "Father Innocent," he called excitedly.

"Yes, yes, what is it, Monsignor?"

"Father Innocent, what is the condition of the torture chamber?" he asked, breathlessly.

"Follow me Monsignor. Somehow, I knew this day would arrive," he responded eagerly.

When they arrived in the bowels of the cathedral, Father Innocent unlocked and opened the heavy, wooden door, lit the lanterns in the musty smelling room, and exclaimed, "Voi*la*!"

The Monsignor was astounded by what he saw. It was as if time had stood still for three decades. "Father Innocent, you have truly done God's work!" he said with gratitude.

"Look here, look here, the rack to stretch out and break the heretic's body, if need be, is in perfect condition," he said, as he demonstrated the workings of the device.

"Perfect... just perfect, Father Innocent."

"And, come here Monsignor... the Scavenger's Daughter, it is the perfect compliment to the rack; it compresses the body instead of stretching it, until it forces blood from the nose and ears, if need be, of course."

The Monsignor nodded his approval, encouraging the priest to continue.

"And the head crusher and knee splitter, both in good condition. Other items are a little rusty but inflict more pain that way. And, the Judas Chair and the Spanish Donkey are both ready for use to extract the truth from the many witches who corrupt the purity of men's souls through their sexuality," he said malevolently.

"And, Father Innocent, are you willing to return to your role as the Torturer of Notre Dame?"

"It is God's will, Monsignor... *it* is God's will," he responded solemnly.

Chapter 31

Jean Marc and the French soldiers awakened early that morning, all were eager to resume their trek back to France. The weather was wet, cold, and dreary. They moved through the muddy streets to the designated place of departure. Lanterns flickered behind the shutters of the wood and stone houses. A few townspeople came out of the houses with pails to fetch water at the nearby river, others simply to relieve themselves. The Poles and the Russians were gathering in the marketplace, and the plan was for the French soldiers to disperse and blend in among the Poles.

Each of Sergeant Moreau's soldiers had been assigned to a Polish worker to make him less conspicuous and to have a Pole nearby if questioned by a Russian soldier. Sergeant Moreau was assigned to a Polish captain, which allowed him to move up and down the convoy to monitor the safety of his men. *Ludwik Goren has done a good job for us,* Jean Marc thought.

The ox carts had been fully loaded a day earlier and the yokes were being fitted to the oxen and attached to the carts. The Russian soldiers merely observed the activity, not lifting a finger to assist the laborers. "Pricks... the Russian soldiers are pricks," a polish worker whispered in broken French to the soldier who had been assigned to him. Luc just smiled and continued with his work.

Among the last to arrive were the butchers, the cooks, and the blacksmiths. The marketplace soon became a hub of activity as many of the wives, lovers, and children came to see their loved ones off. "Der she is," the laborer said to Luc, "my lover, she will not soon forget last night... look at dat smile on her face!"

"She's just happy to see you leave!" Luc responded with a chuckle.

The Polish laborer stared harshly at Luc for a few

seconds and then broke out in muffled laughter. "It's a good ting you Frenchies have a sense of humor because the Polish women say you are lousy lovers!" he retorted, as both broke out into muffled laughter just as a Russian soldier moved in their direction.

"I will take care of da prick... you stay right ere," the laborer said as he stood up and walked toward the Russian soldier. In a few seconds, he was back and the Russian was walking away.

"What did you tell him?"

"I told em my girlfriend would ave someting special for em when e returned. Da ugly prick believed me!"

The order came down for the convoy to start its march. The rain had not let up, and the convoy moved slowly through the muddy road. "How much ground will we cover in a day?" Jean Marc asked the captain.

"In weather like this, maybe ten miles a day, but if the weather lifts, maybe twenty miles a day. The Russians will drive us hard."

Jean Marc looked far into the horizon and all that was visible were dark, foreboding clouds. However, the convoy was moving west toward home, and that brought him a flicker of hope. He left the captain to check on his men, and by the time he had ridden his horse the length of the convoy, he had spotted all of his soldiers. All seemed to have blended in quite well with their loose, peasant garments serving not only as a disguise but also as a camouflage for their weapons. He had briefed them all, that if one French soldier was found out, they were to draw their weapons, create chaos, and flee to the woods. The Poles would create a diversion to cover their escape. He also banked on the Russians not leaving the convoy, for fear of being deterred from their mission.

The rain poured hard the entire first day and by nightfall the convoy had not covered ten miles. "I need vodka," the Polish laborer told his newfound friend.

"Where will you find vodka?" Luc asked

'"From the ugly Russian, I will tell him again what my girl friend will do for im when we return. Wait ere."

A few minutes later he returned and tossed a pint of vodka to his friend. "Ere, you take the first nip," he said, as he watched the French soldier take a long swig. "If we're going to share dat vodka, I should know your name."

"Luc, and yours?'

"Stephan… and when we get to France, you can show me off to all the beautiful French women."

"They will love you Stephan… they will love you," Luc said as they both settled in drinking vodka and eating kielbasa.

After they were done, Luc asked, "Will you get vodka every night?"

"Just for a few days, Luc. I ate the Russians. Poland is a small country wit friendly people… all we want is to care for our families, raise our animals, cultivate our farms, make our kielbasa, celebrate our holidays, drink our earty beer, and, most of all, govern ourselves. But, da fuckin' Russians will not let us do dat! Dey invade our country and ruin our lives."

"Fight them off!" Luc urged.

"Der soldiers outnumber us forty to one. But when I kill dat Russian, for me, it will only be tirdy nine to one."

"When will you kill him?"

"After I drink all his vodka," he responded, as they shared a laugh.

After a few minutes of silence, Luc asked, "How will you do it?"

"I will slit is troat."

"But the Russians will catch you!"

"The dumb Russians do not have a roll call in the morning. I will slit his troat, drag his body into da field, and leave him for da vultures. It will be days before dey realize the ugly prick is dead. And dey will not go looking for him," he said, taking the last swig of vodka.

The rain did not let up the next morning. The ruts were deep and wheels were falling off the over loaded ox carts. Many carts were abandoned, to the delight of the local villagers. It also gave Jean Marc a chance to check on his soldiers, giving him a sense of security. Upon his return, he said to the captain, "It seems like it will be another slow day, sir"

"There will be many slow days Sergeant. We will make it as disruptive as possible for the Russians. For the time being, it is our only weapon."

Jean Marc nodded.

"Follow me, Sergeant," he said, as he led Jean Marc to his tent. He unfolded two maps. "This is a map of Poland before it was dismembered. So perfect in its setting but with no natural boundaries and surrounded by aggressive countries who could easily cross our borders."

"So vulnerable, unlike France, which has an ocean, rivers, and mountains as protective natural barriers."

"This is a map of the Poland today. It shows what once had been Poland, now dismembered by our belligerent neighbors — Russia, Prussia, Austria — now vanished from the earth."

"Do you think your country will be reunited?"

"I dream of that every day of my life and ask myself, *when?* "

Chapter 32

Father Martin looked crushed, like one who had heard bad news, or suffered a death in the family. He seemed unable to think about anything other than the hellish scene he had witnessed the previous day in the museum.

Neither spoke as the two walked to the waterfront, only a short distance from the rectory. They boarded the small ship, which set sail at noon for Napoli. The city had been the scene of a cruel civil war involving Napoleonic France and the Austrian Empire. Following Napoleon's defeat, Napoli and Sicily were combined to form the Kingdom of the two Sicilies, with Napoli as its capitol.

The impact of Christianity will be evident to Martin as he observes the hundreds of churches scattered throughout the city, Thomas thought. His friend had been distant since the incident at the museum, and he found it best to leave him to his thoughts.

Martin was relieved when they were finally at sea, for it helped him withdraw temporarily from the world around him. He sat alone at the bow of the ship, away from the other passengers. The sea was calm, the sky was cloudless, and a slight breeze was carrying them away from Marseilles. He knew he would have to find the strength to rectify the mistakes of his beloved Church but was frustrated as to how to do it and not violate his vow of obedience. Even though, he clearly knew that torture was wrong, he felt it was justifiable if it led to salvation.

The two days at sea did not reveal the answer for him, but it did provide the serenity he needed at this time. He started to feel hopeful again at the sight of the magnificent city of Napoli rising from the sea. He admired Thomas but felt that the journey was placing a strain on their relationship.

"Every journey has its low point but, hopefully, we can move on, Thomas!" he told his friend as they prepared to disembark.

Much to Martin's surprise, a servant was waiting to take his bag as he stepped off the gangplank. He welcomed Father Thomas home and ushered them to a waiting carriage. The carriage worked its way to the top of the city and turned onto a long drive displaying a spectacular view of the bay. At the end of the drive was a palazzo, so gorgeous it left Martin breathless. Another servant ushered them into the palazzo where Thomas' family was gathered in the elegant foyer to greet them. Thomas went first to his mother, sister and brothers and then a little more formally to his father.

Father Martin was envious not at the splendor of his surroundings but of the intimacy of the family. After Thomas introduced Martin to the family, his father, Lorenzo, said, "Father Martin, let me show you to the chapel; you may want to say a private mass before dinner."

"Thank you, traveling with Thomas leaves little time for mass," he said, as the family chuckled at the remark. Entering the chapel, the stained glass windows brought a rainbow of colors to his eyes and led them to the vaulted ceiling depicting heaven with its scattered clouds, numerous angels, and an explosion of light representing God. Next to the marble altar was a replica of the *Veiled Christ*, Napoli's most famous sculpture. *How will I ever concentrate on mass surrounded by all this beauty?* he asked himself.

He read the inscription below the sculpture. *Giuseppe Sanmartino was appointed to make the original life-sized marble statue, representing Our Lord Jesus Christ dead, and covered by a transparent shroud carved from the same block as the statue.*

During mass, his eyes wandered to the lifeless body of Christ covered by a soft veil but still showing the deep suffering of Jesus almost as if the light veil gave emphasis to the tortured body.

Before the consecration, he gazed at the instruments of the passion at the feet of Jesus, the nails, the leather whip and the crown of thorns.

After the bread and wine changed to the body and blood of Christ, he glanced at the statue, the swollen veins still pulsating on the forehead, the wounds of the nails on the hands and feet, and the sunken side finally relaxed in the freedom of death.

At the end of mass, he realized how the sculptor had turned the suffering of Christ into a symbol of redemption for all humanity.

This veil of truth is a far cry from the veil of deceit woven by the Church over the centuries, he thought.

Dinner with Thomas' family was animated as the family members engaged in lively and heated conversation about current issues, including politics, religion, the economy, the papacy, and the Two Sicilies. No topic was sacrosanct, and Father Martin was content listening and learning from the far-reaching conversation until Lorenzo asked, "Farther Martin, how would you change the Church if you were pope?"

Before he could answer, Thomas' sister asked, "And, also, how would you improve the Church's treatment of women?"

"One question at a time," Thomas interrupted, "let us not scare our guest away before he gets to know us."

"My ambition is limited. I wish only to be a parish priest. However, if I were pope, I would remove the Church from politics and return it to its spiritual roots. As I admired the *Veiled Christ* today, I realized that Jesus had but one mission, to redeem all of humanity, including women, Sophia."

"Art has its purpose... it transcends language,

touches hearts, and opens minds!" Paulo asserted.

"He is the artist of the family," Lorenzo said, "and he has yet to earn a lira from his artwork!" The family coming to his support raised their wine glasses in unison and toasted the young artist.

"Such is the life of an artist!" Paulo rejoined.

"And how would you include women?" Sophia persisted.

"I would emulate Jesus," he answered quickly but wondered if maybe the wine was taking hold.

"Well father, we must rise early tomorrow for our journey to the Vatican, but once we complete our work, we will return for a few days."

"What work has to be done at the Vatican?" Sophia asked.

"Father Martin must file an accusation of witchcraft on behalf of the Monsignor," Thomas responded.

"No woman was ever accused of witchcraft by Jesus, Father Martin," Sophia responded sharply.

"Sophia, our guest is tired; it is time to retire for the evening."

Sleep did not come easily for Martin that night. He was conflicted by thoughts of torture, the role of women, and his vow of obedience. His only solace was the recollection of the *Veiled Christ*, which eventually brought sleep to his weary body and anxious mind.

Chapter 33

When not engaged in caring for her children or searching for Jean Marc, Madeleine was engrossed in the business endeavors of her mentor, Madame LeBlanc. However, she was still left with an empty feeling, for it was not that long ago that she lived in abject poverty. She often thought of those miserable days and all of the people who were left behind — victims of Napoleon's wars. Millions of soldiers had died leaving widows, children, and dependents who could not care for themselves. Thousands had returned as invalids, who also could not care for themselves without assistance. Her children often talked to her of their friends at school, who were always hungry and wore tattered clothes. Slums were everywhere in Paris with filthy, muddy, foul smelling streets, people living in wretched squalor, and the rat count greater than the population. "Madame LeBlanc, before we discuss your business ventures…"

"*Our* business ventures, Madeleine" she interrupted.

"Very well, before we discuss our business ventures, there's something I need to discuss with you."

"But, of course, Madeleine, what is on your mind?"

"I would like to help feed and clothe the poor people of Paris. You have seen the squalor, the starvation, and the suffering in many sections of Paris… and the hopelessness of its people."

"I do make a weekly contribution to Notre Dame for the poor people of Paris."

"We must do more, Madame LeBlanc, but in such a way as to bring hope to these once-proud people."

"And how would we do that, Madeleine?" she asked with compassion in her voice.

"The open markets are close by and food is available… we should provide the means for the people in these deprived areas to buy, prepare and distribute the food. People will both take pride in this effort and will function better on a full stomach, and it will bring them hope!"

"Let us start with one neighborhood, and if your plan is successful, we will move on to the next." Madame LeBlanc affirmed. "Now, these charitable efforts will be costly, how will we pay for them?"

"I have saved money... "

"No, no Madeleine, I meant from my money."

"It will be more meaningful to me if I can make a contribution to this effort, Madame LeBlanc."

"I know, and you are right. We all have a moral obligation to help. But where will my contribution come from, Madeleine?"

"Initially, from *La Banque de France*, most of your savings are held there, and many of your investments are financed through *La Banque*."

"And how will we continue to finance this worthy cause?"

"You have vast holdings in the Bordeaux region, and your vineyards grow only white grapes to produce the Sauterne wines of Chateau LeBlanc. Nearly ninety percent of the grapes grown in the region are red grapes, and the red Bordeaux wines are the best in Europe."

"And what do you suggest, Madeleine?"

"I suggest that we cultivate red grapes, as well as white grapes, and produce a red Bordeaux wine."

"There are many families who produce red Bordeaux wines, and the competition is very intense. It would be very difficult to rival these established producers." Madame LeBlanc asserted.

"There is a new variety of grape, which is easy to cultivate. The grapes have a thick, black skin. The vines are hardy and resistant to rot and frost."

"And, what is the name of the grape?" Madame LeBlanc asked, her curiosity obviously piqued.

"It is called the Cabernet Sauvignon grape."

"And what do you propose we do with this new grape?"

"I propose that you expand existing vineyards, purchase new lands, cultivate the Cabernet Sauvignon grape, and produce a red Cabernet Sauvignon wine." Madeleine responded.

"You have an excellent business mind Madeleine... and I assume you will want me to re-name Chateau LeBlanc to Chateau LeRouge," she said in jest.

"Nothing so drastic... but Chateau LeBlanc has an excellent reputation, which would give this new venture immediate status."

"Very well Madeleine, once we have determined the fate of Jean Marc, we will visit the Bordeaux region and decide how to expand our presence in the region with this new undertaking. In the meantime, I will hire people to identify vineyards and properties in the Bordeaux countryside, which are best-suited to grow the Cabernet Sauvignon grape."

"Yes, and tomorrow, we have an appointment with the deputy minister to be briefed as to the deployment of the envoys. Pierre has introduced the veteran soldiers to the deputy and, reluctantly, he accepted the entire group of a dozen men."

"Very good!"

"Pierre has asked to join us tomorrow."

"By all means, he can be very helpful. You know how men in high places talk down to women!" Madame LeBlanc responded.

"The bias against women is as strong in our society as it is in the Catholic Church." Madeleine responded.

"However, the Church is supposed to provide the example... the guidance... the teaching for society to become better."

Madeleine looked at Madame LeBlanc with a frown

on her face, exasperated as to why the Church had not yet, after eighteen hundred years, grasped the true message of Jesus.

Early the next day, the three met with the Deputy Minister. They were ushered into his bureau before he arrived. A few moments later a clerk entered the room and asked Madame LeBlanc for the money. She handed the satchel with the money to the clerk, who immediately left the bureau. After enough time had passed to count the money, the Deputy Minister entered the room, and was very cordial to the three visitors.

"I have met with the envoys, and they are eager to get started. Pierre has developed a good strategy for them to follow, and I have arranged the necessary documents to ensure their safe passage. However, even though the Russian ambassador is willing to provide the envoys with safe passage, he is not willing to provide safe passage to France to Jean Marc or any other soldier who invaded Russian soil."

Madeleine gasped!

"That is not what we paid for!" Madame LeBlanc exclaimed.

"That is all the money will buy... at least, at this time!" The deputy responded delicately.

Madame LeBlanc understood that now was not the time to be difficult. The bribe was merely the first installment. If Jean Marc were found more bribe money would be expected by both the Deputy Minister and the Russian Ambassador. "When can the envoys depart?" Pierre asked.

"As soon as we conclude this meeting," the deputy answered.

Madame LeBlanc sensing that Pierre had an underlying reason for his question, said, "Then, for the time being, our business is done!"

They went to the courtyard where Pierre informed them of the loyalty of the group. "They all volunteered for this mission, first and foremost, to find one of their own and second for the money. If they find Jean Marc, they will smuggle him back into France before they contact anyone. If need be, they will bribe the Russian soldiers or the Russian guards, which will be a pittance in contrast to the bribes for the deputy and the ambassador."

"And what is the strategy that was referred to by the deputy?' Madeleine asked.

"The deputy was not told the entire plan. He was informed that we will meet with the generals as we begin our search in Germany. But instead we will go directly to Poland and work our way back."

"Why go directly to Poland?" Madeleine asked.

"When I met with the veteran soldiers, they all felt that Poland was a safe haven for French soldiers. Poland had been an ally. It is hostile to both the Russians and the Prussians, and French soldiers would be protected in Poland."

Chapter 34

The Monsignor was more arrogant than usual following his weekly confession. He believed that pride was his greatest sin and felt relieved after he confessed his failing. He also believed that pride was his strongest quality because the Church needed confident leaders, like himself, to guide its flock. Confession was not only a way to purify oneself, but it also gave the clergy power over the followers. *If confession is needed for salvation, and only priests can administer confession, then priests are needed for salvation,* he mused.

The Monsignor had a keen understanding of the history of sacraments and was aware that the sacrament of Penance had changed dramatically since the time of Jesus. He was fond of quoting the Gospel of John: "If you forgive the sins of any, they are forgiven; if you retain the sins of any, they are retained." But the Monsignor knew that, by itself, the text did not prove that Jesus instituted the Sacrament of Penance nor that He conferred the power to forgive sins only to the Apostles, their successors, and their chosen delegates.

Furthermore, for the first few centuries after the death of Christ, the writings suggest that Penance was available to the baptized, but only once in a lifetime. The once-in-a-lifetime Penance was always reserved for serious sins. These were matters of common public knowledge. The offender would receive a form of excommunication, and could not participate in the celebration of the Eucharist. Penance was then obligatory, and the sinner was required to appear before the bishop, to present himself to the local community, and join the local group of penitents. Then after a suitable period of probation, the sinner would be readmitted to the Christian community by a rite known as reconciliation. An additional penance was sometimes imposed, such as celibacy for adulterers. This led to the breakup of marriages and resistance by the laity, who would postpone the sacrament until they were near death. It became officially the sacrament of the dying. As circumstances and the needs of the Church changed, private penance became more popular as did the actual confession of sins to a priest.

The once-in-a-lifetime Penance officially ended in 1215 with the Fourth Lateran Council's decree that all the baptized must confess their sins and receive Holy Communion at least once a year. *A long time after the death of Christ but certainly divinely inspired,* the Monsignor thought.

It was also during this period that theologians gave the power of absolution, or forgiveness, after oral confession, to the priest. Since absolution was not part of the practice of Penance in the early Church there was some dispute about its place in the sacrament. Gradually, however, absolution came to be regarded as essential to the forgiveness of sins — and only priests could give absolution.

During the Protestant Reformation, Martin Luther rejected this reservation of forgiveness to the priest, but it did not matter since all the Protestant reformers were heretics, the Monsignor ruminated.

His arrogance persisted as he arrived unannounced at Sister Superior's office. "Sister, how are the Moreau children doing in school?" he asked.

"They are all good students, and their conduct is admirable," she said, surprised by both the visit and the question.

"Where are they?" he asked, disdainfully. "I would like to see them."

"The children are at recess in the schoolyard, and we can see them at play from my window," she responded as she rose from her desk, walked to the large window, and scanned the yard. "There is Jean, the oldest of the three. The children follow his lead. However, he is very strong willed and sometimes a little headstrong."

"Does he ever influence the other children in an evil way?"

"Not at all Monsignor, he is very protective of the other children," she responded, still curious of the reason for his visit.

"He appears a little aggressive to me," the Monsignor persisted.

"Well, he is all boy, Monsignor," she insisted. It always upset her, the way priests talked down to nuns. "Oh, and there is Marc... he is more quiet than Jean but very thoughtful."

"What does he think about Sister Superior?"

"Probably what every six year old thinks about, Monsignor. However, I do worry that he keeps everything to himself!"

"Bring him to me," he ordered.

"Recess is almost over, and he will be returning to class in a few minutes... maybe at a more convenient time, Monsignor."

"Bring him to me now, Sister Superior. And be discreet so that Jean does not observe you," he ordered. "And tell no one of my visit."

"Where are we going, sister?" Marc asked.

"The Monsignor would like to compliment you on your school work," she responded tentatively.

"Monsignor, this is Marc Moreau," Sister Superior said as she re-entered the bureau.

"Thank you, Sister Superior. You may leave now," he responded curtly.

"I will work at my desk while you talk, Monsignor."

"You may leave, Sister Superior," he repeated

harshly.

"Yes, Monsignor," she said, feeling intimidated not for herself but for Marc Moreau, who seemed scared at the Monsignor's harsh tone of voice. Reluctantly, she left the room.

"What is you name?" the Monsignor asked gravely.

"Marc... Marc Moreau, Father," he responded.

"And, your mother's name?"

"Madeleine... Madeleine Moreau, Father."

"And where do you live?"

"We live with Madame LeBlanc," he said as he heard a knock at the door.

"I am sorry Monsignor, I will be but a moment," she said as she picked up a book from her desk.

"Please do not disturb us again Sister," he said as he closed the door behind her and then locked it. "Come here Marc, sit next to me."

Hesitantly the young boy sat next to the Monsignor. "Do you believe in God?" the Monsignor asked.

"Yes."

"Well, God is watching us, and He will be very mad at you if you ever tell anybody about this. Do you understand?"

"Yes."

"And if you tell anyone about this, then something very bad could happen to your brother, or sister, or even your mother. Do you understand?"

"Yes," Marc responded on the verge of tears.

"Good. Now just relax and sit a little closer to me."

"No, father, I am afraid."

"Do not be afraid. I am a priest, and I will protect you," he said as he moved closer to the young boy and put his arm around him.

Marc started to cry, which irritated the Monsignor.

"God will get mad at you if you cry Marc."

"I am afraid," Marc responded.

Just as the Monsignor moved even closer, a loud rap came from the door. "Monsignor, Monsignor, there is a fire in the school!"

The Monsignor rushed to the door and unlocked it. As he flung it open, he saw Sister Superior pointing down the hallway. Just then Marc rushed past them and ran down the hallway in the opposite direction. The Monsignor hesitated, but Sister Superior took his arm and led him down the hallway toward the smoke billowing at the end of the hallway. He looked back and saw Marc rush out the door at the end of the hallway and out into the schoolyard. As they arrived at the scene of the fire, he noticed that it was merely paper burning in a trashcan and obviously set. He glowered at Sister Superior and said harshly, "Would you like me to hear your confession, Sister Superior?"

"Oh, no Monsignor. My confession was heard early this morning, and all of my sins were absolved," she responded in a very kindly way, a smile gracing her saintly face.

He walked away, obviously angry at being foiled in his unholy endeavor.

She reflected upon his words: "Would you like me to hear your confession, Sister Superior?" She had always thought that many priests took advantage of the confessional to assert their authority. She recalled her early years in the rectory, when she had many thoughts about sexuality. It almost seemed natural, but whenever she confessed her sins, the priest made her feel ashamed of her sexuality, to the point where she obsessed about suppressing these thoughts. The thoughts still came but less frequently now — and they still seemed very natural to her. This was obviously the way God had created men and women, so that they could fall in love and procreate. She no longer confessed these thoughts because she did not think of them as sinful — that was just the way God had created women.

Marc hid in the schoolyard until Sister Superior found him. "Come Marc, the Monsignor is gone, all will be fine."

When Marc came home later that day, Madeleine noticed that he was quieter than usual but did not pay too much attention to it — and Marc said nothing.

Chapter 35

The sun was about to rise when the Russian Sergeant barked out orders for the convoy to move out. The objective was to cover twenty miles on that day. So they started early and would end late, if need be. As they marched, dozens of Russians on horseback patrolled constantly, heading the convoy in the right direction, keeping the formation tight, rounding up stragglers, and watching for sabotage by the Poles.

As the sun appeared, Jean Marc saw the land rising gently in front of him. He studied the landscape trying to determine how far they could travel in the next few days. There were no foothills or mountains on the horizon. The sky was clear, and he was optimistic that they could cover a lot of ground. His recollection was that Poland was mostly flat plains. It seemed so long ago that the *Grande Armee* marched proudly through Poland on its way to conquer the enemy. In every village, the crowds had cheered at what seemed an inevitable victory over the hated Russians. Now they were returning to France — defeated, humbled, and disgraced!

"Captain, let us make our rounds." Sergeant Moreau requested. He was encouraged by what he observed that morning. The roads were not as muddy. The convoy was moving steadily, and the sun was bright. Both the Poles and the French soldiers appeared to be in good humor even though the Russians were merciless in ordering them around.

"All seems well Captain," Sergeant Moreau said after they had completed the inspection of the convoy.

"But, there is much underlying hatred. Something will go wrong. The Russians will take their revenge. The Poles will cause disruption, and the convoy will move along slowly and haltingly. Sergeant, just keep in mind that we Poles have revenge on our minds."

"Luc, tonight I will slit his troat," Stefan said.

"Why? He has vodka left, and he is sharing it with us."

"He knows you are a French soldier ... e ask me to locate all of you Frenchies ... I told em I would!"

"Why has he not taken me into custody?"

"E wants to get all of you ... he as not told is comrades ... the dumb fuck wants all da reward!"

"Let me help you!"

"Your war is over Luc ... ours is just beginning. You are returning to your omeland. I am returning to my village and the Russian pigs. I will kill dis one myself, and I will kill a few more before we reach France."

The convoy covered its twenty miles by sunset. Fires were started. The aroma of food wafted in the air; vodka was being passed around, and laughter abounded. "Have a drink of vodka, Stefan," Luc urged.

"Not tonight my friend!" And as the sun set Stefan slipped away. In the darkness he could spy on the Russians without being observed. Although he understood very little Russian, he could tell that they were berating the Poles. Patiently, he waited for the group to retire for the night. He kept a lookout as to where they all went. He continued to wait until he heard the snoring of drunken soldiers. "Now is the time," he said under his breath as he moved stealthily towards his target. He reached for his knife and slowly pulled it out of its scabbard.
He froze as he heard a sound behind him.

"Stefan ... it's me, Luc," he heard someone whisper.

"Don't move ... don't say another word ... or we are bot dead," he whispered back. Luc froze as he observed Stefan crawl toward his prey. In an instant, the knife slashed the throat of the Russian soldier, and he heard Stefan whisper in the Russian's ear before he died, "This is for my mother dat you killed and my sister dat you raped … burn in ell forever you Russian prick!"

Everything was still for what seemed the longest time until Stefan waved to Luc to assist him. "Help me drag the body away," Stefan said calmly.

The two inched the body toward the gully and rolled it over the side. They heard a splash when it hit bottom. "At da bottom of da gutter where e belongs," Stefan whispered.

"Where is the fuckin' vodka?" Stefan asked irritably after they returned to their bunks.

"I was so worried when you were gone, I drank it all!"

"Frenchy, if you ever do dat again, you will be sleeping in da gutter with da Russian."

On the other side of Europe, Pierre and his friends were preparing to cross from France into enemy territory. "We will enter the Rhine Province, travel through the provinces of Saxony, Prussia, and Posen to reach Poland. We will keep to the main roads until we arrive in Warsaw. If Jean Marc is not found, we will return to France by way of the countryside searching every nook and cranny," Pierre explained to his companions.

"My guess is that they will either be a part of or nearby the Russian convoys. That way, they will track the Russian troops and react to their every move," a member of the group responded.

"Yes, Gerard, they are veteran soldiers and will want to know where the enemy is at all times."

As they observed from a distance, they were awestruck by the size of the Russian-Austrian base camp. "It's no time for France to return to war, we would be crushed by these armies sitting on our borders," Pierre told his men.

"It will take a massive effort to keep them supplied, which means more opportunities for Jean Marc Moreau and his soldiers to slip back to France," Gerard responded.

"I will present our papers to the Generals while you and the others snoop around for information. Security is sound outside the camp, but it appears lax inside. Gather whatever intelligence you can!"

When Pierre presented the documents to the generals, they were uncompromising in that the envoys could proceed no farther.

"The documents are valid and authorize us to travel throughout Germany and Poland," Pierre insisted.

"We will have to verify whether the documents are authentic," one of the generals responded.

"That will take time," Pierre said.

"Keep in mind, that France invaded Russia and killed millions of our countrymen. Something that we can not soon forget."

"But our countries will soon be at peace."

"We will not be at peace until Napoleon is dead or in prison. Return to your men and await our orders. And, remember, we are still at war," the general emphasized.

"Gerard, I should have offered them the bribe," Pierre said as he rejoined his men.

"No, Pierre, there were too many generals present. It would have been taken as an insult to the incorruptible ones. Do not worry, one of the greedy generals will contact you soon."

"I hope you are right because we do not have time to waste. But how was your reconnaissance?" Pierre asked.

"There are many French soldiers in hiding in Poland. Most are in Warsaw and the surrounding villages.

Whenever they are found, they are immediately executed. If we locate Jean Marc, or other soldiers, we must avoid the Russians, for they will show no mercy!" Gerard answered.

"How often do the convoys leave Warsaw?" Pierre asked.

"With such large encampments along our borders, the logistics are critical, and convoys are leaving Poland every twenty days. The last one arrived two days ago. There is another en route now."

"That is encouraging."

"We were told that the Poles are constantly sabotaging the convoys. We encountered a group of Poles who delighted in telling us of their exploits. They are very clever!"

"Did they suggest how we might break away from this encampment?"

"Yes, they said to sleep well tonight … the Russian generals are impatient and will soon be looking for their bribe money!"

In Paris, the buzz was all about the upcoming debate in the Senate.

"Talleyrand has invited us to attend the debate with him," Madame LeBlanc told Madeleine.

"When will it take place?"

"On Friday of this week?"

"Three days from now. Will Napoleon attend?"

Chapter 36

As they left Napoli for Rome, Martin asked about the territories ruled by the popes. "They are referred to as the Papal States and include most of central Italy with Rome as its seat of power," Thomas responded.

"But Napoleon dissolved the Papal States and incorporated the territories into his French Empire."

"He did more than that, Napoleon also abolished the temporal power of the popes and the Church. The popes had ruled over the vast territories since the ninth century, and this was commonly referred to as the temporal power of the Church."

"What is the difference?" Martin asked.

"The temporal powers are the political and governmental activities of the Church as distinguished from its spiritual and pastoral activity."

"And why was Napoleon opposed to the temporal power of the Church?" Martin persisted.

"Napoleon, as well as many others, claimed that this corrupted the Church due to its involvement in worldly activities at the expense of its spiritual mission."

"And, how do you feel about the Church's temporal powers, Thomas?"

"It is obvious that Jesus' mission was a spiritual mission. He even warned against involvement in political affairs: 'Give to Caesar what is Caesar's and to God what is God's'"

"And how do we give to God what is God's?" Martin questioned.

"We remove ourselves from worldly politics and follow the example of Jesus. But even in its spiritual role, the Church has oftentimes not followed the example of Jesus. The Protestant Reformation occurred because of the papacy's abuses in both worldly and spiritual matters."

Martin was confused, as he had been so many times during this journey. A vague idea was taking shape in his mind that his friend had something even more startling in store for him once they reached Rome. He was concerned about how he would react once confronted with Thomas' inevitable challenge. He reminded himself that the reason he had come to Rome was to file the accusation against Madeleine Moreau.

"Once you have filed the accusation with the Holy Office," Thomas said, as if reading his mind, " I have something to show you!"

The travelers crossed the yellowish waters of the Tiber River on the Ponte Sant' Angelo. As they walked the horses across the bridge, they stopped to admire a tall cylindrical building on the right bank of the river. "What is that structure?" Martin asked.

"Originally, it was tomb of a Roman emperor. The popes converted it into a castle and connected the castle to St Peter's Basilica by a covered fortified corridor called the *Passetto di Borgo*. Executions were performed in the inner courtyard," Thomas responded.

"Who ordered the executions?"

"The Bishop of Rome, the pope," Thomas responded.

"And who does the executions?"

"The pope has a papal executioner, who executes the condemned prisoners."

"And how are they executed?" Martin inquired.

"They are beheaded by an ax or a guillotine or burned at the stake!"

Martin just shook his head.

"Let us cross the bridge and climb the stairs to the top of the castle to better observe the bronze statue of the Archangel Michael, which is set atop the castle."

As they arrived at the top of the castle, Father

Martin's eyes were drawn to the splendor of St Peter's Basilica in the distance while Thomas' eyes were drawn to the darkness of the inner courtyard below.

On the next day, Martin appeared at the bureau of the Holy Office. He was aware of the dark history of the Inquisition and that its name had been changed to the Congregation of the Holy Office — *the Unholy Office*, as Thomas referred to it. After the introductions had been made and amenities exchanged, Father Martin explained why he had been sent from Paris to Rome and asked whether the Inquisition would return to France.

"The Inquisition has combated heresies for over 400 years and has been very effective, but it has acquired a bad reputation. During the French Revolution and the Napoleonic era, the Inquisition was temporarily abolished. In 1814, papal rule was restored, and the Inquisition was reestablished in the Papal States. The Church through the Congregation of the Holy Office will continue to combat heresies but in a more humane manner. I am confident the policy of the Holy Office will emanate from the Papal States to other countries. In the meantime, we will continue to combat heresies from the Papal States through the Holy Office," explained the Deputy Secretariat.

"There are some who say that the Inquisition is the symbol of the papacy's ambition and ruthlessness," Father Martin responded.

"The papacy recognizes that the Inquisition has been a powerful weapon against heretics and that it has been wrongly accused of ruthlessness. The Holy Office will continue to confront those who challenge the orthodox beliefs of the Church," the Deputy insisted.

Father Martin nodded his assent.

"And now to the business of the day. What accusation do you bring to us from the Monsignor in Paris?"

"The accusation involves the heresy of witchcraft against Madeleine Moreau," Father Martin responded.

"Superstition, sorcery, and magic are very prevalent among women. A large number of accusations involve the heresy of witchcraft. In many instances, if a person of good reputation reports a heresy he might not have to support a full accusation. And, obviously, the Monsignor is a person of good reputation."

"Some say he will be the next Bishop of Paris," Father Martin asserted.

"And what evidence do you have for my consideration?" the deputy asked.

"Madeleine Moreau is a married woman, and she is living openly with another man."

"Her sexuality, influenced by demons, has caused another into a state of mortal sin," the deputy added.

"There are also three children of tender age who are living with them," Father Martin said.

"Three children exposed to an adulterous relationship. Truly the work of the devil," the deputy insisted. "Are there other witnesses?"

"The Monsignor assigned someone to follow Madeleine Moreau, he will testify to the adulterous relationship and her devious ways with men."

"Then there are two eye witnesses to the adultery. Are there any details as to unusual behavior?"

"The Monsignor has also observed very unusual behavior by Madeleine Moreau. He heard her call upon the devil in church … she was often seen in church without a head cover … she talked to spirits in church and not holy spirits … she brought a book listed on the Index into Church and left it there to wreak havoc with the faithful."

"And who was the author of the book?"

"Voltaire!"

"It was Voltaire who said *Ecrasez l'infame,* meaning that Christianity must be wiped out entirely … not only the hierarchy of bishops, cardinals, and popes but Christianity itself, which Voltaire claims is merely superstition."

"He referred to the Church as a *tower of falsehood* and a *fortress of superstition*," Father Martin added.

After taking a brief recess the deputy returned and addressed Father Martin. "My assessment is that the Monsignor is a person of good reputation, has conducted a thorough investigation, and has other witnesses to corroborate his findings. There are ample partial proofs to provide justification for seeking of a full proof. I will accept the accusation from the Monsignor. However, at the trial the Monsignor will be required to provide two eyewitnesses to the heresy. And, if there are sufficient partial proofs the tribunal may order torture to obtain a confession from the heretic."

"And where will the trial be held?" Father Martin asked.

"At this time, the tribunal can convene only within the territories of the Papal States ... and the accused will be notified of the date for trial."

"And if she is not present can she be tried *in absentia*?" Father Martin inquired.

"No, the accused must be present. If she does not appear, the accusations will remain outstanding until either the Inquisition is extended into France or she voluntarily comes to Rome."

"And, for what length of time will the accusation remain outstanding?" Father Martin persisted.

"Until the death of the heretic. Keep in mind, that our task is not only to convict the heretic but to save her soul and preserve the unity of the Church," the deputy explained.

There was a pause as Father Martin reflected upon the good works of the Holy Office. *The salvation of souls is the ultimate purpose of the Church*, he thought. He stared across the table at the deputy and wondered about the age of the deputy secretariat. Young people have difficulty in determining the age of their elders. W*as he sixty or maybe eighty*, he wondered. *And the leaders of the Church were all old men — maybe wisdom comes with age,* he surmised. The voice of the deputy brought him back to the purpose of his visit.

"In conclusion, I have determined, based on the information that you provided to me today, that it is likely that these acts occurred, that they present a grave matter, and that they could lead to the punishment of the accused. The Holy Office will serve the accused, Madeleine Moreau, with a written account of the charges against her. The Holy Office will issue a writ ordering that she appear before a tribunal in Rome. And, the Holy Office will request that she either confess to, or defend herself against, the charge of witchcraft before an impartial tribunal."

Father Martin always felt most comfortable working within the established order, and he was pleased with the progress of the meeting with the deputy secretariat. He had been allowed to present his case; the deputy was impartial in his judgment, and Madeleine Moreau would get a fair trial. *The Church was not perfect*, he thought, *but it is the best way to salvation.*

Chapter 37

Madeleine noticed a change in Marc's behavior but felt it was a phase he was going through. She had discussed the matter with his teacher and was told that he seemed sad and was shying away from his playmates. Jean and Angeline, who continued to blossom and be happy, tried to get him involved, but he showed little interest. She prayed on a daily basis for Jean Marc, Michel, and her children, and now she included a special prayer for Marc. *With God's help I will find the strength to cope with my hardships and raise my children properly.*

As she approached the parochial school with the children in tow, she spotted the Monsignor walking toward them. A chill gripped her heart. Marc moved closer to his mother and held her hand tightly. The other two children continued in their playful way. As he approached them, Madeleine did not know whether to turn and run or stand her ground. Before she could decide, a smile came over his countenance and he said, "Bonjour Madame Moreau, you have a lovely family."

Caught off guard, she froze and did not respond.

"Mama, mama…hurry, or we will be late for school," Jean yelled breaking the trance.

"Yes, yes …" she responded, and with Marc in hand, she hurried toward her children, not realizing how tightly Marc was gripping her hand. She turned back to see the Monsignor, not looking at her but rather at Marc.

Madeleine watched her children at play that evening — the image of the Monsignor still vivid in her mind. Jean was sculpting a piece of marble with tools given to him by Michel. He moved naturally around the marble, sculpting a little here and a little there, trying to find the image within the marble; the hammer in his right hand, the chisel in his left, his movements graceful and natural. Angeline was collecting pieces of marble scattered around the studio. She would place them in a little bag until it was full and then pick out the ones that weren't flawed. She seemed to find beauty in the stones. Marc was sitting by his mother's side holding her hand gently. He looked up at her, a tear in his eye, and a sad expression on his face. "What is the matter Marc?" she asked caringly.

"Is God going to take you away, Mama?"

In northern France, Michel was recovering from his wounds. He had been promoted to the rank of colonel and put in charge of an infantry battalion. He knew they would be tested by the advancing troops, but he felt confident. They would now be defending their homeland.

"The odds could be five to one, so long as we have a strong position to defend," he briefed his staff. "The generals are analyzing the best defensive positions between us and the enemy. If our defensive fronts are close to our frontier the enemy will ravage less of France."

"I have heard that a few generals are advocating for the defense of Paris," a captain mentioned.

"That is a bad strategy. The rest of France would be ravaged, and Paris would come under siege, one it could not long withstand."

"We will know by Friday once the Senate votes on the abdication of Napoleon," the captain added.

"Napoleon will not abdicate. Prepare our battalion to return to battle." Michel ordered.

"Yes, sir," they responded eagerly as they left for their units.

They have all come a long way and suffered many hardships. This was the last leg of their journey, and the most critical. The odds are against them. But that seems to make them more determine, Michel thought.

In Paris, Talleyrand visited with Madame LeBlanc. "It took two armies to defeat Napoleon at Waterloo. What remains of his army to the north is battle tested and will fight to the death for him. But they cannot defend against four Allied armies. Our only hope is for him to abdicate and for me to negotiate a peaceful settlement."

"Are the Allies willing to leave France intact." Madame LeBlanc asked.

"They will demand territory and money, but there is an underlying animosity amongst the Allied countries. I will take advantage of the situation and pit one against the other. Under the circumstances, the results will be good for France."

"How can you be so confident?" Madeleine asked.

"Napoleon's enemies happen to be my friends. They will be indebted to me when I convince the Senate to vote for his abdication. And they will treat France favorably." Talleyrand said, taking Jeannette's hand in his.

"And if I may be so bold, how did the two of you become friends?" Madeleine asked.

"Our friendship goes back to our childhood. We were both born into aristocratic families in Paris. Our parents were in the same social circle. I had a limp from early childhood and because of that infirmity, other kids made fun of me, but not Jeannette. She was kind and came to my defense. I don't know what I admired more, her love or her strength."

"A little later in life, Charles-Maurice went off to the priesthood, where he quickly rose in the church hierarchy and became Agent-General of the clergy and represented the Catholic Church to the French King. Later, he was appointed as the Bishop of Autun. I avidly followed his rise in power."

"Ironically, we were reunited during the French Revolution. Jeannette found the love of her life in that handsome lieutenant. I was so envious!"

"Charles, you never told me."

"I have been in love with you since the age of four. But even with all of my diplomatic skills, I could not bring myself to tell you, Jeannette."

"Charles was such an inspiration to all of us. He supported the anti-clericalism of the revolutionaries. He was influential in the writing of the Declaration of the Rights of Man. He proposed the Civil Constitution of the Clergy, which nationalized the Church. It was at that point that Pope Pius VI excommunicated him."

"And, as I was working on these documents, Jeannette was storming the Bastille, protesting against the monarchy, and fighting for justice, liberty and equality. We saw each other often. Until... '

"Until Robespierre issued a warrant for Maurice's arrest because he would not support the horrors of the new government. He fled to the United States and befriended many revolutionaries there, such as, Aaron Burr and Alexander Hamilton."

"When I returned to France two years later, I became a close ally to Napoleon and became France's Foreign Minister."

"We lived in a time of extraordinary change — not willing to adhere to the dogmas of the past."

"He served France with grace, dignity, and aplomb, until his falling out with Napoleon. It was at about that time that you were quoted as saying '... black as the devil, hot as hell, pure as an angel, sweet as love.' I have often wondered what you meant by those words."

"At the time, my words were taken out of context, but what I was referring to was Napoleon and you, Jeannette. Napoleon being the former and you the latter."

"Rather, I think you were referring to your mistress."

Madeleine gasped, "Your mistress," she said.

"Charles Maurice de Talleyrand-Perigord had a

reputation as a womanizer. When he returned to France from his American exile, he lived with Catherine Worlee Grand, who was married and had a reputation of her own. She divorced her husband to marry Talleyrand. After many delays by Maurice, Napoleon forced his hand into marriage."

"With such a close relationship with Napoleon, why do you oppose him now?' Madeleine asked.

"I disapproved of his continuing initiative to triumph over other nations. It could only lead France to ruin. I was also vocal in my opposition to the Russian invasion."

"Which, we now admit, was disastrous for France," Madame LeBlanc added.

"And now you are leading the charge for his abdication. Why?"

"Now is the time for diplomacy not war. If Napoleon does not abdicate, the Allies will crush our army. Then the victors will partition France just as they have partitioned Poland."

"Poland no longer exists," Madame LeBlanc added.

"And, neither will France, if Napoleon returns to power."

Chapter 38

The convoy made very slow progress. The Poles were very good at sabotaging the journey without getting caught. Jean Marc, although frustrated with the pace, had come to admire the Poles — their sense of country, family, and friends. It was such a small country, with no natural borders for defense, surrounded by its enemies, but having too much heart and courage to succumb. He thought back to the time when Napoleon beckoned the youth of his nation to return France to its glory. Given time, a savior would one day rise from the country's ashes and return Poland to its former glory.

Daily, wheels fell off the carts, supplies disappeared, horses pulled up lame, and Russian soldiers went missing — all slowing the pace of the convoy. With each setback, Russian discipline became harsher, food allocations smaller, rest periods shorter, and punishment more severe. *It is a test of wills, and the Poles are winning*, Jean Marc thought

Early the next morning, the Polish captain rode up to Jean Marc. He checked whether the Russians were within earshot, and said, "Sergeant, there will be a full assault on the convoy before it leaves Poland."

"Will we be warned?" Sergeant Moreau asked with concern.

"You will be given the opportunity to fight with us or flee the convoy before the assault."

That night, after Jean Marc had spoken to his men, he informed the captain that they would join the fight.

The following day, the convoy moved smoothly. Jean Marc surmised the Poles wanted to reach the point of attack by sunset. Although he had not been told the plan, it was obvious to him that along the way Polish soldiers were lying in wait to attack the Russian convoy. The Russian officers, also suspicious, cantered up and down the convoy barking out orders and huddling often to confer. They posted sentries to the front, rear, and sides. At dusk, a Russian officer ordered the convoy to halt, the sentries were called in for chow, and the Russian officers gloated about how much ground they had covered. Jean Marc observed the terrain — hills on both side of the road, thick forest within a hundred yards of the road, and no cover between the road and the forest. *The perfect place for an ambush*, Jean Marc surmised.

Within a few minutes, the Polish captain ordered Jean Marc to follow him."

"Not without my soldiers," Jean Marc responded.

"There is a Polish soldier with every one of them. Before sunset, we will make a dash to the woods just as the canon balls rain down upon the Russians. When we reach the woods, we will link up with a Polish company and assault the Russians as soon as the artillery ceases. The Russians will retreat to the woods on the other side where another Polish company lies in wait to mow them down."

Suddenly, the captain spurred his horse, and Jean Marc followed. He could see the Polish and French soldiers scampering through the field heading for the woods. The Russians reacted quickly, shots soon filled the air, some cracking overhead but many finding the backs of the runaway soldiers. Then came the deafening roar of the cannons. Jean Marc looked back and saw the spray of earth gush from the soft sand, body parts and wagons soaring through the air. He reached the woods and waited for the sounds of the cannons to cease.

He prodded his horse as the Polish company began their assault. *Many will die rushing across the open field*, he thought. His instincts took over ordering the soldiers forward. Rifle rounds sprayed the assaulting company. He heard a scream beside him and saw the captain fall.

"Charge," he yelled at the soldiers. The firing intensified as they neared the Russian line with soldiers falling all around him. He knew if they stopped they would all be killed. "Keep moving," he hollered in French hoping the Poles would understand. He took the lead and the Poles followed. The Russians turned and retreated towards the woods on the other side. Sergeant Moreau halted the troops at the road. The gunfire ceased for a few moments and then echoed from the other side. The Russians were trapped and were not allowed to surrender. The Poles exacted their revenge, slaughtering the enemy soldiers. A loud cheer erupted from the Poles as the last rays of sun left the sky.

The groans, cries, and sobs of the wounded soldiers could be heard coming from the bloody field of battle. Luc, and other medics, spent the dark night with lanterns moving from one wounded soldier to the next, some writhing in pain, others lying in the stillness of death. They worked feverishly through the night healing some and consoling others.

In the early morning, Luc found Sergeant Moreau, "One French soldier and nearly two dozen Poles were killed..." he said as his voice trailed off, overcome with grief and exhaustion.

"Nearly a hundred Russian soldiers were killed, but some escaped and will return with reinforcements. The Poles will take the food, supplies, and ammunition from the convoy and return to their villages. We will go south to the roads less travelled until we are safely away from the Russians and then turn west towards France."

"Do we have maps?" Luc asked.

"Better yet, we have a guide," he said, as Stephan rose from a group of soldiers huddled nearby.

"Sergeant, let's bury our dead, treat da wounded, gater our supplies, and march south." Stephan said.

"The men need rest," Luc responded.

"The Russian cavalry will be upon us soon. We have no time to rest." Stephan responded.

"He is right... we will rest later. Luc, assign the men specific tasks and be back here by noon," Sergeant Moreau ordered.

Word of the Russian defeat spread rapidly. In East Prussia a company of cavalry and a company of infantry were dispatched to Poland. Their mission, to punish the Poles and capture or kill the remaining French soldiers. Word also reached Pierre, where his group was still being delayed at the border. "They will hold us up even more now," Pierre told the others.

"Just at a time when the French soldiers will be most vulnerable!" another added.

"I suggest we return to France and cross the border elsewhere. We can go south and reach Poland through Austria."

"We could also go north and reach Poland through Belgium and Holland" one from the group suggested.

"I have studied the available maps and believe it is more plausible that the French soldiers will flee to the south. I fear if we divide our group, we will not be of any help to our comrades." Pierre advised.

"And, together we will be safer," another reaffirmed.

"It is a good plan, and let's not waste any more time. We will ride the horses hard and use the bribe money to buy fresh horses along the way," Pierre added.

"Time is of the essence... we will leave immediately. Once we reach the French border we will go south and slip into Germany," another said.

The men nodded their assent.

"I will meet with the Russian generals and inform them that we are returning to France." Pierre said.

"Fuck the Russians… they will not let us return to France, anyway. Let us slip away. " All agreed.

"God willing, we will find our brothers before the Russians do," Pierre said.

"God has nothing to do with it," another added.

Chapter 39

Martin was surprised by Thomas' reaction to the indictment of the Holy Office against Madeleine Moreau. *It had been a fair process, and she would receive a fair trial — what more could he expect*, he wondered.

"I doubt the decision would have been the same if the roles had been reversed," Thomas said.

"What do you mean?"

"If Madeleine Moreau had accused the Monsignor of witchcraft with the same evidence, I believe the decision would have been different. First, the deputy would not have accepted that she was a person of good reputation just on your say so. Second, he would have questioned Madeleine's interpretation of the events. Third, he would have given the Monsignor the benefit of every doubt. "

"And why do you say that?"

"The deputy mirrors the values of a Church that looks upon men as honorable and women as shameful."

"Thomas Aquinas concluded that women are inferior by nature to men... that is why the deputy gives more weight to the testimony of men," Martin asserted.

"More important, the history of the Church ignores Jesus' egalitarian treatment of women and grasp on to a philosophy that denigrates women, like those of Augustine and Aquinas. Then the Church elevates these people to sainthood to reinforce their philosophies while those who disagree are condemned as heretics."

"What if they are right?" Martin asked.

"Tomorrow, I will show you what happens when one accepts a philosophy that discriminates against others, come with me, Martin!"

"Where are we going?"

"First to the Vatican Library then to the Vatican Secret Archives."

"I thought the Archives were closed to outsiders."

"During the Seventeenth century the Secret Archives were separated from the Vatican Library and were closed to outsiders under the orders of Pope Paul V." Thomas responded.

"Then how will we get in?"

"I am not an outsider. Whoever occupies the papacy is the owner of the Archives until death or resignation. I have been to the Archives many times, and I have taken guests on several occasions. We will gain access through my family's contacts with the papacy."

Martin reflected what his friend said concerning Aquinas and Augustine, as they entered the opulent Vatican Library. It always upset him when Thomas belittled the great saints of the Church. "Let me study a few of Aquinas' works before we visit the Archives," Martin suggested.

"Then, I will see the guardian of the Archives and prepare a few documents for our review. We will begin our studies tomorrow."

Martin knew this was another test of his vow of obedience, and he was determined not to fail. He had completed the Monsignor's mission and he would not falter in his personal loyalty to the Church. Immediately, he went to the works of Thomas Aquinas and immersed himself in study, which confirmed the Church's view of Christian theology. Aquinas's greatest quest was *truth,* and his greatest achievement was his *Summa Theologica,* a summation of theological knowledge. Aquinas concluded that man is a sinner and in need of special grace from God. Jesus earned grace for mankind by his death on the cross and imparts it daily through the Church. This saving grace flows through men exclusively by their dispensation of divinely appointed sacraments in a Church led by a male pope. So convinced was Aquinas of the divine role of the papacy, that he insisted that submission to the pope was necessary for salvation.

In his search for truth and salvation Aquinas placed the pope as the key to salvation, Martin mused. *My vow of obedience is to the pope. Without his grace, we are doomed to hell.*

Aquinas concludes that men are superior to women not only because they are stronger but also smarter. Aquinas cites Scripture as support for his position: "Man was not created for the sake of women, but woman was created for the sake of man... It is not good that man should be alone; I will give him a helpmate... Man is the head of a woman... A husband is the head of his wife." Based on Scripture, Aquinas reasons that when one thing exists for the sake of another, it is inferior to that other; and, that if men are meant to rule, they do by virtue of intellectual superiority.

Aquinas' view on the inferiority of women was also influenced by Aristotle's view that the male was the active principle and that the female was the passive principle in the act of procreation. The active principle was perfect and the passive principle was imperfect. Therefore, male was perfect and female was imperfect.

Aquinas also noted that women have difficulty in sticking to their decisions and change their minds quickly out of desire, anger or fear.

All persuasive arguments, Martin thought.

Martin's studies were interrupted by Thomas' voice, "Oh, you are still here," he said. "I see you are reading Aquinas' *Summa.*"

"Yes, and I am impressed by his reasoning."

"He is very adamant about the inferior nature of women!" Thomas noted.

"And his arguments are very logical."

"And so are the arguments of Augustine, the most influential of the early church fathers, who was born a thousand years before Aquinas. Augustine viewed women not only as threatening to men, but also as intellectually and morally inferior. He has written, '... what is the difference whether it is in a wife or a mother, it is still Eve the temptress that we must beware of in any woman... I fail to see what use woman can be to man, if one excludes the function of child bearing.'"

"Aquinas and Augustine are great scholars and have made a significant contribution to Church theology, philosophy, and doctrine. Both dedicated to God and Christian truth," Martin asserted.

"The dogma of the Church is based on their theology, which limits the role of women in today's Church! So it is not from Jesus, but rather from Augustine and Aquinas, that the Church has formulated a doctrine that discriminates against women."

Martin did not respond.

"Tomorrow, you will learn how a religion changed by bias, prejudice, and intolerance led to the persecution and death of thousands of Jews, Muslims, Christians and, yes, women!"

Chapter 40

"All of Paris is anxious about the future of France. If Napoleon does not abdicate, we are faced with the reality of several armies advancing to the gates of Paris," Talleyrand told his guests as he ushered them to their seats in the Chamber of Representatives. "The debate will take place in a few moments between the Marquis de Lafayette and Lucien Bonaparte."

"But Napoleon controls the army, what difference can a debate make?" Madeleine asked.

"Public opinion is turning against Napoleon. He should have remained in the field with his army but, instead, he chose to return to Paris to fight the political battle. He believes that the Chambers of the Estates will unite with him to confront the enemy and secure the independence of France. However, both the Chamber of Representatives and the Chamber of Peers are prepared, if need be, to depose the Emperor."

"Who will be first to address the Representatives?' Madame LeBlanc asked.

"Lucien Bonaparte will call upon the Chambers to unite with his brother to annihilate the enemy," he said, as he directed his guests to seats in the first row of the balcony.

"These have the best view of the chamber," Madame LeBlanc whispered to her host.

"The better for me to orchestrate the deliberations of the representatives," he responded slyly.

The murmur of the chamber hushed, and Madeleine looked over the rail to see what was happening.

"Lafayette has arrived," Talleyrand said.

Madeleine observed a distinguished looking gentleman, working the room, on his way to the center of the chamber. As he arrived at his desk, he looked up toward

Talleyrand.

"He is looking in your direction," Madeleine said to Talleyrand.

"No, his eyes are searching for Jeannette LeBlanc," he responded.

Madeleine was stunned as she saw Madame LeBlanc move toward the rail.

"How do they know each other?" Madeleine whispered to Talleyrand.

"The Marquis de Lafayette went to the United States and served as a field officer to General George Washington. Another young Frenchman fought with valor alongside the American rebels. The two formed a friendship that can only be forged by the fires of war. They returned to France with a lust for liberty and spearheaded the French Revolution."

Madeleine looked curiously at Talleyrand.

"The young lieutenant fell in love with Jeanette LeBlanc as the four of us joined in the cause of bringing liberty and equality to our country."

Lafayette smiled at Jeannette.

Madeleine saw tears running from Madame LeBlanc's cheeks as she blew a kiss to her friend. "We will soon be reunited," she whispered.

The sound of a gavel, echoing through the hall, brought the chamber to attention. As order came to the crowd, Lucien Bonaparte rose from his chair to address the representatives.

"I have been sent here as a Commissioner Extraordinaire to collaborate with the Chambers for the safety of our country. Now that the enemy is in France is not the time for interminable debate but, rather, it is time to invest Napoleon with absolute power, that of a temporary dictator. Of course, with the support of the army, he could assume this power — but it would be better for France if it were conferred upon him by the representatives of the people."

A murmur rippled through the hall. "Which means he would also dissolve the two Chambers," Talleyrand whispered to Jeannette.

"The Representatives must unite with the Emperor to save France from a fate similar to Poland." Lucien continued. "A strong military, led by the Emperor, will ensure the public safety and bring the Allies to the peace table. It is the duty of the Chambers to adopt immediate and decisive measures to secure the honor and independence of France."

A light applause followed as he left the podium.

Madeleine observed intently as the Marquis de Lafayette ascended the tribune to address the Chamber amidst the suspense of the gathering.

"Representatives! For the first time during many years you hear a voice, which the old friends of liberty will yet recognize. I rise to address you concerning the dangers to which the country is exposed. The sinister reports, which have been circulated during the past two days, are unhappily confirmed. This is the moment to rally around the national colours — the Tricoloured Standard of 1788 — the standard of liberty, equality and public order. It is you alone who can now protect the country from foreign attacks, and internal dissensions. It is you alone who can secure the independence and honour of France.

Permit a veteran in the sacred cause of liberty, in all times a stranger to the spirit of faction, to submit to you some resolutions, which appear to him to be demanded by a sense of the public danger and by the love of our country. They are such as, I feel persuaded, and you will see the necessity of adopting:

First, the Chamber of Representatives declares that the independence of the nation is menaced.

Second, the Chamber declares its sittings permanent. Any attempt to dissolve it, shall be considered high treason. Whosoever shall render himself culpable of such an attempt shall be considered a traitor to his country.

Third, the Army of the Line, the National Guard, who have fought, and still fight, for the liberty, the independence, and the territory of France, have merited well of the country.

Fourth, the Minister of the Interior is invited to assemble the principal officers of the Parisian National Guard, in order to consult on the means of providing it with arms, and of completing this corps of citizens, whose tried patriotism and zeal offer a sure guarantee for the liberty, prosperity, and tranquility of the capital, and for the inviolability of the national representatives.

Fifth, the Ministers of War, of Foreign Affairs, of Police, and of the Interior are invited to repair immediately to the Sittings of the Chamber."

The Chamber rose in unison and carried the resolutions by acclamation. They were next transmitted to the Chamber of Peers, where they were adopted without amendment.

"What will happen now?" Madeleine asked Talleyrand.

"The Resolutions are being sent to Napoleon. He has been given an hour to respond.

Within the hour, Lucien Bonaparte returned to address the Chamber. "The safety of the country demands that the Emperor participate with a Commission appointed by the Chambers to negotiate directly with the enemy and that these negotiations should be supported by the prompt deployment of the national force. That this means should first be tried; and that, should Napoleon then prove an insuperable obstacle to the nation, he will be ready to make whatever sacrifice may be demanded of him."

"Napoleon is attempting to destroy our independence and re-establish his despotism," cried a representative.

"His plan cannot succeed," cried another, as the Chamber fell into disorder.

Talleyrand nodded to Lafayette, who rose and went deliberately to the podium. A hush came over the hall.

"The Chambers cannot offer negotiations to the Allied Powers," Lafayette began. "The documents that have been communicated to us demonstrate that they have uniformly refused all the overtures which have been made to them, and they have declared that they will not deal with the French, as long as they shall have the Emperor at their head."

Madeleine observed Lucien Bonaparte shaking his head in disapproval and preparing to leave the Chamber.

"You know," Lafayette continued, "as well as I do, that it is against Napoleon alone that Europe has declared war. From this moment, separate the cause of Napoleon from that of the nation. There remains one individual who stands in the way between us and peace. Let him pronounce the word, and the country will be saved."

Madame Leblanc clutched the hand of Talleyrand as Lucien Bonaparte turned his back to Lafayette and walked toward the rear of the chamber.

Lafayette's voice rose as Bonaparte opened the large wooden door.

"We have only one certain means left, which is to engage the Emperor, in the name of the safety of the State, in the sacred name of a suffering country, to declare his Abdication!"

The crashing of the chamber door startled Madeleine, just as the last word was spoken.

In Laon, the general staff of the Army was placed on high alert. "Napoleon is enraged by the Chambers actions and was heard to say that 'the Chambers are composed of intriguers who are seeking disorder to enhance their status," Michel told his company commanders. "He will denounce them to the nation and give them their dismissal. The time we have lost may yet be recovered. Prepare the battalion to march on Paris."

Chapter 41

In Paris, Madeleine and Madame LeBlanc talked animatedly as they walked back from church with the children on Sunday morning.

"I have been told by Talleyrand that Napoleon will soon have a response for the Chambers," Madame LeBlanc said.

"Rumors abound that the northern army is preparing to march on Paris."

"Talleyrand and Lafayette are attempting to ease the panic in Paris."

"That sense of panic was evident in church today." Madeleine added.

"In a lot of ways, the confusion that permeates Paris resembles the confusion inherent in the Church."

"What do you mean?" Madeleine asked.

"I believe most priests are very sincere about their vocation and desire to accurately present the word of Jesus to the parishioners. However, I sometimes have my doubts about the accuracy of their homilies." Madame LeBlanc responded.

"And why do you say that?" Madeleine asked, while keeping an eye on the children running ahead of them.

"I don't think the priests deliberately mislead the parishioners, but the Church does not have the original writings of the New Testament. What it has are copies of the originals made many years, even centuries, later. None of these copies is completely accurate, and the scribes who copied them have been known to make mistakes — some inadvertently others intentionally. Also, many of the early writings were translated from the original language to Greek and Latin, and the scribes at times rendered their own interpretation in the translation. So there are errors in the New Testament — both actual and interpretive."

"Well, it does lend credence to the Church's belief that the believer needs the priests to properly interpret the Bible," Madeleine added.

"Yes, and it also lends credence to the fact that we should at times be critical of what is said from the pulpit for the spoken word might not be Jesus' original words."

Suddenly, Madeleine darted away from her friend and toward the children where Marc was on the ground crying with Jean standing over him.

"What happened Jean?" Madeleine asked sternly.

"I pushed him to the ground," Jean responded defiantly.

"But why?" She asked as she picked Marc off the ground and cradled him in her arms.

"Because he said you were going to die, Mama," he responded, just as they heard a piercing cry from Madame LeBlanc's direction.

They turned and saw her on the ground and rushed to her side. Madeleine was the first to arrive and as she picked her up she felt her bones through her clothes and for the first time realized she was old and frail. "What's the matter... what's the matter?" she asked repeatedly, as the children panicked upon seeing blood flowing freely from her nose and forehead.

"I will be fine... I tripped and hit my head rushing to your side. Take the children away and come back for me in the carriage," she said weakly.

"Madame LeBlanc sit here on the bench, and I will wait with you as Mama goes for the carriage." Jean urged.

Madeleine left with the two children and hurrying to fetch the carriage. "Jean go back to the fountain and wet this handkerchief... and bring it back to me." Madame LeBlanc said haltingly.

"Where is the fountain?' he asked with a panicked look on his face.

"A few hundred meters back toward the church," she said.

When he returned he found her slumped on the bench, unconscious. He wiped the blood from her face as tears flowed down his cheeks. "Please wake up, please wake up, Madame LeBlanc," he sobbed. It seemed like forever before Madeleine returned with the carriage. "Mama, mama… she is not breathing."

The funeral was attended by both the upper crust of Paris and the peasantry. Madeleine speculated that thousands paid their respects to one who had contributed so much to the Paris community. At the funeral service, the cathedral of Notre Dame overflowed with friends, associates, and the curious. The Bishop of Paris celebrated the High Mass with other bishops attending him. It was pageantry of the highest scale for Paris. The elite spoke of her cultural, social and business contributions to Paris, while the commoners waiting outside spoke of her valor during the French Revolution and her kindness to the poor people of Paris. The last words spoken in church were those of Talleyrand who described her character as human, kind, and filled with a spirit of tolerance and compassion.

As the casket was carried from the cathedral to the square, where the horse drawn carriage awaited, the crowd erupted into a chorus of revolutionary and patriotic songs, much to the chagrin of the nobility and the clergy. "This is what Madame LeBlanc would most enjoy," Madeleine whispered to her children.

"Yes, yes Mama she would!" Jean responded, happy for the change from the solemnity of the funeral service.

The procession was led by carts filled with flowers, then the carriages of the nobility, followed by the coach carrying the body of Madame LeBlanc, and finally, the commoners bringing some gaiety to an otherwise sad occasion.

After most of the people had left the cemetery, a man approached Madeleine and said, "I am Jeannette LeBlanc's avocat, Normand L'Heureux. There is considerable speculation concerning the disposition of her personal wealth and her vast business holdings."

"She has mentioned your name," Madeleine responded.

"Please take a few days to mourn her death and then come to my bureau on the Boulevard Saint-Germain," he said, as he turned and walked away.

The children wandered toward the waiting carriage. She stood, a solitary figure, before the open crypt and sighed to her friend, "I have never felt so alone."

Chapter 42

The next day the Russian cavalry arrived in force at the site of the ambush — two platoons of Russian soldiers, ready to exact revenge. They had come in from the west and determined that the French contingent had either gone north or south to find a westerly route to France.

The commanding officer interrogated the Poles in the nearby village but received little information. He tortured the villagers but, still, received little information.

Short on time, he divided the unit into two groups and sent one in each direction. But before he departed, he ordered the village burned to the ground and its inhabitants killed.

Jean Marc knew the Russians would not be far behind as he urged Stephan to pick up the pace.

"Yes, Sergeant," Stephan responded as he spurred his horse and shouted to Luc, "If da Russians catch up to us dey will flay us alive, Luc…" he said, as he flashed Luc a wide grin.

"The sergeant also said to travel light, what do you have in your bags, Stephan?"

"Sausages and vodka my friend, sausages and vodka… and I will kill any soldier who tries to steal it — French or Russian."

"Well, you don't have to worry about anybody stealing your Polish sausage Stephan," Luc smirked as he kicked his horse on its side to stay up with Stephan.

"You will see tonight by da camp fire when you smell da sweet aroma of my kielbasa," he said as he looked back to see the French soldiers bounding awkwardly on the horses. "Our women ride orses bedder dan you Frenchies."

"We are foot soldiers, not cavalry," Luc responded, nearly falling off the horse.

"I bedder slow down… even da orses are laughing!"

214

An hour later Sergeant Moreau came to the front of the column. "Stephan, we must take a break!" he implored.

"Not 'til noon Sergeant... by den da orses will be tired. Tel da men to keep hips and shoulders over der feet... and to keep der hands off da saddle... settle in... relax. Tel dem to look at Luc and do nothing like im!" he said as he burst out in laughter. "Now da men walk da orses... by dis afternoon dey will gallop... tomorrow dey will run like da wind!"

At nightfall, the horses were cared for, a campfire was lit, and Stephan cooked kielbasa for his friends. His prediction was right. The soldiers savored the sausages and vodka. They retired early as Jean Marc took the first three hours of guard duty, which gave him an opportunity not only to plan the strategy for the next day but also to ponder what he would do when they reached France. He listened to the banter of his soldiers as they lightheartedly called to the medic for ointment for their sore butts. Soldiers had a sixth sense about danger, and tonight it was not in the air. They had left the battleground quickly and the Russian replacements would not catch up for a few days. However, the days ahead would bring more danger, and the soldiers would be more vigilant. He would break camp early and would push hard until nightfall. So long as they maintained their distance from the Russians, they would reach France safely. If not, they faced slaughter!

They had come so far since their escape from the Russian camp, that now he could let down his guard for a few hours to think about a reunion with his family. The night was clear. The moon was full, and the stars were brilliant. He wondered whether Madeleine was looking at the same moon and thinking of him. Would she still love him? And the children, would they even remember him? He looked up at the stars and thought of matters that had been out of his mind for months. He had been a soldier all of his adult life. What would he do for work? How could they ever afford to buy a farm? He watched the moon rise in the sky as these uncertainties ran through his mind.

"Sergeant, your watch is over."

Sergeant Moreau looked toward the sound of the voice and noticed the ghostly figure in the moonlight. "Luc, go back to sleep. I am wide-awake and will take your watch. Who's next?"

"Pierre. He's under the tree over there."

Sergeant Moreau spent the next few hours thinking about Madeleine — so young… so strong… so beautiful. All wonderful qualities but also why she could be with another.

How would I react if I found her with another man? He tried to discard these thoughts, but they kept returning. *My conscience is dull from seeing so many die. It would not be difficult for me to kill a man who shared her bed*, he thought, as he stood up and walked down the road from which they had come, attempting to shake these thoughts. When he returned, he awakened Pierre, and with his back against a tree, he finally fell asleep.

By daybreak, the horses were saddled, and the small troop of soldiers was on its way. Stephan was focused on moving fast, and the French foot soldiers were getting accustomed to the horses. They did not stop until they found a stream at midday where there was a large meadow for the horses to graze after they had taken their fill of water. The soldiers drank from the stream and filled their canteens. They ate crusty bread and rested in the shade of nearby trees.

"The last I heard, the French army was encamped north of Paris. We have gone south and now we have turned west. How do you plan to reunite us with the northern army, Stephan?" Jean Marc asked.

"Da enemy is nort of us, and if we go nort, we will

bump into dem. Look at da map. If we stay sout, we will enter Germany ere. Den you can take dese back roads until you reach France. Once you cross into your country, go nort to join your army."

"When will you be leaving us, Stephan?"

"We are almost at da Polish border, and dat is where I will leave you. I have my own war to fight"

"We can only hope that our separate battles work out well for us!"

"Dat's for sure!"

Chapter 43

"The Secret Archives were raided by Napoleon during the French conquest of the Papal State and many of the documents were disseminated throughout Europe. However, what remains is still impressive. The oldest surviving text dates back to the end of the eighth century, and over 35,000 volumes of information are stored in the vast secret library. Obviously, most of these documents have little relevance to our research, but a few examples of abuse will help to set the backdrop for our evaluation."

Martin nodded his assent.

"First, in 1559 Pope Paul IV devised a process whereby all Christians who went to confession were first interrogated about both their knowledge of heretics and prohibited books, which gave impetus to the Inquisition." Thomas explained.

"The sacrament of confession was used to identify heretics?" Martin asked curiously.

"Yes, and if something out of the ordinary emerged from the interrogation, the person was sent to a tribunal of the Inquisition and oftentimes subject to torture and even execution."

"Surely the Church did not condone these atrocities?"

"My second example shows how these actions were promulgated at the Council of Trent, during the pontificate of Pope Pius V, who had more executions staining his record than any other sixteenth century pope. Nevertheless, he was canonized as a saint."

"Did the Council of Trent influence this period of terror by the popes?" Martin asked.

"The Council of Trent, considered to be one of the most important councils in Church history, took place between 1545 and 1563. Twenty-five sessions were held, in three separate phases, and was presided over by three different popes."

"What was its significance?"

"The Council condemned Protestantism, and it empowered the papacy to implement its findings. As a result, the papacy issued the Tridentine Creed, declaring that outside of the Catholic faith *no one can be saved.*"

"The Creed is something I recite daily, and that I adhere to without fail. And I firmly believe that no one can be saved without the Catholic faith!" Martin replied adamantly.

Thomas paused for a few moments and said, "Sadly, as in my first example it was driven by intolerance!"

"But it saved souls!" Martin asserted.

"Follow me to the Index Room, and I will give you another example as to how intolerance led to ungodly results."

"You have my attention but not my conviction!"

"My third example deals with intolerance toward women. For centuries, the clergy perceived women as inferior. It viewed female sexuality as a threatening and uncontrollable force. To support its position, a philosophy was adopted that condemned female sexuality by attributing its power to the devil. And, when female sexuality was characterized as demonic, a new view of women was created — that of the medieval witch!"

"And it is obviously your conclusion that its intolerance brought about the persecution of innocent people!"

"What was a largely egalitarian institution founded by Jesus had evolved into a very chauvinistic one — growing crueler and more heartless with every passing year — due largely to the abuses of its leaders, such as those that I have alluded to."

"But Jesus was aware of the threat being posed by

women when he instituted the virtue of celibacy to make priests pure." Martin retorted.

"That is a myth Martin, celibacy did not find widespread acceptance until a thousand years after Jesus. In the eleventh century, Pope Gregory VII condemned priestly marriage and promoted celibacy as a standard for the clergy. He declared that married priests were guilty of the sin of fornication and ordered parishioners to boycott their masses. In 1139, Pope Innocent III persecuted the wives of priests, declaring all marriages after ordination invalid. Overnight, women who had been legal wives were now labeled concubines, whores, or adulterers. And the struggle to impose celibacy on the clergy continued for another five centuries — but obviously many did not heed the pope's word. Many were perplexed as to why they had to separate the natural act of sexuality from the pursuit of God."

"Why do you refer to sexuality as a 'natural act'?"

"It is certainly a more natural act than celibacy, Martin!"

Martin ignored the statement, feeling that Thomas was single-minded in promoting his own interests, flagrantly violating his vow of obedience, and disregarding the authority of his superiors. "What do you have in store for me now?" he asked attempting to change the subject.

"Search the Indexes for *witchcraft and women*. Start with the fifteenth century. It was in 1484 that Pope Innocent VIII issued the Witches' Bull, enlisting the Inquisition to arbitrarily prosecute witches."

"If it was decreed by a pope, why do you qualify it as arbitrary?" Martin asked.

"The Bull was written in response to the request of a Dominican Inquisitor for explicit authority to prosecute witchcraft in Germany, after he was refused support by the local clergy. It gave approval for the Inquisition to proceed in Germany. It urged the local priests to cooperate with the inquisitors, and threatened excommunication to those who obstructed their work."

"The local clerics should always obey the pope or face excommunication. That is obvious to me!" Martin retorted. "Obviously, the outbreak of witchcraft in Germany had to be crushed."

"It was a test of the pope's authority, but the German clerics refused to give their support to the inquisitors." Thomas responded.

"How sad."

"How courageous! They opposed a Bull that opened the door to horrifying witch-hunts. They denounced the politics which usurped the authority of the local clergy."

"The purpose of the Bull was to save the witches from eternal damnation, certainly a sufficient justification for the witch-hunts!"

"The language of the Bull clearly supports that conclusion. Let me read parts of it to you: *Many persons of both sexes, unmindful of their own salvation and straying from the Catholic Faith, have abandoned themselves to the devil... and by their incantations, spells, conjurations, and other accursed charms and crafts, enormities and horrid offences, have slain infants yet in the mother's womb... these wretches furthermore afflict and torment men and women... with terrible and piteous pains and sore diseases, both internal and external; they hinder men from performing the sexual act and women from conceiving, whence husbands cannot know their wives nor wives receive their husbands; over and above this, they blasphemously renounce that Faith which is theirs by the sacrament of Baptism, and at the instigation of the Enemy of Mankind they do not shrink from committing and perpetrating the foulest abominations and filthiest excesses to the deadly peril of their own souls, whereby they outrage the Divine Majesty and are a cause of scandal and danger to very many... the abominations and enormities in question remain unpunished not without open danger to the souls of many and peril of eternal damnation."*

"*Not without open danger to the souls of many and peril of eternal damnation*, which is what the papacy was attempting to eradicate." Martin asserted.

"As terror swept through Europe following the issuance of the Witches Bull, hundreds of thousands of women were burned at the stake for the heresy of witchcraft." He paused and looked at his friend intently, and said, "Martin, it is not whether the *danger* was eradicated, but rather, whether the *danger* ever existed!"

Chapter 44

As the two friends arrived at the archives, Thomas was the first to speak. "The Inquisition was set on a course to vigorously prosecute the heresies of witchcraft and sorcery. The popes, the clergy, and the inquisitors created a well-organized and proficient mechanism to weed out, identify, and prosecute the women who were possessed by demons. Folk beliefs about the magical powers of sorcerers and witches had existed for many centuries among the peasants — and it was a short step from branding women as shameful persons publicly to the idea that female sexuality itself could be a demonic power. The judicial proceedings of the Inquisition were duly recorded by a secretary and are indexed here in this room. A large percentage of trials dealt with superstition, magic, and sorcery. Before we review the written record of these trials involving the crimes of witchcraft and sorcery, let us explore the frenzy that erupted throughout Europe during the six centuries of the Inquisition." Thomas suggested.

Martin nodded affirmatively, his action belying his thoughts.

"Witches were burned no longer in ones and twos, but in tens and hundreds. The Bishop of Geneva is alleged to have burned five hundred within three months. The bishop of Bamburg burned six hundred in one year. The Bishop of Wurzburg nine hundred in ten years. Eight hundred were condemned and burned in one group in Savoy. The inquisitor in Lorraine boasted he had sent to death nine hundred people for the crime of witchcraft. The Archbishop of Treves burned a hundred eighteen women and two men for prolonging the winter through their incantations. Paramo boasted that in a century and a half, the Holy Office had burned at least 30,000 witches. And Strasbourg burned 5000 in a period of twenty years. It was reported that in Valcamonica, those suspected or accused of witchcraft amounted to one fourth of the inhabitants of the valley. In Germany in 1516 and 1517, five hundred witches were burned. A thousand witches died at Como. In France, the fires for the execution of witches blazed in almost every town. In Piedmont, there was not a family that had not lost a member. In Vemiuel, women were burned on the charge of having changed themselves into cats. The executioner of Neisse invented an oven in which he roasted to death forty-two women and young girls in one year. Within nine years, he had roasted over a 1,000 people, including children 2 to 4 years old."

"Spain, Germany, France, Portugal, and Rome... it appears that not many regions in Western Europe were spared. But there had to be a reason for these grave events?" Martin asked, obviously taken aback by these facts!

"Besides the Church's deep prejudice against women, a main function of the Inquisition was to deprive the heretics of their estates and assets which, in turn, became the property of the Catholic Church."

"Are you accusing the Church of both bigotry and greed?" Martin asked.

"I am accusing the men of the Church of disobeying the teachings of Jesus... and I will continue to condemn their actions until the Church returns to the ways of love and tolerance left to us by Jesus!"

"I believe their actions were justifiable, but I will keep an open mind. Tell me more about these centuries of horror."

"In many cases, if the victims refused to confess at the first hearing, they were remanded to prisons for several months. The dungeons were situated underground. The prisoners were bound in stocks or chains, unable to move about and forced to sleep standing up or on the damp ground. In many cases, there was no light or ventilation, inmates were starved and kept in solitary confinement in the dark and allowed no contact with the outside world, including that of their families."

"Were the prisoners ever set free?" Martin asked.

"Acquittals were rarely granted. After the papacy officially authorized the use of *torture chambers*, the inquisitors were free to explore the depths of horror and cruelty. The prisoners were either left in the dungeons or convicted and burned at the stake. The inquisitors were fiendish and invented every conceivable device to inflict pain by slowly dismembering and dislocating the body. Very few who entered the torture chambers emerged whole in mind and body. Many went mad in captivity, others committed suicide, and the few who were released were left maimed physically and mentally, forever."

"But some survived the torture chambers?"

"By implicating others… fear was rampant… so they condemned friends, parents, siblings, and even their children as heretics!"

"It is difficult to conceive that the Church could be so cruel!" Martin responded.

"Martin, the evidence is all around you in the Secret Archives. The Church not only condemned women, but it also took steps to protect the clergy. To establish an accusation against a bishop required 72 witnesses, against a priest 27, against a dignitary it was 7, while for a layperson, 2 witnesses were sufficient to convict. Whole communities went mad with the grief and fear of being denounced to the Inquisition. It spread all over Europe. Men, women, and children were sentenced to death on flimsy evidence. During the trial the accused had no right to counsel and were denied the right to know their accusers."

"Who could testify against them?"

"Criminals, heretics, and even children were among those who testified against them. Some inquisitors especially valued child witnesses for extracting confessions, as they were easily persuaded to confess. And children were no exception to prosecution and torture. The treatment of witches' children was especially brutal."

"In the eyes of the Church, children reach the age of reason at seven. It is at that age that they can tell the difference between good and evil," Martin interposed.

"For the Inquisition, when a girl turned nine and a boy ten, they were liable to inquiry. But children below this age were still tortured to elicit testimony, which was oftentimes used against their parents. A French inquisitor was known to have regretted his leniency when, instead of having young children accused of witchcraft burned, he sentenced them to be flogged while watching their parents burn at the stake."

Martin sat pensively, thinking what to do next! Now was not the time to antagonize Thomas, but he felt guilt-ridden, not about what the Church had done to the victims of the Inquisition but rather his complicity with Thomas in undermining his superiors. He felt compelled to discuss this matter with Deputy Secretary but did not want to let on to his friend.

"Now that you have some history about the procedures of the Inquisition let us review a few individual cases." Thomas suggested.

Martin somehow still felt inextricably bound to his companion and complied.

After gathering a few files from the Archives they set about reviewing each file. "What, in particular, are we looking for in these files?" Martin inquired.

"Simply, whether women were treated fairly."

"And, if we conclude they were not treated fairly, what will that prove, Thomas?"

"It will be another example of the clergy's bigotry toward women." Thomas responded. "Jesus treated people with dignity and this will give us a clear picture as to how far the Church has wandered from his teachings! So let us get on with our work!"

Martin took offense at the reference that it was *his work* but ignored the comment. The two priests each took a few files for review. The details in the files allowed Martin to visualize what happened to the victims. A young woman had been charged by a person of good reputation with making potions used by women to bewitch men. Other witnesses of doubtful reputation supported the accusation. However, there were no eyewitnesses and no confession. The inquisitor was faced with the dilemma of either dismissing the case or acquiring a confession from the accused person. The inquisitor found there was enough credible proof to extract a confession from the defendant. Still, when asked, she refused to confess and claimed her innocence. At this point, the doctrine of torture was called into play. The inquisitor determined that a confession was likely and the accused was turned over to the torturer.

Following a week in the dungeon, the emaciated prisoner was asked by the torturer to confess. She refused. Her clothes were removed and she stood naked before the torturer. She was taken to a room with a giant wheel at the end of a platform. She was placed on the platform on her back. Her limbs were tied to stakes on the ground. Slices of wood were placed beneath her ankles, knees, hips, elbows and wrists. The torturer stared at the naked body on the platform, and asked for a confession. She again refused. He placed himself to the rear of the wheel and with all his strength pushed the heavy wheel towards the accused. The iron edge of the wheel rolled over the witch's feet and crushed both ankles. She screamed in pain but no confession was forthcoming. The torturer resumed the motion of the wheel up both legs until the knees were crushed by the weight of the wheel. The piercing cry of pain shrieked through the torture chamber as a plea for a confession was heard, between the cries of pain. The torturer asked the witch to repeat the confession, which she did. He rolled the wheel back revealing raw, bloody, shapeless flesh, mixed with splinters of bones.

The following day she was taken before the inquisitor to repeat her confession. She repeated her confession and was turned over to the civil authorities for sentence. That same day she was burned at the stake.

Martin was troubled by the brutality of the torture. In the next case he read, the alleged witch had been heard to speak in strange tongues and it was evident to the witnesses that she was calling for the secret aid of Lucifer. The inquisitor inquired as to whether witches had their own language that could not be understood by others. The accused responded but the inquisitor did not understand. He asked if she was a witch. She said no. A witness testified that she spoke a strange language to him and his sexual desire became uncontrollable. Another testified that his impotence could be traced to a potion she had given him. Another witness testified that she aborted her child after the witch touched her stomach. The inquisitor concluded that she was sexually dangerous to men, had an inferior intellect, and was deceitful. Again, he asked her if she was a witch. She said no. He requested that the torturer delve into whether she had sexual intercourse with demons. She was stripped and examined by the torturer and two nuns for signs of the Devil's Mark. They found a mole near her vagina and identified it as a Devil's Mark. She was asked whether she had sexual intercourse with demons. She said no. A device called *the Pear* was inserted in her vagina by the inquisitor and expanded by the force of a screw. She was asked to confess. She said no. The screw was turned and the vagina started to bleed. She was asked to confess. She said no. The screw was turned and more blood flowed from the vagina. She was asked to admit her sins. She said no. The screw was turned to its maximum level with the prongs fully extended into her cervix. The blood now gushed from the vagina. She was asked whether she had intercourse with demons. She said no. The torturer left the chamber. When he returned the witch was dead. When told of her fate the inquisitor expressed sadness — not for her death but because she had not repented and was damned to hell for eternity.

Martin next read the record of a village attempting to root out witchcraft in the region. Among the accused were twelve women who were tried together. The testimony was that they flew through the air, travelled thousands of leagues in one hour, got through a space not big enough for a fly, swam in a river without getting wet, turned into ravens, changed into any shape they fancied, and called on a demon in the form of a he-goat. All twelve were sent to the torture chambers to extract confessions. All were eventually found guilty of witchcraft. The sentence was for the twelve to be burned at the stake together, five in effigy for they had died in the torture chambers. The executioner explained that they could be burned in one of two ways: To make the fire large enough so that death came soon. Or, to control the fire so the witches would burn for a long time. The body would then burn progressively in the following way: the calves, thighs, and hands would burn first; next, the torso, forearms, and breasts; and, finally, the upper chest and face, until death came. The inquisitor ordered the executioner to burn the witches slowly. The record shows that the witches burned for two hours before they died. Martin visibly upset, threw the record towards Thomas and cried out, "What is the purpose for all of this?"

"To lay bare the Church's prejudice against women and ask for their forgiveness... "

"For having saved their souls, for following the guidance of St. Augustine, for adopting the philosophy of St. Thomas Aquinas, for preserving the sacred nature of the priesthood... no never!" Martin responded sharply.

"*Mea culpa, mea culpa, mea maxima culpa...* let us

admit our fault in denigrating women, in imprisoning and torturing hundreds of thousands of witches, in sending to their deaths armies of women to wash the world clean of their foul blood. And for what purpose — for we now know there is no such thing as a witch and never has been! As a first step, let us accept our guilt and ask the women of the world for forgiveness."

Chapter 45

"Madeleine, the Church, and possibly the government, is laying claim to your vast inheritance. It has petitioned the Tribunal to freeze all the assets of Madame LeBlanc's estate. It alleges that you coerced her to sign a last will and testament."

"That is a lie!" Madeleine exclaimed.

"The magistrate, who will preside over the trial, is a close friend of the Bishop of Rome."

"The inheritance is of little consequence to me, but her intention is sacred. I will not give in to these threats," Madeleine replied adamantly.

"The process can take many years before a final decision is reached. The case has been filed in the *Tribunal de Grande Instance*. Once a decision is rendered, either party may demand a review by the Court of Appeals. In exceptional cases, a judgment of the Court may be further appealed to the French Supreme Court. Because the case will drag on for such a long time, I believe I can extract concessions from your adversaries, which would still leave you with a substantial inheritance."

"How can they possibly prove that I coerced her to change her will?" she asked.

"The petition states that you have special powers… demonic powers… and that you cast a spell upon her!"

"How absurd!" Madeleine responded.

"Absurd to us but not to others. A trial of this magnitude could re-awaken old prejudices, which is both beneficial to the church and the government, let alone bring great wealth to these institutions."

"So there is a chance that the Church will prevail?"

"Not only is it likely that it will prevail, but it might also destroy you in the process."

"Then why would you take on such a case on my

behalf?"

"Because I know the truth!"

"How should we proceed, Monsieur l'Heureux?"

"First, I will deny the allegations in their petition. Then, I will try to ascertain the extent of the bribes to the magistrate."

"It is a sad state of affairs when bribes can trump justice," Madeleine remarked.

"My greatest fear is that they will also bring criminal charges against you under the Penal Code."

"On what grounds?" Madeleine asked, visibly upset.

"Fraud, theft, robbery… anything they can come up with. At which point, the burden of proof shifts to you, the defendant, to prove that you are not guilty. Under French law, if charged with a crime, you are presumed guilty until you can prove your innocence!"

"When would I be charged?"

"Anytime it is convenient for them."

"What will occur if I am charged?"

"You will be incarcerated until I can post bail."

"You mean I could go to prison."

"Yes."

"And, my children, what would become of them?"

"Their father is missing in action. There are no relatives. They would become wards of the State."

"My God, please do not let that happen."

"I will do what I can, Madeleine… I will do what I can."

With these words resonating in her mind, Madeleine left the bureau with both the burden of litigation on her shoulders and a grave concern for what might happen to her children.

The Bishop of Paris now met daily with his new confidante, the Monsignor. "The case of witchcraft against

Madeleine Moreau is significant in our claim for the Estate of Jeannette LeBlanc. Have you received any word from Rome?" the bishop asked.

"Father Martin should return any day now with the official accusation in hand," the Monsignor responded.

"My office has commenced civil litigation claiming to be the beneficiary of the LeBlanc estate. Criminal charges will soon follow. The indictment from Rome will lend credibility to both proceedings."

"What if Rome denies the accusation?" the Monsignor asked.

"The church in Paris wields significant influence with Rome. It is one of the Church's leading dioceses and, furthermore, I am held in high esteem by the pope. Rome will not easily deny the accusation, when it has my endorsement."

"Father Martin will not fail us, particularly with your support behind the case."

"The barrister, Richard Levesque, is representing my office. He is both aggressive and ruthless. He has represented the church in all its major legal battles for the past decades. His team of barristers rarely loses a case, either at trial or on appeal. His strategy in this matter is to protract the proceedings as long as possible, bombard the opposition with every conceivable motion, and destroy Madeleine Moreau's reputation in the process. Our plan is in place, and the only missing link is the accusation from Rome. It is imperative that we hear from Father Martin soon," the bishop re-emphasized.

"As I said earlier, I expect him back soon," the Monsignor responded, feeling uneasy about the bishop's demand.

"It would be a setback to our case if he returns without the accusation. The court magistrate will see it our way, but it is also important to convince the public that Madeleine Moreau is a fraud. Madame LeBlanc was beloved by the common people of Paris for her charitable works, and the last thing we need is a public outcry against our cause. An accusation of witchcraft will solidify our case."

"The government can also lay claim to the estate if the will is declared null and void by the tribunal. And, if it is found that there are no beneficiaries, then the estate would escheat to the legitimate government of France."

"And that could either be the emperor or the king, depending, on whether Napoleon abdicates," the bishop added.

"What news have you received from the chambers?"

"I have been informed that Napoleon will abdicate…"

"That is good news," the Monsignor interrupted.

"But, Napoleon will only abdicate in favor of his son, under the title Napoleon II, Emperor of France."

"But that will not be acceptable to the chambers."

"It might not be their decision… Napoleon still controls the Army."

"Would Napoleon join in the suit?" the Monsignor asked.

"Yes, but he will claim that the entire estate should escheat to the State and not the Church."

"What can be done?"

"The church will give its support to the Chambers. And, you Monsignor, will be responsible for the accusation against Madeleine Moreau."

"But that is beyond my control."

"Let me remind you Monsignor, that over my objection you insisted on sending Father Martin to Rome. It might now be beyond your control, but it is still your responsibility… and you will bear the consequences, whether good or bad!"

The Monsignor left the bishop's office enraged at

Father Martin for the delay in obtaining the accusation against Madeleine Moreau. Not only was his dream of rising in the hierarchy of the Church in jeopardy, but his vendetta against Madeleine Moreau was at risk.

Chapter 46

Things started to go wrong when Jean Marc's group reached a tributary of the Danube River where they found the bridge destroyed. They marched upstream to find a crossing, but after a half a day's journey, they discovered the road to be impassable. They retraced their steps and found livestock and farmers departing on a ferry heading to the village across the river. Jean Marc yelled to the captain asking when he would return.

"In two days… unless you make it worthwhile to return tomorrow!" he hollered.

"We will double your fare," Jean Marc hollered back.

"I will return in the morning," the captain responded.

"Do we have the money to pay for the ferry?" Luc asked.

"No, but the captain doesn't know that."

The soldiers spent a restless night knowing that they were losing valuable time with the enemy closing in on them. Two scouts were sent back a few kilometers to provide a warning if the Russian soldiers were sighted. When they returned in the early morning, they reported that they had not seen the enemy. As promised, the ferry arrived a few hours after sunrise.

"You can come on board, but only after I receive payment. Throw me your bag of coins and once I count them, I will come ashore!"

"Once you get the coins, you will leave without us. We will go down river to the next bridge," Jean Marc responded.

"Gather your gear, saddle up, we are heading down river," Sergeant Moreau barked out.

The men gathered their gear and moved toward

their horses following Jean Mark's order. The ferry captain observed the movement and saw his fare slipping away.

"All right, come on board. Pay me before we leave the shore," he said grudgingly.

The soldiers walked cautiously toward the landing. As the ferry came to the shore of the river, Luc jumped on board, pulled out a dagger from beneath his tunic, and put it to the captain's throat.

"I am commandeering your boat captain," Luc said.

"I should have fuckin' known," the captain responded.

"Sit back captain, we will pull your ferry across the river and be on our way," Sergeant Moreau interrupted.

The opposite shore was about a half a kilometer away. One rope secured the ferry to boulders on opposite shores and a second was attached to a winch used to pull it across the river. The soldier grunted as he pulled on the rope propelling the ferry forward. The tumultuous waters and the strong current slapped the sides of the ferry making the ride rough on man and beast. Upon landing on the opposite bank, the soldiers took time to steady their legs. When ready, they walked the horses off the ferry and rode away. Luc looked back to see the ferry returning to the other side.

"Sergeant... sergeant, look to the other bank!" Luc hollered.

Jean Marc turned to see the Russian soldiers on the opposite bank and the ferry heading in their direction.

"Don't worry sergeant, I'll take care of it," Luc barked out, as he spurred his horse toward the ferry landing.

Sergeant Moreau watched as Luc jumped from his horse, pulled out his dagger, and cut through the thick rope securing the ferry to the landing. The rope broke and the swift current instantly changed the course of the ferry.

"Damn you," the captain's voice echoed as his ferry

was carried swiftly downstream.

The Russians quickly turned their horses south to find a bridge or ferry to cross the river. They had been within sight of the fleeing soldiers but were foiled by Luc's quick action. They knew the location of the French soldiers and were rushing off to overtake them before they reached France.

"They are Cossacks, good horsemen, and will be in hot pursuit as soon as they find a crossing." Jean Marc said. "We cannot delay in reaching the border."

The band of French mercenaries, sent to find Jean Marc Moreau and others, found a route into Germany. They were heavily armed, rode swift horses, and carried food and ammunition. They were motivated to find their comrades before the Russians did.

Back in Laon, the army was tensely awaiting orders to march on Paris. But there was dead time, when Michel's mind wandered as to how he had gotten to this point in his life. *I could be back in Paris sculpting my statues, being with the person I love, nurturing three children I adore, and living a peaceful life. Instead, I am now doing what I left many years ago. Is it the thrill of battle? Is it dedication to the country? Is it part of a Master Plan? Or, is it just the right thing to do?*

These questions left unanswered, his thoughts returned to the times he spent with Madeleine. *In my mind, I sometimes change the course of events, so that instead of leaving her, I spend the rest of my life with her. But in reality, I know that her heart belongs to Jean Marc.*

Chapter 47

Father Martin opened his eyes just as the morning light was seeping into his bedroom. The room was drab. It had a shade with no drapes, a crucifix hung on one wall, and ironically, in every way, it conformed to his vow of poverty. As he lay in bed, he recalled the events of the past few weeks and was convinced as to what he had to do. It had been an enlightening period for him, and he now saw things more clearly.

For the first twenty-five years of his life, he had been sheltered from worldly matters, first by his family and then by the priestly order. But the past few weeks had changed his life; he had been exposed to the real world by both his friend and his observations. Because of this newfound perspective, he was confident about the decision he was about to make between maintaining his vow of obedience and joining Father Thomas' cause.

He rose from the bed with a heavy heart knowing that for the rest of his life he would have to live with the consequences of this day! It was early, and he decided to walk to his destination. The day was cold and wet, but all the same there was a sense of purpose in his step. He stopped at a small cafe for a café au lait and a croissant.

As he sipped his coffee and ate his pastry, he observed the crowd on the street rushing to work. At their workplace, most of these people are told what to do and how to do it. *People are weak. They need guidance. That is the way of life, a few select people directing the masses; much like the Church and its priests directing men and women to find God. And, that is the reason God gave them the Church and its priests*, Father Martin thought.

He arrived at the bureau for his meeting with the deputy director on time and well prepared to make his presentation. However, he was nervous and uncertain as to whether the deputy would be amenable to his views. Whatever the reaction, there would be consequences, and he knew the deputy had a foot in both camps. He was appointed by the pope but received gratuities from the nobility. He had thought about the repercussions to everyone else, but suddenly he thought of the repercussions to himself. He might be relegated to a remote parish, be defrocked, or even prosecuted by the Inquisition. *No matter, I must do what is right*, he thought.

"Good morning Father Martin," the deputy said as he ushered Martin to his bureau.

After the two exchanged pleasantries, Father Martin began a detailed narrative of his journey with Father Thomas. It included the quaint village and the mingling with villagers; Orleans and the execution of Joan of Arc; Avignon and the corruption of the papacy; the Church's prejudice against Jews, Protestants, and women; Marseille and Mary Magdalene; the exclusion of women from the priesthood; torture devices of the Inquisition; Napoli, witchcraft, and the vow of obedience; temporal and spiritual powers of the popes; executions by the Holy Office; the accusation against Madeleine Moreau and Father Thomas' reaction; the Secret Archives; the execution of hundreds of thousands of women; the heresy of witchcraft; the cruelty of the Inquisition; and, the bigotry of the Church.

The deputy sat motionless for what seemed like an eternity to Father Martin. He rose from his chair, said nothing, and left the room. Father Martin expected Swiss Guards to enter the room, arrest him, and take him to the dungeon. He was terrified and regretted his actions. He was incensed at the Monsignor for having assigned him this task. He was angry with Father Thomas for having exposed him to the realities of the past. And, he cursed the day he took the vow of obedience. He wanted to run away from it all, to somewhere safe, to the country, to his mother and father. The wait was interminable, the silence unbearable, and the future intimidating.

Suddenly, the door burst open, four Swiss Guards rushed in, followed by the deputy who stared intently at Father Martin, and said, "God bless you my son for keeping your vow of obedience. Take this official document to the Archbishop of Paris, it is the signed accusation against Madeleine Moreau. Inform the bishop that once she is served with the accusation, she is expected to leave for Rome immediately to stand trial for the heresy of witchcraft. If she refuses, she is to be excommunicated."

Stunned, Martin stood silent.

"Now, follow the Swiss Guard, and they will escort you to our swiftest carriage to transport you back to Paris. The pope has been informed of your courageous actions and he sends his blessings. Bon voyage, Father Martin."

Three of the Swiss Guards escorted him from the bureau before he could respond. The last words he heard were from the deputy to the captain of the Swiss Guards.

"Arrest Father Thomas and lock him away in the most secluded cell of the dungeon. Tell no one where he is and speak his name no more!"

Chapter 48

Madeleine experienced another sleepless night. The events of the last few weeks had taken their toll both physically and emotionally. What was most troubling was the uncertainty of the future. But, in spite of her problems, she resolved to be positive. Her children were thriving and Marc seemed to have overcome his sadness. She would face the obstacles of each day and not think beyond the next.

But now, she had to make a decision, whether to stay in Paris or pursue her dream of living in the country. The children were doing well in school and seemed well adjusted. A dramatic change could set them back. If Michel returned, his preference would be Paris. If Jean Marc returned, his preference would be a farm or a vineyard. If she remained in Paris, she could be of assistance to her barrister. If she left Paris, she could get away from the daily anxiety of litigation. If she resided at the LeBlanc residence, she could manage the legal and business matters of the estate she might some day inherit. If she lived in Bordeaux, she could cultivate the vineyards to produce the region's finest grapes. She considered her options and reluctantly decided to remain in Paris.

"Children… children wake up, it's time to get ready for school," she said loudly enough to awaken them. And soon, they were walking to school. As they approached Notre Dame, she caught sight of the Monsignor rushing off somewhere. She slowed her pace hoping that he would not observe them. A carriage pulled up, he entered, and was driven away without catching sight of the family.

Monsieur l'Heureux awaited her as she returned to the LeBlanc residence. "I have bad news, Madeleine. The Court has appointed a master to supervise all of the estate's business and investments."

"And what does that mean?" Madeleine asked.

"It means that you have been removed from any supervisory duties in regard to any of the estate's financial matters. The master has the discretion to keep you off the premises entirely. He will administer all business activities and report to the Court periodically."

"And the bank accounts?" she inquired.

"The master will also oversee all activities in these accounts. You will be given a small allowance for your basic needs."

"We must resist with all of our strength," she responded with indignation. "And the country estates, what will become of them?" she asked.

"They are also under the control of the master," he responded.

"Can I visit the estates to reassure the staff?" she persisted.

"My advice is for you to remain in Paris. I am still concerned about the criminal charges that might be brought against you! It will be much simpler to deal with your arrest if you are in Paris," he advised.

"Is my arrest imminent?" she asked, visibly upset.

"I believe it is Madeleine... I believe it is."

"Who will care for the children? They need their mother... Madame LeBlanc is no longer here for them... they are without their father. No, no, I cannot be taken from them."

"I will have a bailiff on call to be there as soon as you are arrested. Once the surety bond is posted, you will be released. I believe their plan is to get you to relinquish your inheritance not, necessarily, to punish you."

"And how long will that take?"

"It depends on your cooperation," he responded.

"Then I must arrange for the servants to care for my children."

That afternoon, while she was talking with the servants, the sheriff burst into the room and cried out for all to hear, "You are under arrest, Madeleine Moreau, for fraud, theft and embezzlement!"

She ran from the room into the arms of a deputy. She fought forcefully, but was subdued and dragged from the house, crying for her children. Jean rushed to her side but was thrown to the ground.

On the same day, the Monsignor met with the Bishop of Paris. He was in a good mood and was anxious to inform the bishop of the news he had just received from Rome. But, the bishop was quick to speak, "Monsignor, Madeleine Moreau has been arrested and she is now in prison. The sheriff will not release her for a number of days. She will get a taste of jail, will not be allowed visitors and will not be treated kindly by the guards. By the time she is released, she will certainly have a change of heart about renouncing her inheritance."

The Monsignor's delight was evident.

"Have you received any news from Rome?" the bishop continued.

"A legate arrived from Rome yesterday to receive the annual tithe from the diocese of Paris. He was extremely pleased with our generosity. He expressed the gratitude of the pope and alluded to the assistance we will continue to receive from Rome."

"Did he mention the accusation?" the bishop persisted.

"Yes, yes he did. He is certain the accusation will be issued, and we will soon have the official document in hand."

The answer was well received by the bishop, and his countenance showed his pleasure. "The young priest, Father Martin, appears to have been the right person for this important assignment. Let's hope your judgment was sound, and his return imminent."

"I am confident he will deliver the accusation during Madeleine Moreau's incarceration," he said haughtily, now back in the bishop's good graces.

"In the meantime, the master of the estate will increase the funds distributed to the poor and the needy, which will enhance our image with the common people."

"That is very generous, your excellency."

"Our generosity will end once we acquire the inheritance," the bishop responded. "And, by the way, the Chambers are prepared to decide Napoleon's fate."

Chapter 49

The bishop and Monsignor sat in the gallery of the Chamber of Representatives awaiting the final deliberations on the fate of Napoleon.

"Napoleon has been warned that if he does not immediately abdicate, the Chamber will depose him. But his brother, Lucien, will make one final plea for the Emperor's son to take the throne," the bishop said.

"If the Chamber refuses will there be a last minute *coup d'etat* by the army?" the Monsignor asked.

"I have been informed that Napoleon refuses to shed blood and lead a revolution, but if the Chamber leaves him no choice, a coup is a real possibility," the bishop responded, just as Lucien Bonaparte reached the podium.

"I hold in my hand a declaration of abdication from the Emperor in favor of his son Napoleon II. It transfers power peacefully. It maintains stability in time of crisis. It allows Napoleon to lead the army against its enemies. It carries on the rule of Bonaparte. To do otherwise is tantamount to treason." He paused, surveyed the Chamber, and ended with the warning: "The Emperor expects your support in the rule of Bonaparte."

"That is but a guise to keep Napoleon in power and at the head of the *Grande Armee*," the bishop whispered to the Monsignor.

The Monsignor observed the Marquis the Lafayette coming to the podium and waiting for the murmurs of the assembly to subside.

Lafayette spoke solemnly. "By what right do you dare accuse the nation of want of perseverance in the emperor's interest? The nation has followed him on the fields of Italy, across the sands of Egypt and the plains of Germany, across the frozen deserts of Russia. The nation has followed him in fifty battles, in his defeats and his victories, and in doing so we have to mourn the blood of three million Frenchmen."

The representatives bellowed their support for Lafayette.

"There is little doubt where the Chamber stands, but Napoleon is suspended between two worlds — that of the people and that of the army. Say your prayers so that he makes the right decision," Talleyrand said, as he walked by the bishop.

"What will happen next, Talleyrand?" the bishop asked.

Talleyrand stopped, looked back at the bishop and said, "The two chambers will form a Provisional Government and demand that Napoleon abdicate. Envoys are being sent to notify both the army in Laon and the enemy in eastern France of our actions."

A few hours later, Talleyrand returned to the balcony. "Your prayers have been answered. Napoleon has left Paris for the Palace of Malmaison. However, the army at Laon is restless and the Allies are poised to attack."

The following day word drifted into Paris that Napoleon was depressed but was still considering his options. Lafayette was contacted by Lucien Bonaparte to make arrangements for two French frigates to take Napoleon and his entourage to America.

"I cannot believe the rumors," the bishop told the Monsignor. "The Genghis Khan of France will not walk away from power. He has been invincible for two decades, controls the army and can still excite the multitude. Go quickly to the chamber to discover first hand what is transpiring."

The chamber was abuzz with rumors: "The Provisional Government has placed him under house arrest... the Prussians are aware of his location and are closing in on Malmaison... he will surrender to the

Allies... he on his way to command the troops at Laon... he will escape to America... "

"What are we to believe?" the Monsignor asked a legislator milling in the halls of the Chambers.

"Believe the worst until we hear otherwise, Monsignor."

"I have been told that he is putting his financial affairs in order and is distributing his estate to his family." another legislator said.

The Monsignor remained overnight with the legislators as the rumors continued to circulate. In early morning, news arrived that the bridge to Malmaison had been destroyed. "Either to protect or isolate him," a legislator said.

Then came word from the clerk, ordering the chamber back into session. The Monsignor made his way to the balcony. The Speaker of the Chamber asked for a motion to restore the Bourbons to the monarchy. The motion was made, seconded and passed by acclamation.

Moments later, the Speaker announced that Napoleon had departed for the coast to sail to America."

"I must get this information to the bishop," he said to those around him.

After delivering the news, he returned to the chamber seeking more information. The Speaker was at the podium announcing the news as it came in. "Napoleon has reached the port at Rochefort... a British squadron is blockading the port... Paris is prepared to surrender to the Allies... Talleyrand has left to bring Louis XVIII back to France."

"It is truly happening," the Monsignor murmured.

The Chambers resolved by acclamation not to allow Napoleon back on French soil. And further resolved that anyone abetting him would be guilty of treason.

The Monsignor nodded in agreement.

"Napoleon has been advised to seek asylum in England, but a few confidantes are urging him to return to the army," a legislator informed the Monsignor.

Later that day, the Speaker read a letter from Napoleon that he had sent to England.

Your Royal Highness,

Exposed to the factions which distract my country and to the enmity of the greatest powers of Europe, I have ended my political career, and I come, like Themistocles, to throw myself on the hospitality of the English people; I put myself under the protection of their laws, which I claim from Your Royal Highness as the most powerful, the most constant and the most generous of my enemies.

Napoleon

"The British hate Napoleon and will not treat him kindly," the bishop said as the Monsignor delivered the news.

Within a few days, the response from England was received:

We wish that the King of France would hang or shoot Bonaparte, as the best termination of the business. If the King of France does not feel himself sufficiently strong to treat him as a rebel, we are willing to take upon ourselves the custody of his person.

At a later time, the Monsignor reported that the British had not allowed Napoleon to step onto British soil. "He insisted he should be allowed to disembark and was dismayed that the British referred to him as a general and not an emperor."

"What was his response?" the bishop asked.

"He said, 'They may as well call me Archbishop, for I am the head of the Church as well as the army.'"

"Will the British execute him?"

"No, he was exiled to the island of St Helena were he will remain for the rest of his life."

Chapter 50

Jean Marc looked back with apprehension when he heard hoof-beats. The sun rising in the east blinded him temporarily as the sound approached quickly. "Sergeant Moreau... Sergeant Moreau" came the cry from one of the two riders who had been assigned to the rear guard. "The Cossacks are only a few miles behind us."

"Spur your horses to high ground!" Sergeant Moreau ordered the troops as he yelled back to the messengers. "How many... how many Cossacks?"

"Twice as many as we have, Sergeant."

"Did they see you?"

"I can't be sure... but they ride like the wind, Sergeant... they will be up our ass in no time!"

As he looked ahead, the band of soldiers veered off the road into the open field and in the direction of a rocky hill. The three hurried to catch up, and when they arrived at the base of the hill, the soldiers were dismounting and taking defensive positions. The horses were scattered to the rear, for the soldiers knew that a battle on horseback against the Cossacks would be futile. Rifles appeared above the boulders as they prepared for the assault. Once in a defensive position, Jean Marc looked to the west and saw a ribbon of road winding across the flat open field. *France is just beyond the horizon, Madeleine and my children are just a few days away, the farm we had dreamed about is within grasp, but could it all end here*? he questioned.

He looked to the east, and there was still no sign of the Cossacks. He had second thoughts about his strategy to defend. He looked in the other direction. They could possibly beat the Cossacks to the French border, if he ordered the retreat now. But, when he looked east again, he saw a cloud of dust in the distance. There was nothing else he could do, and he realized, that but for a miracle, they would die today! He lowered his head and silently prayed. When he looked up, he could make out the profiles of horsemen at full gallop coming in their direction.

Instinctively, the Cossacks turned off the road into the open field and toward the hill. The horses divided into three groups. Jean Marc had seen enough battles to know what the Cossack tactics would be at this point. The two outside units would attack the flanks as the middle unit made a direct assault.

He ordered soldiers to both sides to reinforce the flanks. He took aim and ordered his soldiers to fire. Horses and men were hit. Cossacks fell crashing to their death and wounded horses thrashed on the ground at the bottom of the hill — but the charge kept coming. There was no time to reload. His flanks were overrun, and the soldiers were pulling back. Jean Marc ordered his soldiers to hold fast, but the onslaught was too great.

The air was filled with the awful sounds of battle: the grunts of powerful horses, gunshots, the screams of wounded men, and the clashing of sabers. The end was near, but the French soldiers were driven to survive and to kill as many Cossacks as they could. Jean Marc saw a nearby soldier fall from a blow to his head by a Cossack saber. He charged the Cossack, but the skillful enemy avoided his thrust and prepared to drive his sword through Jean Marc's chest just as the retreat was sounded. The Cossacks turned to face another enemy.

Coming across the field toward the hill Jean Marc saw a unit of well-armed soldiers driving warhorses to the battle scene. The Cossacks were caught off guard. The first volley of gunshots from the rear surprised them as many fell from their horses and were seized upon by Jean Marc and his soldiers. The remaining Cossacks spurred their horses toward the enemy's charge. They drew their spears, drove their horses to the limit, and attacked with a rage that was a warrior's last gasp when confronted with death!

Jean Marc watched the battle unfold before him — brave soldiers, pushing forward, joining in battle with a tremendous clash, impaled by spears and sabers, never slowing the swiftness of the attack, until a handful of Cossacks broke through the line in full retreat.

A field that moments before had been tranquil was now scarred by war, carpeted by dead and dying bodies. The Cossacks were routed, but at the cost of many lives. It was a scene that memorialized the bravery of men but also symbolized the folly of war, as so many other fields did throughout the history of civilization. Wars fought for money, honor, land, politics, and religion — and always at the cost of the lives of brave young men! he thought

"Bring Jean Marc Moreau to me... please bring him to me," came the gurgling plea of a fallen soldier.

"Sergeant Moreau! Come quickly. There's a wounded soldier who is calling for you!" Luc hollered as he applied a compress to the gaping wound in the soldier's chest.

"I am Jean Marc Moreau," he said, as he arrived at the side of the wounded soldier.

"Madeleine Moreau... and the children... await your return," he said in the gurgling voice of one who is about to die. He grasped Jean Marc's arm, "She sent us to rescue you... you and your soldiers."

"Don't talk, let Luc do his work," he said, as he wondered how this brave man knew Madeleine.

"No ... no ... I must ... " he said, as he began to cough convulsively and died suddenly in Jean Marc Moreau's arms.

Jean Marc clutched this soldier who had died bravely, so others might live. He wondered from where he came and where he might have gone.

News of Napoleon's flight to England reached Laon. "The man who tried to unify Europe is no longer in the realm," Michel told his company commanders. "Peace talks have commenced. We have no idea what will become of the *Grande Armee*, but one thing is certain, the Allies will disband the French Army."

"We are owed back pay... our families are destitute... what will become us, sir?" a soldier asked.

"The Allies will demand large reparations from France and our money will go to them."

"Foreign soldiers will remain in France," another added, and we will have to house, feed and pay them."

"French soldiers have died, others are disabled, and now, the survivors must return to their families... destitute."

"We will become the forgotten generation abandoned by the country that asked us to sacrifice so much!" Michel said.

"Fuck that... this weapon is coming home with me... and I'll take what I need," another said.

Michel watched many of them walk away — defeated, low in morale, abandoned by their country, but with an instinct to find their way.

Paul R. Dionne

Chapter 51

Father Martin felt some remorse as his speedy carriage retraced the steps of his recent trip from Rome to Paris. He was uncertain as to what would happen to Thomas, but he appeased his conscience by thinking that he would only be defrocked — and truly, he was better suited for a worldly life. He was uncertain as to what would happen to Madeleine Moreau, but he appeased his conscience by thinking she would not be prosecuted in France — and truly, she deserved to be exposed. Also, he was uncertain as to what would happen to himself, but he appeased his fear by thinking he had accomplished his mission — and truly, he deserved to be rewarded.

Both the Monsignor and the bishop will be pleased with the results and, if so, he might even be assigned to a parish as its pastor. Whatever the outcome, he was pleased with the way he had conducted himself: The lure to break his vow of obedience had been strong, but he did not yield to the temptations of the devil; he had presented a cogent argument to the deputy director and had prevailed; and, although incited by Father Thomas' arguments, he had resisted.

The papacy, the bishops, and the young priests would restore the Church to its former glory, but first the dominance of the clergy and the nobility had to be restored. Prior to the French Revolution, most of the wealth, land, and power belonged to the nobility and the clergy. Through the Revolution, the middle class secured the right to vote, to participate in government, and to express itself freely and was now seeking its share of wealth, land, and power — causing the Church to fall further from its position of power. The personal liberties of the emerging middle class must be limited — and that will now be my calling, he vowed.

However, the American Revolution had also

255

embraced the philosophy of freedom, equality, and justice, and its people had wrested independence from a formidable power, which continued to inspire radicals in Europe. But to capture true freedom, people had to be in a state of salvation, and for that they needed the Church, he thought.

He looked down at the satchel by his side containing the official accusation indicting Madeleine Moreau of witchcraft. He was amazed how the devil influenced others to sin: sometimes through individuals, like Madeleine Moreau; sometimes through a revolution, like the French and American Revolutions; and sometimes, through a philosophy condemning the Church, like Voltaire's. The latter being the most insidious because it left the freedom of worship to personal choice. The accusation against Madeleine Moreau would remove one of the devil's tools, but if he were to be assigned to a parish, he would preach to the multitudes about the evils of religious freedom.

Madeleine Moreau was arrested and detained. She was taken to a small cell, which was dark and dank, hay on the masonry floor serving as a bed, and a hole in a corner serving as a toilet. She was fed a watery soup and stale bread sporadically. However, she had not yet been coupled to the wall by the manacles that hung there like a beast ready to seize its victim.

She walked back and forth in her cell to maintain her strength and break the monotony. She worried about her children… even though she knew the servants would be kind to them, they were not a substitute for a mother. Furthermore, the children had experienced many losses in the past few years — Jean Marc, Michel, Madame LeBlanc, and now their mother. They were scarred but, hopefully, not for life. And for now, her goal was to survive this ordeal in order to return to her children. She was in prison not for punishment, not for rehabilitation, not to be removed as a threat to society, but only to renounce her inheritance. She was determined to uphold Madame LeBlanc's intent but not at the expense of her children, and she knew deep in her heart that Madame LeBlanc would understand.

Time had passed very slowly, but she assumed it was near nightfall and gathered the hay in a pile to sleep on. Then she heard voices, drunken voices, coming toward her cell. A key was inserted in the lock. The door was flung open. To her horror, she saw the shadows of three men from the light of their lantern and smelled the alcohol on their breath. They stumbled toward her as she quickly rose from her bed of hay.

"Take your clothes off!" a grotesquely disfigured guard yelled at her.

"No, no!" she screamed.

"Then I will fuckin' do it for you," a guard said as the other two broke out in drunken laughter as they moved toward her. One lunged to grab her, but she dodged, and he stumbled to the floor. The other two laughed at the drunken guard. Enraged, he grabbed Madeleine's ankle while another ripped off her tunic, and the third attempted to fondle her. They threw her onto the hay and tore off the rest of her clothes — their desire inflamed by the sight of her nakedness.

As they readied to pounce on their victim, a loud cry came from behind them: "Get off her, you drunken pigs!"

She turned to see the shadow of a giant coming into the cell. He grabbed the closest guard and threw him headlong into the stone wall. The other two remained motionless, frozen with fear, hearing the moans of their cohort coming from the corner.

"Never touch her again... and if you do, my fist will be the last thing you see before you reach the gates of hell!"

The two ran out of the cell as fast as their legs

would carry them. The giant tossed the injured guard from the cell, as he walked away.

"Wait, wait, who are you?" Madeleine asked as she grabbed for her clothes to cover herself.

"My name is Emile Fortin, Madame Moreau."

"Why did you do this?"

" I would have done it for any prisoner Madame but especially for you!"

"Why Emile, why for me?"

"Many years ago, I was fallen on the field of battle and as my unit retreated one man, called Jean Marc, fought on by my side keeping the enemy from killing me. When our soldiers regrouped and pushed the enemy back, they took me from the field. Today, I am married and have five children — a joy that I never thought possible that day on the field of battle. I never had the chance to thank the soldier who saved my life… until today! No one will harm you while you are here I assure you of that, Madame Moreau."

"Merci, merci Emile!" she said as he lumbered from the cell and locked the door behind him.

As the carriage came to a halt before the Cathedral of Notre Dame, a rumpled Father Martin leaped out, the satchel flung over his shoulder, rushing headlong to the rectory. Monsignor… Monsignor, I have the accusation!" he said excitedly, moving hastily into the large office.

The Monsignor was delighted to see Father Martin. "You've done well father, and I am pleased with your accomplishments," he said, bringing a glow to the young priest's countenance.

"Thank you, thank you, Monsignor."

"And, where is Father Thomas?" the Monsignor asked.

"He was consumed by pride and besieged by Satan! From the time we left Paris, his objective was to spoil your

258

plan and change the mission of the Church. I listened to him intently and was nearly swayed by his arguments, but the strength of God prevailed."

The Monsignor looked puzzled.

"At one point, he insisted the Church should confess its sins against women. He even blasphemed by altering the sacred words of the Mass to say: 'We confess to almighty God, *and to you my sisters*, that we have greatly offended, in our thoughts and in our deeds, in what we have done and in what we have failed to do, through our fault, through our fault, through our most grievous fault; therefore, we ask for forgiveness from God and *from our sisters* and ask the blessed Mary ever-virgin, all the angels and the saints, and you my brothers and sisters, to pray for us to the Lord our God.'"

"Blasphemy… to be so presumptuous as to ask the Church to excuse its treatment of women through a *mea-culpa* is blasphemy; blasphemy of the gravest kind, I swear!" the Monsignor blurted.

Chapter 52

Madeleine was released after serving six days in prison. She hurried home to see her children, only to be intercepted at her doorsteps by attorney l'Heureux. "You have been served with a writ of accusation, and we are scheduled for a hearing tomorrow before a magistrate, summarily convened by the Bishop of Paris."

"Then all the more reason for me to spend every second that I can with my children," she responded as she heard the cries of her children rushing toward her.

"Mama, mama, where have you been?" Angeline yelled as she ran to her mother.

"Mama, mama, we missed you so much," Jean shouted just a few steps behind his sister.

She fell to her knees and embraced all three as they rushed up to her. Tears flowed freely from her eyes as she hugged them tightly, in fear of letting go and losing them again. She pulled back a little to see their faces. Angeline had a bruise on her forehead, which concerned her mother. "What happened to you, my dear Angeline?" she asked as she gently kissed the bruise.

"It is nothing mama. I bumped into Marc when we were playing yesterday. We were too sad to play, but Jean told us you would want us to keep active."

"I did mama, I knew you would not want us being sad and crying all the time, so we tried to stay busy."

"Jean, you have become my little gentleman. I am so proud of you," she said as she stood up gathering her children under her arms and leading them to the house.

"Madeleine, we must prepare for tomorrow's hearing." Monsieur l'Heureux pleaded.

"Not now Monsieur l'Heureux, I must spend time with my children," she responded while entering the house. He followed her and went directly to the library to prepare for the hearing.

"What are the charges?' she asked as she walked by the library.

"The complaint is very vague."

"Come children, let's go out to play," she said as the children rushed outdoors.

In an instant, they were in the gardens running and playing with their mother. They frolicked from one game to another while Madeleine was like a child again — forgetting her time in prison and the ordeal soon to come.

"Mama, let us sit on the bench and talk," Angeline said breathlessly.

"Yes, let us sit and talk, come boys and join us on the bench."

"And take that leaf out of your ear Marc... you look silly," Angeline said with a giggle in her voice.

For a few moments Madeleine just admired her children. She loved them so and never wanted to be separated from them again. She thought about the hearing to come, sensing the bishop wanted to shorten the civil litigation in order to obtain the LeBlanc fortune quickly. *If it means separation from my children, I will concede promptly!* she thought.

After putting the children to bed, she worked well into the night preparing for the hearing with her barrister.

The next morning, as her carriage turned on to la Rue de la Ville l'Eveque and passed by the Church of the Madeleine, she called for the coachman to stop, jumped out of the carriage, ran up the steps of the neoclassical building, entered the church, bowed her head, and asked God to watch over her children. While departing the church, she directed the coachman to move the carriage ahead as she walked to the bishop's office building. Approaching her destination, she spotted Monsieur l'Heureux waiting for her at the front of the building. His look of confidence inspired her.

"This is an ecclesiastical hearing and its orders must be enforced by the civil courts. Today, the magistrate may charge you, may judge you, may condemn you, but he cannot carry out any punishment without the approval of the civil authorities."

"So at the end of the day, I will walk away from the hearing, no matter the results," she said, breathing a sigh of relief.

"We will argue that we have not received enough notice to prepare for trial and that the charges are too vague to defend against, and we will ignore any adverse decision rendered by the magistrate. Yes, today you will walk away from this hearing, no matter the results."

"Who is the magistrate?" she asked.

"A former inquisitor chosen by the bishop," he responded.

"And, who will present the case for the bishop?" she continued.

"A lawyer trained in Canon Law."

"And what is Canon Law?"

"It is a code of law established by the Church," he responded. "The laws regulate the actions of the magistrate but any punishment is governed by the country in which the tribunal presides. For example, France forbids the execution of a person who violates Canon Law. Whereas, the Papal States permit the execution of a person who violates of Canon Law."

The two walked up the granite steps, entered the building, and went directly to the courtroom. They were the first to arrive and settled in at the defendant's table. The bishop's attorney came next and went directly to the prosecutor's table.

A few spectators entered and took seats at the back of the courtroom. Madeleine turned to see who had entered and to her dismay she saw the Monsignor and Father

Martin taking their seats.

The court crier announced the entry of the magistrate. All in the courtroom rose to their feet, as was the common practice. The magistrate took his seat behind the bench. He addressed the parties and asked the prosecutor to summarize the charges.

"Your honor, on behalf of the Bishop of Paris, the charges consist of an accusation from Rome against Madeleine Moreau for the heresy of witchcraft."

Madeleine gasped audibly as the blood drained from her face. She was stunned by the accusation and looked to her attorney for support.

"Your honor, I demand to inspect the document accusing my client of witchcraft."

"Please hand the writ of accusation to Monsieur l'Heureux for his review," the magistrate directed.

Madeleine looked over his shoulder as her attorney examined the document. It was official looking and embossed with a large seal. When finished, he handed it back to the prosecutor.

"What does it say?" Madeleine blurted out.

"The prosecutor will read it to the magistrate. Listen closely to the charges." he responded.

"If it please the Court, I will continue," the prosecutor said.

"You may continue, Monsieur Coulombe."

"The accusation against Madeleine Moreau reads as follows: The dual purpose of an inquisition is to save the soul of the heretic and protect the unity of the Church. Those who conceive morbid and depraved doctrines in the Church of Christ and who resist defiantly and refuse to change their troublesome and deadly doctrines and persist in defending them are heretics. In the instant case, Madeleine Moreau is accused, by a person of good reputation, of heretical behavior, and after due consideration of the evidence by a papal official, the accused is found to be triable for the offense and is charged with the heresy of witchcraft. The accused is ordered to appear for trial before a papal legate in Rome to answer the accusations. The failure of the accused to provide a legitimate defense will result in the condemnation and punishment of the accused.

"The accused, Madeleine Moreau, is entitled to an account of the specific charges against her," the magistrate ordered.

"Madeleine Moreau was observed in church, on numerous occasions, without a veil on her head and consorting with the devil. Madeleine Moreau incited men to commit sexual transgressions in public places. Madeleine Moreau committed adultery by cohabiting with Michel Bois while married to Jean Marc Moreau. For these and other transgressions, Madeleine Moreau is accused of witchcraft. "

"Monsieur l'Heureux do you wish to address the Court," the magistrate inquired.

"Your honor, I request to know who made these accusations against Madeleine Moreau?"

"The person was determined to be one of good reputation, and his identity need not be revealed," the magistrate responded.

"Your honor, in what way did Madeleine Moreau consort with the devil in church?"

"The allegations in the accusation are sufficient to apprise the accused of the offense."

"Your honor, who were the men who were allegedly solicited in public places by Madeleine Moreau?'

"The men will be called as witnesses at trial to confront Madeleine Moreau, when she appears before the Roman tribunal."

"Your honor, who will testify to the allegations of adultery?"

"If she does not confess to the charges and there are

enough partial proofs, the Roman tribunal may invoke the doctrine of torture against Madeleine Moreau to determine the truth. Is there anything else, Monsieur l'Heureux?"

"No, your honor."

"Monsieur Coulombe, please present the official accusation document to the Court, at this time."

The magistrate received and examined the document. Once the document was examined, the magistrate directed that Madeleine examine the official accusation. The document was delivered to the defendant's table by the court's clerk for review by the defendant. "They will do whatever they want no matter what objections I may have," she whispered to her attorney.

"I will object to the charges for the record, Madeleine. If I do not, Rome might not accept our appeal."

"You may appeal to Rome, but that is a place I do not intend to visit!" she responded adamantly.

"I object to the charges in the accusation as being vague, groundless, and without substance, your honor," Monsieur l'Heureux said as he handed the document back to the court clerk.

"The defendant will stand and face the court," the magistrate ordered.

Madeleine complied.

"Madeleine Moreau, you have heard the charges, and you have read the accusation. Do you admit to the charges against you?"

She looked at her attorney, turned to face the magistrate, looked him directly in the eye, and said boldly: "I do not admit to any of the charges in the accusation!"

"Madeleine Moreau, do you confess to the charges in the accusation?" the magistrate asked sternly.

"I will never confess to the false charges in the accusation," she responded defiantly, to the obvious dismay of the magistrate.

"Madeleine Moreau, do you have anything to say in

your defense to the charges of the accusation?" the magistrate continued.

"I deny each and every charge alleged in the accusation," she said, leaving little doubt where she stood.

The magistrate sounded the gavel on the hardwood bench. "The Court will adjourn for one hour. The parties are not to leave the courtroom. The court officers will stand guard at the door."

The court crier called for all to rise. The magistrate rose and left the courtroom through the door at the back of the bench. The court officers, complying with the magistrate's order, moved to the exit doors to prevent the defendant from leaving the room.

At the appointed time, the magistrate returned, and all rose at the call of the court crier. Madeleine scanned the back of the courtroom and noticed the Monsignor had left.

"Madeleine Moreau, stand and face the court," the magistrate ordered.

Madeleine stood and faced the magistrate.

"Madeleine Moreau, I find that you have been properly notified of the charges against you. I further find that a person of good reputation has brought the charges. And, I further find that the partial proofs against you provide justification for the seeking of a full proof by a tribunal in the Papal States. Therefore, I order that you leave immediately for Rome to stand trial for the accusation of witchcraft."

"Madeleine Moreau will remain in France and will not go to Rome to face the charge of witchcraft as ordered by the magistrate!" Monsieur l'Heureux interjected.

Silence fell upon the courtroom, momentarily.

"Madeleine Moreau due to your disrespect for this court, your disregard of Canon Law, your disobedience of the rules of the Church, and the threat you pose to those around you, this Court pronounces your excommunication from the Catholic Church," the magistrate declared.

Both Madeleine and her barrister remained silent and stoic.

The magistrate continued: "The dual purpose of excommunication is ultimately to bring salvation to the heretic and to protect the faith of the community. Madeleine Moreau, from this day forward and until such time as you present yourself for trial in the Papal States, you are excluded from the Christian community. You are deprived of participating in church services, and you are prohibited from receiving any of the sacraments of the Church. Furthermore, you will be publicly condemned from every pulpit, of every church, in every diocese of France. And, finally, if you should die under the order of excommunication, your soul will be damned to the fires of hell for eternity!"

The magistrate paused briefly and then continued, "Is there anything you wish to say in your defense?"

"If I were a man, I would not be deemed a heretic for not wearing a veil in church. If I were a man and approached a woman, I would not be charged with transgressions in public places. If I were a man, and I cohabited with women, I would not be charged with witchcraft. But, alas, I am not a man, and unlike Jesus, the Church will condemn me for no other reason except that I am a woman!"

"You will stand accountable before this court and before God, Madeleine Moreau. This hearing is adjourned!" the magistrate ordered.

The court crier called for all to rise, and the magistrate left the courtroom believing that God's will had been done.

Madeleine departed satisfied that she could not be punished in France. She requested the coachman to take her to the parochial school to pick up her children. When she arrived, she saw Jean and Angeline in the schoolyard with

Sister Superior at their side.

"Where is Marc?" Madeleine asked frantically.

"The Monsignor has taken him to Rome," Sister Superior responded.

"No, no dear God, this cannot be happening!" Madeleine shrieked.

Chapter 53

Jean Marc completed the service honoring the dead who had been so brave on the field of battle just as the sky was beginning to change from gray to blue. The horses were saddled, the gear was packed, and the recent victory gave them heart. "We will follow the Danube into the Middle Black Forest. The terrain is low and hilly. We will travel through the forest to the Rhine River... and cross the Rhine into France."

The mention of France brought smiles to the soldiers' faces.

"How many days to France?" Luc asked

"One maybe two days," Jean Marc responded. "The enemy is no longer in pursuit. The goal is now speed, not safety, and we will move at a brisk pace. Our families and Napoleon await us."

Jean Marc led his men at a furious pace to reach the French border. They arrived at the Rhine River at dusk and crossed the bridge into the city of Strasbourg.

"Tonight we will celebrate our freedom with French Champagne," Jean Marc told his men. But as they rode into the heart of the city their joy turned to fear as they spotted a Prussian soldier addressing a crowd.

Jean Marc took the lead and ordered his men to proceed cautiously. He listened closely as the soldier addressed the townspeople. "Napoleon has abdicated and is a prisoner of the British Navy on his way to the island of Saint Helena. The Bourbons have been restored and Louis XVIII is the King of France. The European countries, including France, have signed the Treaty of Paris of 1815. The terms of the treaty are posted in the town square."

Jean Marc and his soldiers followed the crowd to the square. He noticed that the spirits of the Frenchmen who read the treaty were flagging. He heard one say, "And this is where Napoleon has taken France after two decades of war."

He approached the board where the treaty was posted. As he read, he verbalized the pertinent parts: "France will shrink in size to its borders of 1790... France will pay an indemnity to the Allies of 700 million francs... France will support an army of occupation for five years at a cost of 150 million francs a year."

He turned to face a crowd that was now blurred by the tears in his eyes. France will be like Poland, a country in servitude, partly ruled by a king following the orders of the Allies. "It is not what I envisioned for France, for you, or for my family."

The thought of defeat brought home strong emotions to Jean Marc. As a young soldier his emotion was fear. As a veteran soldier his emotion was exhilaration. And as a defeated soldier his emotion was remorse — remorse for the lost and shattered lives of war. He knew now, that he could set aside the weapons of war, but he wondered if he could ever set aside the memories of war.

In Laon, the soldiers were deserting in droves, weapons in hand. Michel could not stop them, nor did he want to. The Duke of Wellington had appeared at the encampment with an army of British and Prussian soldiers. "To the victor goes the spoils," he mumbled to himself.

Orders came down from Wellington that the combined forces would escort the King into Paris, as a show of support. "The combined armies will open the route to Paris and the King will follow in Wellington's train. We will be the lead unit bringing the King into Paris," Michel told his company commanders. "Not too bad for a defeated army."

"A sign of unity, perhaps?" the captain asked.

"Until after the parade, captain. Then we will be disbanded."

"The bastards know what they are doing," the captain added.

"But we are fortunate, we have survived, more or less, intact. At the briefing this morning, we were informed that the king will soon issue a proclamation saying that all those who served Napoleon will not be prosecuted."

"And if you are not prosecuted, what will you do, major?" the captain asked, half in jest.

"Upon my return to Paris, I will resign from the army and return to my family," Michel responded.

The captain looked confused.

"My sculptures, captain, they are my family — I should never have left them," he said, as his thoughts wandered not to his sculptures but to Madeleine — and whether he would ever see her again. *I am still in love,* he thought, just as the order came down for his battalion to fall in for the march. He straightened out his uniform and walked from of his tent to lead his unit for the last time.

Within an hour, Michel and his battalion moved out, but he was not ready to follow his order to clear the route to Paris, if it meant engaging French troops. It was on the second day of the march, that the unit encountered a fortress defended by approximately two hundred French soldiers. When the order came down from an Allied general to assault the fortress, Michel told his company commanders, "Do not turn against your countrymen."

"But if we do not assault the fortress, the Prussians will annihilate our unit," the captain asserted.

"Drop your weapons and follow me," Michel ordered.

The disarmed officers walked across the open field toward the fortress.

"This is suicide," the captain said.

But as they approached the fortress, a gate opened

and three French officers walked toward them.

Michel and his officers breathed a sigh of relief and resumed their walk toward their French counterparts. An errant shot rang out from a British soldier. The French rifles appeared in the portals of the fortress. All froze momentarily. When they met, Michel reach out and embraced his comrade. "I am sad to say that our war is lost. We must not shed more French blood. Come to Paris, and let us join together to rebuild our nation."

The French officer broke the embraced, "My soldiers are tired of war and want to return to their homes… we will join you colonel!"

This scene was repeated numerous times on the way to Paris, and in this manner the route was cleared. "Not for the king," Michel told his soldiers, "but, rather, for the restoration of France."

Chapter 54

Madeleine Moreau was frantic about Marc's abduction, but she had the wherewithal to call upon Monsieur l'Heureux for help. "I need for you to take care of my children and the affairs of the estate while I search for Marc. The servants will help care for my children and keep them out of harm's way, but I am still so worried about them. During my stay in prison, a guard by the name of Emile Fortin protected me. I know he might do the same for my children."

"And what else?"

"I have very little time to explain, but if the opportunity arises, inform the court that I will renounce my entire inheritance with one exception."

"And what is that?" he asked.

"I will keep the vineyards in the Bordeaux region. That is but a pittance in comparison to the remainder of the estate."

"The bishop and the king stand to inherit an enormous fortune."

" How they divide it is up to them," she responded."

"And if they insist on the vineyards?"

"Then I will not renounce the inheritance."

"It might be years before they receive any benefit from the estate," he said.

"And if, perhaps, we find a fair judge, then they will get nothing!"

"Finding a fair judge in Paris is like finding a whale in the Seine," he responded.

"Then we will fight… and ironically, it will then be their inheritance that is at stake."

"When do you leave?"

"Right now, I am going to Rome to find Marc."

"It 's too dangerous, let me go with you," he urged.

"No, stay here Monsieur l'Heureux... protect Jean and Angeline and save my vineyards!"

"And who will accompany you to Rome?"

"The coachman and my maidservant," she responded.

"I insist that you get more protection."

"My fate is in God's hands."

"God has not treated you fairly in the past," he rejoined.

" God has always treated me fairly, Monsieur l'Heureux... it is the Church that has not treated me fairly."

"Yes, there is a difference!"

Within a few hours, Madeleine departed. *How calculating the Monsignor has been in his plan to bring me to trial for witchcraft. I have been so naïve about the ways of the Inquisition, but I believe I can sway the inquisitor in my favor*, she thought.

As the carriage reached the outskirts of Paris, she scanned the dark woods at the side of the road and thought how much more secure she would be if Jean Marc were at her side on this perilous journey. They had been separated for nearly two years and she had no idea if he was still alive.

Darkness was setting as she heard the sound of galloping horses in the distance. The carriage pulled to the side to allow the oncoming band of ragged soldiers to pass unhindered. As they rushed by, a few tilted their caps in respect for the lady in the carriage. She observed their bearded faces and her heart froze when she caught sight of a blurred figure, which resembled Jean Marc. Speechless, she poked her head out of the carriage window only to see the soldiers vanish into the darkness.

Could it be? she asked herself, instinctively ordering the coachman to turn around to pursue the fleeting figures. *But I have chased so many shadows in the past, only to be disappointed*, she thought.

"What is it Madame?" her maidservant asked.

"Oh, nothing… nothing but the imagination of one clinging to the past."

"What shall I tell the coachman, Madame?

"Tell him to continue toward Rome," she responded, her voice trailing off, thinking of the danger her son was in at this hour. "Tell him time is of the essence and to drive through the night."

"It is unusual Sergeant to see a carriage with two damsels leaving Paris at this time of day… there are many highwaymen afoot, should we turn back and provide an escort to the nearest village?" Luc urged.

"Luc, I wish we could be so honorable, but our soldiers have had a long and dangerous journey, and their only thought is to reach Paris. I can no longer deny them what they have so bravely earned!" he replied as he looked back into the darkness to see the dust rising from the road hiding the carriage from sight.

Sleep did not come easily for Madeleine that night with the rough ride of the carriage, the concern for her son's safety, and the thought of facing the inquisitor. She felt so alone and so terrified — a commoner facing the almighty Church with both her life and her son's in the balance. *Where would she find the words, how would she express herself, what would she say, and how would she convince the inquisitor? Jesus' words of love, compassion, and justice were her only solace. Certainly the Church of Rome would follow the guidance of its Founder.*

She looked over at the young maidservant sleeping soundly without a care in the world. Life had been as peaceful for her a few years ago before Jean Marc's departure. *How could it have become so complicated in such a short time?* she wondered.

The glow of Paris could be seen in the distance. The soldiers sat by the fire swapping stories about their trek from Russia to France. Tomorrow, they would be in Paris — most reunited with their loved ones. Jean Marc had spent months away from Madeleine, and he ached for her now more than ever. The banter coming from the soldiers did not disrupt his thoughts, but the rustling of the leaves coming from behind startled him.

"It's just me, Sergeant." Luc said as he sat down next to Jean Marc.

"What will you do now, Luc?" Jean Mark asked.

Luc was slow to respond. "I have no family... I am not coming home to anyone ...."

"You have a family now Luc... there is a bond here... we are your family!" Jean Marc responded as silence fell upon them — both peering through the darkness toward Paris.

Chapter 55

Upon his arrival in Paris, Jean Marc found directions to Madame LeBlanc's home. As they stood before the grandest of the mansions, Jean Marc wondered whether Madeleine would be happy in their small farmhouse after experiencing such wealth and opulence. It was a fleeting thought, for every cell in his body now yearned to see his beloved family. A soft glow came from the windows of the grand mansion. But as they arrived at the entrance, they found the gate locked tight. Jean Marc rang the bell, and within seconds a giant of a man appeared. As he walked toward them, a large grin came upon his face. "Sergeant Moreau, it has been such a long time. You may not remember me, but you saved my life in battle. My name is Emile Fortin and Madeleine hired me to protect Jean and Angeline while she is away."

"Where are Madeleine and Marc?" he asked apprehensively.

"They are in Rome to appear before a Papal Tribunal. I fear for their safety, as does the staff and Monsieur L'Heureux. They are gathered inside and will brief you on the situation... but before, you must see your children."

Jean Marc's concern deepened, *why would Emile fear for their safety*, he wondered.

"Jean, Angeline, your Papa is home," Emile said in a stentorian voice that could be heard throughout the neighborhood.

They rushed from the house clamoring to see their father. "Papa, papa, papa!" they shouted and rushed toward him as Emile swung open the gate.

Jean Marc gathered them in his strong arms, and for a few moments, all was right in their lives. "You have grown so much Jean and Angeline."

"And so has your beard, Papa," Jean rejoined as their sobs receded.

"But Mama and Marc are gone, Papa... what shall we do?" Jean asked.

"We will find them!"

"Who is this Papa?" Jean asked.

Jean Marc looked back, "This is your uncle Luc, he has come a long way with me," he responded.

"Will he help us to find Mama and Marc?" Angeline asked.

Luc smiled.

"Papa, Uncle Luc, come inside, it is much warmer, and we can plan how to find Mama and Marc!" Jean implored, as they walked toward the back entrance.

At the rear of the mansion, Luc observed a coach parked in front of the carriage house. It was similar to the carriage they had seen leaving Paris the night before. He hesitated to tell Jean Marc sensing that his friend would blame himself for not having pursued the carriage.

"Come Luc, come follow us into the house," Emile said holding the door open for Luc to enter.

"The carriage that took Madeleine to Rome, is it similar to the one by the carriage house?" Luc asked Emile.

"Yes, yes... exactly like that one," he responded pointing to the carriage in the yard. "But, why?" Emile asked.

"Just wondering Emile... just wondering," he responded.

What he had envisioned as a joyous reunion with his family had turned into a nightmare, and he knew he could not delay his departure to Rome. After a few minutes, he told his children to wait for him in the room and went directly to the library.

Monsieur l'Heureux was quick to respond to his presence. "Jean Marc, it disappoints me to ruin this homecoming but, believe me, Madeleine and Marc are in imminent danger."

"Tell me… tell me about it!" he said impatiently.

"The Monsignor abducted Marc and fled to Rome. Madeleine rushed after them to save her son, even though she had been formally accused of witchcraft and faced certain prosecution by a papal tribunal. And, if she is convicted, she will be executed!"

"But Madeleine is not a witch; she cannot not be convicted of witchcraft!"

"The Inquisition has not dealt fairly with women. I fear the tribunal will convict her," Monsieur l'Heureux responded.

"Then I will depart for Rome immediately!" Jean Marc exclaimed.

"I will go with you!" Luc said.

"And me too!" Emile added.

"No… no, this is my fight," Jean Marc objected.

"It is our fight, Jean Marc, for we are family." Luc reminded him.

"But… " Jean Marc said before being interrupted by Emile.

"There is no time to argue, Sergeant Moreau!"

Jean Marc knew he was right and turned to a servant, "Saddle fresh horses and prepare provisions for our journey." He turned back to Monsieur l'Heureux, "Will you join us?"

"No, but heed this advice, it shall not be the law but rather bribes that will free Madeleine and Marc.

"Bribes?" Jean Marc said with a quizzical look on his face.

"The Roman Church is renown for its corruption… a little money will go a long way. Here is a purse of liras to grease the palms of the greedy officials."

"Emile, safeguard the money," Jean Marc said.

"Papa, I will go with you," Jean implored as he burst into the room from the hallway where he had been eavesdropping.

"No Jean, you will stay with your sister, Angeline," he said as he hugged his children, hoping that it would not be their last.

"Now be on your way and Godspeed," Monsieur l'Heureux urged.

A few days later, Madeleine's carriage arrived at Saint Peter's Basilica around noon. She stepped from the carriage and onto the Piazza San Pietro, immediately overwhelmed by her surroundings. She did not stop to admire the beauty around her as she rushed through the square, her eyes avoiding the tall colonnades on either side; her only diversions were quick glances at the young boys in the square in hopes of finding Marc. She ignored the huge statues of the saints sitting upon the porticos high above the square staring down upon her and remained focused on the basilica ahead, which seemed so distant. She saw at the top the stairs two Swiss Guards standing as sentries before the huge doors of the basilica. She caught her breath as she reached the stairs. She paused, then walked up to the guards standing at attention and looking beyond her.

"My name is Madeleine Moreau," she said breathlessly. "I have been accused of witchcraft and ordered to come to Rome for a trial before a papal court," she said in French, hoping she would be understood.

"Do you have the accusation with you, Madame?" a guard asked in fluent French.

"I do not."

"Then follow me, Madame!" the guard responded, as he led her along the front of the basilica to a small edifice. He repeated in Italian through a window what he had been told. Moments later, four guards rushed from a side door. One seized her bag, another tied her hands with a rope, and the other two grabbed her arms and led her roughly away from the basilica. She was thrown into a carriage, which rushed off as soon as the coachman received his order from a Swiss Guard.

From a distance, Madeleine's coachman and maidservant observed her plight but felt helpless. "We must return to Paris immediately!" the coachman said as he turned the carriage around whipping the horses to get away from the area as quickly as possible.

Madeleine was taken to the *Castel Sant' Angelo,* which was being utilized as a courtroom and prison. She was brought to a small room and told she would face the judges in the morning. They stripped off her clothes and gave her a drab, woolen uniform to wear. She was left alone in a room that looked out onto an adjacent foyer. She sat idly for a period of time observing people coming in and out while searching frantically for sight of her son.

She walked to a window at the rear of the room. Outside, people were walking by idly, seemingly carefree. Young children played games, with parents nearby. Dark clouds were rolling in from the east. In the distance, she saw the profile of a tall man with a young child in tow. They stopped and looked back toward the magnificent basilica. As they came closer, she noted that the tall figure was wearing priestly clothes. The other was Marc's height. She lost sight of them in the crowd. Her eyes strained for another glimpse of the figures. "Marc... Marc," she shouted as they appeared below her window.

He looked apprehensively in the direction of the sound just as a guard yanked her forcibly from the window.

Chapter 56

The weather turned stormy, it was cold, and the snow was blinding, but Jean Marc was determined to push the horses and the men to their limits. He was driven by the fear that he might arrive too late to save his wife and son. Although not a religious man, he vowed to God that if He spared his loved ones, he would never fight again!

"Jean Marc, we must rest the horses, they are foaming at the mouth... they need water. We must stop for the night." Luc insisted.

Jean Marc gave him a cold stare and spurred his horse to a faster pace. Luc drove his horse, grabbed the reins and pulled them with all his might. The horses slowed to a gallop and stopped suddenly.

"No Luc... "he shouted over the heavy snorts of the horses.

"The horses must rest Jean Marc, or you will kill them... we can continue our journey before sunrise tomorrow."

Jean Marc shook his head, a look of despair on his face. "But my wife, my son... I must save them!" he said frustrated and helpless.

"Look ahead there is an abandoned barn... let us rest for a few hours." Luc said.

Jean Marc knew his friend was right. He moved toward the building and opened the creaky door. The horses trotted into the barn scavenging the loose hay on the floor even before the saddles were taken off their backs.

"Unsaddle and dry down the horses before they freeze to death." Luc said as all three pitched in.

"I will look for water," Emile said as he picked up two old wooden buckets.

"Let's start a fire to keep warm." Jean Marc said with little enthusiasm in his voice.

"I will prepare a meal and find a little cognac to warm us up." Luc said, trying to cheer up his friend.

Jean Marc nodded.

"These are fine horses and they will get us to Rome."

"I am too worried to think straight, Luc," he said.

"Here, have a drink of cognac; it will help you relax."

Jean Marc sat close the fire sipping cognac. It warmed his insides and provided a brief escape from his haunting thoughts.

Emile returned with two filled buckets. He brought them directly to the horses, and they drank ravenously. He picked up the empty buckets and said as he was walking out of the barn, "The stream is only a few hundred feet away, and the ice is thin… a few trips should take care of the horses… and a few more gulps of cognac should take care of you Jean Marc!"

A slight smile came over Jean Marc's face.

When Emile returned, he placed the buckets before the horses and gathered more loose hay for them. He sat next to Jean Marc but said nothing as they both watched Luc prepare supper.

"Luc will lead us to Rome?" Jean Marc said in a slightly slurred speech. "He knows the horses much better than I do!"

"Then pass the bottle of cognac to celebrate my friend's promotion." Emile said reaching for the bottle.

"Just get us there in time Luc." Jean Marc implored.

The next morning, Luc was the first to rise. He checked the horses. Kicked both Emile and Jean Marc in the back and said, "Let's get moving. Douse the fire, saddle the horses, we can eat on the road." .

In Rome, Madeleine was transferred to the prison

located in the underground part of the Castel. Her cell was small, dark, and cold. Her sleep was fitful, interrupted by thoughts of the cruelty of the Monsignor and the cries of pain of other prisoners. She knew she would not find sympathy for herself from the tribunal but hoped to find mercy for Marc. That was her plan — to beg for mercy, not for herself but for her son.

Suddenly, a prisoner was dragged by her cell pleading with the guard: "I would rather die than be tortured again… please, please, I will confess to anything!"

"Confess to the priest today," the guard said. "Confess to the tribunal tomorrow, and rid yourself of the demons who infest your soul, and then the torture will stop," he said as he kicked her in the buttock with a loud thud that resounded throughout the chamber, inducing a searing scream of pain from the prisoner.

Madeleine peered through the small, barred window, she pleaded with the guard to show mercy.

"The same mercy I will show you when it is your time. There will be no mercy until you confess!" he yelled back.

"I will not beg for mercy!" she shouted for all to hear.

"Just one day in my chamber, and you will change your mind you fucking witch!" came the harsh response from the passageway.

"Never, you cruel bastard!" she responded as other prisoners joined her in shouting their feelings to the torturer.

"Shout today, for tomorrow I will rip the tongue from your mouth with my tongs," came the response from the guard.

"Augustine, let us first pray that the heretics confess their sins so there is no need for torture." came a calming voice from the passageway.

"Yes, father, let us pray," came the now docile

voice of the torturer.

"What's your name?" a prisoner asked from a nearby cell.

"Madeleine Moreau."

"Madeleine Moreau!" The cry went from cell to cell down the corridor and deep into the bowels of the prison.

It was heard by a frail prisoner, chained to the walls of the darkest, deepest cell in the dungeon. *I cannot understand why the Church prosecutes, tortures, and executes innocent men and women. But now I know my dream of equality and fairness will not die in this cell... it will not die because strong women, like Madeleine Moreau, will not let it die,* he thought, as he coughed persistently, feeling a warm liquid spilling into his mouth with each cough. He knew it was blood, and he knew he would soon die — but a smile crossed his face as the name of Madeleine Moreau reverberated in his mind.

For days Madeleine challenged the torturer until one morning, she heard a guard unlock her door. He grabbed her roughly, groping for her breast as he pushed her out of the cell. She turned, faced her assailant, and a thousand years of misdirected hatred and bigotry came through her stare. The guard stepped back obviously intimidated by her temerity and said feebly, "The tribunal awaits your arrival, move along."

As she walked from her cell, the shouts of the prisoners filled the corridor, "Madeleine... Madeleine... Madeleine..." the cries came unremittingly, bringing the prisoners a cause and Madeleine courage.

She was ushered into the marbled courtroom, its splendor serving to diminish the self-esteem of defendants who come to the court in their tattered clothes and woolen dresses. Nonetheless, the grandeur of her surroundings did not shake her sense of self-worth and confidence. Neither did the courtroom packed with clerics in their fine clothes. To her left, she spotted the Monsignor, gloating and obviously regaling his fellow priests about his accomplishments. She stood erect at the defendant's table awaiting the announcement of the tribunal.

The court crier ordered all in the courtroom to stand and moments later the three magistrates entered the courtroom and took their seats behind a massive oak bench. The court crier directed all to be seated. Madeleine remained standing, looking directly at the chief magistrate.

She listened closely as the chief magistrate read the indictment. He asked whether she would confess to the accusation against her.

"No!" she responded firmly.

"Do you have counsel?"

"Not in Rome," she said.

"Have you read the accusation from France?"

"No," she said.

The chief magistrate looked to the other two magistrates to determine whether they had any comments. Neither commented. His gaze turned to the spectators, whose demeanor encouraged him to proceed. He next turned to the defendant.

She had not taken her eyes off him since he entered the room. He stared back at her for a long time and, at last, said in a firm voice, "A person of good reputation has through the procedure of *denuntiatio* accused you, Madeleine Moreau, of the heresy of witchcraft. What say you to this accusation?"

"I request that the person of good reputation confront me before this tribunal with his accusations!"

"The tribunal will not identify the person of good reputation for fear that a witch's curse be placed upon him," the chief magistrate responded.

The Monsignor sat haughtily, surrounded by his allies.

"Then, I will confront my accuser," she said as she turned toward the gallery and with an outstretched hand pointed directly at the Monsignor.

All heads turned in the direction she was pointing. "The Monsignor is my accuser, and he does not have the fortitude to confront me," she said as he glowered at her.

"He is a person of bad reputation. He is a liar. He is a coward. He is an abductor of a young boy," she said, as a murmur spread through the courtroom.

She turned quickly and looked directly to the chief magistrate, and said, "Order him to confront me... let me examine him... and, I will expose the corruption of his nature."

The chief magistrate slammed the gavel on the bench so forcefully that it shattered, "I will direct this trial, and you will confess to the heresy of witchcraft, or you will be sent to the torture chamber!" he said firmly.

"Then send my accuser to the torture chamber with me, and you will truly get the truth!" she bellowed at the chief magistrate.

"Take the defendant from the courtroom and return her to this court once she has confessed to the heresy!" the chief magistrate ordered as the bailiffs closed in on her.

They escorted her through the courtyard on the way to the prison. Less than a kilometer away, she saw the Basilica, standing as a magnificent symbol of Christianity; the holiest site of the Catholic Church, condoning and fostering the torture of human beings. *The Church has replaced love and compassion with hatred and cruelty!* she thought, as the guard pushed her in the direction of the torture chamber.

Chapter 57

Jean Marc marveled at how well Luc handled the journey. Although the horses did not travel at breakneck speed, their steady pace covered much ground in the course of a day. They rose early, took ample rest stops, and retired late. In this way, the horses never seemed to tire. Jean Marc understood his two friends were at risk and appreciated their sacrifice. But they knew how much Jean Marc had done for them, and they were prepared to walk to the end of the earth for their friend. Jean Marc wondered whether the strongest friendships were forged on the field of battle — for the crucible of war was the ultimate test.

When they arrived at Marseille, they were told that the next available ship to Italy would not leave for two days. The port was busy during Christmas week, and the last ship to Napoli was sailing at noon. "Tend to the horses; I will scour the wharfs to see what I can find." Emile said as he rushed off, purse in hand. Within an hour he returned waving boarding passes. "It's not only the bishops and the priests who are disposed to bribes, but also the ship captains!" he exclaimed with a broad smile on his face.

"But, but... that money was to be used in Rome." Jean Marc questioned.

"Fear not my friend, Monsieur l'Heureux padded the purse very well!" Emile responded.

Within a few hours, they were on a ship sailing towards Napoli.

"Let us rest during the sea journey. I was told that the distance between Napoli and Rome is about 180 kilometers, and the roads are good." Luc indicated to his friends. "We will be travelling on Christmas Day and should arrive in Rome one or two days later, depending on the weather."

Jean Marc took advantage of the time he had on the ship to question a few Italian passengers. In broken Italian, he asked about the design of Rome and inquired where papal inquisitors might hold a trial. He learned that most trials were public and held at various sites throughout the city, but there seemed to be consensus that a witchcraft case would be heard at the Castel Sant Angelo for a number of reasons: the prisoners were confined within its walls, a large public courtroom was accessible, and it was heavily fortified. He concluded that their strategy would be to go directly to the Castel.

His friends liked his plan but, more important, they were encouraged that Jean Marc seemed to be back to his old self. "Now, let us rest, for we will not get much rest once we dock." Jean Marc added.

Emile reached into his leather bag and pulled out a bottle of cognac. After taking a large gulp, he passed the bottle on to his comrades. It was soon empty, and the three gathered straw to soften the wooden beds. Jean Marc fell into a deep sleep and awakened the next morning refreshed but still worried. The journey took two more days, and as they descended the gangplank, Luc spotted the carriage that they had seen outside of Paris. A man and a young woman stood beside the horses and were preparing to embark a nearby ship.

Jean Marc saw Luc rush from the ship toward the ornate carriage. "Madeleine Moreau, Madeleine Moreau, where is she?" Luc hollered, as he approached the carriage.

"How do you know Madame Moreau?" the coachman asked.

"That is her husband coming off the gangplank. We fear for her safety. Do you know where she is?"

"She is in danger!" responded the maidservant, just as Jean Marc arrived.

"What kind of danger?" Jean Marc asked anxiously.

"All we saw were the soldiers taking her from Saint

Peter's basilica, tying her hands, pushing her into a carriage, and whisking her away," the coachman responded.

"Where did they take her?"

"Fearing for our safety, we rushed out of Rome," the coachman responded. "We do not know where they took her."

"Will you come back to Rome with us?" Jean Marc asked.

They looked at each other for a few seconds, and then the maidservant spoke, "Madame LeBlanc took us both off the streets. We were poor, penniless, and lived in the slums of Paris. She gave us work and treated us with dignity. Madame Moreau was also respectful. Yes, we are scared and do not know what we can do to help, but we will go back to Rome with you."

"Are the horses fresh?" Luc asked.

"Yes, the horses are fresh," the coachman answered.

"Then turn the coach around… we are heading for Rome!" Jean Marc ordered.

Once on the road to Rome, Jean Marc looked ahead at the rag tag band and wondered, whether this motley group could foil the might of the Catholic Church?

Christmas was the saddest of days. Madeleine was alone in the bowels of a dungeon. She was to be tortured the very next day. Jean Marc had never returned. Jean and Angeline were without their parents. And, Marc was in the clutches of a madman. If she confessed to witchcraft, she would be executed. If she did not confess, she would be tortured.

I must survive; she thought, *but how? A confession would bring a quick execution. Torture, on the other hand, might take a few days. A confession made under torture had to be freely repeated the next day without torture, or it would be considered invalid by the tribunal. It gives me time, and time is my only ally.*

"Madeleine... Madeleine..." came a call from a nearby cell.

"Yes, yes what is it?"

"A priest from Paris died today in the deepest cell of the dungeon," the prisoner responded.

"A priest from Paris... what's his name?" she asked.

"Father Thomas."

"Oh, my God!" she gasped. "That wonderful young priest... how... why?"

"He was brutally tortured Madeleine. We could hear his screams from our cells. He confessed many times, but they continued to torture him, day after day, night after night."

"And Father Martin, was he tortured too?"

"No, there was only one priest, Father Thomas... and he died today! They threw his broken body in the Tiber River."

"He died on Christmas day," she said, her voice dropping to a whisper as she crawled to the darkest corner of her cell and cried herself to sleep.

The thick, wooden door crashed open early the next morning. Startled, Madeleine stood up just as a punch to the stomach buckled her over. She struggled to breath as the torturer dragged her by the hair from the cell. "You bitch, you are mine now!"

She fought to keep her balance as she was pulled down the dark corridor to the torture chamber. Her dress was ripped off. She stood in the cold chamber before three men — the torturer, a priest, and the Monsignor. The blow to her stomach was still painful, and she was slightly bowed over, but she was not ready for her antagonists to get the best of her, so she stood erect fully exposing her naked body. She could tell they were aroused as their eyes scanned her body. They were committing a mortal sin not because they were about to torture a human being but because they were all having an impure thought — *how warped the Church's morality had become when it is a mortal sin to view a naked body, God's creation, and not sinful to afflict severe harm to that same body.*

The supervising priest was the first to speak. "Madeleine Moreau the Tribunal has sent you here so that we can determine the truth about the accusation against you. You have been accused of witchcraft, and if you confess to this heresy you will not be subjected to torture. Do you wish at this time to confess to the heresy of witchcraft?"

Her eyes shifted from the priest to the Monsignor who was still staring at her naked body. "Look at me in the eye you bastard! You stand there lusting for me after you have accused me of these wrongdoings, ripped my family apart, abducted my son, and allowed them to torture me — all because of your warped view of women. Tell them the truth and end this farce that the Church has started and that you perpetuate. Tell them the truth... just tell them the truth... I beg of you!"

He said nothing. She spat on his face and reached for him, but the torturer was too quick. He hit her with a powerful blow to the face, shattering her nose. She staggered backwards, falling to the floor, her naked body splattered with blood.

"Take the other prisoner to the rack and let her witness the torture that awaits her," the priest ordered.

An emaciated male was dragged to the rack, which consisted of a rectangular, wooden frame, slightly raised from the floor, with rollers at both ends. He was placed outstretched on the rack. His ankles were fastened to a roller at one end and his wrists were fastened by chains to a roller at the other end. The torturer took his place beside a handle attached to the top roller. The priest gave him the nod to start. He turned the handle stretching the body and putting tension on the arms and legs. As the rollers rotated the muscles and the joints were strained causing screams of pain from the prisoner, which went unheeded. The torturer continued to slowly turn the handle until loud popping noises were heard from the snapping of cartilage, ligaments, joints, and bones. The prisoner's cries echoed off the walls the chamber.

Madeleine looked away sickened by the terrible sight.

The priest nodded for the torturer to stop. The victim's arms and legs were untied and a guard picked up the limp body, its muscles and joints rendered useless.

"Confess to the heresy of witchcraft, and you will not be subjected to the rack," the priest offered.

"No!" she responded.

"Take her to her cell, and let her ponder what she has just witnessed. Bring her back in the morning.

The next day, she was returned to the torture chamber, her eyes blackened and her nose swollen.

"Confess to the heresy of witchcraft, and you will not be subjected to the rack," the priest threatened.

"No!" she responded.

"Take her to the rack!" the priest ordered.

"You are a wicked man!" she cried out.

"Our purpose is to eradicate the heretics of the world!" the priest snapped back.

"The Church marks women as sinful... alleges that they are witches... tortures them to confess... and executes them for heresy. Is that what you mean about eradicating heresy?" she questioned.

"We have our methods... we search for the truth... and the rack brings it out," the priest retorted.

The torturer removed Madeleine's bloodied, woolen dress. He placed her on the wooden rack and tied her wrists above her head with chains attached to a roller. He then tied her ankles with the chains on the lower roller of the rack.

She stared at the Monsignor, who was obviously enjoying the sadistic scene.

She saw the torturer move to the handle that extended from the rack. He turned the wheel slowly, and she felt tautness in her body, but the pain from her broken nose overwhelmed the pull of the rack.

"Confess to the heresy of witchcraft, and the torture will end," the priest said.

"No, no, never," she responded.

The priest nodded and on cue, the torturer turned the wheel extending the rack and stretching her body. She felt pain extend to her arms and legs.

"Confess to the heresy of witchcraft, and the torture will end," the priest repeated.

"No!"

The priest nodded and the torturer turned the wheel stretching her body even more. She felt a spike of pain radiating through her body.

"Confess to the heresy of witchcraft, and the torture will end," the priest repeated.

"No," she responded.

The priest nodded and the torturer turned the wheel a full turn. Her screams echoed in the chamber as the pain wracked her arms and legs.

"Confess to the heresy of witchcraft, and the torture will end," the priest whispered in her ear.

She did not respond, to the Monsignor's delight.

The priest nodded and the torturer turned the wheel as muscles snapped in her arms.

"Stop… please stop… " she sobbed.

"Confess to the heresy of witchcraft, and the torture will end."

"Please stop… please stop!" she cried.

The priest nodded, the torturer turned the wheel as the Monsignor's emotions piqued.

The sound of a bone shattering filled the chamber. Madeleine screamed. The torturer continued to turn the wheel. She closed her eyes and lost consciousness. The priest motioned to the torturer to release the pressure. Silence filled the room. No one spoke.

"We will continue the torture tomorrow," the priest said as Madeleine regained consciousness, his words barely audible to her.

The torturer grinned, looking down at Madeleine's broken body.

"No, no, there will be no more torture!" the Monsignor said contritely.

It is an act of God. I have met the test. I will be with my son soon! Madeleine thought.

The Monsignor walked away and said over his shoulder, "Tomorrow, torture her son!"

Chapter 58

In December the snow fell and the streets of Paris were cold and wet. King Louis XVIII had been in power for nearly six months. Michel's unit had been bivouacked north of Paris and kept under strict scrutiny, surrounded by Wellington's army.

There had been much anxiety leading to the day when Michel met with his officers. "Our unit is to disband," he informed them.

"Why, major?" a captain asked.

"The king has dissolved all the units of the army that he deems to be rebellious."

"Will we be compensated for our months of back pay?" another asked.

"France is laboring under a huge debt brought about by the Treaty of Paris, and foreign soldiers remain in our country to insure these payments. It is doubtful that that we will be paid our wages." Michel said.

"Are we free to leave, major?"

"You have fought bravely for France but, unfortunately, your sacrifice goes unnoticed. Shed your uniform, and turn in your weapons and you are free to leave." Michel responded.

The next day, Michel arrived in Paris going directly to the LeBlanc mansion. Somehow, it felt right going to the place where he had spent many memorable days with Madeleine and her children. He rang the bell and waited for a servant to open the gate. He turned toward the park and saw foreign troops going through their drills.

"Monsieur Bois, it is so nice to see you," the servant said as she opened the gate.

"I have come to visit with Madeleine and the children."

"You have not heard?"

He shook his head.

Madeleine and Marc are in terrible danger. Jean Marc is back and he has gone to Rome to save them."

"Then, I must speak with Madame LeBlanc, to see if I can help."

"Monsieur Bois, Madame LeBlanc died weeks ago."

"Where are the other children?"

"Follow me... it is Christmas Eve... perhaps, you can cheer them up."

In Rome, Jean Marc used the dome of St Peter's basilica as a landmark and led the group to the heart of the city. Luc had handled the horses well, and they were still spirited. He felt certain they could manage an escape through Rome. Luc and Emile were tested soldiers, and he felt confident they would carry out their assigned mission. He worried about the coachman and maidservant, they were young and untested — but they were eager. As they approached St. Peter's Square, he looked to the east and saw the tower of the Castel in the distance. He turned his horse in that direction and the others followed.

The sensation of going into battle surged through his being, but he had learned many years before not to let it control his actions — his senses were heightened, but they had to be channeled, especially while leading others. He looked back at Emile and Luc, both with determination on their faces. He looked at the two young people atop the carriage, both with anxiety on their faces — if possible, he would stay close by to protect them.

As they arrived at the front of the imposing structure, he saw a crowd at its gates.

"What's going on?" he shouted in broken Italian to a passerby.

"The witch from Paris has confessed, and it appears

that she and her son will be sentenced and burned at the stake today!"

Emotions of hope and fear filled his soul. *They are alive, thank you God! Now give me the strength to save them.*

He scanned the area and gestured to Emile to have the coachman park the carriage in an open space near the entrance.

"But the guard is saving that space for somebody." Emile said.

"Grease his palm, Emile!"

"Bien oui sergeant, bien oui," he said leading the carriage to the assigned location. He jumped off his horse and walked directly to the soldier, who was already gesturing to the coachman to move out of the area.

"Scusi!" Emile said as he placed liras in the soldier's palm.

"Grazie!" the guard responded.

Emile waved the maidservant into the carriage and instructed the coachman to be ready to go at a moment's notice. He returned to his friends, who had already taken their place in a queue.

The area was abuzz, and the three pieced together what little they could about the activities of the day. Priests, bishops, and notables were ushered into the building, but many civilians were being turned away.

A few minutes later, a guard exited with his hand out for money.

"Pay him and get us in Emile." Jean Marc said as the three walked to the front of the line.

Deep in the bowels of the building, Madeleine felt that time was running out. She closed her eyes fighting the pain, the nausea, and most of all the fear — fear for her son, Marc. She had confessed to the heresy of witchcraft to spare him from the Monsignor's abuse and was prepared to confess to the tribunal, if it set him free.

Her eyes were swollen and discolored, her nose was disfigured, she could not draw a breath through her swollen nostrils; her muscles had been stretched to the limit; her shoulder was broken, and her left arm hung by her side. The only action not causing her pain were the soft tears rolling down her cheeks.

The door opened and two guards walked in and picked her up off the floor. She could barely stand. They threw a baggy sackcloth over her naked body. She fell to her knees, her weakened muscles now useless. They picked her up and dragged her from the cell, up the stone stairs, and into a space just outside of the courtroom, the bright sun coming through the barred window temporarily blinding her. She moved toward a nearby stool but collapsed and fell hard on her buttocks. Sharp pain radiated through her body!

The three companions walked into the courtroom and found seats just outside the judicial bar and a few feet from the defendant's table. Jean Marc surveyed the large room and noticed that the guards were stationed around the perimeter.

"Can you make it to the judges' bench?" he whispered to Emile.

"To take a hostage?"

"We can't get out of here without a hostage."

"Don't worry; I will get us a judge."

Jean Marc nodded.

"Look to your left, that is the Monsignor. It's rumored in Paris that he is the bastard who brought the accusation against Madeleine," Emile said.

"Then, I will take him hostage!" Jean Marc replied.

"No, Jean Marc… let Luc take him hostage. '

"You're right Emile; now is not the time for revenge."

"Luc, when you reach the Monsignor there will be many people around you. Show the crowd your gun... and let them know the first to approach you will be shot. Once I get to Madeleine and Marc, we will move swiftly toward the door at the rear. The commoners hate the inquisitors. They might even assist us in the rescue!" Jean Marc said.

Just then, the side door opened, and two guards brought a prisoner into the courtroom. Jean Marc recoiled at the sight of this badly beaten woman. He watched as she limped into the courtroom assisted by the two guards. When she got closer, he realized that it was his once beautiful wife — disfigured and lame!

Another side door opened, and a young boy was led to the prisoner.

Madeleine reached out for him. He jumped back in fright. She spoke to him, and he ran to her arms.

Emile kept a firm hand on Jean Marc's shoulder controlling his friend's emotions.

The court crier announced the entry of the inquisitors as they entered the courtroom.

"Now, Emile, now is the time... let's take advantage of the situation." Jean Marc ordered, as Emile leaped over the enclosed bar.

"Now, Luc... capture that sonavobitch!"

In a flash, Luc was at the Monsignor's side with a gun pointed at his temple. The bailiff lunged at Emile, and with one mighty blow Emile dropped him to his knees and rushed toward the inquisitors. The three ran for safety, but he was too quick and blocked their exit. He drew his knife and put it to the chief inquisitor's neck.

Jean Marc jumped the rail and rushed forward. "I'm here to take you home, Madeleine."

She gasped in disbelief at the sight of her husband.

The guards moved slowly toward the center of the courtroom just as Emile shouted, "Stand back, or I will kill the hostages!"

"Stand back!" echoed the chief inquisitor.

"Come this way... we will shield your escape!" came a voice from the crowd as the commoners formed a passage to the rear door.

Jean Marc took Madeleine in his arms and turned toward his Marc. "Come with mama and papa," he said softly to his son.

"Follow them, Monsignor," Luc said as he pushed him forward.

The Monsignor moved ahead looking for his chance to escape.

Jean Marc anxiously scanned the crowd as they moved toward the door.

Emile pushed his hostage forward keeping the knife to his back. The judge moved ahead feeling the prick of the knife.

"Burn him at the stake!" a commoner shouted.

"Burn him at the stake!" the crowd echoed.

"The witch has inflamed them," the chief inquisitor said nervously.

Emile urged him forward with still another jab of the knife to his back.

Jean Marc reached the carriage and placed Madeleine on the back seat. Marc jumped in next to her.

"Put the hostages in the carriage!" Jean Marc ordered just as he saw the Monsignor bolting from Luc's grasp.

"Let him be, Luc... we don't have the time."

Emile shoved the other hostage into the carriage.

"Move out quickly," Jean Marc hollered.

The coachman cracked the whip as the three mounted their horses and followed close behind. The Monsignor slithered back into the Castel as the crowd cheered the escape.

Chapter 59

As they reached the outskirts of Rome, they stopped to rest the horses and check on Madeleine. Jean Marc leaned over to Emile and whispered, "If the Monsignor ever steps into France again, he is going to pay for what he did to my family."

Suddenly, he turned away as he heard a terrible scream coming from inside the carriage. "What's wrong?" he shouted as he ran toward the noise.

Luc poke his head outside the carriage window and said with a sly grin, "No need to worry Jean Marc. I snapped her nose back in place. She can now breathe normally... and it looks much better."

Jean Marc peered into the carriage seeing his wife in obvious pain, "We are both scarred... but somehow we will heal together, my beautiful Madeleine."

"Our love will heal us both, Jean Marc... and it will heal our children," she said as she drew Marc to her side.

"Only if you make it out of Italy," the hostage interrupted from the dark corner of the carriage. "I am certain that at this time, the Swiss Guard is detaching a cavalry unit that will soon overtake us."

"That is why we have taken a hostage!" Jean Marc said.

"Do not deceive yourself; they will never let you leave Italy."

Jean Marc pushed away from the carriage and ordered, "Luc, take the point. Emile, stay with the carriage. I will fall back to check on the enemy. If they get too close, I will fire a warning shot. There will not be much time... so find cover and hold the hostage in full view."

Inside the carriage, Madeleine attempted to get comfortable but with every bump in the road, bolts of pain surged through her body! Her only solace was the sight of her son and the thought of Jean Marc nearby

Gray skies and light snow crept into the area. Jean Marc feared that it gave the enemy an advantage, for if visibility was poor they could spring a surprise attack, at any time.

Within a few seconds, Jean Marc vanished from sight. He waited patiently for over an hour, until he heard the beat of hooves in the distance. He planned to stay ahead of the cavalry, unobserved, for as long as possible. He moved stealthily keeping the enemy within earshot. He estimated they were only a few kilometers from his group. If they came too close, he considered setting an ambush to delay the advance. One, well aimed shot at the lead horseman would send the troops scattering and cause delay until the area was cleared.

As he arrived at a small village, he went to the common well, where he saw a man drawing water. He called to him in broken Italian.

The villager broke into a smile and said in fluent French, "Your friends watered their horses and said you were close behind. They paid me well to divert the pursuing cavalry. Something I would have done for nothing."

"But why, you are Italian?"

"I am an Italian Jew. The Pope has ordered the confiscation of our property and has confined many us to the ghetto... that is why I will help."

"The Jews have been harshly treated by the Papacy," Jean Marc said.

"Over two hundred years ago, Pope Paul IV forced the Jews of Rome into a ghetto, limiting their economic activity, and forcing them to wear yellow hats in the streets. Conditions were so harsh that within five years half the population was dead."

"History seems to be repeating itself."

Abraham nodded.

"I'm curious; do you have a plan?" Jean Marc asked.

"I will tell them that you passed through the village a few hour ago, that I directed you to a fork in the road, and told you to take the road to the left, which would lead you directly to Napoli."

"And how will that help?"

"The road to the left does not lead to Napoli but far south of the city, and there is only one way back."

Jean Marc smiled.

"Then I will ply them with my best Chianti, which will delay them as you make your escape."

"But when they find out you deceived them, they will come back and exact their revenge."

"My property has been confiscated by the pope. My wife and children are in a papal ghetto in Rome. I have nothing left but my pride. I will be prepared when they return!"

"What can you do against a unit of cavalry?"

"Go to your friends and family, Jean Marc. We both have a battle to fight… and we are not alone!"

"We are allies with a common enemy!"

"Go my brother, and wage your war… as I will soon wage mine!"

Within a few minutes, the cavalry arrived and went to the common well to water the horses and fill their canteens. The captain called out to a bystander and asked whether he had seen a carriage and its escort.

"I have, captain."

"How long ago?"

"Maybe, two hours."

"Then, we must be on our way."

"You have time: I lied to them. I told them to go left at the fork. It will be hours before they discover their mistake, and by then you will have blocked their return."

"Very commendable."

"I was just doing my duty, captain. And now, let me serve you my finest Chianti, which I have reserved for a special occasion."

The captain ordered his men to rest the horses. They were soon eating local food and drinking the fine wine from Greve.

"The village is deserted; where are the villagers?" the captain asked.

"Some are caring for the livestock... others are in the ghetto in Rome," he responded.

"Ah yes, the Jews. This pope is not as tolerant of the Jews as was Pius, his predecessor," the captain responded.

"Yes, but Pius was intolerant of the Protestants and the Freemasons."

"What is your name by the way?" the captain asked.

"Abraham... "

"Ah, an Italian Jew," the captain interrupted. "And when will you be going to the ghetto?"

"Whenever you take me, captain!"

"I am a professional soldier... it makes no difference to me if you are a Jew, a Protestant, or a Freemason. Unless, that is, you hamper my mission. So far, you have been very helpful... you have foiled the enemy, and you have been a gracious host."

"Shall I bring you another bottle of Chianti, captain?"

"Maybe, one more Abraham."

Once he had finished the wine, the captain ordered the unit to mount up. The drunk and disgruntled soldiers responded slowly. "We have a f-few h-hours of daylight l-left, then we will c-camp for the night. We, we must b-block the road before they r-return!" the captain slurred.

Abraham watched the soldiers depart from the village — unruly and undisciplined. *I have delayed their advance by half a day. Tonight, they will head in the wrong direction, and by the grace of God, my friends will make it back to France — certainly not the god of the popes but maybe the Jewish-Christian God!*

Chapter 60

On Christmas day, Michel took the children to the studio. "I have presents for the both of you."

"When can we see them?" Angeline asked anxiously.

"Here for you, Angeline," he said as he handed here a perfectly sculptured miniature angel."

"Did you make it, Michel?" she asked

"Yes, just for you, Angeline."

She smiled precociously and took the sculpture to a table to admire it."

"Come with me, Jean… your present is unfinished," he said as he pointed to the floor of his workshop..

"A block of marble?"

"It is what is inside that is your present."

"You will sculpt it for me?"

"No, Jean. You will sculpt it with these tools," he said as he handed Jean a hammer and chisel.

"But how, Michel?'

"First, your mind must imagine what is inside. Then, your hands must bring it out. And, finally, your heart must make it glow."

Jean turned to Michel and hugged him with all his might.

"Joyeux Noel, Jean… et Joyeux Noel, Angeline!"

The Monsignor wasted little time in making preparations to return from Rome. The Papal Curia was disturbed by the escape of the witch but impressed by the Monsignor's courage in the face of adversity, and was more than willing to help him return to Notre Dame.

"We will provide an escort for you to Paris," the papal aide informed him.

"And the witch, what will happen to her?" the

Monsignor asked.

"The civil authorities at our request issued arrest warrants for her and the accomplices. The warrants are not valid in France, but it will lend some legitimacy to our order of excommunication."

"We may not be able to keep her out of France, but we can certainly keep her out of Heaven!" the Monsignor responded wryly.

"Louis XVIII supports the Catholic Church, and it will soon regain its former glory. When that happens, the Church will need strong leaders like you."

"Thank you," the Monsignor said with a grin.

"And along with the other documents, there is a letter of commendation reflecting your dedication to the Church in combating heresy. May God be with you."

Jean Marc waited for the cavalry to reach the fork to make sure they fell for the deception set by Abraham. Once he saw them take the road to the left, he spurred his horse to catch up to his friends.

It would be his first night with Madeleine in nearly two years. He knew he had little time, for they still had to escape from Italy. *Madeleine is badly battered, but she is free of her tormentors. Marc is emotionally scared, but will heal with the love of his family,* he thought.

As he arrived at the campsite, all were eager to learn what happened. "They fell for the trap set by Abraham, but they will not take this lying down. Once they sober up and realize they have been duped, they will return to the village to find Abraham… and then they will come after us with a vengeance. Let us sleep for a few hours and then be on our way."

"What is our plan if they catch up to us?" Emile asked.

"I will continue as the rearguard and give a warning as they approach. That will give you time to find high ground for our defense!"

"And time to place our hostage in an open and exposed position!" Luc added.

The inquisitor squirmed and asked Jean Marc, "When will you let me go?"

"When we are safely in France."

"And only after we conduct an inquisition of your past actions... giving you due process of course!" Luc added, bringing a muffled laughter from the group and angst to the inquisitor.

As the moon rose, Jean Marc walked to the carriage to be with Madeleine. He entered and checked on Marc, who was already sound asleep. He delighted in his son for a few moments, the light of a full moon shining on his face. He then turned toward Madeleine, and saw a faint smile on her face.

"Can it be that our family will be together once again?" she asked softly.

He looked beyond her battered face and knew that it was her kind heart and warm love that he had missed the most — and it was such a joy to have her by his side. They talked about their separation and the children. And he longed to take her in his arms.

Sensing his feelings, she said, "Hold me Jean Marc, but be gentle and in time we will recapture our intimacy."

He gently kissed her forehead, her swollen eyelids, and her broken nose. She put an arm around him and squeezed gently. "We will make love again soon, Jean Marc."

The next day, the cavalry unit broke camp to continue their pursuit of the rebels. Within a few miles, they arrived at a village, and the captain inquired as to the passage of a carriage and its escort. When he was told that no carriage had come through the village in days, he realized he had been duped by the Jew. Anger flowed through his veins as the cavalry retraced its steps to the fork in the road.

"Sergeant, take two squads and burn the village and be sure to kill the Jew. Join us when you have accomplished your mission," the captain ordered. "I will pursue the rebels with the remaining squads."

"First and second squads, follow me," the sergeant commanded.

Throwing caution to the wind, they approached the village at full gallop and funneled into a narrow path between two small slopes. Instantly, bullets rained down upon them from left and right. Instinctively, they spurred the horses to get beyond the killing field. The few that survived turned and charged the slopes.

"Shoot the horses!" Abraham ordered.

The horses fell, and the riders stumbled to the ground.

"Charge!" Abraham yelled.

The villagers overran the dazed cavalrymen and quickly slaughtered them. The battle lasted only a few minutes, the Swiss unit completely annihilated.

Abraham surveyed the battle scene, and said gravely, "Let us now go to Rome and free our families from the papal ghetto!"

Jean Marc awakened his motley group early the next morning, "Eat quickly and let's be on our way!" he ordered.

Luc tied his horse behind the carriage and jumped inside. "I will wrap your broken arm in a sling to keep it still and to ease the pain during the rough ride," he said to Madeleine.

When he was done, he turned to the inquisitor and said, "I am a little confused."

"Confused about what?" he asked.

"About the role of priests in our society?"

"A priest's primary responsibility is the salvation of souls."

"And why is that so difficult?" Luc persisted.

"Because it is only through the Church and its priests that men and women can find God!"

"It sounds like you are playing God!" Luc said as he paused to collect his thoughts. "But bear with me, Father, I have a different view of the role the clergy."

The priest waited impatiently for Luc to continue.

"Jesus left us with a very simple message, *Love God and love thy neighbor*. If the clergy adhered to this simple message it would reach out to the Jews, who have been persecuted for centuries; it would be tolerant of Protestants, who brought reforms to a corrupt Church; and it would treat women as equals, who are as capable as men, all as Jesus envisaged."

The priest did not respond.

"Love God and love thy neighbor," Luc repeated. "However, it is not this message of love that the clergy is spreading but, rather, one of persecution, intolerance and bigotry."

"That is blasphemy!" the priest retorted. "And what legacy will soldiers like you leave?"

"I have been a soldier all of my adult life. I now view war as mankind's worst creation. But within this framework, I was able to do some good as a medic. I saved many from death; I mended their ghastly wounds, and I consoled the dying. However, I now realize that war is evil, and I will spend the rest of my life opposing war." He paused for a few seconds and continued. "You should realize that the Church has lost its way... and you should spend the rest of your life opposing persecution, intolerance and bigotry."

"Blasphemy... blasphemy! I will remember your words when you are judged by my Tribunal!"

"And my only defense will be the simple message

of Jesus: *Love God and love thy neighbor.*"

Chapter 61

As dawn broke, it was not only the enemy that Jean Marc worried about but also the weather. As he looked to the west, he saw storm clouds gathering. Soon the pouring rain made the travel more difficult. The center of the road was solid, but the sides were muddied and rutted. The carriage edged toward the mud whenever it encountered oncoming traffic.

Progress was slow, and Jean Marc worried about the papal troops catching up to them. His training as a soldier made him prepare for any eventuality. At this time, he knew speed was critical, and he thought of abandoning the carriage and using the four horses to carry the passengers. But he knew Madeleine could not endure a long journey on horseback.

He dropped back, still not seeing pursuing soldiers in the distance and feeling more optimistic with the passing of time. The rain let up around noon, and he thought it safe to return to the convoy to check on its progress. He was chagrined when he spotted the carriage off to the side of the road.

"What happened?" he hollered as he approached the carriage at full gallop. "A wheel fell off, Jean Marc," came Emile's reply

"Can it be fixed?"

"Yes, but it will take time."

"Was anybody hurt?"

"No… but Marc was scared. Madeleine is trying to console him." Emile said.

Jean Marc jumped off his horse and rushed to the carriage — reassured of their well being when both smiled timidly.

With the help of a nearby farmer the wheel was repaired within a few hours. They had lost valuable time, and Jean Marc did not know how to make it up!

"Luc, drive the horses as hard as you can. We are nearing the port of Napoli, and the papal soldiers cannot be far behind."

"The horses are still strong, and I will push them hard. We are too close to our destination to see our escape turn to dust!" Luc responded.

Jean Marc ordered Luc to lead the way as he dropped back to ascertain the proximity of the cavalry.

He positioned himself at an elevated spot in the road where he could see to the east nearly two kilometers. His spirits rose as time passed with no sight of the enemy. But, in a split second, his spirits plummeted when he saw a band of horsemen crest a hill riding at full gallop. He turned his horse and fled in the direction from where he came. He made a quick calculation and feared the enemy would soon catch up to them.

"Push the men harder, sergeant."

"But captain, they've been driving hard all day... they're hungry, thirsty, and tired," the sergeant responded.

"They will eat, drink, and rest once we capture the witch and her collaborators. Entice them with a reward if we intercept them before they sail for France."

"That's what they need to hear, captain... they will sacrifice food, water, and sleep in exchange for a bounty."

The grueling ride was having its effect on Madeleine. Even though she did not complain, Luc knew she was in intense pain. He ordered the coachman to stop to give her a respite from the arduous journey. She exited the carriage slowly while gripping the door. On the ground, she steadied her weakened legs and tried to catch her breath. She was scantily dressed for the winter, and the cold penetrated her frail body.

"We have to slow down for Madeleine's sake," Luc

told Emile.

"But we have our orders!"

"Madeleine is in pain... she cannot survive at this pace!"

"Then we will slow down!"

Jean Marc was back and forth between the two groups. He dropped back until he saw the enemy, and then moved ahead to determine the distance between the two. The gap was shrinking, and he was now certain they would be overtaken before reaching Napoli.

Jean Marc understood cavalry tactics. He had fought both with and against these charging units. They were trained to fight on horseback, to be mobile, to terrify, to overrun, and to overwhelm. *On level ground the large warhorses will crush our defensive position. We must find terrain to our advantage — a hill, a stream, a gulley, a wall — anything to slow them down,* he thought as he rushed off to join his friends.

When he arrived, he ordered the carriage to increase its speed and directed it to the top of the steep hill, which stood ahead of them. As they reached the top, he led the carriage to the rear, to protect Madeleine and Marc.

"Can you fire a gun?" Jean Marc asked the coachman and the handmaiden.

"No," the coachman answered for both of them.

"Then, come with us to the large boulders at the crest of the hill and reload the guns as we fire them." He looked to the west and to his amazement the Bay of Naples was in sight — the ships and the port were in full view. *We are so close but yet so far!* he thought just as he turned to see the oncoming cavalry.

The cavalrymen stopped at the bottom of the hill to survey the situation. They looked intimidating on their huge warhorses, fully armed and uniformed.

The captain raised his saber, pointing it to the sky,

in preparation of the order to charge. The cavalrymen unsheathed their sabers pointing them directly at their foe.

Chapter 62

Jean Marc looked around and saw Emile and Luc both ready to die for his family, the coachman and the maidservant, too young to die, Madeleine writhing in pain, Marc quivering with fear, and the inquisitor with a smirk on his face. Jean Marc peered at the enemy cavalrymen, their sabers unheathed, the warhorses restless, the captain ready to order the charge.

"Luc, bring the hostage to the front," Jean Marc ordered.

The captain watched from below as the hostage was brought to an exposed position. "Take care not to harm the hostage as we charge the enemy," the captain ordered.

We are about to be slaughtered, Jean Marc thought.

"Wave the white flag... we will surrender... our fate is now in the hands of God!" Jean Marc shouted as he stood up waving a white rag he had taken from his pocket.

The captain hesitated in ordering the charge, apparently not wanting to ignore the universal sign of surrender but sensing his men were now hungering for the kill.

No one moved. Then all eyes turned to the clatter of approaching horses from Napoli. A military unit was trotting in their direction in their bright uniforms of yellow and green. Each horseman armed with a long lance held in his right hand, all pointing to the sky. Each soldier riding a magnificent warhorse, all in perfect cadence.

Jean Marc lowered the white flag.

The captain lowered and sheathed his saber as the unit crested the hill. His soldiers followed suit.

The intruding unit broke ranks going to either side of the carriage and coming to a halt in perfect formation between the cavalrymen and Jean Marc's group.

At the head of the unit, an officer addressed the

captain. "I am Major Paulo Thomaso."

Madeleine gasped upon hearing the familiar name.

"You are in the Kingdom of the Two Sicilies. You are an army without authority to be on our sovereign soil. I will consider you to be invaders unless you discard your weapons."

"I am Captain Remy of the Swiss Guard... "

Upon the command of the major, all the lances were lowered to an assault position and aimed directly at the outmanned Swiss cavalry. "There will be no discussion until your arms are surrendered," the major barked out.

The captain looked back but caught no sight of his missing squads. He knew it was foolish to resist. He ordered his unit to comply. The soldiers disarmed and dropped their weapons to the ground.

"Now get down from the horses!" the major ordered.

The cavalrymen dismounted standing to the front of their horses.

"Now captain, tell me why you violated our soil without following proper diplomatic protocol!"

"We are here at the direction of the pope to capture an escaped prisoner and her accomplices," the captain said.

"And what was the prisoner charged with?"

"Charged with and tried for the heresy of witchcraft," the captain responded.

"Witchcraft... that is a myth of the Middle Ages," the major rejoined harshly.

The captain remained silent.

"Where is this person charged with witchcraft?" the major asked.

The captain pointed to the carriage, "She is Madeleine Moreau."

"Madeleine Moreau, come to the front of my squadron!" the major ordered.

"She can barely walk, sir," came the response from

Jean Marc.

"Then carry her to me."

Emile went to Madeleine's side. She winced as he picked her up. He carried her to the front of the squadron.

The major looked down and cringed at the sight of the mutilated body. "Who would be so cruel as to mutilate a human being in this manner?" he asked.

The inquisitor slouched, fearful that he would be identified.

"The Inquisition in its search of truth and the elimination of heresy," the captain responded.

"The heresies of the Church are as mythical as witchcraft," the major responded sarcastically.

"The Grand Inquisitor is in the carriage!" Jean Marc declared.

"And who are you?" the major asked.

"I am her husband."

"Bring the inquisitor to me," the major ordered.

Luc grabbed the inquisitor and pushed him to stand in front of the major.

"So you are the one who had this poor woman tortured."

"Only to rid the Church of a heresy and help her find salvation," he replied.

"I am not a priest... but as I look upon this poor soul, I am convinced that you and others like you have forsaken both the teachings and the spirit of Christ."

He then turned to the captain, "I am not here to judge the actions of the pope, the Church, or its priests but it seems to me that unlike Jesus who was filled with love and forgiveness they are consumed by hatred and vengeance."

The inquisitor said nothing.

"But, unfortunately, I am here only to protect the sovereignty of the Kingdom of the Two Sicilies. I will escort you and your prisoners from our kingdom. Leave your weapons, mount your horses, take your prisoners, and let us take our leave!"

"Wait… " came a weak call.

The major looked down at Madeleine.

"Ask the inquisitor the whereabouts of Father Thomaso," she said.

Shock came to the face of the major and fear came to the face of the inquisitor as the name of Father Thomaso was spoken.

"I have no knowledge of his whereabouts!" the inquisitor responded quavering with fear.

"Ask him how much time he spent in the darkest part of the dungeon."

The major looked harshly at the inquisitor, awaiting a response.

"I… I… have no knowledge of that… "

"Ask him how many times he was taken to the torture chamber because of his belief that women should be treated as equals," she persisted.

"He always spoke strongly of the role and strength of women," the major said as he stared coldly at the inquisitor.

"Ask him how Father Thomaso died in the dungeon!"

The major shuddered. "We have been looking for him for weeks but in Paris not Rome, because we were told by a papal aide that he had returned to Paris. Please tell me that my dear brother is not dead!"

"Ask him why they threw his ravaged body in the Tiber River," she said, now nearly breathless.

"Speak up! You are the Grand Inquisitor. You bear some responsibility in the fate of my brother! Does this woman speak the truth?" the major glowered.

"I had no involvement in your brother's death… I played no role in his torture… and I have no knowledge whether his body is in the Tiber," the inquisitor said defensively.

No one spoke. The major looked to the heavens, tears rolling down his cheeks.

"Captain, you and your men will be taken to prison. You will be charged with invading our kingdom. And, if you are convicted, you will be executed!"

"And the Grand Inquisitor?" Madeleine asked.

"I have done nothing wrong! I did not invade your kingdom… I am not to blame for your brother's death!" the inquisitor pleaded.

"Your crime is worse than that of the invading force; you will soon find out whether Dante was right when he said, 'the darkest places in hell are reserved for those who maintain their neutrality in times of moral crisis'!"

"What shall we do with the woman and her friends?" a lieutenant asked.

"I will escort them to my father's palace where she can heal from the wounds unjustly inflicted upon her. And, sadly, we will break the news to my father that his beloved son is dead."

Chapter 63

Michel saw the children on a daily basis. He was at the mansion waiting for them as they returned from school. On most days, he took them to his studio where they played and grew closer to him

Jean's block of marble was taking shape as he worked deftly under Michel's tutelage. When Angeline tired of playing, she would join them to watch her brother break off chips of marble.

"Would you like to learn?" Michel asked her.

"Can girls sculpt?" she asked.

"But, of course, Angeline, girls can sculpt as well as boys, but they are not given the opportunity."

"What is opportunity?" she asked.

"Let's see," he said as he paused to think of an example. "If I give you a block of marble and the tools, that is an opportunity."

"Can I have an opportunity?"

"I have many blocks of marble at the rear of the studio. Let's go find one," he said as they walked toward the marble.

"When will Mama return?" she asked.

Soon, very soon, I hope."

"Will we go for our picnics in the park when she returns?"

"Here are the blocks of marble... pick the one you like," Michel said, hoping to get her mind off the picnics.

"I would like this one, Michel," she said as she pointed to one of the smaller blocks.

"It's a small block, but the marble is pure. What do you see within the marble?'

"Another angel, Michel."

"Let me bring it to the front of the studio for you."

Michel noticed a curious look on Jean's face when

he placed the block of marble next to his. "It's for your sister... she would like to learn to sculpt."

Satisfied with the answer, Jean returned to chipping away at the marble.

On Sunday of that week, Michel brought the children to church at Notre Dame. They sat in Madame LeBlanc's pew, which was still held by her estate. During mass, Angeline tapped Michel's arm to get his attention and whispered in his ear, "I am praying so that Mama will join us for our picnic today."

Michel nodded and smiled.

Before the homily, the bishop came up to the pulpit, "Official documents were recently delivered to me from Rome. The Monsignor received a letter of commendation from the pope for his courageous effort in combating heresy. And the Papal Curia issued a warrant of arrest and a writ of excommunication for the witch, Madeleine Moreau."

A murmur rippled through the cavernous church. Michel looked at both children, who were not paying attention. Disgusted at the bishop, he rose and led the children out of church, as he heard the whispers from the congregation.

In the hospitable ambience of the palace, Madeleine's fear faded, her physical condition improved, and her emotions stabilized. A physician tended to her medical needs and the companionship of Jean Marc and her son caused her spirits to soar.

She settled into a daily routine as the discoloration and puffiness of her face faded, the damaged muscles of her body strengthened, and her broken shoulder set in a splint mended. Every morning she went to the chapel spellbound by the sculpture of the Veiled Jesus. *The wounds on his feet and hands, the sunken side, the crown of* *thorns all symbolize the suffering of Christ for the redemption of humanity, s*he thought. *But what did the transparent veil symbolize?*

One morning as she prayed near the sculpture, Lorenzo Thomaso entered the chapel. "I come here often to grieve the death of my son, where I find some solace and some peace." He paused, ostensibly reflecting on the memory of his son. "He became a priest because of me... I thought that eventually he would be named as a cardinal of the Church... a Church he was not very fond of but one he wanted to reform."

"In what way, Monsieur Thomaso?"

"He was troubled by the destruction of documents tracing the history of women as priests, bishops, and leaders in the early Christian communities and women being an integral part in the spread of Christianity for nearly three centuries. But when Christianity became the religion of Rome, the male leaders demanded the same subjugation of women in the Church as prevailed in Roman society."

"Apparently, women were not only fighting against the men in the Church but also in Roman society," Madeleine said.

"The women leaders quoted Scripture for support...'In Christ there is no male or female.'"

"St. Paul, I believe." Madeleine commented.

"Nonetheless, the male clergy cited other scriptural passages to support their position."

"Sounds to me like it is still an open question!"

"The controversy persisted until the year 493 when Pope Gelasius issued an edict prohibiting the further ordination of women."

"What did the edict say?"

"I have my son's notes here in the chapel, wait just a moment," he said as he went to a drawer by the altar.

"Yes, here are his notes. The edict issued by

Gelasius reads, in part: 'Nevertheless, we have heard to our annoyance that divine affairs have come to such a low state that women are encouraged to officiate at the sacred altars, and to take part in all matters imputed to the male sex, to which they do not belong."

"Very chauvinistic," Madeleine commented.

"Not only did it prohibit the ordination of women, it also condemned the bishops who ordained women."

"It sounds like the ordination of women was widespread," Madeleine commented.

"Otherwise, the pope would not have issued an edict condemning the practice."

"And, obviously, the edict served the purpose of excluding women from the priesthood," Madeleine rejoined.

"But not overnight, Madeleine. Women priests continued for many centuries but gradually they lost their status as equal partners... and sadly, the Church's prejudice against women prevailed."

Madeleine turned her attention to the statue of the Veiled Christ.

"It is an incredible sculpture. As you walk from Christ's feet to his head, notice how the expression on Jesus' face goes from suffering to peace." Lorenzo remarked.

"While the teachings of the Church have gone from peace to suffering!"

"My son was fond of saying that the suffering will continue until the veil of hypocrisy is lifted."

As he walked from the chapel with a heavy step, his words echoed in her mind. *The suffering will continue until the veil of hypocrisy is lifted.*

Chapter 64

"As you leave us Madeleine, let us pray that at some point in time, the Church will view the intelligence and capability of women as equal to that of men, which would vindicate the death of my son and your suffering," Lorenzo said as his guests prepared to leave for France. "Your physical scars have healed well, but I fear that the emotional ones will haunt both of our families for some time to come."

"The rage that burns within me is subsiding because of the love and understanding your family has shown us. I can only imagine the change that would have come to the Church had your son become a cardinal."

As the two embraced, they somehow knew that Thomas' spirit would not die — he had given his life for the sake of a better Church.

She entered the carriage with Marc and the maidservant. Luc and Emile took the lead and Jean Marc soon joined them. "For the first time in many years, I need not worry about the enemy behind us!" Jean Marc told his friends.

They nodded their assent.

"I have seen enough bloodshed and suffering for a lifetime. I never want to see another battle. And I hope my children will grow up in a peaceful world."

"Bless you," Emile said.

"I am married to a extraordinary woman and want to spend the rest of my life with her — while putting behind me my time as a soldier."

It was the start of a new year and Madeleine was anxious to return to Paris, both to settle her affairs and settle in with her family. But she took advantage of the time she had with Jean Marc. In the evening, the carriage was their domain. Their conversations would last long into the night — some happy and some sad.

Whenever Jean Marc fell asleep before her, she observed him sleeping fitfully often waking up in a cold sweat. She questioned him about this, but he shrugged it off, merely saying that his nightmares would soon subside. She had nightmares of her own but was not as certain they would soon subside. Fortunately, now they could comfort each other. "We will have to be strong for the children, but during our private moments we must confide our fears to each other." Madeleine advised Jean Marc.

After the second day of travel in France, she told him of her relationship with Michel Bois, how they had met, his bond with the children, his talents as a sculptor, and the kindness of his soul.

He was quiet for a long time. "I cannot deny feeling pangs of jealousy, but I was away for nearly two years while he was there for you and our children."

"Yes, he was... "

"Is he still in Paris?' he interrupted.

"No, he volunteered to fight with Napoleon at Waterloo."

"As an enlisted man?"

"No, as an officer... a major, I believe."

"How did you meet him?"

"Whether it was a twist of fate or loneliness that brought us together is not important. What is important is my love for you, which will get us beyond this."

He longed to take her in his arms and make love to her. But at that moment they heard the call, "Mama, Papa come outside and play," from their son, Marc.

In Paris, the Monsignor's favor with the Bishop of Paris rose meteorically. He was lauded for exposing a heretic within the clergy and obtaining an indictment of witchcraft against Madeleine Moreau. *Now, the Church stands to gain a vast inheritance from the LeBlanc estate,* the Monsignor thought, prideful in what he had accomplished and exuberant about his future.

He shared the hardline conservative views of the Church that opposed the changes of the modern world; and he worked closely with the bishop to revive the blind orthodoxy of the past by appointing conservative priest, to perpetuate the disdain for both women and modernism.

"Monsignor, I have good news!" the bishop said.

"Does it concern our proposal to divide the LeBlanc estate evenly between the Church and the King?"

"Yes, it has been accepted by the king. Now it need only be approved by the court."

"Our timing is perfect. The case is scheduled for a hearing tomorrow," the Monsignor added. "And, Madeleine Moreau is not in Paris."

"Who is the judge?"

"With both the Church and the King behind the effort, it really does not matter who presides over the case!"

"But Madame LeBlanc's last will and testament names Madeleine Moreau as the sole heir to her estate?"

"Our petition alleges that Madeleine Moreau coerced Madame LeBlanc to sign her last will and testament; and, we have witnesses who will corroborate that!" the Monsignor responded.

"God works in mysterious ways… and apparently he will deny a heretic of this vast inheritance… and reward the Church for its good actions!" the bishop said.

"And what will the people of Paris think of this turn of events?"

"Time will serve to dull their memory… like so many other matters in our history!"

Chapter 65

They arrived in Paris early in the morning. Jean Marc's soul was haunted by the thoughts of war. He constantly worried about the wounded and forsaken veterans. He had heard that many injured soldiers were in *l'Hopital des Invalides* and many more were beggars on the streets of Paris. The primary purpose of *l'Hopital* was as a retirement home for veterans who had served in the military twenty years or more. But now it served mainly as a hospital for sick and wounded soldiers, with many discharged prematurely because of the large numbers awaiting treatment. And, once released from the hospital, no provisions were made for them.

"Then let us go directly to *l'Hopital des Invalides,*" Madeleine insisted after Jean Marc expressed his concerns to her.

Depression set in as they walked through the halls of the hospital: The hundreds of mutilated bodies waiting to die with hundreds more walking the halls aimlessly, oblivious to the world beyond them. Others confined in locked and padded rooms, for their safety and the safety of others. "I saw so many maimed and wounded on the fields of battle but never gave much thought to their lives afterwards — this is the real tragedy of war!" he said somberly.

"Not so sergeant," replied the attendant who was accompanying them. "They are cared for in the hospital. They receive treatment, food and shelter. If you want to see the real tragedies of war, walk the streets of Paris!"

"But the government has to provide for them." Madeleine said.

"The government's policy is to let them rot in the streets… the thought is that in ten, twenty, or thirty years they will all be dead and then the streets of Paris will be clean again. That is their dastardly policy... the veterans are treated like trash... when they die, they are tossed in a common burial pit... that is what our veteran soldiers can expect on the streets of Paris."

"That is my nightmare Madeleine... that is my recurring nightmare. How can I rest when my brothers are suffering?"

"Come Jean Marc let us go to the streets of Paris. Let us see for ourselves the suffering of your brothers."

It was a sunless day, the sky full of low, gray clouds. Within a few blocks of the hospital they saw crippled soldiers roaming the streets panhandling for food and money, many on crutches, some in wheelchairs, and others slumped on the sidewalks with a cup beside them.

One called out to him, "Sergeant, you saved my life in Italy! Do you remember?"

"I believe I do, corporal," he responded as he placed a coin in the soldier's cup.

"Merci... merci, sergeant," he said as Jean Marc and Madeleine walked away.

"Sergeant!" the wounded soldier called.

Madeleine and Jean Marc turned to the soldier

"You should have let me die!"

As they turned the corner, the situation worsened. Peddlers were everywhere. Madeleine and Jean Marc sat against a building next to a legless man. "Don't sit too close to me," he said. "I haven't taken a bath in months."

Nonetheless, they sat next to him, the stench of urine and feces filling their nostrils.

"How do you survive?" Jean Marc asked.

"I sit here during the day and beg for coins. When night comes, I crawl into that alley to sleep."

Madeleine rose and stepped into the alley. "There are nothing but rags there," she said.

"That is my bed, Madame!"

"What do you eat?" Jean Marc asked.

"If I have a few coins, I buy cheese and a baguette... if not, I trap rats and cook them."

Madeleine looked away.

Noticing her cringe, he added: "You know the French Madame, we can make anything taste good!" he said with a sly grin.

She returned his smile.

"And sometimes, when I have a really good day, I pay a prostitute. She bathes me and..." he stopped in mid-sentence, not wanting to embarrass Madeleine.

"Do you ever think of... "

"Of killing myself. Yes, every day," the beggar responded.

"And what stops you?" Madeleine asked.

"God... God does. You see, I believe in God and I believe in heaven. I will suffer today in return for an eternity in heaven."

A few yards away, a man started to play an accordion.

"What is that?" Madeleine asked.

"That is the sound of money."

"The sound of money?" Jean Marc inquired.

"When he plays he brings attention to us... and people toss coins in our cups. Just wait and see."

As he had predicted, the people walking by tossed coins in their direction.

"Sonofabitch!" the beggar exclaimed, obviously agitated.

"What's the matter?" Jean Marc asked.

"Watch the *Brute*!" he said pointing to a beast of a man picking up the coins from the walkway. "The bastard always robs us of our coins."

"Why do you put up with it?" Jean Marc asked.

"Are you fucking blind... look around, we are a bunch of cripples!"

The music stopped. Groans could be heard up the

street as the *Brute* picked up the coins. After he was done, the *Brute* took his place at the head of the street, waiting for more coins to be tossed by those passing by.

What kind of man would steal money from crippled veterans? Jean Marc thought as he stood and walked in the direction of the *Brute*.

All eyes were upon him. *What was this stranger doing in their neighborhood?*

Jean Marc spoke a few words to the *Brute* and both walked into the alley. A cold arrow of fear pierced Madeleine's heart as she realized what might happen — as did the beggars on the street. Moments later, Jean Marc reappeared. He placed the coins in the cup of the accordion player. "Distribute these as you see fit!" he said.

Jean Marc returned to Madeleine's side. "What is your name?" he asked the beggar.

"Albert... Albert, Sergeant."

"The home of brave soldiers will not be defiled again, Albert," he said as he walked away holding Madeleine's hand.

"Merci... merci, sergeant."

Madeleine looked over her shoulder but saw no sign of the *Brute* coming from the alley.

Chapter 66

Still haunted by their visit of the streets of Paris, Madeleine and Jean Marc rushed to the LeBlanc residence. As the gate opened, Madeleine saw Jean running down the drive to greet them. She noticed that Angeline was holding back — holding tightly to Michel's hand. Jean Marc grabbed his son and twirled him around, like he was a feather. He put him down, looked up the drive and motioned for his daughter to come to him.

She resisted and held on to Michel's hand more tightly.

He moved toward her as Madeleine watched from behind. Angeline let go of Michel's hand and ran by Jean Marc to her mother's side.

Jean Marc continued to walk toward Michel.

Madeleine watched helplessly as the gap between the two warriors shrunk. They stood face-to-face, neither blinking. It was a moment in time when lives could be changed forever.

Jean Marc reached into his tunic and pulled out a knife. Madeleine screamed and Michel jumped back.

Jean Marc paused for what seemed like an eternity then threw the knife to the ground. He opened his arms, and the two proud men embraced.

Seated at the Plaintiff's table were the agents of the king and bishop and their barristers. The Monsignor represented the bishop, and a senior aide represented the king. Seated at the Defendant's table were Monsieur l'Heureux and another barrister.

The courtroom was crowded as the trial went into its final day. The Plaintiffs rested their case. Their witnesses had testified that Madame Leblanc was coerced by Madeleine Moreau to change her last will and testament.

The credibility of the witnesses was questionable — but there was little evidence to rebut their testimony.

Monsieur L'Heureux had worked tirelessly on the case since Madeleine's departure. He was drained of energy and weakened by his adversaries' onslaught. He was listless as he testified to Jeannette LeBlanc signing her will and swearing that it was her free act and deed before two witnesses; however, his testimony lacked conviction. When cross-examined, he admitted that the witnesses to the signing had mysteriously disappeared.

The Monsignor sat sanctimoniously at the plaintiffs' table, and when he heard the witnesses to the will could not be located, he leaned over to the barrister and whispered, "We have done our work well!"

The barrister nodded his assent.

The trial nearing its end, the judge focused on the defendant's table. "Call your next witness," the judge ordered.

Monsieur l'Heureux clearly understood that without further evidence, the judge would find for the plaintiffs, and the LeBlanc estate would escheat to the king, who had agreed to share the windfall with the bishop.

"If we could have a short recess, your honor?" the defendant asked.

"The court will adjourn for an hour. When we return the defense will either call another witness or rest its case!" the judge ordered.

The judge had been appointed to the bench by Napoleon's regime and was one of the few remaining judges from that era. *He has been impartial during the trial and will be objective in his decision. But we have not presented enough evidence for him to decide in our favor,* Monsieur l'Heureux concluded.

The sound of the gavel took him suddenly back to the reality of the courtroom.

"What is the pleasure of the defense?" the judge

inquired, following the recess.

"The defense moves the court to continue the trial for one week, your honor!"

"We object, your honor." came the cry from the bishop's barrister.

"Objection sustained," the judge responded immediately.

"But, your honor… "

"Call your next witness," the judge interrupted.

"We do not have another witness, your honor!"

"Then rest your case, counsel!"

Monsieur l'Heureux was feeling that he had an ethical responsibility to bring out the truth, but he was powerless to do so. "Tell the judge that the defense rests it case," he told his barrister.

At that moment, loud voices were heard coming from outside the courtroom.

"I don't give a damn if the court is in session!" came the muffled sound from the lobby. "Open the door!" the judge ordered.

"All eyes turned toward the rear of the courtroom."

"I object, your honor, the defense must rest!" the bishop's barrister bellowed.

All eyes returned to the judge.

"Open the door to the courtroom," the judge repeated — obviously enjoying the drama.

Jean Marc Moreau and Michel Bois entered the courtroom followed by Madeleine Moreau.

The Monsignor gasped at the sight of his nemesis.

Monsieur L'Heureux swung open the bar door and escorted her to the witness stand.

She walked with a noticeable limp, and her left arm hung unnaturally by her side.

"The defendant calls Madeleine Moreau to the stand, your honor!" the barrister said with a newfound firmness to his voice.

"We object, your honor," came the response from the plaintiff's table.

"Objection overruled," the judge ruled.

Once sworn in, her eyes locked in on the Monsignor.

He stared back defiantly.

"Madame Moreau, were you tried for the heresy of witchcraft?" the barrister asked.

"I was arrested and tried by a papal court in Rome."

"And what happened?"

"During the trial, I was freed by a few brave soldiers, thus escaping the wrath of Rome."

"Objection, your honor. I move that this witness be returned to Rome to be tried for the heresy of witchcraft!" the bishop's barrister moved.

"Unlike you, I do not believe she came in on a broom," the judge responded, provoking laughter from the gallery. "France and most of Europe have dismissed this myth of witchcraft — but the Church perpetuates it for the sole purpose of demeaning women. Furthermore, this court does not recognize the jurisdiction of the papal courts in these matters. The objection is overruled, you may continue," he directed the defendant's barrister.

"Tell us of your relationship with Madame LeBlanc," the barrister urged.

Madeleine Moreau felt a strong emotion for Madame LeBlanc but feared she was not capable of expressing it well. Nonetheless, she brushed aside her doubts while reminding herself that so much depended on her testimony. With a trembling voice, she described the kindness Madame LeBlanc had shown her family at their first encounter at Notre Dame; and, when Madame LeBlanc discovered Madeleine was her niece, how they became a family. And, even though, Madame LeBlanc embraced Michel Bois and became a sponsor of his artwork, she encouraged her to continue the search for Jean Marc

Moreau, knowing that her soul would remain restless until she learned the truth.

She paused to catch her breath and then testified about the business ventures they had planned, including, the expansion of the vineyards in Bordeaux and the special grape they would introduce to their winemaking.

As her testimony wore on, her voice lost its quaver and gained in strength, up until she related the events of that fateful Sunday, when Madame LeBlanc died in the arms of her son, Jean.

"Tell us about the accusation of witchcraft that was brought against you," the barrister said.

She testified that upon the death of Madame LeBlanc, her journey took an unexpected turn, as rumors of heresy and witchcraft sabotaged her life; and, how the Monsignor abducted Marc, in order to induce her to Rome.

"Do you need to rest?" the judge interrupted.

"No, I can continue, your honor," she responded.

She spoke of the journey to Rome and of her concern for the safety of her son.

"How old was he?" the judge asked.

"Marc was six, your honor."

She testified about her incarceration, the torture of prisoners and the death of Father Thomas. She talked more about the suffering of others then she did of her own torment.

"Tell the court what they did to you, Madeleine," the barrister urged.

As she described the torture that was exacted upon her, some left the courtroom appalled by the brutality, others contorted in their seats sickened by the wickedness of the Church, but still others sat stoically — seemingly condoning these horrific acts.

"Did you confess to the accusation?" the judge asked.

"No, not right away, your honor!"

"Then when... when did you confess to the accusation," he persisted.

"When they threatened to torture my son... that is when I confessed. I would have confessed to anything to protect him!" she said as she completed her testimony.

"Cross examination by the Plaintiff?" the judge asked.

"Tear into her, make her out to be a liar, show her to be a heretic and a witch," insisted the Monsignor.

The barrister rose, anxious to attack her credibility.

Madeleine braced herself for the onslaught.

The Monsignor yearned for her impeachment.

"There will be no cross-examination, your honor!" a stentorian voice declared.

"Of course there will be cross examination of the witch," the Monsignor blurted out.

"There will be no cross-examination!" the king's agent repeated.

The bishop's barrister stood still, not foolish enough to take on the king's representative

"Does the defendant rest it case?" the judge asked.

"Yes, the defendant rests its case."

"Then let's proceed to closing arguments?" the judge ordered.

"There will be no closing arguments from the plaintiffs, your honor!" the king's representative responded. "However, we would like to hear from Madeleine Moreau as to her thoughts on the disposition of the estate."

"This is unusual, but the witness may share her thoughts with the court," the judge directed.

Madeleine knew exactly what she had to say. "The spirit of Madame LeBlanc's last will and testament should be honored, in part. The vineyards in Bordeaux should be set aside to my family, to be cultivated and worked in harmony with our shared dream."

A smile came to Jean Marc's face.

"The remainder of the estate, which I will renounce, should be divided equally: One share going to the King of France to be distributed at his absolute discretion."

The king's agent nodded his approval.

"The other share to be distributed to the Bishop of Paris."

The Monsignor sat up straight, knowing that this result would keep him in good graces with the bishop.

"The bishop will be pleased!" he whispered to the barrister.

The barrister nodded in agreement.

Madeleine continued, "Conditioned upon the bishop distributing the funds exclusively for the needs of the veteran soldiers on the streets of Paris, who have fought so bravely for France!"

"It is so ordered!" the judge stated emphatically.

The Monsignor jumped to his feet, "The bishop will appeal the decision of this court!"

All eyes went to the solitary figure now standing in the middle of the room-alone in his quest for power.

All in the courtroom were silent.

The king's representative rose and addressed the court: "Your honor, there will be no appeal of the court's decision by either the King or the Bishop of Paris!"

Chapter 67

The bells of the cathedral rang out early in the morning as the small convoy left the LeBlanc home for its journey to Bordeaux. "Look at the headline Madeleine," Jean Marc said as he showed the newspaper to her.

The Monsignor of Notre Dame Charged With Abduction

"The *Moniteur*, Paris' largest newspaper, exposes the Monsignor's illicit acts in abducting our son. He was arrested yesterday after attending the bishop at high mass." Jean Marc told Madeleine as he handed her the newspaper.

"He will be out in no time," Madeleine responded.

"The judge denied his release."

"The Bishop of Paris will use his influence to free him."

"Quite the contrary, the bishop has abandoned him, telling the *Moniteur* that if he is convicted he will be defrocked."

She read the article and placed the paper on her lap, the hint of a smile on her face.

Jean Marc looked at his wife and thought of the torment she had recently undergone. He was astonished by the strength of the human spirit to endure hardship. "Is that a smile I see on your face?" he asked.

"It reflects my thoughts for our family, my love. We cannot forget the past but we can ease its burden with our dreams of the future."

As the caravan arrived at Michel's studio, a wagon loaded with the sculpture of Mary Magdalene awaited them. "This is a gift to you, my friends," Michel said standing by the wagon to greet them.

"Michel, join us in Bordeaux," Jean Marc said.

"A sculptor in Bordeaux is like a vineyard in Paris,"

he responded. "I would wither on the vine in Bordeaux, but I will flourish in Paris… that is the nature of things."

"We will miss you Michel," Madeleine said.

"I will visit often," he said. "*Au revoir.*"

"*Au revoir*, Michel."

As they arrived at the city of Bordeaux, Madeleine explained what she had learned during her childhood. "Wine has been produced in the area since the Eight century, and its red wine is recognized as the finest in the world. Red wines are made from a blend of grapes that include Merlot, Cabernet Franc, Petit verdot, and Malbec." Madeleine explained to the eager listeners.

"Tell them how our wine will be different from the others," Jean Marc interjected.

"The Cabernet Sauvignon grape is a relatively new variety, and it is not produced by many vineyards. The grape is dark blue, has a thick skin, and is easy to cultivate. We will blend it with the Merlot and Cabernet Franc grapes to make the finest of red wines!"

"It's all so foreign to me," Luc remarked.

"Our vineyards are located in the Medoc area which is home to many of the finest chateaux in France. In comparison, our buildings are simple, but our soil is the best in the region. When I surveyed the properties with Madame LeBlanc, she was firm about the soil being more important than the buildings. So our plan is not to build a chateau but rather to grow a family, farm the land, and produce unique red and white wines. We will first restore the dwelling house, the tradesmen's yard, the cooperage, the vat room, and the wine cellars." Madeleine asserted.

"What is that ahead of us. Mama?" Jean asked.

"That is the Chateau Margeaux. It is called *le Versailles de la Medoc.*"

"It's like a palace!" Luc said, in awe of its splendor.

"Its vineyards are on both sides of the road we now

341

travel." Madeleine explained.

"And who will harvest our grapes?" Emile asked as he observed the workers in the vineyards tending to the vines.

"Ah yes… and Madame LeBlanc was also firm that we hire the villagers to cultivate and harvest our vineyards and local winemakers to mature our wine."

"Why then have you brought me and Luc along?" Emile asked jovially.

"For only one reason, Emile. To take advantage of your talents." Jean Marc responded.

"And what talents might those be, Jean Marc?' Emile asked.

"Your formidable talents as wine tasters." Jean Marc quipped, a sly grin on his face, as the group broke out into loud laughter.

Not to be outdone, Emile responded: "And to maintain our formidable talents, tasting must be a daily task."

"And what will the children do?" Angeline asked as the laughter subsided.

Madeleine saw clearly the value of hard work, but she was broad-minded enough to include the work of the mind as well as the work of the hands. "There are times when work on the farm will come first, such as, planting and harvest times; but there are other times, when learning will come first, such as the winter months. And, Sundays will be set aside for worship and play."

"I like the play part, Mama." Marc quipped.

All eyes turned to the long avenue of old plane trees that marked both sides of the long approach to the magnificent Chateau Margeaux. All were in awe of both the splendor of the chateau and its surroundings, in stark contrast to the poor appearance of its soil.

As the small caravan wound its way through the vineyards, the pine forests, the flat lands, and the sandy beaches formed by the Atlantic Ocean, Madeleine continued her explanation, "Madame LeBlanc had been interested in the *terroir* of the land, its sense of place, which imparted a certain quality to the wine — and that is what became our primary focus."

"How were you able to buy such valuable land?" Luc asked.

"There is a certain irony involved in the transaction, in that, the vineyard was owned by the Church. Its monastery had maintained and developed strict vine growing practices, which resulted in superior wines. But it had fallen on hard times during the reign of Napoleon and the abbot of the monastery readily accepted Madame LeBlanc's generous offer."

"Initially, Madame LeBlanc was not convinced it was a wise investment," Jean Marc remarked.

"She voiced her opinion that the vineyards did not appear to be as rich as those in the surrounding areas. And, I gently reproached her with a common saying in this area, *the worse the soil, the better the wine.*"

During the quiet moments of the journey, Madeleine reflected upon her recent life — whether it was fate, the human spirit, or divine intervention that brought them to this point, she was not sure, but she felt certain that the simple message of Jesus, *love God and love thy neighbor,* had something to do with it. And, she truly believed the spirit of this simple message would some day prevail over the bigotry and corruption of the Church!

As the caravan approached its destination, Madeleine observed the look of disappointment on the faces of her family. Instead of a magnificent chateau there was a dilapidated monastery, instead of a tradesman's yard there were run down buildings, and instead of rich soil around the vines there were rocks and gravel.

"The monastery will become our home, the buildings will be repaired, the rocks and gravel will give us good drainage, and our southerly exposure will ripen our grapes!" Madeleine said. "And always remember, *the worse the soil, the better the wine*," which words seemed to invigorate her family.

Jean Marc called for the last wagon in the caravan to come forward. It stopped in front of the entranceway and the canvas top was removed, revealing Michel Bois' unfinished sculpture of Mary Magdalene.

"Place it to the side of the entranceway to greet our visitors." Madeleine directed.

Once in place on the pedestal, it loomed over the countryside and graced the entranceway! "Jean, are you prepared to carve the inscription into the pedestal?"

"Yes Mama... I will carve the name *Chateau Mary Magdalene* into the marble of the pedestal."

"And who will complete the sculpture?" Luc asked.

Madeleine looked up at the imposing sculpture for a long time, much of Mary Magdalene's body still hidden in the marble, a remarkable symbol of the unfulfilled journey of women. At last, she said softly: "Mary Magdalene will emerge from the marble only when the Church embraces Jesus' message of *love* and *inclusion*!"

Made in the USA
Coppell, TX
09 July 2021

58756967R00204